Once Upon a Time there was a Girl…

Troubles at Blue Bayou

By
JF Kearney

Prologue

Blue Bayou, Louisiana, is a fictional small town situated across the bridge from Thibodaux, Louisiana, in Lafourche Parish. Its history mirrors many Louisiana towns with a rich but complicated history of slavery and agriculture, including Thibodaux and Raceland, Louisiana.

The also fictional body of water referred to as "Blue Bayou" is based on the very real Toledo Bend Reservoir, whose unusually clear, blue water is in deep contrast to the many brown and murky bayous of Louisiana and Lafourche Parish. Toledo Bend Reservoir is located on the Sabine River between Louisiana and Texas. The 185,000-acre lake is the largest man-made reservoir in Texas and one of the largest in the country.

The population of the fictional Blue Bayou fluctuates between 10,000 and 15,000 people, dependent on the season. Residents include a majority white population, followed by Blacks, Asians, Native Americans, Cajuns, and a growing population of Hispanics. Most workers in Blue Bayou work in agriculture, forestry, fishing, hunting, mining, quarrying, oil and gas extraction, construction, and manufacturing.

Table of Contents

PART I: Police Chief Thomas "Tom" Mallory 9

    Chapter 1: Autumn in Daphne 10

PART II: Blue Bayou, Louisiana 24

    Chapter 2: That Town in Southeast Louisiana 27

PART III: Pastor Tucker, of Miracle Way Missionary Baptist Church 34

    Chapter 3: Evangelist Tucker Spreading the Word around the World 35

PART IV: Mrs. Virginia 46

    Chapter 4: Reclaiming her Roots 47

PART V: Maia 54

    Chapter 5: What Southern Love looks Like… 55

PART VI: Yesterday Is Calling 64

    Chapter 6: A Midnight Call 65

    Chapter 7: The Morning After 71

    Chapter 8: Weldon Solder 77

    Chapter 9: Manna from Heaven 84

PART VII: The Evangelist's Return 104

Chapter 10: God's Eyes on Blue Bayou 105
Chapter 11: A Young Calli's Turning Point 108

PART VIII: Lucia Benet 113

Chapter 12: What we Carry. What we Leave Behind 114
Chapter 13: A Haunting Goodbye 118

PART IX: When God Ghostwrites our Message 127

Chapter 14: A Vessel For God's Message 128
Chapter 15: Remembering the Journey 137
Chapter 16: God Messin' with His Loyal Soldier 146

PART X: Clyde Thomas Vann 153

Chapter 17: New Beginnings 154
Chapter 18: Winter Love 171

PART XI: Calli's Missing 177

Chapter 19: Almost Perfect Road Trip 178

PART XII: The Haunting of Old Times and Places 191

Chapter 20: A Mother's Cry for Help 192
Chapter 21: Delia's Place 197
Chapter 22: Coming Home to Good friends, Hard Memories 204
Chapter 23: Growing up Delia 217

Chapter 24: Missing You. Missing Me 226

PART XIII: A Storm in the Forecast **237**

Chapter 25: Looking Backward through a Broken Mirror 238

Chapter 26: A Healthy Serving of Memories 250

PART XIV: Remembering Calli Tucker **260**

Chapter 27: A Mother's Loss 261

Chapter 28: De Ja 'Vu all over again in Blue Bayou 269

PART XV: I am Calli **275**

Chapter 29: A Different Kind of Homecoming 277

Chapter 30: Telling the Tucker Women's Stories 289

Chapter 31: Inside Calli's World 299

PART XVI: What Tomorrow Brings **320**

Chapter 32: Nurse Nancy 321

Chapter 33: What Loyalty Gone Wrong Looks Like 325

PART XIV: Luke 8:17 .... **329**

Chapter 34: Charlie's Secrets 330

Chapter 35: No Way Back 346

Epilogue: Again, With Love **349**

A sailor went to see, see, see...

To see what he could see, see, see. But all that he could see, see, see
Was the bottom of the ocean, sea, sea, sea...

The cold breeze traveling across the water embraces the woman's body, not gently, but like the caresses of a hurried lover. The tide leaves small rivulets of water and tiny creatures behind to decorate the woman's hair.

The ethereal shadow of the early morning moonlight creates a portrait of a woman sleeping peacefully after a long, exhausting night. Except there is the barely visible stream of blood beneath her neck and scars along her jawline. The body is eerily still, and only a whisper of breathing can be heard. The peaceful songs of the cicadas and southern nightbirds and lovely reflections of the autumn moon on the slowly rolling Bayou belies the truth of what has happened here.

If there is something good at this moment, it is that Callindra Tucker is yet breathing and unaware that she is left to die on the banks of Blue Bayou, the place that holds the sweetest memories of her childhood. The midnight canoe rides with a young Tom Mallory, holding hands as they watched the trail of waves like moon drops on the water. They would laugh that the townspeople stubbornly referred to the 800-mile reservoir as a bayou because 'Louisiana is known for its bayous, not reservoirs.'

Had life not changed in these past moments, Calli might be staring across the water, thanking God for the blessing of this moonlight's romantic cast on this bounteous water that fed families and was home to fish. The crescent birds already singing their morning arias, and the egrets gracefully diving low for a morning drink and a place to nestle for the morning. She would *remember with a smile how as a child, she'd gaze across the bayou in the night and imagined the hundreds of oxbows were the Indians and slaves she'd learned were once an integral part of this world; but now were trudging across the waters back to their faraway homes.*

It has been months, maybe years, since Calli has spent time simply enjoying the beauty of Blue Bayou. When was the last time she'd had the free time for a still and quiet moment such as this one? The foundation of her perfect, story-book life was a schedule of endless meetings, counseling sessions, public speeches, and weekly messages to her parish. Amidst it all, the evangelist welcomed her days with grace and gratitude for her life, her church, and the gifts beyond her wildest dreams.

Callindra Tucker didn't hear the night sounds of wildlife echoing through the air or the animal mating calls across the swampland. Her eyes, however, fluttered as she sensed a change in her surroundings. Somewhere in her half-consciousness, she feels a presence here. Someone's ginger touch, someone's quiet sobs. As quick as it appeared, she was falling back into darkness, just this side of the alive.

It is fourteen days now since the tragedy befell Callindra Tucker. She is yet just this side of living, fighting against the blackness that threatens to pull her back into its orbit. She half-awakens from a dreamless pit to a tiny sliver of memory fluttering in the place where full and living thoughts resided not long ago.

It is day again. Again, she senses a presence emanating body warmth and human smell.

She feels the tenderness of butterfly wings as they soothe her burning skin. Weightless hands remove the small creatures violating her body. The whisper, once more, of her name. She is yet alive, at least for now. The presence evaporates, and Callindra's questions disappear into the air, out to the bayou, unheard. She struggles to hold onto the sliver of light whose one purpose must be to guide her safely out of the darkness swallowing her yet again.

Callindra. A voice, or simply a memory, forces its way to the forefront of her brain. Her body stills itself, tenses, trying, trying, trying to understand.

Callindra...she repeats the word someone whispered, with parched and flaccid lips. There is a faint familiarity to its feel. But her mind aches with trying, and she gives up, embracing the sweet and comforting darkness.

PART I: Police Chief Thomas "Tom" Mallory

CHAPTER 1

Autumn in Daphne

Police Chief Tom Mallory leaned back in his office chair, staring across his office and through the opened window. He frowned at the cool breeze that blew through the room from time to time. Not often enough. How many weeks had it been? He couldn't remember; just knew it had been too long. His town had suffered a terrible drought this summer, and the police chief was suffering with the rest of his staff as they waited for the air conditioning repairmen to come.

"Thank God for small miracles," he mumbled on this lazy southern afternoon. "At least we got an air conditioner to fix. Think of the thousands of people in this county alone who don't have a thing except a ceiling fan, a window fan…or, God forbid, just a paper fan. We don't have a right to complain," he complained as he wiped the dribble of sweat from his forehead.

Tom Mallory had hoped for a real autumn this year. He was worn out with the fall- wannabes' that kept the temperatures up to around 60 and 70 through December. He had long believed that human beings were doing all the wrong things to keep this world around for future generations now. He could see the ramifications of it more and more each year. Whoever chose to believe there was no such a thing as climate change was living with their heads…buried in the sand, he thought. He could show them his boxes of winter clothing he hadn't unpacked in years, to prove it.

Finally, Tom breathed a sigh of relief as he sensed the breeze growing cooler – a teaser that a break in the hot Alabama weather was forthcoming. Tom walked to the opposite wall and stood in front of the large window that took up most of that wall.

Forgetting the dreadful autumn heat wave, there was a bemused look on his face as he watched his city at its busiest. The cars—like tiny, colored ants—scurried from one end of the slickly tarred Highway to the other. Hurrying and hurrying. To where, and for what? It seemed just plain strange that 45 years ago, this city was looked down on as too "slow" and "rural."

Tom had thought seriously about leaving Daphne, Alabama. He'd been courted by larger southern cities and a few in the Midwest. He must have received ten invitations after the 2005 racial murder that threatened to sever the town down its racial lines. He had stayed then because Mayor Mavis Simmonds had begged him to and offered him more than he'd ever have the nerve to ask for. "I need you here, Tom, the city needs you," she'd said. He couldn't tell for sure but thought he'd detected tears in the corners of her eyes.

He remembered it had been hard for this independent woman to share her fears with even him, though they'd been friends for more than 20 years. Tom had stayed for Mavis and himself. The murder had wrenched his own heart, tugged at the strings that bound him to the town he'd now long ago named home. Angel's parents had gone on to their glory, and siblings had settled in other parts of the state. He knew Daphne could never be the same for them.

It hadn't been much more than a year ago that the clouds had slowly parted in the city. The girl's murder had been the unspoken elephant in every mixed race meeting for most of the four years before. Many times, to the community's credit, a conversation around the murder was the reason for meetings. Relationships that didn't end altogether grew stronger more meaningful. A memorial to Angel had been placed on the school's lawn where she'd taught. For years, vigils were held on the anniversary of her death, led by Mayor Simmonds and her good friend Clarice. Whether Daphne was what he'd been looking for all those years ago, he now knew it would be the last job he'd ever hold.

Tom peered further out his office window. Most of what he saw these days was light years from what he'd witnessed on Main Street 10 years ago. There were noticeable changes in what was outside his window today and what was there two decades ago. He refused to believe he was simply an aging man still stuck in yesterday. That certainly wouldn't explain away the brazen changes on just about every street in downtown Daphne. *Sun tanning cafes? My God*, Tom thought to himself.

It was almost six years ago that Mavis Simmonds had given up the mayor's seat, telling Tom she didn't want to spend her 62nd birthday still tied to that oakwood desk in City Hall. "I ought to be able to tell folk something more than how many meetings I sat through or how many city ordinances I argued for!" she grumbled.

Mavis and Tom still met every Friday for lunch at Cracker Barrel, and she was still shaking her head at her friend Tom's grumbles about the city imploding from change. "All you're witnessing, Tom Mallory, is growing pains," she chuckled. "You, being the most liberal law man in this part of the country, it's just a bit ironic to hear you grumbling about change – something you wanted to see happen around here since you set foot here."

"That was something completely different, Mayor, and you know it. That was about changing how we treat people, about fairness, seeing people the same no matter who they are. I wasn't pushing for electric cars and uber taxis and male beauty shops. And now, they're ready to bring a gambling casino here!"

"But think about it, Tom. No change happens without some growing pains, whether they're bad changes or good changes. Every little town that decides not to be so little anymore goes through this very same thing."

Tom shook his head. "If growing is this damn painful, why do it…why not just stay as you are?"

"Tom Mallory, do I detect someone I've always considered pretty much ageless, finally growing old?" Mavis laughed, and Tom wondered if she was serious.

"As I recall from a certain document that came across my desk some years ago, you were born a total of five months and 22 days before me, Mayor Simmonds…*so*, speak for yourself. I still got a few years left in me."

As he looked over at his friend, he was surprised at the truth: Mavis Simmonds was truly ageless. She hadn't changed a lick in the 25 years he'd known her. She didn't look young then, and she didn't look old now. Tom tried to hide the smile that snuck up on his face.

"Do you remember the first time we met in that restaurant for breakfast, and you were giving me the lay of the land, and I was trying to figure out whether I wanted to get stuck in this little redneck town with the hardnosed woman mayor?"

Mavis chuckled and rolled her eyes. "I knew you would stay after the first few minutes...I just needed to convince you that it was a good idea. The only thing I thought would happen over these 25 years is you settling down with some nice woman and having a brood of children. I guess everybody thought Maia would be that nice little woman."

Tom blushed and took a sip of his tea. Mavis laughed. The non-response told her she was treading outside the boundary of hers and Tom's friendship, on what Tom called his `sacred ground.' Mavis had made a habit of reading people pretty good, and she'd never dipped into Tom's personal life, never dared criticize the way he did things, and she wouldn't start now.

A few minutes later, Tom dropped his napkin onto the table and offered her a crooked smile. "Enough arguing for a day, Mayor. But, say what you want, I've heard enough about what change does to small towns. Most of these towns don't have the foundation for change, and they won't fare so well trying to mix what they are with what they want to be."

He saw the relief in her face that they were back on safe territory. "I've seen it done, Tom. Look at Mobile, up there; Birmingham...they are bigger, but they're made up of some of the same people we got here. Some towns, with the right leadership, can handle change...can even thrive with it."

"I think our young mayor is alright even if he did live up north most of his years out of college. But I can promise you that for every town that thrives with change, I can name you ten than don't. At least that many who grew too fast for their own good, and ended up with horrible education systems, bad leadership, crime out of the kazoo...and rampant joblessness, to boot. Is that what we want in our town?"

He was sure his position had nothing to do with age or his politics. He knew some of the lawmen in other parts of the state complained he was too soft on crime and too progressive in how he dealt with the community. He didn't pay them much mind. He just wanted a safe community that didn't grow too fast for many people who couldn't keep up. He just didn't think it made much sense to ignore what made a town work all these years and jump on the first passing train that rolls through.

Tom remembered Bill London's column in the town's daily just a few years ago. The columnist had taken up almost a full page extolling the still small and innocent virtues of Daphne, which was so unlike the quickly changing city of Mobile. The headline, **"Something to be said for Bedroom Communities,"** had quotes from all the town leaders, including Tom, who agreed that the people of Daphne were lucky to still have such a great quality of life, even as they moved into the 21st Century.

It was the very next year Tom began noticing changes showing up in Daphne. Within five years of the column, Daphne no longer fit the bedroom community description.

To Chief Mallory's disdain, the first notices of change appeared outside his office window. Harmless little things, so far...cute little boutiques; franchise restaurants that advertised all over the country; and banks, whose owners may have never set foot in the town, cropping up on opposite ends of town.

But later, the small changes became more noticeable, more ostentatious – shouting their arrival. At the same time, Tom realized there was a consistent trickle of strangers moving into town, mainly on the outskirts. As the changes grew bolder, Tom's concerns grew along with them. Concerns, he told Mavis, no more or less than any small-town chief of police, any conscientious protector of the community.

Hell, he wasn't afraid of change, and he wasn't quite ready to give over his badge to some younger man with spit-slick hair or Izod shirts with Khakis and a North Wind jacket. Not until he was good and ready to.

Truthfully, it did sometimes take him by surprise to remember just how long he'd been doing this -- all of his adult life. He had protected the good people of Daphne for 25 of those years and was proud of what he and the other town leaders had done here.

Wasn't it simple common sense, or at least human nature, that what you've built, you protect with every fiber of your being? That the people who helped the town survive through its most dangerous eras wouldn't want outsiders coming in to annihilate all they'd done. Not one good lawman worth his salt would ever tout "change is good," not when they knew good and darn well it most times brought a scrap of evil with it.

The mostly foreign cars, the fast, pretty ones built low to the ground, or the Humpty-Dumpty trucks with oversized tires or oversized cabins – all, seemed to be in a frantic hurry as they raced down the town's Main Street. Tom remembered it wasn't so long ago when some paved streets were gravel, and traffic jams happened just once or twice a year—around the busy festival seasons.

Now, heavy traffic in their small town was the norm. The whoosh of tires on the pavement and the short, timid horn beeps ushered in

Daphne's mornings, now. The din began early on weekday mornings and hit its crescendo around 5 p.m. Tom watched the cars race into the small parking lots that housed the coffee shop. They made such desperate turns into the small buildings as if this one was the most important stop they had that morning.

Tom shook his head, remembering how Java Joe, Mocha Joe, Java-Java, Java Café...all names that belonged in Seattle, L.A., or Miami, seemed to have all magically appeared on every corner around the same time a couple of years ago. Around 8 a.m., the long line of cars, many that had left the coffee shops, began nudging their way across the bridge to Mobile or onto the freeway for work or business further away. Some dawdled at the Java joints, catching up with gossip or taking their time, as their Java cravings quieted.

Tearing himself from the window and his thoughts, Tom moved back to his desk that was covered with multi-level piles of paper waiting to be dealt with or moved on to another resting place. Tom was sure his position couldn't have had anything to do with his age, because he never thought about his age; never liked thinking about how fast the years were coming at him.

Suddenly he admitted, he was feeling his age and remembering how close he'd come to that permanent "Gone Fishing" sign and a mortgage on a cabin on the lake some years ago. Maybe the sign and the cabin were items he should seriously consider putting back on his "To Do" list this year.

Tom wiped the small trickle of moisture from his wide, creased forehead. It had been a bruising summer they'd suffered through. Even the once-upon-a-time northeastern snowbirds who darted back and forth between their homes and the Bay complained about the hot, sweltering summer. Some were even known to vacation away from their vacation homes to escape the steamy southern heat.

Tom wasn't one of the natives who sneered at the newcomers' northern airs. He knew what it was like to fall in love with the slow, innocent beauty of the shore area. He didn't resent their ability to pay for opulent privacy while still enjoying the quiet splendor, the calm, and unsophisticated charm of Daphne and Mobile Bay.

Tom was never 100% certain of the snowbirds' motives. How could it be that simple to shift a life so drastically? Sure, he had moved from one area of the southeast to another, but from the cold, frigid climate of the north, or Midwest, to the southeast? To uproot yourself and leave a whole world behind? But the truth was the majority of the noveau eastern-shorers had no intention of completely overhauling their lives even when their addresses changed. Most of the newcomers, he realized, never bothered trying to fit into the community. They lived not so much inside the town as residing just beyond the town, forever remaining "elusive residents" or "permanent voyeurs."

Tom couldn't wait for a real change in season, including quieting the loud, raucous noises he always assigned to summertime. He had a reverence for natural, dependable changes, from the cold winters to the sticky heat of Alabama summers. Tom was sure the extreme summer heat acted on Alabamians' souls and spirits, the same as saunas: sweated out the things that found their way inside us throughout the year; the evil thoughts, hate, prejudices, the hopelessness, fear, and general malevolence that festered during the often sunshine-less winter days.

He smiled, remembering some of the conversations he'd had over the years about how New Orleans had brazenly stolen the Mardi Gras – and the spotlight—from east Alabama with their elaborate, sex-tinged parades and traditions, which included prancing half-naked through the quarters and bearing their boobs for beads. A much tamer Mardi Gras celebration, the Mobilians declared, was birthed and nurtured on Alabama soil—not on Louisiana's strange, exotic soil. There would always be something to claim or fight about, he figured.

Tom began reading the City Hall Update and found himself frowning as he followed the long list of upcoming festivals. He'd never looked forward to public parties or festivals. He had a lawman's serious disdain for big crowds –uncontrollable numbers of people he didn't know. His years in Alabama had taught him that while Mardi Gras was the most outwardly sacrilegious of the festivals, there was an inherent other-worldly taint surrounding the Jubilee celebrations.

* * *

Tom Mallory was turning 62 this year. He wasn't looking forward to the old folks' jokes or sitting through yet another office birthday party. He felt it was a cruel way of making him admit to his own mortality. Once again, he'd tried and failed to find a way to avoid the party.

It was just plain unfair to force an aging man to stand up in a crowd of folk who knew you when you were much younger, and you both knew that each year you moved one step closer to being a scrap of dirt in the earth. No one had ever written a manual on becoming an aging lawman with grace.

Tom chuckled to himself, thinking how he'd begun studying his aging body in the bathroom mirror, and admittedly, and found less and less that looked the same as 10 years ago. His memory and eyesight, thank God, were still pretty much intact, though his doctor kept hinting he might need cataract surgery and reading glasses. *When Elephants fly*, Tom thought...a four-eyed police chief? No way. He'd immediately become the Barney Fife of Daphne.

As Tom lay in bed on the night of his birthday, he realized he was finally accepting that he wasn't the man he was 10 years ago, not even five years ago. He still often preferred falling asleep and waking up in his own bed rather than at Maia's. It was purely a matter of ensuring he got the sleep he required for a clear head the next day. No one needed to know he still enjoyed reading in bed at night, which most times meant he'd find a pair of broken glasses in bed with him the next morning.

Tom remembered all the birthdays he'd reluctantly celebrated since moving to Daphne. Good years, most of them...not good things always happening, but good people to have around when bad things happen. The birthdays he couldn't remember were probably the most memorable, given he was too young to realize he would one day grow old and become someone else.

Those were the days when his hair was thick and almost had a life of its own; his body was lean and strong and never pained him, no matter how hard he worked. And, yes, there had been a vibrancy about him that he only now realized it was simply because there were fewer years on him.

With the years came something more. Finally, introspection, the thing he'd run from most of his life, had become a sometimes enjoyable pastime. He spent many a night remembering, even analyzing memories he'd long ago stowed away.

Tonight, as he awaited sleep to overtake him, the memory he'd been chasing for some 45 years arrived as if on cue. He was never surprised when it visited. It was always near his birthdays. Never mind that he'd so meticulously wrapped that part of his past in fine tissue paper and hidden it deep inside himself. Here it was.

Calli Tucker of Blue Bayou had been the one most important things in his young life when he was searching for who he was. It was only his fear of repeating what he'd grown up with that he'd abruptly ended the affair. Yes, he had explained to her that the affair ended, not his love for her. That hadn't eased her misery, and he knew it.

Though Calli Tucker didn't overtake his memories regularly, now, she was still an important part of his treasured memories of that past. He wondered, now, if she was experiencing some of the same vagaries of growing older, though he found it difficult to imagine Calli as anything beyond the young girl he'd loved so much. He hoped she'd found happiness as an adult, something he nor her mother did a good job of supplying.

Just as he always did when the memory visited, Tom wondered how things might have been different had Calli remained in his life. For certain, there would be no Maia. Maia, the best-known secret in Tom's personal life, had claimed him the first week, maybe the first day, he'd walked into Daphne's sheriff's office. How many times since then had she tried convincing him their love was written into destiny. Good and long-suffering Maia, still holding out hope that one day she'd be Mrs. Tom Mallory.

Tom had come close many times to sharing Calli Tucker with Maia. Close, but not close enough. It had even crossed his mind to tell his best friend Mavis about the girl. He knew for a fact the former mayor wouldn't understand that younger Tom.

He would dream about that early relationship tonight, just as he always did around his birthday. It was never a happily ever after remembrance. In fact, he always woke with a feeling of guilt and loss. He relived young Calli's hurt and anger, the cold tears that fell from her face onto his.

The look on the girl's face as he told her he was leaving pained him. "Did something happen, Tom? Is there something you're not telling me? I don't believe you would just up and decide to leave like this…out of the blue!"

She had cried, and he hadn't been able to explain his reason, though it made perfect sense to him. It had nothing to do with her but with his dogged fear of repeating his own ugly history. What he knew about love between a man and a woman wasn't something he wanted to repeat.

Later, after he'd finally pulled himself away and walked to the bus stop, the tears had begun. No longer having to stay strong for Calli, his heart had burst open. He'd boarded the bus and found a seat at the back of the bus. For the next few hours, he'd replayed the final hour he'd spent with Calli, the hardest hour he'd experienced in his life.

Tom's real pain was in knowing he'd acted out of cowardice, fear of what could happen. Somehow, he knew that too much happiness was a trap. Growing up in the Mallory home in New Orleans had taught him that. Was this his future? Would love always be partnered with fear and distrust? Now, the fear became never finding a love that would last.

Calli would be 59 now. Tom imagined she was somebody's mother, grandmother, and maybe even a great grandmother. She wouldn't be that same girl he'd known and loved, and more importantly, she would be able to fall in love and stay in love.

Though he'd reluctantly learned the basics of Google and other internet search engines, Tom had never once searched for Calli Tucker. He knew Maia would have done all the necessary work for him if he'd ever asked. He would never connect the two women, and he had no right to reconnect with the girl he left behind.

When he woke the next morning, Tom was still tired from a restless sleep. He sat on the side of his bed and sighed, thankful that the dream didn't happen more than once each year. He looked over at the clock and saw he could get by with 30 more minutes of sleep. As he felt himself falling asleep again, he realized Calli had left him…maybe until next year.

* * *

PART II: Blue Bayou, Louisiana

A Sailor went to market

To see what he could market But all that he could market
Was the bottom of the ocean... market

She knew she couldn't do anything to leave a trace that she had been there and attended Callindra Tucker. She would do what she could to stave the bleeding. To attend to the surface wounds. She coddled the injured woman and forced water down her throat that must be as parched as her lips.

More than anything, the woman cried and prayed. This had all been her fault, she told herself, but nothing she'd ever wanted or imagined. She sat on the mostly mud beside Callindra Tucker and imagined a time when things could have turned out so different.

Nothing could change what was and wasn't. Now, all she could do was try and save the woman's life, assuage her own guilt and complicity in this crime. She knew it was a weak attempt, given she could only spend a short time here before returning to her home and job in New Orleans.

She was a coward. She admitted that. If not, she would go to the police and tell them there was a dying woman lying on the banks of the Bayou. She wouldn't because she realized her knowledge of the crime would lead to other questions, and she would have to answer those questions – about how she knew the woman and how could she possibly know she was in this isolated bank of the bayou. Courage was not one of her gifts, not yet. She would have to build up the courage to share her whole story and her unknowing but very real complicity in this crime.

As she sat, the tears fell freely down her face, onto her breasts. She spied a gleaming gold chain through her tears, attached to a ring. As she picked it up, she saw the clasp had been broken, likely torn from the woman's neck. She turned it in her hand. A beautiful sapphire ring she'd obviously worn around her neck. She wouldn't leave the items to be washed away by the rain, the tides, or some curious drifter. More than that, it was a part of this woman. Something she'd never had before. She'd hold it for now, just until…

* * *

CHAPTER 2

That Town in Southeast Louisiana

In 1804, all of Louisiana became the Orleans territory. In 1805 the Territorial Legislature created ten counties, including the County of Lafourche, which would later become Lafourche Parish. Blue Bayou, Louisiana, would become a town and then a city inside Lafourche Parish.

By 1808, a trading post and small village, known as "Thibodeauxville," was established on the west bank of Bayou Lafourche – which ran 100 miles from beginning to end. The village location was a strategic move, given the confluence of Bayou Lafourche and Bayou Terrebonne. By the 1820s, the village, which included a small community known as Blue Bayou, was an allusion to the fact that most of the houses were built right along Bayou Lafourche. This branch of the bayou was as clear and pristine blue as any lake in southern Louisiana.

In time, the town became a growing community and local center of the sugar cane industry. The settlement was formally incorporated in 1830 under the name "Thibodeauxville," named in honor of Henry Schuyler Thibodaux, who provided the land for the original village center.

Thibodaux, the son of Acadian exiles, served as lieutenant governor for the state and briefly as acting governor of Louisiana.

The town's name was shortened to Thibodeaux in 1838, then officially changed its spelling to Thibodaux in 1918.

Blue Bayou, like Thibodaux, was recognized for a time throughout the south for its rice and sugar cane production. The Cajun syrup industry at a time was of interest internationally. A stranger entering Lafourche Parish might question whether he was indeed, in the "land of cotton," after seeing the miles and miles of rice and sugarcane fields.

The Laurel Valley Sugar Plantation, located just outside Thibodaux, was one of the largest 19th and 20th-century sugar plantations in Louisiana, known for the miles of sugarcane fields and the ingenuity in its operation. To this day, it has not fully relinquished its history. Visitors can still see rows and rows of slave cabins, a schoolhouse for Negro children, a church, and a general store featuring many of the antique tools used for harvesting sugar cane.

Thibodaux nicknamed the "Queen City of Lafourche," was separated from Blue Bayou only by a mile-long wooden bridge. The water changed from one consistency to another depending on the county it flowed. Wildlife was abundant along the bayou, bats, raccoon, opossum, deer, beaver, otters, alligator, bear, and a wide range of snakes.

Part of the region's wetland, including the Bayou itself, was home to old, tall trees such as the Bald Cypress, the historical symbol of the Louisiana wetlands. There was also the Southern live oak, Southern magnolia, crape myrtles, deciduous oaks, Southern sugar maple, hollies, Sweet bay magnolia, pines, and the Tupelo trees. Spanish moss was often found inside the swamplands and near the trees.

The bayou was populated for miles by oxbows, or trees that were nesting homes to a wide array of large and small birds, including the pelicans, stork, osprey, heron, kingfisher, barred Owl, woodpeckers, yellow-throated Warbler, and Painted Bunting.

For anyone with a hunger for fish, there was a diversity of species found in the waters of southern Louisiana—the red drum, black drum, sheepshead, alligator gar, jack crevalle, redfish, catfish, and even the Spanish Mackerel.

Though visitors snickered that the local folk had it all wrong and that the so-called Blue Bayou was more likely a lake or river. The talk didn't change residents own position on the body of water. It was their water, and they'd name it whatever they felt most comfortable, regardless of the clear, blue waters bore no similarities to the muddy brown bayous that made up most of southern Louisiana.

At last count, there were over 100 miles of the Bayou in Lafourche Parish, and a large percentage of the twin cities' populations lived along the banks of the bayou. The former slaves built temporary lean-tos where they lived and worked and raised families until something or somebody caused them to up and move further down the bayou or to another part of the county.

* * *

While the first documented inhabitants of Lafourche Parish were the Chawasha, a small tribe of Native Americans related to the Chitimacha of the upper Bayou Lafourche, all traces of this tribe were erased from the area and replaced by white European settlers-- the French nationals and Louisiana-born French and German creoles. The next wave of immigrants would be Spanish and French

Arcadian immigrants who arrived in the 18th century when Louisiana was the Spanish province of Louisiana.

The next wave of immigrants into south Louisiana were the Africans, imported in slave ships into the southern states of the US. European and Spanish colonists were convinced the Africans were the missing link to their successful rice and sugar cane industries. As far as they were concerned, these men, women, and children delivered to Louisiana from the dark African continent in droves were good for only one thing, taking care of the hardest and most critical manual labor that ensured successful farms and crops. European, which they believed would ensure successful farms and crops.

Lafourche county even had its share of government leaders to grace their towns. U.S. Senator Henry Clay visited Thibodaux as a presidential candidate in 1844. Following his visit, local leaders saw fit to name a residential lane along the canal connecting Bayou Lafourche to Bayou Terrebonne in his honor.

Confederate General Braxton Bragg, the victor at Chickamauga, and his wife had a plantation, "Bivouac," just north of Thibodaux. They attended services at St. John's Episcopal Church on Jackson Street. The church was founded by Bishop Leonidas Polk, the "Leighton" plantation owner, and later a Confederate lieutenant general who was killed in action.

In 1896, the first rural free delivery of mail-in Louisiana began in Thibodaux. It was only the second such RFD in the United States. Ironically, the town suffered irreparable damages during the Civil War. In October 1862, following the Battle of Georgia Landing (Labadieville), Thibodaux was occupied by the Union Army under

Brigadier General Godfrey Weitzel. Before the Confederates left the city under the command of General Alfred Mouton, they burned the depot, the bridge, sugar, and supplies that they could not carry with them to prevent Union forces from benefitting from them.

On June 20, 1863, Texas Confederate cavalry forces attacked the Union forces occupying Thibodaux and captured the town. Per one report, 'terrified Negroes and whites raced into the town announcing that 3,000 Confederate cavalrymen were enroute to attack Thibodaux and Lafourche Crossing. Union Colonel Thomas W. Cahill ordered an immediate retreat. The bayou bridges were burned, three field guns were destroyed, and as many of the men and the horses as possible were loaded . . . and ordered to the adjoining town of Raceland. It was recorded that the soldiers destroyed ammunition, abandoned horses, and left four field pieces or weapons of artillery were left behind.

It was also reported that once the Union regained control of the area, they ordered that all enslaved people be freed and paid wages as free laborers. White planters in Thibodaux complained about negotiating labor contracts for the African-American workers. Alexander F. Pugh, a major sugar planter near Thibodaux, complained but agreed to pay former slaves' monthly wages only because everybody else in the neighborhood had agreed to do the same.

There is seldom southern history without racial atrocities inside southern towns. The "Thibodaux massacre" of November 23, 1887, is considered the second bloodiest labor dispute in U.S. history. Some claimed casualties, including wounded and missing, to be in the hundreds.

The massacre occurred in the late 19th century after the south took back control of the state government following the Reconstruction era by using election fraud and violence by paramilitary forces such as the White League, which suppressed black voting. White Democrats continued to consolidate their power over the state government. In the late 1880s, they were challenged temporarily by a biracial coalition of Populists and Republicans. Because blacks were skilled sugar workers, they briefly retained more rights and political power than northern Blacks and other southerners who worked as tenant farmers or sharecroppers on cotton plantations.

Post-Reconstruction, the Louisiana Sugar Producers Association, made up of some 200 major planters, worked to regain slave conditions and control of workers, adopting uniform pay, withholding 80 percent of the workers' pay until after harvest, and making them accept scrip, redeemable only at plantation stores owned by the planters, rather than cash. Cane workers struck intermittently against these conditions.

The Knights of Labor organized a chapter in 1886 in Shreveport, Louisiana, and attracted many cane workers seeking better conditions. A sugar cane workers' strike in Lafourche and three neighboring parishes involved 10,000 workers, 1,000 of whom were white, taking place during the critical "rolling period" of the sugar cane harvest.

Planters were alarmed both by outside labor organizations infiltrating the area and the thought of losing their total crops. The governor called in the state militia at the planters' request. The militia protected strikebreakers and evicted black workers. The strike was broken in Terrebonne Parish.

On November 23, after the ambush and wounding of two whites posted in the southern section of town, the militia committee began to indiscriminately shoot black workers and some family members, killing an estimated 35 black workers.

Black cane workers eventually returned to the plantations under slavery conditions created by white planters. The massacre and subsequent disenfranchisement of blacks in Louisiana at the turn of the century included white Democrats' imposition of Jim Crow throughout the region and making voter registration more difficult for Blacks. This brought a halt to labor organizing of cane workers until the 1940s.

PART III: Pastor Tucker, of Miracle Way Missionary Baptist Church

CHAPTER 3

Evangelist Tucker Spreading the Word around the World

On Friday night, Pastor Callindra Tucker and her entourage of twelve arrived back in Blue Bayou, Louisiana. It was the first day of fall in their beautiful corner of Louisiana. Thank Goodness Weldon, her counsel, had talked her into purchasing the land behind the church to build a landing strip. If not, they would have had to land in Shreveport and drive into Blue Bayou.

Their arrival brought the two-week Miracle Campaign that took them across the African continent to a close. The private jet loaned to Miracle Way Baptist Church for this special trip landed at 11:43 p.m., just seven minutes before morning.

It was an admirably smooth landing, and the pastor and her travel-weary entourage gave the pilot a warm round of thankful applause. Before she stepped off the plane, Pastor Tucker offered the young pilot a personally inscribed bible to take on his next journey and a very generous tip for his kindness.

As they left the plane, the travelers' unrestrained groans drew good-natured laughter, light jokes about their ages, and forecasts of stiff and achy muscles the next day. The eight women and four men gingerly made their way down the jetway of the sleek, private plane, chattering but exhausted.

The conversations lulled slightly as they were met by a brisk, fall breeze transporting the pungent aroma of crude oil and sea fish. They remembered now just how far from home they'd traveled and how good it was to be home again. They had left during Louisiana's summer end and returned to a pleasant autumn night.

The trip had been both exhilarating and exhausting. How could it be any different, they'd laughed, when you travel with someone like Pastor Tucker who had more energy than women half her age.

The group would never say it, but they felt there was something special about being chosen to travel across the world as Pastor Tucker's entourage. She was such a dynamic and charismatic messenger. The African ministers had all fallen in love with her. They had begged her to stay in their country longer. Though she didn't change her mind, she was kind in her refusals.

Callindra Tucker represented her congregation and the state of Louisiana so well, greeting the leaders of that world as if she was, in fact, a member of their congregation. She'd even learned a few words to respond in their language. She had learned to use the Swahili greeting, "asubuhi njema," and the Yoruba's Thank you, "E Se."

The African leaders were utterly charmed by her southern style of speech and delivery. It was that warm and open way that melted their hearts. They completely accepted and trusted her. As she did each Sunday in her own church, Callindra Tucker touched thousands of hearts. More importantly, on this trip, she saved hundreds of children and women throughout the seven African continents.

Her entourage quieted, smiling as Callindra Tucker walked carefully down the jet way, wearing a weary smile of contentment.

"Can you believe it? We're back home in Louisiana." Her voice was hoarse, almost a whisper, but she stood at the foot of the steps, smiling up at the star-filled Louisiana sky.

Though Callindra Tucker's warm heart drew strangers to her, few could describe themselves as close confidantes and certainly not close friends. Callindra kept her own counsel, rarely extending friendship beyond a business or spiritual friendship.

A tired smile lingered on her lips as she looked at her loyal entourage. "Thank you," she whispered to the group. The Louisiana fall came with cool night breezes, and as happy as they were to be home, they had somehow not prepared for the cool night.

They shivered delightfully in the embrace of the September night. One member, so full of good grace, began to speak; but Callindra softly touched her shoulder as she bowed her head. The group followed her lead, closed their circle around the woman as she reached for the hands nearest her.

"Oh! Masterful Savior, you have kept your promise, again…and, smiled on our journey; bringing us across your globe, all the way back to our sweet Louisiana soil. We thank you for the safe trip and for the bountiful Campaign. I thank you for these amazing ministers of your word who joined me on this trip. You have blessed us beyond our needs or our expectations, and, as we go our separate ways tonight, we ask that you guide each of us safely home…for this, and so much more, we give you the glory and our gratitude…Amen"

Barely had "Amen," slipped from the pastor's lips before her aides began to offer, one by one, their expressions of gratitude and goodnights. She hurried them along with warm well wishes for a sound and dreamless sleep. She turned and walked toward the waiting car.

* * *

"Good evening, Saul." Pastor Tucker's voice was a sweet but tired whisper as she looked warmly into her chauffer's eyes. Saul grinned. He would have loved to have given his boss a huge welcome back hug, but he knew better. Public hugs weren't something the boss generally didn't stand for. Not from Saul or others.

Callindra patted his back gently, then slid across the seat of her limousine, settling her purse and satchel beside her. Saul quietly slammed the door closed and walked to the back of the car to deposit her bags. As he settled into the driver's seat, he stole a glance back at Pastor Tucker.

"We all so happy you back safe and sound, Pastor Tucker...we been prayin' for your safe deliverance back here." A wide smile was plastered across the man's pleasantly round face.

Callindra smiled at her driver through the rearview mirror.

"Thank you, Saul. Gratefully, your prayers were answered. We had a wonderful trip, and we did make it back safe and sound. We all are just plum worn out. Traveling halfway around the world is for young folks, Saul...not old people like most of us."

They both laughed. He thought what she said was more funny than true. He never thought of the pastor as old. He doubted if any of her parishioners did.

"Boss, you just tired, nothing close to old." the man offered.

"Saul...don't you dare try to make me feel good about growing old. But, you'll get here one day, and then you'll see what I'm talking about."

"Pastor, I'm just a coupl'a years behind you."

She did remember, now, and smiled. Saul's 53rd birthday was just a month away.

Callindra drew out a long sigh of exhaustion as if the sudden memory of just how far they'd traveled over the last 20 hours was adding to the bone-tiredness. She covered a yawn with her hand, combed her hands through the thick mane of silver hair that had a mind of its own, and slipped further down into the curve of the leather seat.

"You know, Saul...at 60, I truly am getting too old for this...Most women my age are spending their weekends at home with a passel of grandchildren. Sometimes I ask myself, 'what good is that big old house, and a pond full of fish out back for an old woman with no one to share it; somebody to come out and help me cook dinner, and catch fish and fry them out back...somebody to spend some time with?'

She looked out into the darkness. Her silver-gray eyes glazed over with something Saul understood but wouldn't address.

"Grandchildren," Saul chuckled and shook his head.

"Yes, Saul... spending weekends with grandchildren rather than galivanting halfway around the world to save souls. Shoot, I can stay right here...we got thousands of lost souls right here in Louisiana."

Saul shrugged. Sure, she had a point, but should he remind the pastor that she had to have children first before she started pining for grandchildren? He decided it was just her exhaustion talking, reminding her of all the empty spaces in her life. Besides, what in the world would she do with a passel of grandchildren on those days and nights when she hardly left the church building? Or, when she jetted away right after service to some church halfway around the country?

Saul remembered the woman had been bowled over with excitement about the Africa trip. Wild horses couldn't have kept her from going. Her rant tonight, he believed, was a sign that she was more tired than she would ever admit. She would be just fine tomorrow after a good night's rest. Two weeks was a bit long for the woman who was exhausted even before she left – as if she'd ever admit it, though.

Saul was sure as rain that she'd wake tomorrow morning singing a completely different song, ready to prepare for a big Sunday at the Miracle Way Ministries Church. And it would, indeed, be a big day on Sunday. Her members would be lined up outside the church well before the message began.

Everyone, including Saul, was excited about having the pastor back in the pulpit on Sunday. Not that anyone had a problem with her assistant ministers' message, but they never measured up to her. Besides, one of the joys of attending Miracle Way was to be serenaded by Callindra Tucker's sweet southern drawl that reverberated throughout the sanctuary.

A few of Saul's buddies hadn't shown up during the two weeks that Callindra was away. While Saul didn't cotton to that kind of conditional religion, he had to admit he understood. Pastor Tucker was the real draw for her members. Not even the beautiful building or the amazing choir could compare. None of that would keep the members coming if Callindra Tucker wasn't there.

Saul knew from personal experience. Her charm and common sense message made him come back after his first visit to the church. In fact, during his second visit to the church, Saul had learned about the minister's need for a chauffeur.

On his way into service that morning, he had seen the notice on the bulletin board and wrote down the phone number on a business card that some pesticide man had left on his windshield last week.

After the service, as he was on his way out the door, Saul had thought, "Why not?" and walked over to the receptionist's desk to ask if the position was still open. The woman at the desk had been young and nicer than most young people sitting behind desks. Unfortunately, she couldn't tell him anything about the position.

"But...if you give me your name, I'll find out for you, and someone will give you a call back tomorrow." When he'd hesitated and given her a "really, now?" look, she'd giggled. "I promise you." He'd left his name.

Saul had been shocked the next morning when he answered his phone and heard the sweet, southern drawl of Pastor Callindra Tucker on the line. As she spoke, he imagined her standing in the pulpit delivering her message in just that same beautiful way.

Saul was even more surprised to realize he was nervous sitting in his living room talking to the minister, who he was pretty sure was sitting in her office. They spoke for less than five minutes, but he found himself searching for the right words. Finally, she said she had a meeting to attend, but if he had time tomorrow, she'd love for him to drop by her office to finish their conversation. Saul was shocked but grateful.

"There won't be any problem getting onto the church grounds, Saul. I'll leave our name with the guard, as well as the receptionist. When you stop at her desk, she'll buzz my office."

Saul's conversation with the pastor that next day was brief...or, it would have been if he hadn't ended up talking 90 miles a minute. He was proud that he got through the meeting without sweat dotting his forehead, but he'd found the pastor even warmer sitting three feet from him than she was when she stood in her pulpit on Sundays. She welcomed him into her office, giving him a short tour of the pastor's suite, making light of all the space that she didn't need as if they had known each other for years, rather than the 24 hours – since their phone conversation.

The receptionist brought in a tray with water and soft drinks when they sat. Saul chose Coca-Cola. The pastor asked him questions about his early life as if she was genuinely interested in learning who he was as a person. What kinds of work he'd done before, and whether he had enjoyed that work?

The pastor seemed just as interested in his family, asking questions about their three children, what they were doing with their lives, now. Saul was amazed at how easy it was to talk to Pastor Tucker. He remembered, though, his children accused him of talking way too much when he felt comfortable enough.

He felt comfortable enough with Pastor Tucker to tell her all she wanted to know and more. That he, Saul Benevido, had grown up in Alexandria, Louisiana. His parents and other family still lived in an Arcadian parish there. He'd left school when he was in ninth grade and soon after left home. For many years, he was something of a drifter, moving from town to town in south Louisiana, picking up seasonal jobs to keep a roof over his head and food in his stomach. None of them, however, held him very long.

Saul suddenly realized he had been sitting there running his mouth for 30 minutes. He placed part of the blame on the minister, who smiled so nicely, clearly enjoying his story. Before Saul had stood to say his goodbyes, Callindra had leaned and offered him her hand, hiring him on the spot. Saul had breathed deeply, silently thanking God that he hadn't mentioned to the woman how scared he was that he'd have to go home and tell Dolly he hadn't gotten the job. "Thank you, Pastor...when do you want me to start?"

"How about tomorrow morning at nine, Saul? I'll need you to pick me up around 8:30 to get me to a meeting at nine." She reached a card over to him, and he read her home address and cell number.

She stood, shook his hand, and promised to be ready when he arrived the next morning. "You can park your car in the garage when you arrive. The pastor's car will be waiting for you," she smiled.

As Saul drove home from the church, he swore never to let the woman down. Of course, he would never say that to her. Somebody probably already had...maybe lots of some bodies who then turned around and let her down. He wouldn't be that person.

It took a matter of months before Saul realized that, like most of the men in her congregation, he was a little smitten by the woman pastor. Of course, it wasn't real love, not the kind that would rile his wife if he ever decided to admit it to her. But there was something about the kindness in her spirit that drew you to her.

There wasn't much that Saul Benevido wouldn't do for his boss if she asked. And, as one of her members, he soon realized that unless you were really careful, a member could find themselves worshipping the messenger rather than the message. As he neared the Pastor's home, he realized that he'd likely never be able to tell her just how happy and relieved he was that she was safely back home. Saul stole a look into the rearview mirror. He noted the small frown on her forehead, subtle signs of weariness on her face. Saul couldn't imagine traveling 16 hours in an airplane. He'd, of course, never flown in an airplane and had no intention of doing so.

Callindra Tucker's eyes fluttered as Saul turned onto the mile-long road that led to her home. She stared through the window as if she hadn't expected the black Louisiana sky, decorated with an endless blanket of stars, or the giant, round autumn moon. It was the kind of night she had missed during her 14 days in Africa, the kind of night that tugged at your heartstrings, especially if you'd not seen it in a while.

Callindra let a long, deep sigh out. She was home, and there was no other place in the world, no matter how beautiful or exotic, she'd rather be. No other sky that could bring tears to her eyes like this one.

"Saul, it was a wonderful trip, and sometime this next week, I'll tell you all about it. But, tonight, right now...I need to just talk to God for a while...there's just so much we need to talk about."

Saul nodded, listening closely to the exhaustion in her voice. He would hold all his questions about Africa until she felt like talking. As he slowed the car in front of her home, he peered into the mirror again. Her eyes were closed.

Saul liked the silence, too, and the nice sound of the Pastor's quiet breathing. He always hated waking the poor woman from her sleep after her long, exhausting days. He knew how hard she drove herself, how exhausted she must be to fall asleep in the back of her car.

Saul Benevido is a very lucky man. He never missed a day reminding himself.

Pastor Tucker was a special kind of woman, more than just a good

Christian, but a good woman. What man wouldn't be happy and lucky to have a woman like her?

Thing was, he couldn't imagine any he knew that was deserving of somebody as good as her...not a pretend bone in her body. Though she often joked about not being a spring chicken anymore, he knew she had a whole lot of life left in her.

PART IV: Mrs. Virginia

CHAPTER 4

Reclaiming her Roots

"Happy Birthday, Dear Tommy. What does this one make you...35, 40?" Virginia Mallory's laughter, soft and girlish, almost made Tom forget that there was surely an underlying reason for this early call.

Tom gave the beautiful Mrs. Mallory credit for having impeccable timing. His mother never called without a good reason, and when she called this early on his birthday, he was well aware that wishing him a happy birthday was the opportunity, not the reason. Yes, the woman most definitely had good timing.

Mrs. Mallory wasn't one of those mothers who sought out excuses to hear her son's voice very often. Her calls almost always had a concrete purpose, and those miraculously turned up around the same time as Tom's birthdays each year.

Tom and Virginia Mallory's brief conversations were still a bit awkward, even though they'd drawn a truce now, relinquishing most of their emotional baggage. Tom visited his mother once or twice a year, a lot more regularly than he had for most of his 60 years. He was sure the getting older was what had spurred the change, leaving enough space between his childhood and now, to see that she wasn't so bad as he had viewed her over the years, and he wasn't quite as innocent as he'd remembered.

No matter how he tried to avoid them, surprises seemed to find Tom. Surprises like his mother's early call on his 62nd birthday and this other one he knew would follow.

"Well, Tommy...while I got you on the phone, I thought I should tell you I've finally made up my mind. I'm moving back home."

Home was Shreveport, Louisiana, and 78-year old Virginia Mallory had left at the tender age of seventeen after threatening to kill herself if she couldn't marry the Cajun boy who was Tom's father.

Tom's father, Thomas Alexander Mallory, had stolen the beautiful Virginia's heart with his sweet poems and exotic accent. He'd married her despite her parents' dismay and moved her a whole world's distance away to New Orleans. She still lived in the home that was, for all of Tom's childhood, a tragically unhappy one.

But Tom rarely ruminated on that time in his life anymore. The years had taken care of the raw pain he'd carried with him into his adulthood. He returned his full attention to his mother's soft southern drawl.

He recalled that Virginia had rarely returned to her hometown, even when her parents were alive. But if she suddenly wanted to make it home again, Tom wouldn't dissuade her. He just hoped this would give her some semblance of happiness. He'd never really known her to be a happy woman, so maybe it was true that Shreveport was the only place she had ever been happy.

Virginia had discussed the possible move with Tom three years ago. But, after all this time, he had assumed his mother had changed her mind decided to live the rest of her years in New Orleans. Not that he was surprised, ever, by what his mother did...like choosing today to announce a decision like this. Never mind that she had been planning the move for months now.

Virginia Radisson Mallory was moving back to Shreveport, and the old Radisson place, into the mansion owned for centuries by her father's family. She had ignored Tom's reminders that it wouldn't be the same Shreveport she'd left, that her name didn't hold the same currency, and the only people she knew there were her cousin Plank, and his business partner, John Rose, Jr., the son of the Radisson family's maid and cook Mary Ann Rose when Virginia was a child. John Jr., Virginia reminded him, was called "John-John" by most of the townspeople back then. "You know I love old Plank dearly, but he was born into that other line of the Radisson family," she said, raising her eyebrows.

Tom moved the conversation back to Virginia's upcoming move. "Oh, Tommy, please don't be so negative...here you go making a mountain out of a molehill.

You always do." Tom chuckled to himself. He'd never understand where Virginia's memories of him came from. How could she forget that he rarely talked at all as a child, let alone having the courage to make mountains out of molehills?

Only in his older age could Tom find humor in his mother's eccentricities. As a child, there had been no humor. It was her eccentricities that had scarred his childhood something terribly. But he had to give Virginia credit for her consistency, never veering from who she was.

The fact that there was little logic to the way she viewed life didn't change the fact that she was genuine in her views. You could always count on her to think that very same way, ten or 20 or 50 years from today. Now, after years of experiencing life and learning that imperfections run rampant in the world, Tom lessened his judgments of Virginia Mallory's humanity. He even admitted to himself that he loved her despite her strange and often ridiculous ways.

"Tommy, are you listening? John-John Rose and Cousin Plank have been working on restoring Papa's house since last year. I thought I told you. Oh well, I can't remember everything, now, can I?

"Even with Plank growing up on the other side of the family, I always just loved him. He was one of my very favorite cousins. You know his mother worked in city hall…I think she was the mayor's secretary or something like that. It was the strangest thing how he and John-John became best friends, way back there when you didn't see a lot of that, though some folks thought John-John was white until summertime."

Tom imagined a mixed-race friendship would not have been acceptable in Shreveport back in the 30s and 40s. "You know, John-John went away and was up north somewhere for a long time. Came back about 20 years ago. They say he must 'a done pretty well for himself cause he built himself a home down there in the new area where blacks and whites lived together and moved his parents in there with him.

"And then, about ten years ago, Plank brought John-John on to work with him in his construction and architecture business. They say John-John went to college up north and got a degree in architecture. Aint' that something? Anyway, they've been working on my house and sent me pictures last week, and it looks just beautiful…almost like I remember it from childhood.

"Plank was talking about sending the pictures through the internet, and I told him don't you dare! I never flipped that thing on since you brought it in the house.

"Tom, let me ask you this...I told Plank I'd talk to you about driving me down there next week so that I can look everything over for myself...and, it won't hurt to have another pair of eyes, too."

Tom winced but sat silently, listening to Virginia tear on through her spiel as if the trip was already a foregone conclusion. *And, it probably is*, he sighed.

"Tommy, I'm finally doing it. Aren't you proud of me? I really believe I would've just died if I had to live out my last days in this place. John-John said the house could be ready to move into in about a month, but they'll have to wait until I take a look at it and make sure about the materials for the bathrooms, kitchen, and floors. I want to choose all that once I get a good look at everything."

Tom would do what his mother asked him to. He'd plan the trip from Daphne to New Orleans, and from New Orleans to Shreveport...and back again. He just hoped he'd be able to get there and back within three or four days. He didn't want to be out of the office any longer. Not that Virginia would understand a little thing like needing to get back to a job because the city of Daphne depended on him to protect them from people just like them; and, most assuredly, those who weren't.

"Tommy...you know I've always said that Papa's house is the only real home I've ever known. After all these years, New Orleans never felt like more than a stopping-off place for me. Your fool of a daddy...never mind, none of that matters now. I feel like I'm halfway home, Tom, and you wouldn't know how good that feels."

Tom was still amazed at the ease with which Virginia Mallory could rewrite the script of her life and make her years of unhappiness in New Orleans her husband's fault. Or, how she could live in a place for 50 years and never have a kind thought, or at least some warm feelings toward it.

"Tommy... you will have time to drive me down to Shreveport, won't you, son? I wouldn't ask, but you know I don't drive, and I'd be scared to death to get on one of those Greyhound buses. They say all kinds of people ride those buses these days."

Tom knew it was no use trying to talk his mother out of anything once she'd set her mind to it. Besides, why should he try? Maybe she was right. At least she'd been consistent in believing that Shreveport was the only home she'd ever truly belonged.

And it was certainly true that Virginia never fit into the New Orleans culture. Yet, he knew it was also true that she hadn't tried to fit into that "culture of heathens."

It had taken Tom so long to get to this point. He truly wanted his mother's happiness and was empathetic with her unhappiness– whether voluntary or involuntary—during the last 50 years. If miracles could happen, then maybe Virginia would find happiness back in Shreveport, the only home she knew.

He would rest easier knowing she enjoyed whatever last years she had on this earth. After all, the beautiful, prejudiced, and still naïve Virginia Mallory was the only mother he'd ever have. He was ashamed that as a child, he'd desperately wished that God had been offering seconds.

Tom might as well get comfortable with the fact: there was no earthly way he would get around chauffeuring his mother from New

Orleans to Shreveport, Louisiana. He had promised her, three years ago—promised to make the drive from Daphne to New Orleans, help pack her up, and drive her "home." Tom's fingers had been crossed for all these years, though, that Virginia would forget the whole thing.

What must he have been thinking? Virginia Mallory never forgot promises, and she never allowed the barer to forget them, either. Tom agreed to the trip, acquiescing to Virginia's sweet, finagling before thanking her for the birthday call and saying goodbye. "I'll call in a few days and let you know when to expect me, Mother."

PART V: Maia

CHAPTER 5

What Southern Love looks Like…

This trip with Virginia, Tom knew, would require some serious rearranging of his schedule. Tom ran his fingers over his calendar, making cryptic notations of what he wanted Maia to do about his various meetings. The ones he'd scheduled himself could wait. They would be canceled outright. Others, he would reschedule for the week he returned.

The more mundane meetings, he would push off on Esau Tavistad, his new young deputy. Tom had a good feeling about this young officer he'd recruited from down in Tuscaloosa. He had graduated from the academy with flying colors, number 2 in his class– and one of the few minorities to win the praise of the academy director.

Esau would make a fine deputy, Tom knew, but he wasn't yet willing to put too much responsibility on him before his probation period was up. Besides, even though he looked good on paper, the boy had come there straight from six months under a really small-town sheriff. He needed a lot more experience under his belt before he could be let loose in his job.

Tom raffled through the paperwork Maia had set at the edge of his desk, adding to the piles already there. Maia had been Tom's clerk for almost 15 years until Tom was finally brave enough to give her a promotion, though he imagined what was going through the coworkers' minds.

Maia was a fine office manager. She had proven her worth twice over—holding the office together by the sheer tenacity of her sunny personality, smoothing out the kinks created by small-town office politics.

If anyone were brave enough to question his reasoning, he would remind them that the woman had worked for him all of his 25 years here in Daphne and been an outstanding employee all of that time. He would deal with the other too if it ever came up; how they had been something more than office colleagues most of those 25 years.

Tom knew it was common knowledge that theirs was a romantic relationship. Because of that, he hadn't been comfortable promoting her until five years ago. Maia had been bursting with pride when that promotion was announced at the Monday morning staff meeting. Later that night, as she thanked Tom for his confidence in her abilities, she also found the courage to tell him that an office promotion wasn't the most important thing to her.

Patience had been Maia's middle name during all those 25 years. Even now, she was still telling herself that Tom would one day wake up to the realization that he wanted to be married to her as much as she wanted to be married to him. She had long ignored the whispers inside and outside the office, of coworkers wondering when Tom would pop the question, or whether one of them tire of the other, and thrown them overboard.

For years, her girlfriends had warned her that she was wasting her youth in the relationship, that Tom Mallory was not the settling down and marrying kind. However, Maia was still certain she was right about Tom and would one day prove them wrong. But, one day was taking a long time, she sometimes sighed.

God knows Tom was not an easy person to know or understand. But Maia had learned him, had grown accustomed to his quiet spells, and the days at a time when she could hardly get a grunt out of him. She had eventually given up trying to explain their relationship to her parents because they would never understand.

Every once in a while, someone would mention they'd seen Mavis and Tom having dinner. Maia rarely responded with anything except, "Oh…that's how they catch up on city business."

She would never understand the strange relationship between Tom and Mavis that seemed to be something deeper than either of them realized. The weekly dinners that Maia was never invited to join had been a source of jealousy for a long time, but she had let it all go. Just as she did the late-night calls that Mavis often made, and Tom never discussed.

After Virginia's call, Maia watched as Tom fiddled with his computer that morning. Rather than the usual frown, Tom's face wore a small smile as he tackled with his keyboard to make it work the way he wanted. She almost asked him if he needed her help, but Tom hated interruptions when he was figuring things out all by himself. She walked over and gingerly placed another bulging file on the edge of his desk.

"Morning." He mumbled, hardly looking up. "How is Miss Virginia?"

"Just fine. If you call picking up lock, stock, and barrel to move from New Orleans, back to Shreveport – after being away 60+ years, fine," he answered with a straight face, but with a small chuckle.

"Hmmm..." Maia never got in the middle of Tom's discussions about his mother; usually, it was a five or ten-minute rant. At least this morning, she heard a bit of humor in his voice.

"Well, just remember your meeting at City Hall at 10 this morning, Chief." "I'm on my way...just need to make a few notes to myself. Seems like I'll be out of the office most of next week. Can you start in on rescheduling some of next week's meetings? Maybe you can get started on that while I'm over at the mayor's office, and we can finish up after I'm back."

"Sure, Chief...I'll get started on it right away. When do you leave, and do you want all your meetings canceled outright or reworked for another day?"

Tom was halfway to the door, pulling on his tan linen jacket. He pointed to the screen that showed his weekly calendar with red highlights. "I left a few notes there. See if you can make any sense out of that, will you? We can fill in the holes when I get back." With that, he was out the door.

As Maia settled into Tom's still-warm chair, she thought to herself that it wouldn't do a bit of good to ask the man for specifics. She was sure he hadn't mentioned a trip out of town last night while they lay in bed talking...and they had talked about his schedule for the week. She was pretty darn certain the new plans had to do with Virginia's call this morning.

Maia bit her lip, wondering about the mysterious Virginia Mallory. Any woman with such a hold on Tom Mallory must be a pretty powerful woman. She had long decided. She was also convinced that Tom must love her a great deal more than he thought he did, even if she did get him all riled up, sometimes.

But even Tom admitted that his and Virginia's relationship had mellowed over the years. She hadn't really been able to rile him at all for some time now. That, Maia decided, was what she called a miracle.

Maia remembered how she'd made the mistake, some ten years earlier, of imagining that she and Virginia might one day cultivate a normal relationship. It was the first and last mistake she'd made about Virginia Mallory. Tom had clarified things for her, though.

It was during one of their rare leisurely trips, fairly early in their relationship. The weekend trip to a New Orleans annual Jazz Festival was Tom's birthday gift to her that year. And, for Maia, it was still the most wonderful memory of their times spent together. But Maia had gone on the trip with a secret: she was more excited about the possibility that Tom would introduce her to Virginia than she was about the jazz festival. In her heart, she knew that meeting Virginia would mean she and Tom's relationship had reached a magical place.

As they neared the old iron bridge that would take them into Bastrop, Louisiana, just outside New Orleans, Maia coyly remembered that Virginia resided in the very city they would be staying in for the weekend.

"Tom, why don't you stop by Miss Virginia's to say hello before we go to the hotel. I bet she'd be so excited to see you. She might even like to join us at the concert tonight."

The smile was still fresh on Maia's face as she looked over and saw the unpleasant scowl on Tom's face. She knew she had said something wrong.

"Maia, I think we better get something straight about my mother. She is not the typical sweet mother who loves the air her son breathes. Of course, she loves me...in her own inexplicable way. In fact, she would be appalled if you ever questioned that love...but, trust me, it's not the kind of motherly love you're accustomed to.

"But that's neither here nor there. What you need to know is that Virginia Mallory would never be accepting of our relationship. She wouldn't treat you with warmth simply because you are my friend...not even because you happen to be a nice young woman.

"In a nutshell, she's probably the most judgmental human being you're ever to meet; very strict in her morals...even with a son moving fast toward 50."

Maia grew quiet, turned, and looked over the concrete bridge into the dirty Louisiana bayou. She wouldn't let Tom know how terribly he had dashed her hopes for a promising weekend...maybe even something traditional like getting introduced as the woman he'd like to make the next Mrs. Mallory.

Tom looked over at her and cleared his throat. He had said too much and said it all wrong. "Look, Maia. I don't mean to make my mother out to be a horrible person. If she got to know you, she'd have to like you. I just don't want to build up false hopes about her. She's not the kind of woman who will even let herself get to know you. And it's because of that, that we won't be staying there. I want this trip to be as enjoyable as possible for both of us."

She allowed a weary half-smile at the hard-to-understand Tom Mallory. They had driven a bit further, and Maia had softened, placing her hand on Tom's leg as he drove. He chuckled to himself, then. "And you can be absolutely certain that you won't run into Virginia Mallory at a crowded jazz concert on a Saturday night."

That was the last time Maia had brought up Virginia Mallory, except simply to ask Tom how she was doing or if she was well. She continued to remind Tom to send holiday cards and call on birthdays.

Though she was sure Tom would get around to telling her more specifics about next week's trip, the fact that it had something to do with Virginia added both a bit of intrigue and a bit of disappointment that she wouldn't get another chance at meeting Tom's mother.

Maia went back to her desk to shut down her own computer and make certain nothing confidential was left lying around. She was always pleased when Tom did something, no matter how off-handedly, to show he trusted her implicitly. Other times, she felt like his middle-aged Girl Friday, trusting her like he might trust his favorite pet.

As she sat reading through, then slowly deciphering his notes, Maia remembered how long it had taken to get to this point with Tom. He had remained wary of anything resembling a relationship for years. It had been a while before he'd spend the night at her place. In ways she couldn't explain, there was vindication in winning over Tom's trust. She was his office confidante, his sounding board when he needed one. He relied on her slow, methodical thoughts on things.

Maia loved knowing Tom valued her worth. More so, because it was so slow in coming. Yet, she couldn't help wishing that the pendulum in their relationship tilted a little more in the other direction: a little less, as his efficient girl Friday, and more toward the girl who was the love of his life and his future bride.

Everyone knew Tom Mallory didn't spread trust around lightly. He had a keen sense of people, and for him to trust her in just about every part of his life meant a great deal. She reminded herself of that as often as she needed to.

In case he hadn't noticed, lately, the pretty young woman who had welcomed Tom into the Daphne Police office and helped him set up his filing system 25 years ago, was no longer that innocent, young thing.

Her mirror reminded her each morning that she would soon be turning 48, a middle-aged woman who had miraculously dated the same man for over 25 years. And all of those years had been filled with dreams of what might be. For most of those 25 years, she'd dreamed of marrying Tom and having his child. Until she woke up one morning and realized she could chunk one part of that dream out the window. Well past 40, she knew there would never be a child. Yet, she held on to the expectation of marriage...one day.

When Tom Mallory walked into the Sheriff's office 25 years ago, a young, handsome, devil-may-care character out of someone's western novel, she'd fallen head over heels in love and had never stopped falling.

Tom was the man she had dreamed of all those years before he'd walked through that door. It was Tom she wanted as the father of her children—the very ones she imagined smothering with love the way her mother had with her. It was Tom who she prayed each night, still, would ask for her hand in marriage before it was too late for them.

How many nights had she lain awake while Tom slept beside her, remembering her early dreams of a perfect life, a perfect family? Those dreams had begun at 14 or 15, and the dreaming hadn't stopped, even now. Was Tom blind, are more callous than she believed he was, that he wouldn't sense the need in her?

Tom, whose sensory perceptions had always been keen, had, in fact, sensed Maia's needs. Yet, his fear of repeating his past would never allow him to take a chance on Maia's dream. He wasn't meant for the traditional kind of happily ever after. More than just feeling guilty about what she'd missed out on, Tom was painfully aware of what he'd never have, as well.

His inalterable position on marriage and families was his way of assuring he wouldn't repeat his parents' mistakes. His childhood was the obstacle to his happily ever after. For Maia's sake, and also for his, he wished things had been different, that things, now, could be different. While he loved Maia completely, he would always leave the door cracked for her to walk away if she ever felt she had to. He would completely understand and wish her happiness.

He wondered would it ever come to that, or would she continue to dream and pray that he'd come to his senses before her clock stopped ticking, or they stopped loving each other? After twenty-five years, Tom thought it wouldn't make sense for either of them to look elsewhere. While their romance had mellowed some, it had also grown stronger, more comfortable...much like it might if they were, in reality, an old, married couple.

* * *

PART VI: Yesterday Is Calling

CHAPTER 6

A Midnight Call

Tom returned from his meeting 30 minutes later than he'd expected. The mayor had stacked too many meetings together. Next up, Tom discerned was something critical, like rounding up city workers to help man the football game tomorrow night.

Maia had finished her work at his desk. He hung his jacket back on the door and began checking his messages. There didn't seem to be anything important enough to merit an immediate call back. He slid the message rack to the far side of his desk and clicked on his computer.

He grunted his approval that Maia had magically worked everything out. He looked over and found her looking back, a confident smirk on her face. "You do good work, lady," he offered.

According to his now updated calendar, the office would be just fine over the next week unless something unexpected and extraordinary happened. As far-fetched as that sounded, unexpected things were known to happen in this once-upon-a-time bedroom community.

Maia had plugged Esau Tavistad's name into more meetings than Tom would have if he'd given it more thought before he turned over his schedule to Maia. He wouldn't change the schedule. This would be a good opportunity for the young man to prove himself. Maia was high on Esau's abilities, and he knew she was likely right about him. He would just have to prove himself to Tom before he placed that level of confidence on him. He'd wavered between hiring Esau, the school principal's son, and the new mayor's grandson. Maia had been adamant that he should hire Esau. "Tom, you of all people, know Esau is the right person for the job…and it's high time you put your money where you say your heart is. I'm sick of hearing you preach about diversity."

In fact, she'd pretty much badgered him until he agreed to give the boy a chance to prove his worth. This might at least give Tom an opportunity to learn whether young Esau was lawman material or not.

Tom chuckled softly to himself when he came to the bottom of the calendar and saw the words:

Missing you, Already!

(Maia)

It wasn't that Tom was dreading this trip. It's just that he wasn't doing flips over it. He hoped it would take less than the full week for Virginia to get her business done. He began mapping the trip in his head…he'd drive to his mother's home and spend the night there on Saturday. They'd prepare to drive to Shreveport Sunday morning since neither he nor Virginia pretended that church-going was part of their Sunday morning routine.

They'd likely arrive in Shreveport on Sunday around noon. Even before talking specifics with Virginia, he imagined that she'd want to spend all of Monday at the old house and maybe part of Tuesday. They'd stay over Tuesday night, get up in time for a good breakfast on Wednesday morning, and prepare to light out for the four-hour drive back to New Orleans by 10 a.m.

The cloud over Tom was evaporating by the moment as he imagined the possibility of depositing Virginia back at home on Wednesday early afternoon, spend a few hours there, then be on his way back to Daphne before dark. He would sleep in his own bed next Wednesday night and arrive in his office before anyone else on Thursday morning.

Tom smiled despite himself. Not bad, just three days out of the office. He was certain not much could happen to close down the city in those three days. And, even if there were small catastrophes, he figured Esau could handle those with just phone supervision.

His plan felt doable. He just had to make sure Virginia didn't throw a wrench in the middle of it. The woman was legendary for her contrariness. He would call her later when he got home tonight. They would compare plans, and he'd decide whether she had any opposing thoughts that deserved consideration. Surely, Virginia wasn't planning to

take any furniture down on this trip. That would require more time in New Orleans than Tom had planned for.

He thought fleetingly of paying a visit to his father's kin, but he knew it wouldn't be possible on this trip. Not with Virginia in the mix. Tom's mood continued to change colors as he realized he and Virginia would be traveling alone together for four hours, the longest time they'd ever been in one space together.

Admittedly, he wouldn't break out in hives at the thought... as he would have ten years ago. Yet, it was a mystery to him why Virginia, who rarely exhibited any natural maternal instincts during his childhood, now seemed to love having her son spend time with her.

Tom wouldn't spend much energy reanalyzing Virginia's unorthodox mothering techniques. His take on his mother had changed so completely that it didn't matter very much. It had taken him almost 60 years to get here, and he'd be damned if he'd mess that up with trying to rethink the woman. He had a good 10 or 15 years left in him, and he meant to make the best of them!

If there was a God above, he'd smiled down on him. He could carry on a civil conversation with his mother. He could sleep under the same roof as the still unpredictable woman without wanting to put a fist through the wall. The truth was, Tom loved the woman despite what she'd been as a mother. Maybe he simply needed to love her because she was his mother...he didn't want to think the whys of things anymore.

New Orleans. With all the dark memories, it was the place he'd always call home. There was a kinship between the soul of this strange city and Tom's strange soul. He'd never questioned the affection he harbored for the place Virginia hated so much. He'd run away once when he was still a boy and equated the city with his unhappy childhood.

Now, Tom found himself drawn to that very same city for what it was, and what it wasn't, and even because it had been home to Virginia Mallory all of these years. Part of his admiration for the city had to do with its tarnished heritage, its inherent tragedies. Besides, there was something to be said about a city that could hold onto a woman like Virginia, even if she hated it with a passion.

There was, of course, more to his fascination with New Orleans. There were yet secrets of his family's past. Unspoken truths, like his great grandparents who had lived just blocks away from where he'd grown up and where his mother yet lived. In all these years, Tom had never broached the subject of his father's relatives with his mother.

He'd wanted to. He'd wondered for years what she knew and didn't know about this other side of her husband's family. He never imagined Virginia could have a civil conversation about her husband's mixed heritage. Now, he was wondering if he underestimated Virginia all these years. Maybe. He wouldn't think about it now.

* * *

Tom would never like surprises, even if he lived another 60 years. Life had taught him that surprises were too often exactly what we feared and rarely what we wanted. Why couldn't he be surprised by winning a million-dollar lottery that would allow him to spend a full month sitting on the lake and reading his favorite James Patterson novels or catching a mess of brim; or experiencing a full week with no crimes – especially the ones that left you trying to decide whether to laugh or kick the perpetrator in the butt for his stupidity.

Like Virginia's birthday call. Not that he was dreading the time he'd be traveling between New Orleans and Shreveport with his mother. But he'd be lying if he said he couldn't think of a few other surprises he would place in front of this one. The real surprise for Tom was that, for the first time in his memory, he hadn't dreaded Virginia's call. He could not have imagined that 10 years ago, or even five years ago.

Tom remembered something else he'd learned over the years. Surprises were like deaths of the rich and famous. They almost always came in threes. Virginia's call had reminded him of that old adage, and now he was waiting for the other shoe to drop.

This morning had to count for surprise number two. It wasn't one that blew him completely out of the water...but it definitely rated as a mild surprise. Maia hadn't awakened him this morning with her now traditional rendition of Marilyn Monroe's "Happy Birthday, Mr. President," Tom recalled that first time she had. It was 20 years ago, and she had, indeed, knocked his socks off with that one.

"Well...aren't you going to say anything, Tom Mallory?" Maia had asked him, half-smiling. "I practiced for a week on that dang song!"

Tom was a man of few words. He had finally pulled himself together enough to show her rather than tell her how moved he was.

* * *

CHAPTER 7

The Morning After

Eric Rayes, Pastor Tucker's audiovisual guru, lay in bed trying to soak in every last second before he rose for the day. The sound of Earth Wind and Fire's sweet melodic, "September," on his cell phone told him somebody wanted him up before he wanted to get up. It was 6:43 a.m. Eric cursed under his breath before answering the call. Whoever it was would be privy to Eric's "forced to get up before my eyes are even open" mood.

He settled the phone next to his ear, his eyes still half-closed. Callindra Tucker's syrupy southern drawl spilled over into his ear. Even with the hint of exhaustion in that voice, he could never mistake it for anyone else's. Eric mumbled a surprised "Good morning, Pastor," tasting the staleness of last night's wine.

"Why, good morning, Eric. Please don't cuss me... it's your friendly pastor calling out of desperation. Sweetie, I know it's early, and I really hope I'm not waking you, but I'm afraid duty doth call."

Eric tried shaking the sleep out of his brain as he recalled that the pastor had arrived back from her Africa trip late last night. He wondered how the woman could possibly be awake at 6 a.m., after a 16-hour flight from Africa that landed at midnight last night.

"Pastor Tucker, it's wonderful to have you back, but...I can't believe you're already up." He pulled himself up, leaning back against the headboard, feeling strangely embarrassed about his bare torso as he spoke with the pastor. Thankfully, she never claimed she was one of those clairvoyant preachers who could see all kinds of things.

Eric blushed to think the woman might have even an inkling of how he'd spent last night – out at the home of Anita, the church secretary. Or that he'd rolled out of her bed at 3 a.m. to take a shower, dress, and let himself out of her apartment. He repressed a groan, realizing that had been just three hours ago.

"Eric, sweetie, I really need you to meet me down at the sanctuary at eight. I have to work on my message, and I'm thinking we'll need to plan to be there at least until noon. I'll call Saul and ask him if Dolly can put together some breakfast snacks and coffee.

"Honey, I am so sorry to intrude on your Saturday morning, really. Unfortunately, this is the only free time I'll have today. By the way...how's your mama doing, sweetie?"

"Oh, Mama's just fine, Pastor Tucker...she's been resting herself since that last visit to the emergency room."

"Well, that's a blessing. You tell her I'll be sending her another care package next week and praying she'll be back with us before long." Eric heard the ragged edge to Callindra Tucker's silky drawl and knew it was a symptom of her soul-saving tour and the long flight home.

He wondered who could talk the pastor into resting every once in a while? He was sure there wasn't a soul she'd listen to. She was like his own mother, a strong, independent woman who was proud of how much she could do without leaning on a man. The difference was that his mama had had a good, strong man most of her adult life until Eric Sr. passed just a few years ago. Now, she lived in his memory and wouldn't think of letting another man try and take his place.

"Thanks, sweetie...now, go on back to sleep. I'll see you around 8." As Callindra clicked off, Eric fell back on his bed and closed his tired eyes. The woman couldn't have gotten more than five hours of sleep, he thought. Anita's cousin had traveled with the pastor and called her from the plane to report they'd be landing around midnight.

Telephoning from the jet was pretty impressive, Eric had to admit. He set his alarm for 7:15 in hopes of getting another hour of sleep before meeting the pastor at the church. As much he as loved the woman, he wished there was a man in her life to divert some of her attention from the church.

Callindra Tucker emerged through the sanctuary's doors at 7:55 a.m., still yawning but smiling. She blew good morning kisses up at Eric and the thin crew he'd been able to recruit at this early hour. Eric was thankful his minister had made it back safe and sound, but what he was most happy about was that she never ventured upstairs into the production area.

Eric would drown himself in large cups of black coffee for the rest of the morning. He'd gotten started before he left home. All he needed, Eric told himself, was for his bladder to hold out. He blew into his third cup of coffee. Miss Dolly had made it strong. The steam brought sweat to his upper lip as he waited for the pastor to signal when she was ready. Right now, she was making last-minute changes to her message.

Where did the woman get so much energy at her age? Not that she was an old woman...and, she certainly wasn't a bad-looking one.

In fact, Callindra Tucker was what the Hollywood folks called an ageless beauty. If you didn't know her age, you could never guess it. When he thought about it, she wasn't what most men would call beautiful at first sighting, but there was something about her that brought the word to bear most times you thought of Callindra Tucker.

Eric was failing at his attempt to block memories of his evening with Anita. Now, Anita...that was a beauty for you. Especially when she wasn't all dressed up like a schoolteacher. He wondered what the girl was doing this morning and what she'd be wearing to church tomorrow morning. She'd be back to Miss prim and proper, he knew. Eric smiled. Thank goodness that wasn't who she was last night.

Eric's memories disappeared as a team member walked over and started a conversation. They made small talk about their weekends while the pastor continued to work on her message. When she signaled that she was ready, the pianist asked about her trip with as much genuine enthusiasm as he could muster that early in the morning. She gave them short but warm responses, intermittently drinking from her coffee.

"You know, Pastor C...we're still waiting for our trip around the world on that jet!" Eric's crew laughed tiredly. "Yeah, we want to go out there and help you save some souls one of these times," someone said.

Callindra looked up with a mock frown on her face, though she couldn't help but giggle at their silly joke. "Your time is coming, guys...I promise. Next time we might end up in Asia." As she worked on her message, she would stop from time to time and talk about the trip, describing the city of Nairobi, the hundreds of baptism services she performed throughout the various cities; and how the flight from Nairobi had truly been as comfortable as sitting in her limousine.

"Wow...that's cold, Pastor C. Thanks for rubbing it in our faces!" they all laughed. She hadn't realized how fascinated young men were by nice airplanes. She had never given much thought to that because she rarely flew in planes. It was truly a miracle that the beautiful Cessna jet had been bequeathed to her just months ago.

Reverend Callindra Tucker stood at the podium peering down at the words she'd scribbled before falling asleep last night and the changes she'd made to them. One of her assistants would type up the revised message later today. This morning, she just needed to clear the cobwebs from her head and practice her delivery for tomorrow and get a tape to take home with her so that she could listen to it tonight.

Eric sat in the production box directly across and above her. He wondered what magic he could conjure up to mask the exhaustion in his bosses' voice. There was certainly enough equipment here to work some magic if he could just figure out the right balance.

He smiled, remembering how quickly the music and sound committee had taken up his campaign to raise funds for the state-of-the-art, round-sound system. They'd ended up raising $20,000...well over the amount he'd estimated a good system should cost.

He frowned, realizing that this morning's task would require some magical maneuvering on his part. The Rev's voice was ragged and strained, but there was no way she'd listen to him about going home, drinking tea, and taking a long nap. His grandma's favorite saying was, `You can beat your head against a brick wall all you want, boy, but you can't squeeze blood from a turnip.'

Eric would have to do exactly that this morning. Callindra Tucker was a perfectionist, and she'd expect nothing less than magic from this recording. He would do whatever it took to give the Rev exactly what she wanted.

The young sound engineer's own pride was wrapped up in his amazing equipment. It had been over a year now, and he was still in awe of the choir's heavenly sound reverberating throughout the huge church each Sunday morning. It was the same for the minister's message, the female version of God's voice. His chest swelled with the crescendo of that voice and the choir's many voices.

This morning, Eric prayed for that kind of magic to transform the Rev's tired voice into the sweet, soothing one her members were most familiar with. Thirty minutes into rehearsal, his prayers were finally being heard. He breathed a sigh of relief as he picked up the change in her voice, the scratchy one moving into the background, and the old, familiar one—mesmerizing and sweet to the ear— growing stronger, steadier.

Eric knew there was no force in the world strong enough to coerce the woman to rest either her body or her voice before throwing herself back into her busy schedule. He figured God surely looked out for her. He knew better than anyone just how little time she gave to herself.

"There is just so much to do!" Callindra always complained, but always with awe and amusement. Besides, she'd gotten by on just a few hours of sleep most of her life.

* * *

CHAPTER 8

Weldon Solder

Callindra was in her late thirties when Weldon Solder met her. He would often tell parishioners about their first meeting. "I remember saying to myself, 'Here is a woman with more life, more spirit than any I've ever met in my life.'" After that first meeting, she'd invited him to her Sunday service. For whatever reason, he had got up that next Sunday morning and walked through the church doors just 10 minutes before service began.

During her goodbye greeting of the parishioners, her face had brightened, and her smile widened when Weldon walked up. She offered him a pastor-like hug and asked if he would call her about a new role she wanted to add to her staff.

Weldon had said yes to Callindra Tucker a second time and called her the next day. What was he thinking? He wasn't a church attorney. That wasn't how he was made? Yet, he had been mulling the possibility of leaving the firm. Still, a church hadn't entered the calculation.

Yet, he found himself intrigued by the woman who didn't exactly fit the profile of a southern preacher. Too open, too pretty, too honest. But he'd said yes during their telephone call. He'd meet her at the church for lunch. They met in her beautiful study. The food was delicious and more than he usually ate in two days.

He was surprised to realize how much he enjoyed his time with the preacher. They'd both asked questions and learned a lot more about each other than they'd expected to learn.

She'd shared that she had answered God's message to start the church from scratch five years earlier, and the church and the congregation had been steadily growing since.

"It's all God, Weldon. I knew nothing about leading a church or a congregation…but he's put this thing in front of me. I can literally feel him holding my hand, guiding me. It's the strangest thing to ever happen in my life."

Weldon smiled, impressed. He told her he knew what he wanted to do since high school. His favorite uncle was a lawyer. After business school, he'd gone straight into law school at Penn State. The offers came in from both private and public organizations. He chose to go to the highest bidder and had been a corporate lawyer for the last 45 years.

He laughed when she admitted she'd hesitated to ask him for the meeting because it was so obvious he was a northerner. Something he said, or maybe the way he said it, had convinced her it didn't really matter in the end.

"No, Ma'am, I'm not a southerner. I was born in the north, but the best job offer I got back then was to join Warner Stone & Pasterik Law Firm, one of the largest corporate firms in the southeast. My only hesitation was the requirement that I move down here to New Orleans for work. They made me an offer I couldn't refuse. I moved and, in time, settled into `N'awlins.'"

Calli laughed out loud to hear his attempt at a southern drawl. "You're still not a southern boy, I'm afraid, Mr. Solder."

"I have to agree with you, there, Pastor. But I can honestly say I've gained a great deal of appreciation for a lot of the southern ways."

Callindra leaned her head. "What is it, Mr. Solder, that you find in us southerners to admire?"

"Oh…honesty. Openness. Those weren't the first things you'd notice back where I came from, but I've decided those are the values you want in your employees or the people who pay your salary."

After their long lunch and endless conversation, Callindra invited Weldon Solder to accept the new counselor's role for the south Louisiana church that was growing by leaps and bounds. "I need someone to organize me, guide me, and take care of my financial stuff." He looked in her silver-gray eyes and wondered if she knew just how effective her charm was.

Mr. Solder, I'm also in terrible need of a personal attorney. I'm just not a very organized person, and the more this thing grows and my way of living changes, the more scared I get that I'm gone find myself in a heap of legal trouble."

He gave a loud sigh pulled his hands through his salt and pepper hair.

"Oh no. I've been known sometimes to talk myself out of my blessings. Did I scare you away by asking you to take on two huge and complicated dual roles at one time, Mr. Solder?"

Weldon was quiet for a moment looked down at his hands. She knew that meant he was at least thinking it over…or trying to find a nice way to say "no." He looked back up and straight into her eyes. "I'll come in and officially apply for the job next week, Pastor Tucker."

* * *

Weldon Solder wasn't a man who acted on whims. He was thorough and sometimes waited weeks thinking offers through before saying "yes." there was something about this woman who clearly needed his help that made him want to say yes much sooner than he should.

Maybe it was simply that she'd met him at a time when he desperately needed a change in his life and his work environment. Leaving Warner Stone & Pasterik had been an emotionally painful change for him. He'd left angry, hurt, and, if he was truthful, pretty burned out. Even the burnout, though, wouldn't have forced him to leave.

It was the fact that he'd be ready to retire even if he ever was offered the managing partner role. Still, it was hard to walk away. Being a high-level corporate attorney in any part of the country, but certainly in the south, meant having access and a certain level of power and gravitas. He'd enjoyed that for more than half his life. How could being the church attorney at Miracle Way compete? It couldn't. He knew that, but still. He was convinced this was the kind of life change he needed for whatever reason.

Weldon Solder, an overachiever since his elementary school days in southern Illinois, had failed to achieve what he had worked towards for many years. Most perplexing given that his abilities as a top-rate attorney had never been questioned. His annual evaluations showed him to be excellent in almost every area of his work.

Whatever the thing that had held him back, it wasn't his intellect or his work. Yet, something clearly made the firm's board pass over him year after year for a role everyone in the firm knew he desperately wanted. He had asked more than once what he wasn't doing or should be doing differently. No one could ever tell him what that was.

It had taken him months to decide, but finally, Weldon had walked into the firm and gave the managing partner his resignation letter, saying he believed he deserved much more from the firm. He fully believed he was the most deserving of the role and had worked hard to prove himself over the years. In his letter, he reminded the board of the cruelty of being told numerous times that he was on the list of top ten partners for the role. Yet, it had never once been offered to him, not even the opportunity to interview.

Three years before he finally left, Weldon was diagnosed with bleeding ulcers and high blood pressure. Even so, it took him those three years to talk himself into leaving the firm. It was late one night as he was preparing for bed and drinking seltzer water to soothe his burning ulcers that he'd finally accepted that he had gone as far as he should with the firm. Leaving was one of the hardest things he'd done in his lifetime. He imagined what some of his friends experienced who'd gone through divorces after long years of marriage.

Callindra didn't know of Weldon's scars he carried with him from the firm. Maybe she did sense some hurt, but it didn't mar her conviction that God had sent him to help her. That had been almost 15 years ago, and she was convinced he was the reason for the church's success and growth.

Weldon Solder was church counsel, chief operating officer, personal attorney, and confidante to Callindra. Theirs was a close business friendship. They were both in the habit of carefully choosing friends. Weldon quickly became Callindra Tucker's right-hand man, offering her his counsel even before she realized she needed it. When she was in the mood for company after a long day, Weldon was the one person she turned to join her for dinner, for a political tete a' tete, and other unexpected events.

He was the one person she trusted to push back, those times when she was pushing for something new for the church. She admired just how many ways he could say no without making her angry because he softened it with reasoning and logic.

In time, yes, they had become mutual admirers. He admired her purity of purpose, her charm that brought in new members every week, her understanding of the bible, and her ability to translate it into something so simple, one wouldn't even have to be able to read to grasp it. Callindra, he thought to himself, was a brilliant messenger.

It wasn't until he had worked with her for a year that he realized his emotions could become a problem. He was very aware of his strong attraction to his employer, while he knew there was no room for it within the church...and, certainly within Callindra's life.

He squashed those thoughts and those feelings each time they dared raise their heads. Their friendship – any substantive friendship- was an unexpected one for Callindra. She had lots of admirers, associates, and colleagues, hordes of people wanting to spend time with her. There were few people she spent any time with outside church business.

Callindra had, from the beginning, impressed with Weldon's intellect and his legal credentials. She was impressed with how fast he taught himself all he needed to know about the operations of a church and what it took to manage a growing operation like the church. Yet, the man was so starched and tucked-in, she laughed. She wondered about Weldon's faith. They'd never really discussed it, and why should they. He was her employee, and the depth of his faith was not her affair. His work was beyond reproach. In time, Callindra realized that her counsel sometimes seemed to know her better than she knew herself... was able to read her at those times when others couldn't figure her out.

* * *

CHAPTER 9

Manna from Heaven

The sleek, midnight blue, customized Cessna 737 had been loaned to Callindra Tucker and the church the week before the pastor and her entourage was to make their Africa Ministry. The loaner was one Mr. Edward Wilson, a gentle soul and a faithful servant of the church for as long as it had existed.

Callindra had long viewed the octogenarian as one of God's gifts to her. He was there sitting with a smile on his face each Sunday. He gave magnanimously to the church and always supported the church's work in the community.

Upon returning from the Africa mission, Callindra learned her benefactor had been hospitalized. Bothered by the news, Callindra made it her business to call him each day despite the six hours difference in time. She made Alana change her appointments around to visit him during the week. They would spend as much as an hour reminiscing about the beginning of their relationship, which coincided with the beginning of the church.

One night, just as she was preparing to visit her friend, she received a phone call. It was Mr. Wilson calling from his hospital room. "Pastor Tucker, I wanted to catch you before you came tonight. Would you please bring your bible with you tonight? There's a little passage in there I've heard you teach so many times.

I'd be so honored if you'd read it tonight."

Callindra said, of course. She would. She'd be there in the next 30 minutes.

In thirty minutes, Callindra was walking into Mr. Wilson's private room that was filled with flowers, plants, and cards. Callindra imagined many of them were from members of her own congregation. She walked to his side, bent, and kissed him on his forehead.

"How are you feeling tonight, Elder Wilson? It seems you always have that same beautiful smile on your face no matter how you're feeling."

"Pastor Tucker, I'm feeling fine. The doctors make sure I am. But, you know, out of all the things in my life, what I miss most these days is your Sunday messages. They have become so much a part of my life. Earlier this morning, I had one of your tapes playing beside my bed but realized I didn't have the one I love so much. It is the message from John:4, of Jesus and the Samaritan woman. I'd love to hear you read that tonight."

Callindra read. It was as if God truly did mark her words tonight, gave them more meaning than she ever could of her own volition. When she came to the end, she looked up and saw that Mr. Wilson's eyes were closed. She was a little startled when he opened his eyes and began to speak.

"Pastor Tucker, God spoke to me this morning. I know…folks say that all the time, but it was His voice. There is no question of that. The good Lord gave me the answer that I had been wrestling with for a long time- how I could repay you for all you've done for me over these last 20 years, all the wonderful spiritual leadership you've blessed me with."

"Oh, Elder Wilson, you don't need to give back because you've already given us so much. Your presence has meant so much for the love we've felt each Sunday. Your generous gifts, your support when we had to go before the county or the city...what more could I possibly ask of you...except you get well and return to us?"

The man chuckled and looked down, quiet for a minute. "Pastor Tucker, your guidance has been the one sustaining thing for me all these years...taking me from one Sunday to the next. I'm just so thankful God showed me how I can repay all those years of spiritual guidance."

When Elder Wilson told Callindra his plans to gift the jet for the church, Callindra found herself speechless, her eyes wide and quickly tearing up. "No...oh no, Mr. Wilson, you can't! Miracle Way doesn't need anything like that. Please, there are so many causes out there, so many other things you can spend that money on!."

The man listened quietly. "Pastor Tucker, it wasn't all my decision...God had a bit to do with it, too." He chuckled and was quiet for a moment. "Please, Pastor Tucker...it's my gift to give. Please let me before I leave this world."

He ignored her gasp of surprise. "Elder Wilson?"

"Well, I had no plans of sharing that little piece of information with you, Pastor, but you're leaving me no alternative... the Lord is making things ready for me, as we speak. He's coming for me very soon, and I'm trying like the dickens to get things straight before he does." She was moved by the lack of panic or urgency in his voice. Callindra couldn't help but wonder if she would accept God's decision to call her home with such grace.

"I'm ready, no doubt about it...but I needed to get this one thing straight with you. Don't make me tell Him I couldn't do this one small thing," he lightly touched the minister's arm, and she covered the small hand with her own. Tears now streamed freely down her face. "Oh, Mr. Wilson. I'm so sorry, so grateful, and so sorry."

Callindra was overwhelmed with gratitude. "You've given so much. But, if it is God directing you, how can I say no...you and God against little old me?"

The man's small laughter lit up his face. He was happy and content. "Reverend Tucker... the plane will be a blessing for your Campaign in Africa next year. And, if you don't mind me prophesying...I have a feeling that this is just the beginning of that Campaign. God is smiling on your good works, and he has plans in store for you. I might even be a little selfish, knowing I won't be able to join you in the flesh. I want to have something to do with this wonderful crusade."

Callindra laughed lightly as she swallowed back her tears. She didn't want to rain on Elder Wilson and God's blessings with tears. She was silent for a while, still speechless. The good man had won. She relented with grace and a heartfelt, "Thank you, Elder Wilson...will you at least let me pray with you?".

The tears fell freely as she prayed fervently. The tears, now, were from her sadness that the man would soon be leaving her and the church. She would never again look down into the sanctuary and catch sight of his warm, sweet smile. The least she could do, she said, was to pray with him before they said goodnight.

* * *

In all the years Callindra had known Edward Wilson, almost as many years as she had pastured the church, she had never given much thought to his monetary worth. There were rumors that he was well off, and she did know he made generous contributions. She didn't think much beyond those facts.

In fact, as pastor of the fast-growing church, she rarely concerned herself with the financial side of things, often telling her board's finance committee that God held her responsible for the souls, and she held them responsible for keeping the finances in order.

Edward Wilson had been one of her earliest supporters. When she'd met him 20 years ago, he was a dapper middle-aged man who she'd learned had recently lost his wife. He told her more than once that coming to church every Sunday made it easier for him to get through his grief. She recalled he'd never remarried, not even bringing a female friend to the church.

Callindra had found it endearing, as she looked out over the sea of faces each Sunday morning, to find Mr. Edward sitting in the same front-row pew, with that same adoring smile on his face. There had been nothing to tell her, however, that the sweet, little man had real wealth. As ostentatious as it was, his parting gift certainly proved her wrong.

After sharing his secret with her, Callindra made daily visits to the hospital praying with Elder Wilson, sometimes holding his hand until he fell asleep. His name had been on the prayer list for the weeks he'd been unable to attend services. A week after she'd learned God was calling him, Callindra walked into the hospital only to be told by the attending nurse he'd been released to hospice. Callindra had hurried home to change and eat dinner, planning to visit Mr. Wilson that evening.

Before she finished dinner, she received a call. It was Mr. Wilson's nurse calling to tell her their patient had expired at 1 p.m. that afternoon. "Pastor Tucker, Mr. Wilson left a request that you meet with his attorney at your earliest convenience." The woman gave the pastor the attorney's phone number before hanging up.

Callindra immediately began a prayer for Mr. Wilson, thanking God for taking care of him for all these years and now bringing him home to spend eternity with Him.

She decided to call the attorney this evening. She was sure the conversation would be about the expensive plane the sweet man had promised her and the church. Likely there were boxes of paperwork she'd need to sign. The attorney's secretary answered and was about to say he wasn't in until Mr. Seaton picked up his line.

"Pastor Tucker, thank you for calling. I was about to walk out the door for the evening...perfect timing. I won't keep you this evening, Pastor Tucker...I know how busy your days are. Your friend and parishioner, Mr. Edward Wilson, shared with me how much of a positive force you've been during the long winter season of his life. And, for some time, he had been trying to find a way to express his gratitude...but, we can talk more about that when we meet.

"What I think would be good is for us to put off our meeting until after Mr. Wilson's service, which brings me to one of his requests. Just a few days before his expiration, he asked if I would convey to you just how grateful he would be if you would deliver his eulogy at the funeral service. If you say yes, I think it would be completely proper for us to meet shortly after the service – or, if you would like at that time, we could set a more appropriate time to discuss the rest of our business."

Callindra imagined the man on the other end of the phone dressed in a dark grey suit, silver-gray hair, and pince-nez glasses. He would be dapper, meticulously- dressed very much in the mode of his deceased client. She agreed to meet with him in his Shreveport offices the day after the services.

"Mr. Seaton, I am more than honored to eulogize my loyal church member's service. Would you make sure that someone will get the details to me tomorrow, and I can prepare to the extent one can, for an event such as this…Edward Wilson was a very special man."

Callindra surprised herself when she felt the tears swell in her eyes, overcome by the man's goodness. She often wondered what made some people's hearts so open and giving, while others were closed, immune to the needs of those around them. She regretted that she had not taken the opportunity to know Mr. Wilson better. Spent more time with him through the years. It warmed her heart to remember that his caretaker had said Mr. Wilson had died in his sleep, in no pain.

* * *

"His departure was the kind that we all aspire to…after a long and fruitful life; to leave knowing that God is smiling on our good works…," Callindra had half-mused during her eulogy of the dear, sweet man.

It had been a pleasant service, even if Callindra was a bit surprised that there were no more than 50 visitors, including Mr. Wilson's children and distant family members. The man had twins—a daughter and son. They were small, diminutive, like their father. Callindra couldn't guess their ages. She estimated they were in their late 40's, or maybe even her age. Their timid smiles and quiet voices reminded Callindra of their father.

Weldon Solder had joined Callindra at the service, wanting to be as inconspicuous as possible. He stood to the back as she greeted family, friends, and other grievers before the service began. The children, she noted, were reserved like their father. There was a shy kindness that permeated from them, that very same aura that ensured she would never forget Edward Wilson.

Though Callindra found it awkward to converse with the twins, she understood it was only because she had never known of their existence. Their father had never mentioned his family except to share that his wife had passed shortly before he'd arrived at the church door.

As the twins prepared to leave for their drive back to Houston that evening, Callindra embraced each of them and whispered condolences into their mildly surprised faces. "It was such a personal blessing to have known your father. He was such a special man, such a loyal Christian. My heart and spirit tell me we can be certain your father got his business straight with God before he said his final goodbyes here," she smiled, with tears sitting in the corner of her eyes.

The twins nodded, almost in unison. "We know how much he loved the church, and you, Pastor Tucker. We are so grateful that you found time to be with us and remember him. I know he's resting in peace."

The younger, female version of Edward Wilson nodded her small head. "He said there was nothing that gave him as much joy as your ministry. Sunday mornings were something he looked forward to each week...he told us as much. We could never get him to visit for long in Houston...he said his life was here because his church was here."

She smiled. "We just can't thank you enough for that...and want you to know that no gift my father might leave is too much in return for the goodness you provided him during his last years. He was truly a happy man, here."

With that, the siblings looked intently into each other's eyes, nodded toward Callindra, and turned to leave. "Goodbye, and Thank you again, Pastor Tucker." Mr. Wilson said.

* * *

The next morning Callindra woke with the thought that she was scheduled to visit the attorney's office. The thought was hardly a pleasant one. Gifts always cost as much as they were worth, she had always believed. Not that she wasn't grateful for the luxury plane Mr. Wilson had left the church, but...well, she just didn't need it. In fact, she thought, rarely do we ever need unsolicited gifts.

Callindra Tucker was not a businesswoman. Decisions that required her implicit attention were the ones that forced her to lean on Weldon Solder. Not that she minded leaning on Weldon. This gift forced her to, and if she had to lean on anyone, she was happy that it was Weldon Solder.

They rode together to Attorney Seaton's office in Shreveport. By the time they arrived, they were both convinced the meeting would be a quick signing of papers for the appropriation of the Cessna Jet.

"Just so you don't panic once we get in there, Pastor, there may be a ton of papers needing your signature. We can either sign them here or just take them back to the office with us…giving us time to scan them more carefully."

There was a hint of a smile on his lips as Callindra seemed to blanch with disappointment. "I do hope you brought your reading glasses."

"Are you insinuating that I'm so vain I wouldn't wear reading glasses, Mr. Solder?" They both smiled, now.

"But seriously…do you think something could have gone wrong, that Mr. Wilson might not have gotten around to getting the paperwork signed before…he left us? You think we might even have to return the plane?"

Callindra shook her head. The thought was incredulous, but funny just the same.

"Well, we can always boast that we owned a Cessna Jet for just a few days.

"Of course, that's probably a good thing that it happened before we got too attached to the idea of traveling in luxury."

They both walked from the car with a smile on their faces. However, the meeting with Mr. Wilson's attorney quickly erased the smile. The matronly secretary offered the visitors a cordial good morning and asked how she could help them. When they told her of their appointment, she gave the couple a look that bespoke her interest, but nothing more. She rose from her desk and asked that they follow her.

Though they had no knowledge of the man, it was obvious simply by walking into his well-appointed office that Mr. Daniel P. Seaton was an important attorney in the city of Shreveport. One wall was glass and looked down upon downtown Shreveport and beyond.

The wall behind his desk was covered from one end to the other with plaques and photos of Dan P. Seaton and the most important men and women in the state and the country. Diplomas from Tulane University and Harvard Law School were quite displayed along the wall.

As his secretary nodded at Mr. Seaton, Callindra realized she must be the woman who had spoken to her on the phone just a few days ago. "May I offer you coffee, or sodas...or water?" she asked before leaving. Both Callindra and Weldon asked for a glass of water.

Their 30-minute meeting with Mr. Seaton turned out to be something quite different from what Callindra and Weldon had prepared themselves for. Callindra had been very wrong about the reason for the meeting. It wasn't about the plane at all. As she sat in complete shock on the soft white leather sofa, Callindra recalled Ed Wilson's son yesterday alluding to a gift her father had left. She had mistakenly assumed he was referring to the plane.

The younger Wilson had been alluding to a $20 million endowment. Callindra found herself completely speechless. Now, she had to depend on Weldon to talk business with the lawyer. Never in a million years would she have imagined Elder Wilson had $20 million to leave to her church or any church.

The lawyer was saying, ".the amount to be disbursed as you, Pastor Tucker, see fit, with only one stipulation, that it is disbursed over the next 20 years." The lawyer stared at her, with a half-smile, as if he had expected her response and was now immensely enjoying her display of shock and surprise.

"Maybe we should have asked for something a little stronger than water, Mr.

Seaton," she joked in a suddenly hoarse voice. The Shreveport Attorney chuckled good-naturedly, his eyes mirroring the shock Callindra felt.

It was times like these, Callindra reminded herself that this was what made Weldon Solder indispensable. Weldon, always cool under fire, always ready and willing to tackle whatever problems arose. As Callindra was thanking God for sending Weldon to her and Miracle Way Ministry, Dan Seaton was analyzing the role of this man who had come with Ed Wilson's pastor.

He immediately recognized that role. There was no shock or awe in Weldon Solder's eyes. Yes, there was a mild surprise, but in conjunction with a mind moving 100 miles an hour. Dan Seaton had lived long enough and dealt with enough people to have a good feeling for people in situations like this.

It didn't take much to see the influence Weldon Solder held over Callindra Tucker. She was a good woman and wouldn't recognize she had relinquished power, and Solder was much too smooth and loyal to blatantly ask for it. But there it was.

Seaton watched the two, deciding the attorney was most surely a positive influence who cared for the messy legal business lawyers were good at. Stuff, their clients, most usually avoided like the plague. Seaton knew full well the blessings of having someone you can give that level of trust. Unfortunately, he was old enough to know the number of times that trust was breached. He wouldn't let what he knew color his thoughts about these two. He preferred to believe theirs was an honest and mutually respectful relationship.

Callindra was valiantly trying to pretend they were leaving just another meeting at an attorney's office. The effort was taking everything she could muster. First came the surprise of the jet, now, this. It was simply more than she could digest. Was God testing her? Or might it be Satan playing one of his evil tricks on her? Someone had to be setting her up. Why of all the ministers in southern Louisiana was she being singled out for a blessing such as this one? There were so many others more deserving.

After their goodbye at the secretary's desk, Weldon and Callindra had found their way outside the office and down the elevator without uttering a word. Callindra was thankful for this time to gather her feelings and her thoughts. She was most thankful, however, that Weldon Solder was there.

He lightly guided her out onto the sidewalk. They paused for just a moment before making their way to the waiting limousine. As always, Saul had circled the streets until he could park as near the doorway as possible.

Dependable men were invaluable, Callindra thought. She had missed that in her childhood. Saul and Weldon were the rocks that held her life stable. Weldon, she knew, would make everything okay with what just happened in Dan Seaton's office. He'd explain it to her and make her understand the smallest of details.

As they approached the car, Saul had looked questioningly at the woman who walked out of the office building. He had expected her warm smile, maybe a small joke. Certainly, he was expecting that light that always exuded from her face. There was no smile and no light...just a look of confusion and some worry. A deep frown furrowed her brow, and instead of light, a dull discomfort.

"Pastor Tucker...you alright?"

Callindra nodded, "Yes, Saul...I'm fine. Just fine." She distractedly patted his arm as he opened her car door. Weldon gingerly guided her through the car door and into her seat as Saul settled himself into the drivers' seat, peering uncomfortably into the rearview mirror.

Weldon stepped into the passenger's side of the seat beside Callindra. After closing himself in, he bent forward, ducking his head inside the partition. Callindra paid only scant attention to her counselor whispering directions into her driver's ear. As he sat back, the partition quickly closed with a soft whisp, separating Saul from his boss and her friend and counsel.

"I think we should go back to the church, Pastor Tucker...I told Saul as much. My car is there, and...I really think we should spend a little time talking, maybe in your study. Maybe a cold glass of chardonnay would be good for both of us."

Callindra smiled faintly and nodded. He noticed the faraway look still on her face. "Callindra...everything will be absolutely fine, I promise you. It's not the first time some eccentric, but devoted parishioner left their church and its minister better off than when they first came. . It happens quite often.

"We'll begin tonight...or tomorrow, if you'd like, sifting through the paperwork. I won't let it overwhelm you, I promise. I know how you hate this part of the church business...that's why you have me, remember?" He tilted his face slightly, peering into her eyes.

Callindra smiled. "Yes, Weldon, and I'm so grateful I have you...that God sent

you to us. I do believe it will be fine. It will just take me a little time to digest it all, just a lot to digest at one time."

Weldon patted her hand lightly, comforting her as if she was a child in need of comforting.

"I have a great idea…why don't we pick up my car, and I'll take you to dinner. We can talk some about all of this only if you want to, or we can skip working tonight altogether. Tell me, would you like that? I can let Saul know that I'll bring you home."

Callindra thought for a moment. She rarely went out to eat with anyone except in a group and even less often with a male. Weldon was the only man she'd been see with outside the church for years. Everyone knew Weldon was her church counsel.

"Why not? Yes, I think I would like that, Weldon."

She turned and stared out of her window at downtown Shreveport, noting it wasn't so different from every southern city she'd visited. The most memorable building was always the courthouse. She wondered why that was so.

Weeping Willows and Cypresses shaded old Victorian houses. Her eyes hardly registered them as she thought of how her life had changed in just these last 30 minutes. This time it wasn't something she'd prayed for, and for the first time, she had an unexplainable dread of this change.

Calli swept stray strands of silver hair from her forehead as they sat in the restaurant. "I'm afraid I won't be able to eat very much, Weldon, but it will be nice to sit and talk and drink a glass of wine."

Yet distracted, she settled back in the seat, quiet, praying; Weldon slipped on his reading glasses and began going through the folder the attorney had given Callindra, and she had immediately passed on to Weldon.

* * *

The attractive couple sat across from each other, sipping their cool glasses of wine, conversing intensely, looking into each other's faces. Middle-aged was not a description anyone would immediately arrive at if they happened upon the couple who had been placed in one of the restaurant's prime sitting areas.

The giant picture window invited the beauty of Louisiana. The sunset captured them in soft light. An innocent observer would assume they were a couple, two people who knew each other very well. The piano music was calming. The waiters were quiet and very good at their jobs, talking in half-whispers.

Weldon called the gift an unexpected blessing. Callindra couldn't put a word to it.

It was nothing she had ever dreamed of or prayed for. She reminded Weldon of her "thing" about unexpected gifts. Her mother had teased her about her "strange ways," even sharing with Weldon, once she felt comfortable enough with him, how "My girl never trusted nice gifts in pretty wrapping. She would immediately tear the wrapping off every gift as soon as she got it. It was like she thought they'd disappear inside the paper."

Callindra smiled weakly. Childhood memories were things she tried very hard to steer clear of. But Ed Wilson's gift...she didn't know if God liked her questioning it the way she was. She had loved the old man, adored him...why couldn't she be happy about his expression of love for her and the church?

His children said he was giving it with a pure heart, that, in a way, it was a repayment for the happiness he found inside that church each Sunday. Wasn't that reason enough to accept the gift with open arms? God blesses us that way. She reprimanded herself. Even sometimes, unexpected blessings fall from the sky.

Callindra had found she could eat, after all, at least a little. Maybe it was the wine that helped settle her nerves. Maybe it was Weldon mesmerizing her with his stories about his childhood.

Calli knew very little about Weldon's past. She'd asked only what she thought she needed to know for his job. He'd offered only what she'd asked. Callindra had joked, "Weldon, I always thought you were born with a dark grey suit on, and those glasses taped to your little face." They both laughed, and he told her that he'd had a very normal childhood up in Southern Illinois.

When they both decided it was time to leave the restaurant, Callindra was almost back to normal, even laughing at Weldon's dry jokes. They were headed back to Callindra's home.

Before he started the car, Callindra touched his sleeve and looked into his eyes. "What would I do without you, Weldon? I know I depend on you much too much. But it's your fault. You make it easy, always helping me through times like these."

Weldon smiled blushed. "For some reason, Callindra...I don't think there's much that I do that you couldn't do yourself if you had to, or you'd find someone else who could do it almost as well.

"Besides, I'm the one who should be thanking you. I'm the blessed one. But... more than anything, I'm grateful for your confidence in me, Calli. That gives me a reason to be here. As long as I'm here, there is no deal for you to deal with any of the stuff that you don't want to deal with. I'll always be here, as long as you need me."

Callindra smiled before delicately removing her hand from

Weldon's arm. She looked up at the star-filled Louisiana sky. "For the first time in my life, I will accept a gift with grace and gratitude...I know that's what God would have me do, isn't it, Weldon?".

"It is, indeed, Pastor Tucker. I'm so happy to hear you say it."

Callindra smiled. "You know, Weldon, I think we're both tied to this church. I know I'm doing what God put me on this earth to do."

Weldon nodded and smiled as he started his car.

They sat for a moment in Callindra's driveway. Weldon had convinced her the best thing for them both was to hold off on sharing this news with the rest of the board until they'd gotten things straight in their own heads; when Weldon saw the question on her face, he'd smiled. "For someone who isn't sure about accepting a gift like this, you seem very anxious to get the news out to the congregation."

"I guess I was thinking, the sooner it becomes the church's gift, the sooner I don't feel so responsible for it...somehow the thought that he gave this directly to me doesn't feel right, Weldon."

"Then, we'll take care of that, Callindra. Please don't get yourself worked up over this. I will make sure everything is spelled out exactly as you want it. It will be an endowment to the church from Brother Wilson. All of that will be very clear, but please, trust me, we shouldn't announce this just yet. Let's cross all of our Ts, and dot all of our I's before we broadcast something like this, even before we meet with the board members to let them know. After that, we can decide how we will move forward, exactly what we should do."

"Yes...I'm sure that is how we should proceed, Weldon. But it doesn't completely change my feeling about such a gift, and the fact that I can think of no reason I should deserve all of this."

"Callindra, which is it...that you don't trust God, or you don't trust blessings that you never prayed for?" Though there was a vague smile on his lips, Weldon seemed more confident and, somehow, more in charge than ever.

Callindra closed her eyes, feeling suddenly exhausted. She nodded. "Of course, you're right, Weldon. We'll talk more tomorrow...I'm feeling pretty exhausted right now."

She began to open the door to make her way to her home when Weldon touched her hand lightly. "Pastor Tucker, as your loyal counselor, may I please be allowed to first open your car door; then, do the gentlemanly thing and escort you to your door?"

Callindra tilted her head in surprise, then settled back into her seat, smiling. She imagined this is what teenagers went through. She hadn't actually gone on dates, not like that...but she could see how it might be. She stood as Weldon opened the door and offered his hand. He continued to hold it lightly as he closed the door and escorted her to her door.

After they'd said goodnight and Weldon walked back to his car, Callindra stood for a moment at the front window, watching him drive off. She couldn't explain how this night had ended so differently from the way it had begun. Yes, the outrageous gift was part of it...but she wondered if there was something more, something that she had little control over happening, now.

Callindra was more convinced than ever that she could not have made it through the years without Weldon's quiet counsel. In time, he had convinced her that she was deserving, and to deny God's goodness was to deny God.

Callindra never missed offering a special prayer to sweet Mr. Wilson as she stood in the pulpit and looked down at the now memorialized seat in Edward Wilson's name. The empty chair reminded Callindra of her self-doubt early in her ministry and how few people believed in her. Mr. Wilson was one of the few who, without articulating it, encouraged her from the very beginning. She was anxious to show her gratitude by announcing Ed Wilson's benevolence to the church.

The members, she knew, would be just as amazed as she was by the man's generosity. They already knew about the Cessna Jet and were still whispering about how wealthy he must have been to afford such a gift.

* * *

PART VII: The Evangelist's Return

CHAPTER 10

God's Eyes on Blue Bayou

Thirty years. Callindra was always struck by the realization that she had been at this for 30 years. She recalled the time just before she embraced this life...when her life could have gone in a different direction. She had stood halfway in the Word and halfway in the world. She was seeking, she told herself, needing to know for certain what it was God had in store for her.

That night He had sent for her, made his plans clear. There had been no turning back, not even an ounce of doubt. All that had gone missing in her life had surfaced that night. The emptiness she'd carried all those years was suddenly filled, smoothed over as if it hadn't existed.

Callindra's first piece of business as a pastor was to search for a church. It took a few weeks, but she ended up finding a small building five miles outside Blue Bayou that was sure God had led her to.

She recruited a few friends to help refurbish the building, paint it and make it worthy of those who would come and spend their Sundays with her. Her artist friends, carpenters, painters, Jacks of all trades bought into her vision.

Within two weeks, they had created a home for all who needed a church home or somewhere to just rest as they listened to her words from God.

The night before her first Sunday service, her friends raised the sign above the roof: "Welcome, All who are weary, to Miracle Way Baptist Ministry."

The Ministry started small, with only dribbles of believers and non-believers for the first year or two. Even then, Callindra had felt His presence in those gatherings each Sunday and Wednesday nights. As she went to bed each night, she thanked God and smiled with happiness.

In what seemed like days but was more like months, lines of members were filing into Callindra's small building, hungering for her messages. The membership seemed to double each Sunday. The pews were full and overflowing. Finally, she admitted to herself and her new leadership that she would have to move from one Sunday service to two. There were new members standing outside the door, listening to Callindra's message over the large speakers.

She knew it was God's way of telling her He approved of the direction she was taking the church when He opened wide the floodgates of her church. Within five years, Pastor Callindra's name was a household name throughout Lafourche County. Her ministry had outgrown two buildings. The current site could hardly be called simply a building anymore. The fifty-foot sign at the entrance said The Miracle Way Baptist Ministry Complex.

One local magazine dubbed Pastor Callindra Mae Tucker of Miracle Way Baptist Ministry "one of the seven wonders of south Louisiana." The article started out with, "The beautiful minister and her Architectural wonder of a church seems to have arisen out of Louisiana's Blue Bayou. One day, a small storefront ministry, and just five years later, a megachurch...".

The Miracle Way Ministry and Complex was a breathtaking architectural design and sat on a prime piece of real estate, annexed by beautiful rolling hills and ancient, majestic trees as background. Ten miles outside Blue Bayou, the complex included five separate buildings, perfectly spaced across the 25 acres of well-kept lawn, gardens, woods, and park.

Callindra would unabashedly admit that the building and land were mostly gifts from her wonderful and loyal members. Not gifts straight out, of course, but much of the work had been donated. Members launched and coordinated weekend work parties for a full year until the Complex was completed.

The obvious and conspicuous wealth that seemed to have magically accumulated over the years had not changed Callindra Tucker—neither the awe-inspiring complex surrounded by all of its natural beauty; nor the church roll of 15,000 active members.

What changed was her depth of gratitude and desperation to deliver in return for her blessings. Twenty years later, her real joy in life remained as pure as it had begun, touching, and changing lives through the word of God.

CHAPTER 11

A Young Calli's Turning Point

As quickly as the words slipped from one part of her brain, another part of her brain joined in, slowly replaying that part of her past she tried so hard to forget. She hadn't meant to let herself wander there. Not there. She rarely did. Never would, if she had more control. During times of stress or exhaustion, she unconsciously sought out those memories. Never mind the hundreds of times over the years she had sent up special prayers for closure.

And, she *had* put it away all those years ago...pushed it far back into the recesses of her memory, found ways to replace the memory with others. Yet, it remained, never completely disappeared. Callindra knew if it had been God's will, the memory would have been removed from her conscious long ago. He hadn't. Not so far.

The young girl in love was fresh in her memories as well. So alive, with a young girl's scorching hot aching with desire. Her desperate love for the boy who walked away.

How hard it was to move on. Callindra feigned a need for water. As she sipped from the cup, she lightly shook her head, remembering just how long ago the memory had been a reality. Even at 16, she understood that she'd likely never experience a love like she had those years with Tom Mallory.

The minister struggled against memories of the exquisite

happiness of those summers in Blue Bayou. Of the girl, foolishly, helplessly in love, blindingly infatuated with the boy who had been both a best friend and caretaker before he was her lover. Nothing could have convinced her he wasn't just as much in love with her.

The memories still brought a sense of loss, grief, and an empty ache that replaced the butterfly sweetness of that young love. How could it be that at 60 years old, Callindra Faye Tucker still missed the boy, still wondered what his world was now, and if...unlike her, he'd finally found someone to call his own. She imagined he had grandchildren running around his house fulfilling him, where she had none to fulfill her.

The tears began as they always did when she remembered the secret. The secret she never shared with anyone. No one knew except the nuns. The secret sometimes jolted her awake at night as she relived the moment she'd learned she was pregnant. More than a stupid mistake, she believed it was God's punishment for her brazen sins. Which sin was it, she sometimes wondered, had God finally punished her for?

Calli had realized she was pregnant when she was dressing one morning and stole a glance at herself in the bedroom mirror. There was the telling bulge under her blouse. She was terrified. What if Delia found out? She knew without a doubt it would be anything good. Once more, Calli knew she'd never let her live this mistake down.

Calli had continued her life as usual as she tried to figure out what she should do. Without complaint she attended school and church and helped Delia around the house. Unlike Delia, Calli wasn't outgoing with loads of friends. She didn't have to worry about keeping the secret from a gaggle of girlfriends peering at the small bulge in her stomach. At night, she didn't sleep but lay awake worrying.

***

Delia Tucker's 32nd birthday came on a balmy Louisiana spring day. She had spent most of the week planning her party. As always, there would be a house full of good friends who were directed to "bring one guest…just make sure they are fun!"

For as long as Calli could remember, the pre-celebration preparations brought out a softer and funnier Delia. She shut down that other side of her as she sang and danced through the day of planning and preparing for a night of fun and music with friends.

Calli hummed along with her as she helped clean and decorate. They started decorating the living room and kitchen early in the day, setting up chairs and tables. Delia always baked her own birthday cake. A huge cake with an extra layer of colorful frosting and 32 candles. Delia's birthday cake would be the talk of the community for the next few weeks. She appointed Calli to call and make sure the musicians were coming early to set up.

There would be just one diversion from all the previous birthday parties Calli could remember. She was finishing up laying out the plates and silverware when she heard the doorbell. "Mama, your guests are coming!" she yelled. This was only the beginning of the doorbell rings this evening. As the designated greeter, she sat at the living room table to wait. Delia hadn't greeted her own guests since Calli was ten years old.

Everyone came with a small or large gift for the "birthday girl" and a warm hug for her daughter, as they held her at arm's length and shook their heads with amazement that she was "all grown up, and what a pretty girl you're growing up to be."

Before she knew it, the large living area spilled over into the kitchen. The drinking and music began early. Thank God Delia lived a full five acres from her closest neighbor. Her annual party didn't bother the neighbors much, though they sometimes joked about the cavalcade of cars passing their homes on their way to Delia's.

By the end of the night, the music was noticeably louder. The conversations were noticeably less cohesive. By early morning, the doors began slamming as guests finally began leaving a lot wobblier than they'd walked in. Delia never expected Calli to hang around once the party moved to second gear. Calli imagined she didn't want her daughter to see just how much she celebrated her birthday.

Since her daughter was old enough to help set up the party, Delia no longer ran in to check on her once the party got started. Calli stood in the doorway to the kitchen and caught Delia's eye, then waved and mouthed, "I'm going to bed." Delia blew her a kiss, then turned back to the friend in the middle of a story.

Calli closed her door and slipped into bed without changing her clothes. Delia wouldn't check. Her small suitcase was packed and pushed to the back of her closet. This was only the second time Calli had used the bright blue suitcase. The other time was a few years back when she and Delia had gone on a short vacation to her Aunt Anne in Baton Rouge. Fighting sleep, she steadily checked the clock on her dresser. When the hands stood at midnight, the Happy Birthday song grew to a crescendo, and she knew the party was at its highest peak. It would last another hour or two.

She dozed, then woke to loud goodbyes. The guests were leaving. It wouldn't be long before Delia made her way to her bedroom and fell asleep. She loved the parties, but they always wore her out, she'd say later. It would be another 30 minutes before the last guest left, and Delia would head off to bed. Calli listened and heard the door slam as the last guest yelled his goodnight and stumbled out the front door.

Calli stared at her ceiling for another 30 minutes, listening for sounds from her mother's room. When the house turned perfectly quiet, she left her bed and slipped through Delia's door to see that she was safely asleep. She was.

She was startled when Delia, her eyes half-closed, looked over at her. "Honey, will you do me a favor and make sure everything's locked up? Don't worry about straightening, I'll do …." She was out.

"Yes, Mama." Calli hugged her mother. "Happy Birthday, Mama. I hope you enjoyed your party." She pulled the covers up around her shoulders and gently kissed her mother goodbye. She stood inside the door as long as it took to ensure Delia was asleep. When she heard her mother's soft snore, she slowly removed Delia's keys from her purse and slipped out of the bedroom.

She had saved her allowance in preparation for this trip but still wasn't sure it would be enough. She left a note on the kitchen partition. Her mother would see it when she came in to make coffee in the morning. "Mama, I'll call you before long. Don't worry about me. Your truck will be sitting at the bus stop. I love you, Calli."

* * *

PART VIII: Lucia Benet

CHAPTER 12

What we Carry. What we Leave Behind

Calli sat in Delia's truck. Her suitcase sat beside her on the passenger side. She pulled her jacket closer around her shoulders against the cool Louisiana morning. She took note of the sun rising behind the towers of trees across the road. It was a perfect fall morning. Almost. She was fighting the fear that threatened to drive her back home and into her bed.

She saw the bus turning the corner and scrambled out of the truck. She was almost at the stop when she remembered to go back, lock the truck, and leave the keys under the floor mat. Mama had a spare key. The Greyhound Bus came to a screeching halt as Calli ran to the bus sign.

"Good morning, young lady, you almost got left…I didn't see you as I drove up." Calli offered the driver a weak smile as she stepped up. Where you headed this fine Saturday morning, young lady?"

"New Orleans."

The small change in the bus driver's face told Calli he wondered about her traveling alone to the city, and while she knew it wasn't his business, she appreciated his concern.

"Got your ticket?"

Calli pulled the ticket she'd bought last week from her jean jacket pocket. She had been thrilled to know it was only $12. The bus driver clipped the ticket and gave her a receipt. Calli made her way to the back of the bus with the suitcase in tow. Only half of the seats were taken this early in the morning, but she wanted to be alone, not forced to carry on a conversation.

She knew it would get warmer in a few hours. The mild temperature would keep rising through the day. But now, Calli seemed not to be able to stop shivering. She regretted she hadn't brought a heavier sweater or jacket. Shortly after the bus took off, she dug into her purse and found the crinkled newspaper article she'd torn from the Blue Bayou Daily newspaper her mother had left on the breakfast table last week.

Calli re-read the article about the Nuns at the New Orleans Catholic Church. It was a part of a series of articles on the New Orleans Catholic Church community. The story centered around the church's orphanage, which had been around for more than 100 years.

It said that the nuns were especially proud they were able to intervene in so many young girls' lives and help parents who wanted to adopt babies. They were also proud that the community had continuously supported their effort to be a temporary safe home for pregnant girls and match their babies with good families. Calli had made up her mind after reading the article.

* * *

She slept most of the two-hour bus ride, only waking when the driver yelled out, "New Orleans! We're entering Crescent City…the great city of New Orleans!" She woke with nervous butterflies and hunger pains. Without any explanation, her eyes began to water as she stared out the window at the dreariness of the bus terminal and the small buildings surrounding it.

Calli wasn't sure what she'd expected, but Delia had always painted the city full of colorful, exciting, and beautiful people. Delia and her closest friends met there once a year to shop, eat, and party. She returned home with souvenirs and small gifts for Calli, exciting stories of the lively streets, jazz music, the outdoor cafes, beautiful mansions, and high-end department stores, not to mention, "Lordy, the good looking men there. The problem is that you never can tell whether they are black or white or something else. And, Oh Lord, the food is to die for…nobody beats New Orleans when it comes to good-looking people and Southern-French cooking!"

The bus driver pulled into his appointed space and parked. She cringed at the loud screech of the brake. The driver stood and stretched, then looked back at his passengers as if to say, "See, I got you here." The numbers had magically grown from a half-full bus. Last Calli had noticed, to a full bus after Calli fell asleep. The driver offered Calli a paternal smile as he stepped down and hollered back, "Y'all watch your steps as you disembark."

The New Orleans bus terminal sat on Loyola Avenue. She'd recognized it and the surrounding streets when she'd studied the map Delia kept in her truck. Calli stepped down and thanked the driver for getting them there safely. He pointed over at the line of cabs in front of the terminal. "If you need a cab, they're all over there, young lady. Be sure you give them the exact address of where you going, too."

"Thank you. I will," she said as he handed her the small suitcase.

"Be safe, now.

This is a good city, but also one that ain't always the best for a young lady all by herself…you get where you goin' and don't tally."

She looked at him longer than she realized, then thanked him again before hurrying towards the line of cabs. Stopping at the first available one, she gave the address to the Orphanage.

* * *

CHAPTER 13

A Haunting Goodbye

Just as the article promised, the nun who greeted her at the door welcomed her with open arms and asked no questions, not even her legal name. The nun's name was Harriet, and the questions she asked had to do with Calli's health and the baby's health, and the term of her pregnancy as far as she knew. She didn't look the least surprised that Calli wasn't sure about the term and hadn't shared her pregnancy with her doctor. The nun's nod told her this was more normal than not.

Harriet noticed the girl was overwhelmed and scared, and the tears began to form in the corner of her eyes. "Everything will be fine, Sara. We have a very good doctor who will examine you and make sure both mother and baby are fine. His name is Dr. Allen.

He comes weekly and will be here tomorrow. I'll put you on his early schedule.

We also have a very capable nurse on call 24-7. Her name is Nancy. She will check in on you as well. But, right now, I'll take you to your room. You can put your things away, wash up and rest. You can join us for dinner downstairs at 5 p.m. – some of the girls do— or, if you prefer, we can bring dinner to you in your room."

"I'd like dinner in my room, please," Calli mumbled.

Harriet nodded smiled. "And…what would you like me to call

you while you're here, dear?"

"Sara," mumbled Calli.

"Of course. Now, you get yourself some rest, Sara. Your dinner will be here at 5p.m."

Over the next days and weeks, Calli met several girls, but gratefully, none

who lived near her community in Blue Bayou. They knew her as Sara. Just Sara, there were no last names shared in the Home. In time, the girls began to share their personal stories. Though the nuns did not forbid this sharing, they did not encourage it. There was always the fear the girls would meet again after leaving home.

Sara chose not to share her story with anyone, though it might have helped. She kept her beloved diary under her pillow and used it to share her most personal thoughts. It was the only thing in the room with her actual name on it. Most of her nights were spent in tears and questions: Was she doing the right thing? Had Tom come back looking for her? How could she keep the truth from her mother for the next few years before she left home for good?

Mostly the tears were for the loss of what she'd dreamed could be. Losing Tom Mallory meant the loss of the best friend she thought she'd ever have. The one person who knew her and still loved her. She stopped questioning why he went. She told herself he had a good reason. Though losing him still hurt every day, she couldn't hate him.

Four months after arriving at the Home, despite her sorrow-filled nights, Calli's baby arrived. It was a beautiful, healthy girl with a head full of curls and soft downy skin. The nuns praised her for her "easy delivery." However, the first day of the child's birth was surely the hardest of all the time she'd carried her. The nuns were used to the girls' emotional rollercoasters after giving birth.

They promised Calli they would find a good home for her child, and as was their policy, they would follow up with the family for the first five years after the child was adopted. "You will never have to worry, Sara. We will never share your information with anyone—not the adopting family, nor with anyone in your own life—unless you personally give us permission to do so. Calli's weak smile belied the turmoil that was still inside her heart.

Harriet sat across from Calli as she cried and told her of her fears and doubts about doing this thing that was so final. "You are experiencing what every girl that comes through our home, experiences. It is natural for you to question if this is the right choice. What you should know is that God has smiled down on our work for over 100 years. We are saving young girls' lives and creating whole families. Please believe that God is smiling down on this exchange of gifts between you and the new parents. He will bless you for your courage and giving heart."

Calli turned away. She liked Harriet and all the nuns here. They had been so kind and wise. Still. Still. She cried until she fell asleep. When she awoke, Harriet was yet there.

"Sara, dear. I have spoken with the Mother Superior. We have discussed your case. It is so very painful to see you in such pain. She agreed that we will allow you to keep your child if this is what you believe in your heart is the right thing to do. We cannot force you, at any rate.

We can only share what we think is best for you and the child. Yet, we feel your pain and guilt and want you to think hard about this decision. We will ask you tomorrow what you'd like to do."

Calli thanked Sara and, shortly after, closed her eyes and fell asleep. Near morning, she found herself half-awake, sensing a presence in the room. She was certain it was Harriet kindly checking in on her. Seconds later, the door softly opened, then closed.

Calli rose early the next morning, intent on leaving early as possible. She knew Harriet wouldn't be happy about her getting up and washing up in the bathroom rather than waiting for the nurse, but she didn't want to have to say goodbye to anyone.

She hurried to the bathroom before any of the girls awoke. When she walked back into her room, she was embarrassed to see that Nurse Nancy was already making up her bed and straightening her room. "Oh. Nurse Nancy. I'm sorry, I just went to wash up."

"Yes, I noticed you were up. You should have waited for me. How are you feeling this morning? Why don't you sit? I'll get my stethoscope and check your vitals before you start moving around today."

Calli always felt compelled to do what Nurse Nancy asked her to do. She wasn't like the rest of the women there. She didn't have the motherly, caring warmth of the other women. Calli avoided as much as possible looking at Nurse Nancy, afraid she'd find herself staring at the dark mark on her forehead. She wondered if it was a birthmark or maybe a scar caused by a childhood accident. She wanted to ask but dared not.

"The wonders of youth. Thankfully, your body is healing just fine. If you keep taking care of yourself, you should be pretty much back to normal within a few weeks, young lady." She turned, picked up the day-old linen, and walked out.

Callie was almost finished dressing when she felt a little weak and decided to sit awhile on the side of the bed. As she turned, she realized her diary was not in its usual place under her pillow. She was sure Nurse Nancy had accidentally moved it while making up the bed. The woman wouldn't be a bit interested in her diary. She searched under the bed and throughout the room but couldn't locate it. She was confident it would show up before she left.

She had nothing to do now but wait for the breakfast bell. Calli looked around the room. She was so grateful to the good women here. She would miss Harriet most of all.

The doctor was kind and gentle but quiet. Nancy was not kind, but she was sure she was good at what she did. She would remember one of the girls, most. She was the youngest in the group. Unlike the older girls who kept their stories to themselves, Linda had shared her ugly story of how she ended up pregnant. Calli felt so sad for the girl and was glad she wouldn't know her real name.

Had it really been four months since she'd arrived? The baby was almost two weeks old, healthy, and beautiful. She swiped the tear off her cheek. She'd promised herself she wouldn't cry today.

After breakfast, Harriet brought the child to Calli. "This is not our usual way of doing things, Sara. But we want you to be absolutely sure of the direction you will take."

She didn't know they would allow her to say goodbye to her child. She'd heard stories some girls never saw their babies once they gave birth. Calli understood. The attachment to your child was physical.

When Harriet brought the child into the room, Calli felt herself stop breathing. The child began to whimper, and Calli's breast began to throb. Harriet handed the child to her. Calli sat on the side of the bed. Oh, how very beautiful the child was. An angel with jet black ringlets and a natural glow to her tawny skin. She didn't want to make a mistake that she'd have to live with for the rest of her life.

Delia would surely fall in love with this beautiful child no matter how it had gotten here. But, what of Calli's bald-faced lies and her sin? She knew her mother. Even if she welcomed Calli and the baby back, she would never let her daughter forget her terrible and stupid mistake. Delia's acceptance of the child would come with a price.

Calli knew some of the girls didn't dare name their babies, not wanting to have that connection after they left. "Harriet, may I give a name to my baby?" The nun was bewildered by the question. What did the question mean?

"Have you decided what you want to do, Sara?" "Yes. I decided last night before I fell asleep." "Very well. What is your decision, Sara?

"The baby will remain with you, Harriet. But I would like to name her, please." "That is acceptable, Sara. I know the Superior Mother would accept that. What would you like to name the child?"

"Lucia Benet. That should be her first and middle name…it is a very special name." She looked down at her child and smiled through her tears.

"Sara, it is a beautiful name. Would you write the name down as you'd like it?

We will encourage the parents to keep the name you have given her."

She hesitated before giving the child back to Harriet. "I'm so sorry, Lucia. I love you and will pray every day that a wonderful family will find you and you will be happy in life."

Calli hugged Harriet long and hard. She thanked all the nuns and nurses who had helped care for her and her baby. They wished her well on her journey and told her they'd work very hard to get the home that little Lucia deserved. Though they offered another week's lodging, Calli knew she couldn't stay if she were to leave her child.

She hugged the nuns and the nurse as if they were long, lost friends. Mostly though, her tears and her pain were because of the loss of her beautiful daughter, knowing she'd never get the chance to see her grow up. In these last minutes at the orphanage, the diary was nowhere in her mind.

"I know we aren't supposed to ask, but I pray you will be safe and find peace in this world," Harriet said. "I will try," Calli answered. Trying, she knew, included forgetting these last few months, or at least putting them behind her. She knew the rest of her life would be built on a lie. The first lie would be telling Delia she had gone in search of Tom, and after failing in that search, had decided to return home.

She said her final goodbyes and walked out of the home. Harriet had called a cab to deliver Sara to the bus terminal on Loyola Street. She'd made sure the girl had enough money to purchase a ticket and for food during her trip. Calli would never forget the kindness of the home for young mothers. In time, she promised, she would find a way to give back to this place that had meant so much to her and Lucia.

***

Delia cried when Calli walked into the door that winter morning. Her tears were a combination of anger and joy four months after her departure. Her emotions throughout the day, even that full week, would fluctuate between the two.

That night, as they sat together in the living room, Delia looked over at her daughter as if she were a ghost. "Where did my baby go? She would never have the courage to run away to look for love. It's funny, baby, I'm so proud of you, and I'm so angry at you. The anger will go away. My pride never will."

Calli knew there was nothing she could say that would make a difference in the hurt she'd caused. The apologies she offered were useless. They just hung out there between them.

Calli had always been a quiet child but a responsible one. Delia had joked with her friends she had to think twice about who was the adult and the child. Then, her daughter went and did something so irresponsible and callous.

It was only during the late nights inside her room that Calli allowed herself to think about what had happened over the last few months. Giving birth to Lucia had changed her in ways even she couldn't explain. Now, she couldn't decide which was more important to go back and claim her daughter or to light out, for real this time, to look for Tom. Deep down, though, she knew it was a futile search.

She wouldn't leave again. She really wasn't brave enough. More importantly, she refused to hurt Delia more than she already had. In time, she might even share her secret with her mother. But not now. She would continue to repeat the lie that she was hurting and decided to go looking for Tom. What was true was that she desperately wished Tom would return. She still dreamed of becoming his wife one day.

Calli's lie rang true for Delia, who had experienced a hopeless love herself, with Calli's father. That understanding allowed the mother to slowly resolve her anger and embrace her daughter because, above all, she was grateful to have her home.

PART IX: When God Ghostwrites our Message

CHAPTER 14

A Vessel For God's Message

Callindra Tucker stood at the podium rehearsing tomorrow's sermon. Her faith and work for the church allowed her to stave off the emptiness produced by leaving her child with the nuns and, before that, losing what she was convinced was her one chance at true love. It had taken some time, but her deep faith allowed her to move past that dark time and thrive despite the losses. After all, she knew God had forgiven her for the sins which led to those losses.

"Through God's grace," she whispered to herself as she moved back to the podium and signaled to Eric and his crew to resume work. She took a deep breath and rubbed her tired eyes. She thanked God for the truly miraculous drug called coffee that allowed her to keep going, for now, four hours with less than five hours of sleep.

She imagined tomorrow's over-filled sanctuary. It would be a festive celebration of her return home. She'd better be prepared to share exciting details of her two-week Africa trek and to deliver a knock-out message to make up for the last two Sundays she was away.

Her congregation had lifted her and her traveling team in a rousing, moving prayer the night before their departure. Without a doubt, they'd continued the prayers throughout the trip up until their return last night. She had lots of ground to cover, far too much work to spend one moment remembering yesterday.

Callindra checked and rechecked her words, voicing them into the microphone just as she would tomorrow. Rather than dwell on her exhaustion, she dwelled on her miraculous transformation from the broken young woman the boy had left behind to the committed messenger for God she was today.

She rarely allowed herself to think about the rumors about how she ended up in the place she was. Rumors ran the gamut, from the broken love affair to the hot and steamy affair with a wealthy benefactor. She was a woman in south Louisiana. How else would she rise in the religious community so fast? She also knew that there were men who questioned the appropriateness of a woman minister leading such a church as Miracle Way.

God saves in mysterious ways, Calli often her congregation – directing her words at the doubters. Not that she hadn't questioned God's blessings herself. At least once each month, Calli drove into the middle of the huge parking lot to sit alone and send up a special prayer to God, thanking Him for all His blessings, the magnificent church, the parishioners who loved her unconditionally, her devoted staff and…yes, Delia, who still tested her religion more than anyone she knew.

Delia Tucker. While she had not been a perfect mother, the truth was that neither had Callindra. What Delia was, was a constant. As constant as a rock. Despite all their differences and complicated history, Delia was there for her through thick and thin.

What Calli found most amazing was how her mother seemed to be going through some immaculate maternal transformation. Most recently, she'd become a doting mother, extolling her daughter's virtues to anyone who'd listen, showing up at church, even volunteering for the least popular services. Calli couldn't help but remember the younger Delia when her role was more of a younger sister to her beautiful mother than a daughter.

As she rehearsed her message one last time, Callindra half-heartedly wondered about Delia changing her stripes so late in life. Her way of motherhood had worked for her all these years, and she'd seemed as set in her ways as any woman could be. Part of it, Callindra knew, was her mother getting older. Not that anyone else thought of her that way, but surely Delia was experiencing some of the same pains that other over-50 women felt from time to time or saw the subtle or not-so-subtle changes in her mirror. It was just hard to get used to a saintly Delia Tucker.

Calli focused back on the sermon, crossing out too-long sentences and scribbling notes outside the margins for the typist. Just as she found herself changing every other sentence, a vibration in her front blouse pocket startled her back into the moment.

She pressed her forefinger to her last edit on the page and pulled the cell phone from her pocket. Callindra sighed. Phones. One of those "Damn if you do. Damn if you don't" necessities of contemporary life. She had fought hard against being saddled with a phone every moment of her waking life. Should anyone be so completely available to the people in their lives?

This wasn't even a phone call, but a blasted text message! She pulled her reading glasses over her nose, tilting her head up slightly to read the message. She gingerly placed her papers inside the folder and closed it. "Eric, can I have just a few minutes?"

"Yes, Mam'! Why don't we all take ten?" the engineer offered his crew.

Minster Tucker squinted out into the dimly lit church as she returned the tiny phone to its hiding place. Why was she not surprised that Weldon Solder had made his way down to the church this morning? He could track her down on the other side of the world.

She smiled despite herself. Catching sight of her messenger, she made a mock-showing of exasperation as she walked across the ecru-colored carpet and down the steps to greet her counsel and attorney.

Weldon stood at the bottom of the steps fidgeting with the slip of paper in his hand, trying to control the grin he was trying to control. Weldon, tall, slim, outrageously fit, was dressed in an illuminatingly white polo shirt tucked into hard-pressed khakis. He searched his pastor's face to gauge the balance between irritation and humor, then slowly let his grin emerge, softening the hard edges of his handsome face.

"Welcome back, Pastor. We're so thankful for your safe trip across the world and back."

Callindra's smile matched Weldon's. She gave her counselor a warm embrace and a quick peck on his cheek. "It's good to be back, Weldon, and it's good to see you… as they say in Kansas, 'there's no place like home.'"

"I hope you'll forgive my interruption, Pastor, but your mother threatened me with bodily harm if I didn't get this message directly to you as soon as you stepped off the plane."

She took the message from Weldon Solder's hand and placed the reading glasses atop her nose again. She read down the slip of paper without comment, folding it neatly and placing it deep into her pocket, along with the telephone.

"Thank you, Weldon. You know, my mother depends upon your efficiency as much as I do."

"Well, I had planned to give you a little more heads up than this, but I wanted to deliver the message rather than leave a voice mail.

"Besides, I wanted to see for myself that you made it back in one piece, the same as you left!" They both laughed, Callindra holding out her arms and pivoting for Weldon.

She suddenly thought of the rumors that swirled around Weldon's coming on board all those years ago. The whispers about Weldon's not-so spiritual affection for her back then. But, like all the other rumors and insinuations, Callindra had ignored them, knowing they would dissolve in time.

"You know, Weldon, I've known my mother for almost 60 years, and you've known her for almost 15 years. We have both experienced her Dr. Jekyll and Mr. Hyde personalities –sweeter than apple pie when she wants to be and more prickly than a desert cactus when she doesn't get her way. Not to mention that other side of her, overbearing and manipulative." The easy laughter, again.

"First, she asks me about my two weeks in Africa and how I must be exhausted, but in the very next sentence, she orders me to come out and spend next week with her. And of course, I must because she has some extremely important news to share with me!"

Weldon beamed at his pastor's good spirits. "Knowing Delia Tucker, her important news is that she has bought a new bedroom set or a new big-screen TV and can't wait to show it off." They both shook their heads, smiling.

Callindra scanned Weldon's face, quickly reading his position on the matter. "Oh, come on, Weldon. You know I have to go, even though we both know the woman will be the death of me. But, I can't say "no," even while the sensible half of my brain is telling me I should go home, crawl in bed, and not reappear for another ten days!"

Despite his efforts to maintain a straight face, Callindra saw the subtle flare in his nostrils, which told her how much he hated seeing her mother manipulate her, once again. "Weldon...You don't think I should go, do you?"

He took a deep breath and shook his head. "What I think bears no weight here...this is between your mother and you."

"I do appreciate your concern, Weldon. If you see Alana, will you ask her to fix my calendar, move next week's meetings around or push them to the week after?

Hopefully, I'll only be there a couple of nights. Saul will drive me down on Monday morning, and I'll return in plenty enough time to be rested up for next Sunday's service."

"Callindra...Pastor Tucker, when will you rest? You have just returned from a two-week trip across the ocean, just landed a few hours ago after a 16-hour flight, and you are already up, and spending God knows how many hours rehearsing this morning.

"When do you rest? I can see in your eyes that you're exhausted, whether you want to admit it or not. Because you won't rest before your sermon, you must rest after tomorrow's sermon. You and I know the lines of parishioners will be a mile long. People wanting to tell you how much they prayed for you and missed you while you were gone."

She sighed and pulled her hair off her face, looping one thick strand around the other to form a ponytail. Weldon remembered the first time he met her. She'd worn that ponytail, a much darker ponytail at the time, allowing those sparkling gray eyes full reign.

Callindra was remembering how Delia had first fussed that her daughter never wanted curls or flips or up-dos but seemed stuck on "that damn ponytail you insisted on wearing all through your childhood." She'd never liked the look for her daughter.

Delia had finally realized her fussing didn't deter Callindra's choices in hairstyles, dress, makeup, or friends. The girl had always had her own mind, and there wasn't a soul who could change it. In time, Delia admitted the simple hairstyle y suited her daughter perfectly and did play well off her sparkling gray eyes.

"You're always right, Weldon...but, while I'm as stubborn as a mule – just like Delia, I'm still her daughter and scared of saying "no," to her. What I will do, is plan to leave the sanctuary no later than 5 tomorrow evening and go directly to bed. I'll be fresh as a daisy on Monday morning. And, while I'm there...I'll get some real rest. Delia Tucker prepares the most nurturing meals and has the most comfortable beds I've ever experienced. Despite everything, there is no place in the world where I feel so at home."

"You're truly a jewel, Weldon Solder," she said before hurrying back toward the pulpit. At the podium, she'd rifled through her notes, readying to resume her work. There was a frown of worry somewhere in the back of her mind, something she couldn't put her finger on. She looked out into the dark and signaled to her sound engineer. It was time to continue rehearsals for her Sunday service.

* * *

"Callindra...Pastor, I know you're just back from your trip, but I was wondering…I really think we should spend some time this evening talking about the gift, the endowment. We definitely should, since you plan to visit your mother on Monday."

Callindra frowned, realizing she had successfully pushed thoughts of the endowment far back in the corners of her mind while she was away. Now, she guessed she'd have to retrieve it, deal with it, decide how she would handle it. And, of course, Weldon would help. She sighed, promising herself she'd have a private talk with God about the whole thing before she met with Weldon.

"Callindra, we have to. It's far too important to keep putting off. I know the trip was extremely important, but it also put us two weeks behind in reviewing the paperwork involved in this transaction. We really can't put it off any longer.

Though she didn't want to, she would. At least getting it done and over with would give her some peace of mind. For some reason, when she was forced to think about the gift, it was with trepidation, not happiness or even gratitude, as she knew was how she should be feeling.

"Weldon, I'll need to spend some time with the members after the message today, and the ministers and board have asked for a little welcome back reception in the Grace Room later…could this possibly wait until tomorrow morning. Maybe you can come out to the house for a breakfast meeting?"

Weldon thought for just a moment before nodding his head. "Actually, I think that would be best for both of us. You can get some rest tonight, and I can take some more time to pull everything together we'll need to discuss."

"Yes, I think that would work a lot better, Weldon…maybe

around 9 in the morning. I should be up and ready to work. Dolly will have breakfast and lots of coffee…or whatever you want." Her spirits suddenly seemed lighter. She quickly swallowed the last of her coffee and picked up the bible her mother had given her for her fifth year anniversary. It was a beautiful bible, with Callindra Faye Tucker embossed in gold stitching across the front cover.

* * *

CHAPTER 15

Remembering the Journey

Callindra pulled the sapphire-colored jacket over the matching sleeveless sheath that skimmed her knees. It was much too sophisticated for her taste, but Alana told her it was perfectly appropriate for someone of her stature. Besides, it fit her body type perfectly. Callindra wasn't sure what that meant. She wasn't tall, yet she was told she had a presence. She wasn't thin, but Alana her body proportions were forgiving in most any style. She supposed these were all pluses, at least it was what Alana told her, and she had to admit that her best friend Alana knew a lot when it came to fashion.

Callindra remembered there was a time when this all mattered, but even then, it was mostly because it mattered to Delia. For all of her childhood, she had acted or reacted based on what Delia wanted or needed from her. Including Delia's decision to enter her daughter into the local Miss Blue Bayou Beauty pageant during her junior year in high school.

Somehow, Calli believed, it was her way of assuring the community that her family was as good and as normal as any in Blue Bayou. Despite the daughter who had run away and stayed away for four months.

"Honey, you are as pretty as any girl who ever won one of those pageants. Why shouldn't you compete?" Calli had argued as effectively as she knew how against a woman who prided herself on not losing arguments. It seemed not to matter one whit that the child's heart wasn't in it. This was more about Delia proving something than proving how pretty her daughter was.

Calli finally relented, telling herself it was the least she could do to make up for the pain she'd caused her mother. And, yes, she'd do just about anything to make up for that. If her competing in a beauty pageant would prove that she and Delia were as good as anyone else in Blue Bayou, then maybe it was worth it.

Besides, way in the back of her young mind, Calli wondered if Tom might learn about her being part of the county's beauty pageant. Maybe…just maybe. A lot of the boys in town already thought she was pretty. More than a few had asked to take her out, but Delia didn't encourage dating after the disastrous relationship with Tom. Besides, Calli wasn't interested.

Delia basked in the light surrounding her beauty queen daughter during Calli's high school years. Calli did as Delia asked, most time feeling as if she was watching her life play out in front of her with no input. The pretty girl with the emptiness inside was suddenly winning pageant after pageant, and Delia's smug "I told you so" was ever- evident. Calli wondered how she could keep winning when she didn't care at all whether she won or lost.

During her senior year, Calli dredged up the courage to tell Delia she wasn't happy being a perpetual beauty contestant. She wasn't prepared for her mother's disappointment. Each of their emotions was raw for a time. Delia wondered aloud why her daughter couldn't appreciate that she was only looking out for her own good. The pageants could help secure a successful college future for her. Truth was, Delia had never understood her daughter and didn't expect she ever would.

Delia finally relented. The Miss Louisiana pageant coming up next fall would be Calli's final competition. She promised her daughter she wouldn't push her to participate in another beauty pageant.

"Honey, you'll have the whole summer to get prepared for the pageant in the fall. But, I promise, no matter what the outcome, it will be the last one" Delia had promised to do the last pageant until she spent the summer volunteering for a youth center with mostly poor children of sharecroppers or farm laborers. At the end of the summer, she told her mother she had changed her mind. She just couldn't see herself traveling across the state to participate in even one more beauty pageant.

Pasted across the top fold of the front page of the local paper was "Louisiana's winningest Beauty Queen Leaves the world of Beauty Pageants." Calli had no idea that the public was that interested in her decision about beauty pageants.

Delia had set up interviews with local and regional papers when she thought Calli would be a contestant. She had to go back to them to share the news that she wouldn't. It turned out they'd seen this as an interesting twist of the pageant world.

Delia played along, not mentioning her own disappointment in her daughter's decision. Her daughter had spent the summer doing outreach work with young, poor children, and somehow that changed her mind, she told the reporters. During the interviews, Calli would never forget the fake smile plastered across Delia's face.

That was so long ago, Callindra thought. No more having to hold her head high, walk with perfect posture, wear only quality attire! Now, when she found herself in public or inside a department store, she was just Calli, not Calli, the beauty contestant. She no longer kept up with the latest styles. Alana often chose the outfits that fit her to the best advantage. No one, it seemed, knew more about style than her assistant.

* * *

Calli stood before the full-length mirror, appraising her suit and agreeing that it did fit her slender, curvaceous body quite well. She was blessed to have a metabolism that jibed well with her appetite. She hated exercise and diets like the plague. Even so., she was pleased to realize she'd lost the few pounds she'd gained last winter.

Close behind her, straightening her jacket, smoothing down stray curls, was her best friend and personal assistant, Alana McGriffin. A beautiful woman who, like Callindra, looked years younger than her age.

The two had been friends since they were children. Calli, the daughter of the local restaurant and pub, and Alana, the niece of the restaurant's cook who had come to spend a summer with the McGriffin family and never left.

Though Callindra was older by five years, they had become friends after high school getting to know each other when it turned out they were both competing in the same beauty pageants. They gravitated towards each other when they learned how different their backgrounds were from the other contestants.

Alana and Calli joked that Alana had spent much of her childhood trying to make Calli play with her. The older girl, however, was already in the throes of puppy love with Tom Mallory. Calli joked that she'd hide and watch them kiss in a corner of the restaurant.

Alana often told her friend there was a real correlation between a woman's looks, and her success, even in the ministry. As much as Calli didn't want to accept this unfair premise, she knew it was true. She turned to inspect herself from the back view just as a knock came at the door.

With a precursory straightening of her dress, Callindra opened the door. A quick smile appeared on her face as she bade Weldon into her suite. "It's you! Come on in. What do you think about this outfit Alana is making me wear, Weldon?" She smiled warmly as she winked at Alana.

Her eyes widened as she realized Weldon Solder was pushing a beautifully placed breakfast cart. "What...how?" She laughed to see her counsel taking on the role of the hotel clerk. The succulent aroma of food and coffee made her stomach growl.

She shook her head in disbelief. "You never leave one leaf unturned when it comes to me or this church, Weldon. What would I do without you?".

He waved away her words and pointed her to the small sitting table, where he calmly placed silverware alongside her napkin as if preparing for a long and leisurely meal. "There is no way you're starting this day without a healthy breakfast, Pastor Tucker...you won't have one minute to yourself the rest of this day."

"But Weldon...you know I can never eat before my message. There's just no way...Alana, tell him. Just look at this spread!" There was bacon, biscuits, eggs, grits, marmalade and jelly, orange juice, and coffee.

Weldon stood with his arms folded and a petulant half-smile. Alana walked over, laughing, and stood beside him. "I agree with Weldon, Pastor. You have to eat something. You've been running since you arrived back, and we don't need you to collapse."

Callindra tried to send her harshest glare their way but found it was simply impossible to pretend she was upset. She knew these two always looked out for her best interests. She sat with a loud sigh as she pulled a small butter plate in front of her. She placed one slice of bacon and a half biscuit on the plate, adding a few grapes from the large bunch. She looked at the plate, let out another loud sigh, then proceeded to eat what she could. Her closest friend and highly valued employee stood across from her, smiling.

Smiling back, Callindra made a show of carefully chewing the grapes, then taking a bite from the bacon. As she chewed, she took note of her counselor's perfectly tailored charcoal suit, his crisp white shirt, with its silver monogram. Weldon Solder could surely vie for the "best-dressed man in the state of Louisiana," title, she thought. She couldn't remember ever seeing one loose thread hanging from his suit or shirt or one hair out of place. She broke off a small piece of the moist biscuit and ate it, then sipped from her orange juice.

Callindra was thinking how much she depended on these two people to get through her days, Weldon's business and legal acumen, and Alana's discerning planning and organizational skills. Others on her staff had formidable skills, but none were as precise or appropriately decisive when she needed exactly what Alana and Weldon offered. No one came close to their ability to get things just right or to read her mind and know exactly what she wanted, sometimes, even before she knew herself.

Weldon casually looked over the paperwork on Callindra's desk as she ate sparingly from her meal. He didn't want to be seen as hovering but knew if he weren't there, she wouldn't touch the food.

"Thank you, Weldon, for the wonderful breakfast...seriously, I know I needed it. I do know how lucky I am to have you guys here to make me do what I need to do."

"Don't mention it, Pastor Tucker, that's what we're here for. And, by the way, I'm not sure whether you'll count it a blessing or a curse, but as I was coming in, the sanctuary was already filling up. There was a line forming in the hallways. From the murmurings, their great anticipation for your first message since your return home. I hope you remembered to include some exciting stories from the trip. The congregation always enjoys those so much."

Callindra patted her mouth with the white napkin and offered Weldon a slight smile. "I did. I did remember, Weldon. And you all did notice that I made a substantial dent in my breakfast?"

He smiled and pushed the cart into the corner.

"Please, Weldon...enough of your maid service, one of the interns will take care of that after we leave out.". He smiled and glanced at his watch. Lori Sanders was Callindra's assistant. Callindra sometimes thought of her as a slightly more laid-back version of Weldon.

Alana had been a member of Callindra's close-knit circle from the start, one of the first to encourage her when she questioned if this was the journey she should embark on. Callindra would always believe God had chosen her team just as he had his own disciples, each bringing with them their own strength...and, to a great extent, their own needs.

Though Weldon hadn't been a part of her early circle, he had turned out to serve in so many roles. His being there, had allowed her to experience personal growth in ways she likely wouldn't, had he not been there to take care of her business affairs.

"Callindra, I really have to remember to thank you for the wonderful blog you sent out during my trip. You really posted some amazing photos and wonderful information. I hope the members took the time to read it. Did you get a chance to read over it, Weldon?"

"Oh...Yes. Of course. Alana does such a wonderful job for you, Callindra."

Alana smiled over at Weldon and lightly hugged Callindra so she wouldn't muss her clothing or hair.

When Alana opened the door in preparation for Callindra to walk to the pulpit, she noticed that Weldon seemed distracted. She made a note to ask him if everything was okay after the service began this morning.

Callindra suddenly remembered she hadn't shared the details of her trip with Weldon and Alana, her most trusted confidantes. However, she would be sharing it with the full congregation in just minutes. She didn't believe they felt slighted. It was simply an oversight on her part.

"Weldon, Alana, I hadn't had time to share a thing about our trip with either of you. Some of it you'll hear this morning, but there was so much..."

Weldon smiled before glancing at his watch. "I'm sure you will find the time to share your experiences with us, Pastor, and I look forward to hearing it. Now, however, I think we need to make our way into the sanctuary."

"Wait. Before we go, Weldon…I just need to tell you both just how grateful I am that you were here to keep things together during the two weeks we were away. If you hadn't been here, there's no way I would have felt comfortable being away so long.

Weldon noted the awe in her face as she smiled over her shoulder at them. He nodded, returning her smile as he and Alana fell in just inches behind her as she walked down the hall and into the sanctuary of Miracle Way Ministries morning service.

* * *

CHAPTER 16

God Messin' with His Loyal Soldier

The expression of love was deafening. The standing ovation, followed by loud shouts of adulation, "Pastor Callindra!" from the upturned faces of her parishioners, was more than she ever expected. She awkwardly waved and smiled as she moved to the pulpit, then to the podium. Tears gathered in the corner of her eyes as she motioned the church members to sit. After another 30 seconds of thunderous applause, it slowly receded, and members began to take their seats.

"Oh, my goodness…what a greeting! Good morning! Thank you for that…. very warm welcome. I think you all really missed me. Well, I missed Y'all, too, and I felt your prayers all those thousands of miles away. You'll never know how important that was to me as we traveled halfway around the world!"

The quieter sounds of members settling comfortably, and tittering floated through the crowd. The pastor took a long breath, a sip of her water, and began a walk down memory lane, sharing about the ten-day Christian trek in the African continent.

"We saved souls for five days and two nights, friends. Some of you weren't with me from the beginning of our journey. You wouldn't know that this was something we never in a million years dreamed we might end up doing, crusading in three continents of the world, ministering to so many different cultures and races of people, and bringing many of them to God.

"It was you, our ministerial alliance, who encouraged us to take this giant step. You, who guided us all the way and are still coming up with new ways to evangelize to the peoples of this world. Somehow, wearing this poor old evangelist out!" Their laughter was filled with warmth and admiration. She stood, looking around the beautiful church.

"I know just how blessed I am that God moved the religious leaders of Africa to accept this strange American woman into their circle of evangelists from around the world. I know that was God, He ordained it all those many years ago when I was lost, and he found me and directed me into his service and blessed me with each of you.

"And it was Him anointing me, and you pushing me, that gave me the courage five years ago to begin this annual spiritual trek and to answer God's call. Thank you, each one of you…those who were with us on the trip, and those who stayed home and offered your prayers and moral support. Thank you for helping us create an extremely successful ministerial experience."

After her ten minutes of sharing about her Christian Trek to Africa, embellished by the awesome audiovisual presentation Alana had created, Callindra took a longer drink from her glass and bowed her head in a quick prayer. She looked up out at the crowded sanctuary. As always, she gave herself over to God, leaning into his strength and guidance.

Callindra Tucker's silver-gray eyes turned dark or light depending on her level of excitement. Today, as she strolled from one side of the pulpit to the other weaving her mesmerizing story of

God's mercy and grace during her 14 days on the other side of the world, her thick mane of silver hair swayed loosely across first one shoulder, then the other as if it held a life of its own. Today, her eyes were wide and shone brightly.

At 60, Callindra Tucker was as beautiful as many much-younger women who worked around her. The silver sheen of her hair was the only thing to belie her age. The one thing she demanded and would not relent on was sensible, comfortable shoes. Alana had scoured the local and regional stores, then resorted to catalogs to find the right shoes for Calli. Finally, she ordered the perfect shoes—attractive but classic pumps with two-inch heels and adequate cushioning that addressed Calli's needs.

Weldon stood at the back of the sanctuary. As always, he was overwhelmed by the pastor's charisma. He had never known anyone who could rouse a crowd the way she could or who possessed such pure and natural love for her fellow man. He watched in awe and satisfaction as he always did, yet today his mind wandered to other business they would need to attend.

Calli felt the butterflies awaken as she looked out into the crowded church. Try as she might plan her messages each week. God always had the last word. It was Him who put this message inside her heart more than two weeks ago, then allowed it to churn inside her spirit throughout her Christian Trek and up until this moment. She hadn't purposely misguided wasted Eric's time at rehearsal yesterday. It was God who awoke her early this morning and repeated that she was to deliver the message He'd sent her two weeks ago.

During her long flight home, Calli had reread, for Lord knows how many times, the story of Judas Iscariot, one of the original

Twelve Apostles of Jesus Christ who betrayed Him to the Sanhedrin in the Garden of Gethsemane when he kissed him and addressed him as "rabbi" to reveal his identity to the crowd who had come to arrest him.

She knew the story, had heard it preached several times during her childhood and studied it during his Bible School days.

She recalled the biblical theorist had dubbed the story the "Kiss of Betrayal," repeating Judas' name over and over. Delia and her classmates often gathered in one of their dorm rooms after classes. They often joked about the professor's obsession with this particular story. Calli had wondered if the story somehow hit close to home for the professor.

* * *

Calli had fought against delivering the message for some unexplainable reason. As it turned out, it was the only one she could deliver today. After a deep sleep, Callindra awoke two hours before her 5:30 alarm buzzed. Her eyes opened on their own, and though she tried resting longer, it was as if there was something she had to do before she began her morning.

She pulled herself up and sat on the side of the bed. Suddenly, she found herself chuckling and shaking her head. "You're messing with me, Lord. You know it, and I know it." It wasn't the first time she'd had such awakenings. She knew for a fact. He had lots of tricks up his sleeve.

"Okay, what is it now, Lord?" she asked as she stood and grabbed her robe from the bed rail. She walked half-asleep into her office, flicked on the light, and walked to her desk. She pulled on her reading glasses and reviewed the large-printed pages that were her message for today.

It was a whisper, maybe not even that. Callindra knew immediately what it was. The message of the Samaritan woman meeting Jesus by the well wouldn't do. She felt herself about the panic but refused that expenditure of emotion this morning.

She sighed heavily, then pushed the typed message into her drawer and grabbed up her purse from the floor. She pulled out the folded pages she'd put there during her plane ride home.

The scribbled sentences had been written almost in a trance as if hurriedly transcribed. Still, as she read, the words became abundantly clear. She had been moved…directed to share the story of Judas, who loved the Lord yet chose to betray him.

"God. You can't mean this…not this harsh message? Who am I delivering this message to? I can't think of one of my parishioners who need to hear this message!" She was nervous and fully awake.

"You've got to be kidding me! This is my welcome home message to my wonderful members? This is what you've placed inside my spirit?" She hadn't discussed this with anyone, hopeful that she had misheard His message. Maybe He'd forget or change his mind.

She couldn't believe she was laughing…at herself or God. One thing she knew for sure, He wouldn't forget or change his mind. Forgetting is what we humans use to excuse our sins. He never forgets. As she continued reading over the message, she had had no plans of delivering. She realized she'd been transcribing His words so fast there were more scribbles than words.

* * *

Callindra couldn't believe it when she peeked at her watch. When was the last time she'd preached a whole hour? Her breathing was slightly labored, and her face glowed with an otherworldly aura. A sheen of perspiration covered her face and her neck and dampened her underarms.

As she felt herself coming out of the glorious daze she'd been in for the last hour, she remembered the sermon was not one she would have chosen for herself. She looked out into her parishioners' faces and imagined they were wondering what happened to her in Africa.

Today's message was different from the moving, uplifting ones she usually shared. Those anointing messages always received unrestrained gratitude and adoration with the joke that the message would take them at least through the week!

Calli was exhausted, wrung out, and still questioning why God made her deliver the message on betrayal. She sensed her congregation wrestling with that same question. For the first time since she took on this role, she found it hard to look her parishioners in the eye. Would they believe she was pointing a finger at them when she preached about Judas? She knew it was wrong to question God's wisdom, but she feared He was stirring up a wasp's nest this time.

She forced herself to look out into the congregation, praying for courage and grace. It began as a timid clap, and then it became warm applause and eventually a rousing ovation. Finally, the "pat on the back" Calli needed. It told her that many, if not all of her parishioners appreciated her message even if they questioned the reasoning behind it. How could she make them know it was God's bright idea, not hers.

"Thank you. Thank you. I just wanted to say…for those of you who found my message this morning completely different from what you expected, just imagine how hard it was for me to deliver it. It was the message God placed in my lap two weeks ago, and truthfully, I had no plans of sharing it with you. I tried my best to ignore it…but who am I to turn from it…Am I not a woman following God's directions?" The applause started again. This time it was familiar, filled with love…and forgiveness. She sighed with relief.

There was genuine laughter from the crowd, and more applause, than a standing ovation. Callindra breathed a sigh of relief and beckoned the choir to begin. She knew the amazing intergenerational choir would resettle the congregation in the spirit and take them to an even higher level of love and acceptance.

As she prepared to leave the pulpit, Callindra looked toward the front pew and spied Weldon sitting with one of their newest parishioners Clyde Vann. She smiled down at the two men. Weldon looked back, but there was no smile in return. So often, she tried to know what her counselor was thinking. Weldon didn't like surprises or being caught off guard. She was sorry she'd surprised him this morning, but there was someone bigger than both of them, and He'd pulled rank today.

* * *

PART X: Clyde Thomas Vann

CHAPTER 17

New Beginnings

Before Callindra began her 15 minutes of hugs and warm wishes from as many congregants as could find a place in the greeting line, Weldon slipped into the Pastor's office to wait for her. He stood taking in the hundreds of photos she had on the walls, desks, and bookcases. The many people she had met and loved over the last 20 years. He noted, once again, there was no photo of any personal relationships among the many. He'd always found that odd for a woman who seemed the epitome of close and loving relationships.

Weldon was remembering how he'd met Callindra Tucker. It had been by pure accident, well before she acquired the fame and name she now possessed as a prominent Louisiana Christian leader. They met at one of her Family Day picnics. He had attended with an old client who was also a Miracle Way Missionary Church member.

Within the time he met her and the time he left the church park, he'd already professed the pastor would be a star one day, in Louisiana and maybe across the country. Her charm and personality outshone anyone he'd ever encountered. There was also the passion that was part of everything she did and such purity that made others gravitate to her.

Weldon and Calli spent several minutes sharing sweet stories about their mutual friend and parishioner. As they began to leave,

Calli had hugged them both, saying to Weldon, "Please come and visit us sometimes, whenever you have an extra Sunday to spare.". He'd laughed, charmed. He'd never heard the phrase before.

After that day, Weldon had stealthily done his background on the beautiful evangelist. Who was this woman, where had she come from, was she...genuine? He was more than a little surprised to learn she was ten years older than him, as Weldon studied

faces like some of his friends studied art. He rarely got women's ages more than a couple of years wrong. There were many women who didn't "show their age," but there was something unique about Callindra's beauty. It was as if God had frozen it at a particular time in her life. The innocence in the eyes and smile. The open affection. Callindra Tucker was one of the few truly age-neutral women he knew. Maybe even timeless, if he wanted to put a romantic spin to it.

Over the last 15 years, Weldon served as general counsel for Miracle Way and personal attorney to Calli Tucker. He had often been pushed for information about her—suggesting reasons for the paucity of relationships in her life or joking that a woman who must have been a real "hottie" in her youth must have a few skeletons in her closet. Weldon only smiled at the harmless yet intrusive allusions about Callindra Tucker's personal life.

Throughout Biblical history, Weldon mused, God had often used beautiful women as catalysts for good. Mightn't Calli Tucker be God's modern-day Ruth or Sarah, or Deborah? He imagined a large number of men joining Miracle Way with an image of Calli tucked in the back of their minds. It never took long for any impure thoughts to be transformed into devotion to Callindra and the Church.

No, there was nothing at Miracle Way Baptist Church for men

with impure hearts to take advantage of, except for the word of God. To her credit, Callindra had never given any of the men a hint that she was personally interested beyond her interest in their spiritual salvation. Not one that he could recall...until Clyde Thomas Vann showed up at Miracle Way.

* * *

Clyde Thomas Vann, football icon and business tycoon, had visited Miracle Way Missionary Baptist Church several Sundays in the last year at the invitation of Weldon Solder. It didn't take many visits before he realized just how at home he felt in the warm and familial environment and, more importantly, how Pastor Tucker's message resonated with him.

Clyde Vann hadn't joined a church since growing up in Ruston, never feeling comfortable enough with the church leadership or the makeup of the congregations. He shied away from most churches once he realized how quickly he became the center of attention after entering the sanctuary.

Clyde met Weldon Solder in Baton Rouge at a Christmas dinner party hosted by Weldon's friend and Clyde's attorney Barr Winston who also happened to be a managing attorney at Weldon's old law firm. Though Weldon had left the firm over a decade earlier, he still had many friends there.

Each year, he was invited to the Christmas gatherings held at a partners' home or one of Baton Rouge's swanky restaurants. The two men were amazed they hadn't met before since Barr had known them both for well over two decades. They spent the evening talking oil and the business of sports. Weldon had off-handedly mentioned

Miracle Way and invited Clyde to visit.

Clyde took him up on the offer. He had been looking for a church he could call home for years now. He had attended the church at least once a month for several months when Weldon invited his new friend to a small, informal Pastors' reception. Weldon found the small gatherings were a great opportunity for the pastor to charm visitors like Clyde into becoming permanent members.

Though he'd never admit it to Clyde, Weldon made it a point to mix in non-wealthy but passionate visitors with potential members who could be big givers, like Clyde. On the day of the Pastor's Meet & Greet, Weldon sent ushers to each of the 15 invitees to escort them to the pastor's reception held in her study. Clyde Vann was one of the first visitors. He pointed out.

Weldon was in his element as the number one representative for Pastor Tucker, greeting guests as they arrived. After small talk, he graciously directed them to where the pastor stood inside a circle of admirers. Clyde hadn't quite made it in before being hijacked by Alana, who had met Clyde before and found him as attractive as the other women in the church did.

He watched as Alana turned on the charm as she talked with Clyde. He always found it interesting that there were so many similarities between Alana and Calli. He guessed it made sense. They were best friends and had grown closer during their years on the beauty pageant circuit

Alana was also a dear friend of the Tucker family, and something like an adopted daughter to Delia Tucker. The Pastor considered the woman the closest thing to a sister.

Though Alana praised Weldon to Calli, it took her some time to warm up to his reserved ways. When the two finally did warm up to each other, they found that they had some things in common, most pointedly, their desire to please and take care of Callindra.

When Weldon forced himself to admit it, he saw Alana as exotic, charming, and smart. For Alana, Weldon was a handsome, good-looking man with lots of power inside the church. As Delia came up and took over with Clyde, Weldon came over and touched Alana on the arm. " I just wanted to tell you that you did a great job with the Pastor this morning. She looks great."

"Thanks, Weldon, but we both know the Pastor doesn't need much help in looking good. The woman has that natural beauty and glow that comes from inside of her."

"And, she has you. She's lucky." Alana smiled and blushed before walking over to a new guest.

Weldon was simply amazed by the crowd Clyde Vann attracted each Sunday as he tried to make his way out of the church. "Like flies to cream," his aunt Clara used to say. He wondered if there was anyone who didn't know who Clyde Vann was, other than Pastor Tucker and himself. They were part of that small contingent of Louisiana residents who didn't follow his career like a map. That is until he met him at the lawyers' dinner just a few months earlier.

The truth was, Weldon had never been a sports buff and hadn't played organized sports unless you called racquetball an organized sport. He'd played as a businessman's game for most of his adult life. He knew very little about football or its icons. He rarely kept up with celebrities unless their lives intersected with his in some way or were associated in a business sense.

He jokingly dubbed it a God-intervention that he met the good-looking football icon who had transformed himself from a nationally recognized athlete into a very wealthy oil businessman. He was especially impressed that Vann had come from a very poor home in Ruston, Louisiana, but was such a standout player that he received both an athletic and academic scholarship to Grambling University, where he broke every college record for rushes, before being courted by most of the NFL teams throughout the country.

Young Clyde had known since he was a youngster playing peewee football that he wanted to be a New Orleans Saint. His friends had laughed and told him he was just dreaming. Somehow, he knew it was more than just a dream. It was meant to be. Within two years of becoming a member of the New Orleans Saints team, he was an unmitigated star, again breaking every rushing record in the NFL.

It wasn't just his skill on the football field. The fans fell in love with the good-looking young man from the poor Louisiana community. "Clyde, Clyde...he's our guy!" was the cry of the impassioned Saints fans most Saturday nights. He was that extraordinary athlete who exuded a simple, boy-next-door humility and grace. His "good little poor boy makes good" story was legendary and had been told and retold during and since his football career.

The Saints and Clyde Vann were synonymous in the minds of most Louisianians. Clyde preferred the media stories that shared his early life growing up in Ruston, his parents, and his community. "Without that poor community and my parents," he often said, "folks wouldn't take a second look at ole Clyde Vann." He never forgot who he was or where he came from. He never forgot the obstacles his family faced growing up in a town where blacks and whites recognized and abided by the separation rules

After retirement, Clyde was overwhelmed by the barrage of offers from companies and products seeking endorsement contracts or wanting him to join their teams. They wanted Clyde to represent this new south, accepting of Black men like Clyde with an innocent sex appeal that didn't threaten the south's old guard, a trusting voice – with just enough of that "good old boy" syrupiness Louisianans loved.

Clyde was nobody's fool. He knew what they were after—and what he wanted in return. He wouldn't work for anyone for the rest of his life, but while he did, it would be on his own terms that included ensuring security for him and his family.

At his attorney's recommendation, Clyde accepted a full partnership with one of the three firms he had settled on—one of the largest oil firms in the southeast. The founding partners were pleasantly surprised at the former athlete's intelligence, excitement to learn all he could about the industry, and discernment about what he wanted out of the business relationship.

Clyde Vann was a quick study in the oil industry. His open and direct personality was attractive to the company, which needed someone like him to open the conversations and close the deal very often. What some in the company had looked at as just a pretty face to sit out front, in time, had to admit it was a smart pick for the company. Clyde quickly learned and began offering calculated strategies that worked in parts of southern Louisiana, Texas, and Arkansas. It didn't hurt that he had a special knack for befriending the ranchers and farmers before they'd sell him their piece of land and wish him good luck.

Clyde had worked with the oil company for 20 years when he

retired at 50. It still amazed him to see his name as one of the 100 richest men in New Orleans. He was surprised and grateful. Who would have thought "Little Clydie" would one day grace the cover of local, regional, and national business magazines?

His retirement created opportunities to take on more personal initiatives, including board roles on two nonprofit organizations he had followed over the years and serving as spokesperson for philanthropy causes that meant a lot to him. Now that he had the legal options, he researched investment options. One of his first investments was in a small Texas oil company. The second investment was in a Louisiana shrimp boating company founded by a former teammate after his retirement. Clyde invested more into his own international sports entertainment firm that had continued growing during his time with the oil firm. Anything with Clyde Vann on its name seemed bound for success.

During their meeting, Weldon had learned about Clyde's early marriage to his high school sweetheart. There hadn't been children, but it was obvious there was still a great deal of love and respect for his ex-wife, Alice Bond. Alice, he learned, had followed her dreams to become an artist. Clyde readily admitted that she was part of his success and had stood beside him throughout their uncertain early years.

Once success was on the horizon, they'd tried hard to get pregnant. After learning they couldn't, they talked about adopting. Somewhere between their talk of adoption and Alice's long hours getting her art career off the ground, their marriage began to unravel. "The marriage ended, not our love for each other. Never our love for each other," he told Weldon.

Clyde's divorce was a news story in New Orleans and Louisiana. He quickly became known as one of Louisiana's most eligible bachelors –and the most sought-after men in the country. He blushed as he admitted to Weldon that he'd dated his share of beauty queens, as well as prominent professional women. None of them long enough to consider marriage material, he said.

* * *

Should there have been a message in the fact that Clyde and Callindra met during the Christmas season -both of their favorite holidays?. It was two months after he'd taken Weldon up on his invitation to visit the church and had visited a couple of times each month. Weldon had begun his soft campaign to persuade his new friend to consider becoming a permanent member. Clyde hadn't said, "yes, so far.

Now, Weldon had invited him to the more exclusive after-service pastor's reception. Clyde smiled at the invitation and asked, "What comes with the invitation, Weldon?" He had said hello to Pastor Tucker before, during the after-service greetings on his way out of the church. That hadn't included any real conversation, just an offer of his name and "I really enjoyed the service." She had smiled, thanked him, and asked him to please keep coming. This time, he'd received a personal invitation to meet the pastor on a more personal basis during the after-service Pastor's reception, an invitations-only affair.

Clyde loved Christmas. It was his favorite time of the year growing up in Ruston when all he and his siblings had to look forward to was their Christmas box with fruit, nuts, candy, a few firecrackers

–and during the best of years, a small toy they treasured for the rest of the year. Nothing brought those sweet memories back like the smell of live Christmas trees and the sight of blinking Christmas bulbs.

This afternoon, the pastor's study was beautifully decorated with festive holly, lights, and aromatic candles sitting at every table. A beautiful Christmas tree stood in the corner, and Christmas music played in the background. Clyde thought as he walked in that this was a perfect way to spend an afternoon leading up to Christmas.

Delia Tucker loved the Christmas season at her daughter's church. She enjoyed the seasonal programs, the caroling, and the opportunity to give to children in need. The older Tucker woman was talking with Weldon when Clyde finally broke free from his admirers and made a beeline to Weldon.

"You're free…at least for a moment," Weldon smiled. "I need you to meet Miss Delia Devereaux Belsen- the first lady of Blue Bayou and known far and wide in Louisiana circles."

Clyde offered his hand, and Delia shook it with gentle firmness. A smile spread across her face. "Well, I'll be dog-gone if I'm not meeting Clyde Vann in the flesh and blood!"

An avid New Orleans Saints football fan, Delia knew just about everything about Clyde Vann, at least the public information. She had followed the younger man throughout his career, and for the next 15 minutes, she amazed him with her recollections of some of his most remembered on-field successes.

Alana walked up with a camera. Smiling at the two of them, she offered first Delia, then Clyde a quick hug. She held her camera out for them to see before asking if she could take a photo of the two for their monthly newsletter.

"I'm fine with it if Mrs. Delia is okay," Clyde offered. Delia's smile grew even wider. "I'm absolutely fine with it, Lana," she told her almost-daughter. Shaking his head, Weldon whispered to Alana before she made her way to another part of the study.

"You, Miss Delia, have an amazing memory for statistics…and bloopers," Clyde laughed. "I have to tell you, some of those memories left me years ago." They laughed about some of the bloopers, most of which he did recall.

"Where is that gorgeous little girl you were married to?"

"Alice and I are no longer married, but she's doing fine, making a name for herself as a very fine artist. We remain good friends."

"I'm happy to hear that. I read that y' all were childhood sweethearts, and you know what they say about first loves…they will always be your first love, right?."

"I kind 'a think that's right, Delia. I might fall in love again one of these days, but I don't think anyone can ever take the place of that first love inside your heart," he agreed.

Weldon was surprised to find just how comfortable Clyde and Delia were with each other. He knew how obsessive Delia was about Louisiana sports and, most specifically, the New Orleans Saints.

Delia looked over and saw that her daughter's line of guests was dwindling. She pointed over and asked Clyde if he would like to go over and meet the "star of this show?"

"Of course…"

Weldon walked back over at that very moment. "Thanks for keeping Mr. Vann entertained, Delia. Why don't you join me while I take him over and introduce him to Pastor Tucker."

Clyde was amused to be escorted to the pastor by Delia and his friend Weldon. Callindra Tucker was also amused as she saw the three approaching.

"Mr. Vann, what an honor! I'm finally getting to meet the man the whole church has been talking about for the last few months. Seriously, thank you so much for joining us."

Clyde smiled, noting how much prettier the pastor was here, less than a foot from him than she was in the pulpit. He found himself looking from Delia to the Pastor, with a frown across his forehead. . "Is there something, Miss Delia, that you failed to mention?"

Delia looked sheepishly from her daughter to Clyde, and they all laughed. Callindra shook her head in mild exasperation at her mother's usual antics.

"Your little sister?" he asked Delia, laughing. "Well...she could be," Delia smiled.

"You two look so much alike. I guess I should have guessed."

Delia and Callindra looked at each other. How often had Delia played this joke on unsuspecting men? Too many times for Callindra to try and remember.

"Mr. Vann, the woman who has been bending your ear for the last 30 minutes, is my mother. I admit she's the sports fan in the family, but I'm more grateful than she is that you're here to worship with us."

The two exchanged smiles and began a conversation that lasted as long as his conversation with Delia, who remained with them and chimed in as she saw fit.

"Oh, by the way, Calli...he's promised to join us for the Feeding the Homeless weekend," on New Year's eve, Delia shared, with a hint of pride. In response to her daughter's surprise, she told her she'd taken the liberty to invite Mr. Vann to the event and promised him she'd personally put his name on the email listing."

"I'm so happy, Mr. Vann. It's a wonderful way to bring the new year in. What better way to begin the year than giving back."

He nodded, mumbling that he'd be happy to take part in the event.

"I'm happy, Mr. Vann, but I hope my mother didn't bully you into saying yes. And please don't allow us to take up too much of your time. We all know how busy you are, and I'm watching that line of folk outside the door, waiting for you to walk out." He turned and smiled out at the line of parishioners.

Clyde shook his head. "You're not taking up too much of my time, Pastor Tucker, and I'll be happy to say hello to everyone who wants me to on my way out."

"That makes me feel better. So, I should tell you that I do have quite a little dossier on you, thanks to my able detectives here at the church."

"I'm not surprised, Pastor. You have one of the best attorneys in Louisiana working for you, and I've learned that the people of Louisiana know just about everything there is to know about Clyde Vann!"

Calli laughed, "Yes…like, we know you vote as a Democrat in most elections, that your favorite song is "September," by Earth Wind and Fire, that you were invited by President Clinton to the African State Dinner with Nelson Mandela, in 2000, and according to my sources, you are even on a first-name basis with a few world leaders. Now, how can little ole Miracle Way compete with all that star power?"

Clyde shook his head in surprise. "I'm truly impressed, Pastor Tucker, but it's really not a matter of competing…that's a whole other part of who I am, nothing to do with spiritual life. I'm more than happy to be visiting your church, and I'm really grateful to your counsel, Solder, for inviting me."

"Oh, I'm so happy to hear that, Mr. Vann. And, on that note, I'm not sure how much Weldon has shared about our little church family here, but I know he'd want me to say that I would be more than happy to share more about our vision and what we hope to accomplish over the next few years."

"I would love that. Weldon gets excited telling me how you've grown the church over the last 25 years, but yes…I'd like to learn more because the truth is I'm in search of a permanent church home. I know it makes no sense, but I hadn't joined a church since I left home in Ruston. For years, I went back there for monthly services. But, I have to tell you…there's a really good, at-home feeling I get when I visit here, Pastor Tucker. "

Callindra smiled, pleased and excited. "I'm glad. Alana will call you and schedule a time that works for you to meet again for lunch here at the church." She couldn't believe that she was jumping ahead of Weldon, setting up her own meeting with the man.

Most surprising to Callindra was her attraction to the man—his good looks, his natural charm, and, what seemed to be, a genuine good heart. She was almost convinced he was exactly who he portrayed himself to be.

"And, while mama is the sports fanatic in the family, I do recall watching you a few of those Sundays I sat with mama during Sunday football games. I can still remember her jumping up in the middle of the room and calling your name. She was definitely one of your biggest fans."

He laughed, and something warm ran through Callindra. He was charmed and a bit embarrassed. "Just wondering, were you a cheerleader, by any chance, Pastor Tucker?" She was blushing now.

"Oh no, Mr. Vann, watching television sports with mama was about as close to cheerleading I ever came."

Delia chimed in, "No, but she could have been. She was pretty enough. I was just thinking, Calli, instead of bringing Clyde out here to this church for lunch, why don't y'all come over for a New Year's dinner with Lance and me? Weldon and Alana can join us if they don't have other New Year's plans. That will give you plenty of opportunity to tell Clyde all about the church and your plans for the future. Plus, you'll get a real Cajun dinner, to boot!"

Clyde grinned as if he had died and gone to heaven. He looked over at Callindra for confirmation that she was okay with the offer. She seemed surprised but pleased. "Thank you, Delia. If you let me double-check with my assistant tomorrow, I can confirm tomorrow afternoon."

Weldon and Callindra looked at each other, bemused by Delia's kind and unusual offer. "Alana, can you make sure I don't have anything on my calendar for new year's day? And, if I do, I'm sure we can rearrange it. Mr. Vann, you have not eaten Cajun food until you eat Delia Tucker's Cajun food."

As he left the pastor's study Clyde Vann promised Pastor Tucker he'd be back next week and looked forward to seeing her on New Year's evening. She noted his easy laughter indicating comfort with whatever surroundings he found himself in and with who he was despite what others thought of him.

As Delia prepared to leave, she hugged Callindra and told her how much she'd enjoyed her message that morning. "You know Weldon usually invites the dullest people he can find, but today…he done good. It's been a while since I enjoyed meeting someone at church. Clyde Vann is certainly different from most of the men who come to your church."

Callindra laughed and kissed her mother as she left. "I'll talk with you this week, mama."

As he walked into the lobby, Clyde ran into his friend. "You do good work, Weldon Solder…investigator and headhunter! You just might be in the wrong field."

Weldon laughed, pleased. "Well…I just want you to know that we're extremely honored to have a man of your stature visit our humble church."

Clyde smiled. "You make me sound a lot more important than I am. I'm just a man who's been highly blessed. I've been coming to your church for a couple of months now, and I want you to know that it has nothing to do with how humble your church is. I come for Pastor Tucker's message, and I take it away with me. It stays with me for the entire week, and by then, I'm always ready for another helping…it's just that simple. We all have to get our spiritual sustenance from somewhere, and right now, your church is doing a good job of that."

The man's words tugged at Weldon's heart. He felt that way about Miracle Way…and about Callindra Tucker. Weldon wasn't a man who quickly liked anyone and hadn't expected to like Clyde without any reserve.

Clyde didn't know much about Delia Tucker, but he was drawn to the woman. She was beautiful, funny, down to earth, and had a huge heart. But it was Pastor Callindra that sparked something inside him he hadn't felt in a long time. There was an undeniable electricity between them. He hadn't expected that at all. It had been a long time since Clyde had felt drawn to a woman beyond physical attraction. His love for Alice had started this way.

Clyde Vann had had a plane to catch later this evening – a weeklong trip to Kenya he was hopeful would be a successful business consummation. He wouldn't change that, but he would be looking forward to New Year's day all the way there and back.

***

CHAPTER 18

Winter Love

Dinner at Delia and Lance's home was the beginning of something neither Calli nor Clyde had anticipated. While neither would admit it, they both had spent part of the last weeks thinking of the day, wondering if the electric charge they'd felt were real would still be alive during today's dinner.

The Cajun dinner was just as Calli had told Clyde it would be. Exquisitely cooked and seasoned. Everyone was admitted they'd eaten far more than they'd planned or wanted to. Delia shooed everyone from the kitchen and into the living room after dinner. "Nobody washes dishes at my house except me. You're all guests!"

There was vocal sighing as they sat. Lance offered after-dinner wine. "That was the absolute best dinner I've had in years, Ms. Delia…you sho'nuff put your foot in that meal," Clyde said.

"There is a lot more where that came from, Clyde Vann. Now that you know your way here come anytime. If you want to pick up my daughter on your way out, we're fine with that." The room filled with laughter. Clyde almost spilled his drink as he laughed.

The conversation was easy, light. Lance told stories about Blue Bayou the history of the town. "Did you know that a lot of people call Blue Bayou the rib God pulled from Thibodaux? It's like we've always been trying to keep up with the larger city. They call us twin cities, but one is a prosperous commercial town, and Blue Bayou got the leftovers. We've also had a really speckled race history. Most folks don't want to remember that, and certainly, they don't want to talk about it.

"But…I know Delia, Calli, and Alana will agree that there are some mighty good people here, blacks and whites. Calli has done so much to bring the races together. I don't think anyone questions that her ministry is the best thing that could happen to our community." Calli blushed and thanked Lance for his kind words.

It was past 10 p.m. when everyone decided they should get home and let Lance and Delia go to bed. There were hugs all around and heartfelt gratitude to the wonderful hosts.

At some point during the after-dinner hour, Clyde had asked Calli if he could drop her by home, and she'd said yes. She walked into the kitchen, away from the group, and called Saul, who was about to drive back to Delia's to pick her up.

"Happy New Year, Saul. I want you to take off the rest of the evening and watch the new year come in with sweet Dolly. Believe it or not, I have an offer from a wonderful man to take me home."

Saul gasped, then giggled with surprise. Calli couldn't help herself. She joined Saul giggling like school children. "Good night, Saul."

"Good night, Pastor. You and Mr. Vann enjoy this New Year's evening."

* * *

As Weldon and Alana walked the Pastor out to Clyde's car, they both seemed to be in shock. Callindra wanted to laugh at the look on

Weldon's face as if he'd created something he had no plans of creating.

"Do you need me to call you tonight, Pastor, to go over anything before your week starts tomorrow?"

"Of course not, Weldon. I need you to enjoy the rest of your weekend. Everything is pretty much in place. Alana and I went over my calendar last week. Most folk won't want to start the year with meetings, after all."

"I understand, but I was thinking of our...."

Callindra touched his arm gently. "It's all taken care of, Weldon. I'll call you tomorrow to see if we should plan to meet on Wednesday. Have a good rest of your night." She looked over at Alana and waved.

Alana smiled. "Good night, Pastor Callindra. You have a good night. Get her home safely, now, Mr. Clyde Vann." She giggled as she turned and headed for her car.

Weldon seemed stuck in place. "I'll talk to you tomorrow, Pastor. Clyde, it was good seeing you." He turned, then and walked away.

Callindra looked over at Clyde and shrugged. Sometimes she gave up trying to figure out what was going on in Weldon's mind.

The 20-minute ride back to Callindra's home was a quiet one. Neither seemed to know exactly what to say. There was that electricity charge they both felt, even stronger now. Callindra looked out the window at the dark sky overfull with stars. She saw her reflection in the window and quickly looked down.

"I hope this isn't taking you too far out of your way, Mr. Vann. I'm sure you have other things to do tonight."

He looked over at her and shook his head. "Not a thing in the world, Pastor Callindra."

She smiled and looked back out into the darkness. She had never learned the first thing about how you act with a man—not how a woman acts with a man. She knew about pastoring and ministering, but…

As they arrived at her house, Calli's heart skipped. Already? She sighed and hoped he didn't hear her. Clyde turned into the circular drive and parked in front of Callindra's home.

"I had a very, very nice evening tonight, Pastor Tucker. Thank you for agreeing to have dinner with…with your mother, stepfather, Weldon, and Alana."

She looked at him and saw that he was joking. He was smiling, and she began giggling. What was this with the schoolgirl giggling tonight?

"Next time…" he began.

"Next time?" she asked

"Next time, I'd love to take you to dinner alone if that's acceptable."

She looked down, then over at him. She realized something was happening inside her because she was already anticipating the next time. She didn't recognize this…desire, need Clyde Vann had brought out in her.

"Next time, we'll have dinner with just the two of us, Mr. Vann."

"Will you please call me Clyde, Pastor Callindra?"

"Only if you call me Callindra, Clyde?"

Their eyes locked, and what might have been laughter got caught in both their throats. Their eyes seemed to have somehow locked on each other. The electric charge escalated several decibels.

Clyde quickly stepped out of the car and walked around to help her out of the door. "My father taught me that you never leave a woman till she's safely inside her home. I'm walking you to your door, and you will go inside, turn your lights on, and let me know when you are sure that everything is fine."

She didn't walk into her home as he'd suggested. She sat in the swing on her beautiful wrap-around porch. Clyde followed suit.

"My mother had this swing built when I was just a child. I loved it so much. It was always my favorite place when things weren't going well." She didn't add that the swing was also where she and Tom Mallory had set so many nights after Delia went off to bed.

"I grew up with a porch swing too. But, I had to share it with a bunch of brothers."

"I'll go and get us a glass of lemon tea…you can't sit in a swing without lemon tea. I'll make it hot to help us both sleep tonight."

Clyde smiled and looked down. "That should help some, Callindra."

They swung and sipped lemon tea and talked well into the morning. Callindra felt as if she was inside a dream. She'd never experienced this before…not since Tom, and that was so very long ago. She hadn't talked to a man about herself, ever. She was telling Clyde things she'd never told a living soul.

Clyde decided he was more interested in listening tonight than talking. There had been so many questions he'd come up with since their meeting at the church. He never in a million years dreamed she would feel comfortable enough to share her life story with him. The more she talked, the more she shared. Clyde felt himself falling…

"Well, I've bent your ear for hours, Clyde. You have to travel to the other side of the world tomorrow. I heard you tell Lance you did.

I'm so sorry to keep you up like this!"

"I could sit here listening to you for another four hours, Callindra. I love listening to you talk. Your story is so fascinating. You have no idea how much I've enjoyed this."

As he stood, Callindra stood. He touched the swing to stop it from moving and, at the same time, moved the few inches that separated Callindra from him.

"I have no idea how to say this, Callindra, but I really do want to kiss you."

She didn't answer but said yes as she timidly pressed her lips to his. She knew her life was changing at that moment and would never be the same.

PART XI: Calli's Missing

CHAPTER 19

Almost Perfect Road Trip

Forty-eight hours before his road trip with Virginia, Tom worked late in his office. He loved this time of the evening when he had the office to himself. Quiet, no phone calls, no one walking in looking to him to solve their problems. A time he could catch up on all the paperwork left undone during the day.

Tom took a bite from the Brisket sandwich Maia had left for him. The deli down the street had excellent sandwiches, and the brisket was Tom's favorite. It also had the best lemonade he'd ever drunk, but he was backing off sweet drinks for as long as he could stand it, he'd had one episode with his high blood pressure whirling out of hand last year, and he wasn't trying to bring another one of those bouts on.

He kept plowing through the over-grown piles of paper on his desk. This was his one New Year's resolution: he'd clean off his desk every day before he left for home, no matter how long it took him. He always hated it when he returned from a business trip or vacation, only to be greeted by the triple mountains of paper on his desk. Tonight, he would tackle the mountains, deep-sixing what he didn't need, and leaving the rest in new, smaller stacks for Maia to place in the appropriate folders.

Two hours later, Tom found himself in a comfortable pattern.

He smiled, impressed with the headway he'd made...until he heard the long ring of the phone. He searched for it and realized it was hidden under the piles of paper he was working on. Why did phones sound twice as loud at night, especially when you were all alone? He shook his head. His concentration would be shattered. Tom thought for a second. Should he simply ignore it, let the message go to voicemail? His lawman's instinct wouldn't let him do it.

"Daphne Sheriff's Office." Tom tried to keep the irritation out of his voice. The person on the other end didn't need to know how much he didn't want to answer that phone. For thirty seconds, there was no voice on the other end.

"Hello, anybody there?"

Finally, the voice came through. The hairs on the back of Tom's neck stood on end. The woman's voice hadn't changed much in 45 years, giving him the same pit in the stomach it had back when he was 18 years old. The southern drawl, he thought, had gotten even deeper.

By the time Delia Tucker spoke her name, Tom was seeing another face, not hers, but a beautiful young girl, and hearing that sweet, innocent laughter that still haunted him sometimes late at night.

Tom spoke to erase the sound and the memory. "Delia...Miss Deveraux. My God, it's been more years than I can count since I heard your voice. How are you?"

Tom wondered if Delia looked the same as she did all those years ago. She was some looker back then. He was in love with Calli but had had an innocent boy's crush on her mother, as well.

"Tom, it was hell finding you. But I had to...I had to, Tom. I need your help." This was Delia, alright. No niceties, just straight to the point.

"What's wrong, Mrs. Deveraux? You sound ... where in the world are you, here in Daphne?"

A heavy silence filled up the airwaves. He had always remembered Delia covering silence with her raw, sexy laughter. She had never allowed life's hard knocks to steal her brave smile. Had something finally been able to do that?

A tiny reminder of his promise to Virginia blinked off and on in the back of Tom's head, a subtle neon sign reminding him that nothing Delia could say could supersede his promise to his mother. Whatever Delia's troubles, they would have to be taken care of before Saturday morning or wait until his return next week.

"Tom, it's Calli" the tired voice was now of an older woman. "It's our Calli.

She's disappeared." Tom hardly recognized this voice, sobbing into the mouthpiece of the phone. Maybe he had believed she never cried. The sobs were interspersed with pain-wracked groans.

Tom waited. He'd never learned what to say to women when they cried or were in emotional misery. He had been paralyzed by his own mother's outbursts as a child and had avoided her during these times at all costs.

Calli was missing. He couldn't think of one thing other than this that would force Delia to call him. Of course, it had to be the worst thing that could happen to her to make her track Tom down, call him up out of the blue. Calli had always been the glue that held the three of them together.

God forgive him, but the cowardly part of Tom Mallory wished he hadn't answered the phone, that he'd let the call go to voice mail. Then, Maia would have scribbled the message on a pink note-it and pasted it to his desk. Tom would have scanned it, been surprised and curious when he saw Delia's name, but wouldn't have been forced to call back until he returned from Shreveport because Delia wouldn't have left the whole message – the whole truth about why she called.

Her calling this late, at a time when she must have guessed the office was closed, made everything different. Her Calling Calli's name, her heart-wrenching sobs… changed how he'd have to deal with her call.

Tom roused himself out of his shock, reminding himself that he couldn't change his plans for next week, and wouldn't let this news intrude on his promise to a mother he knew from experience wasn't the forgiving kind.

"Tom, I need you to come. Please," Delia Tucker's very human grief shocked him even more. Delia was a woman Tom had believed confronted life much the same as most men he knew – steering clear of human emotions that hampered the female race.

"My girl's nowhere to be found, Tom, and I need your help to find her. We've been searching for her for over two weeks, and there's not a trace of her anywhere. The mayor, my husband, has done everything in the book—community searches, helicopters, those new-fangled things…drones, search dogs. You name it, and we've done it…still, no Calli," she was sobbing uncontrollably, now.

"Tommy…you know I wouldn't ask if I didn't have to. You're the only one I can entrust with this. You're the only man who really knew her, the only one who can help."

Tom felt the stirrings of something he had buried deep inside him. He unconsciously shook his head. Now wasn't the time. He couldn't take that something out and dissect it, not now, after all this time.

Tom sat as if glued to the chair, unmoving. He had worked hard to bury the memory of Calli Tucker, to forget the consuming desire he'd had for her. He hadn't called her name in all those years, had thought of her only when she forced herself into his dreams once or twice a year. How was it that hearing Delia's voice reawakened everything? He wondered who Calli Tucker was now, 45 years later.

"I'm on my way home, Miss Deveraux. Let me get home and call you in an hour.

I can't come there, now. I have a commitment, something I have to do next week...a promise I have to keep."

"When...Tom? When can you come? Will you really call me back tonight? Please call me back, Tom."

Tom promised to call Delia Tucker later that night. He gently placed the phone on its cradle as he realized he was experiencing a strange sensation – as if he'd drank on an empty stomach. His memories tumbled and whirled thickly in his head. The past was the present... memories of Calli, Delia, and moonlit nights in Blue Bayou.

Tom hadn't told Delia his commitment was to his mother because he dared not introduce her into his real life. Neither would he use Virginia as his excuse not to help. Yet, he wouldn't lie to himself. He already knew what his answer to Delia would be. He couldn't turn his back on her because she was the mother of the girl he'd loved all those years ago.

They, the three of them, had been almost a family, though family wasn't an institution Delia paid much homage to. There had, though, been a lot between them, and Tom had realized almost too late that there might have been too much between them.

Tom took a deep breath forced his mind outside the filmy past, back to his real-life here in Daphne. He needed to sleep, to think clearly before he called Delia. Before he could tell her, he would help.

* * *

"You're driving like a maniac, Tommy! Slow down before you kill both of us out on this highway."

"Sorry, Mother…I'm just trying to get us down there before too late. If we get there early enough, Plank can take us by the house, and we can get some things done before dark."

"Hmmm…that's true. But we have to get there first."

Virginia smiled, then placed her reading glasses back on her eyes. As he drove, Tom realized there was something different about his mother. Nothing he could quite put his finger on right away, but something.

She read the **Picayune Times** for ten minutes at a time, then stopped to stare out of the window for another 10 minutes in a reflective mood. Virginia Malloy, reflective? What might Virginia be reflecting on, Tom wondered, her life, her future, her relationship with Tom? There was most certainly something new about his mother, a new sense of calm in the way she reclined in her seat, held the newspaper to her breast…and smiled to herself.

As they turned off the Shreveport Exit, Tom found himself smiling too, thinking that at last, Virginia was going home of her own volition, with no chance of recriminations from her father or sad looks from her mother. Now, finally, she wouldn't have to explain to anyone about her unhappy marriage.

His mother, he felt, was as near being happy as he'd ever seen her. He had missed this in all those years in New Orleans. Now, he knew. It hadn't been hatred for the place that kept her from moving home; it was ghosts of her failures she'd surely see in her parents' eyes and her own fear of facing them.

That fear had kept her away from the father she adored and the mother whose love had always made her believe she was special. And there had been the guilt too, of all she had kept from them, that they had never met their only grandchild. By the time they began to ask, she had hardened her heart against their years of refusal to recognize her husband or her marriage.

Now, she would never have to tell her father he had been right about her marriage. Finally, the place she had loved so much as a child but turned her back on during her darkest years would be home again, the home she so needed.

"Tommy, I've already been working out in my mind what kind of flowers I want planted in my front yard. You remember how pretty my mama's chrysanthemums were?"

She giggled, "Oh...of course, you don't. You weren't even born...never saw them." Her face clouded some, for just a moment as she remembered,

"Oh, Tommy...I so wish you had met my mama and papa. They would have loved you so much better than I knew how." She took a deep breath as if she was willing the ugly memories out the window again.

"Your papa loved my mama's flowers. He loved that pretty blue and white color they had and how good they smelled when he came to visit."

Tom didn't let on just how shocked he was to hear Virginia mention her husband with even a hint of fondness. He turned just enough to catch a glimpse of the face that was suddenly soft, almost girl-like in its beauty.

Tom could see by the coloring that came up in her face that she was remembering young Thomas Alexander, who had come to Shreveport, had swept her off her feet, then stolen her from the home she loved, to a strange world she hated.

"Did you love papa, Mother, even a little?"

"Oh, Tommy…" She turned her head, pretending to look out the window. He imagined she was trying, now, to slow the rush of poignant memories.

"The truth is, son, it's near about impossible to hate a man as much as I hated your father in the end unless you loved him at least that much in the beginning."

* * *

Plank Masterson was as wide as he was tall, with dirty blond hair streaked through and through with gray. His white painters' pants looked as if they had been soaked for years on end with paints of every hue. With his wide grin, the man hurried across the road to Tom's Honda Element. He grabbed Tom's hand in both of his own, shaking it with all his might.

"This is Tommy Mallory, I presume?" with that wide smile, he half-pulled Tom from the car and gave him a clench of a bear hug.

"Boy, nobody – men or women-- in this family leave it at just shaking hands...we a hugging family. Ask Ginny." Tom wouldn't show his complete surprise.

Plank stood back with the wide grin still on his face.

"Ginny's boy! I swear, the way she talks about you, I imagined you weren't no more'n 20 years old, most."

Tom half-grinned and shook his head. He wondered how in the world Virginia might have described her 62-year old son to her cousins.

"She's talked about you a lot, too, Plank." Tom smiled, "I almost feel like I grew up with you all out on grandfather's rice plantation."

Plank laughed before hurrying over to swallow up Virginia in his arms. "You must be John Jr.," Tom said as the shorter, slimmer of the partnership walked up. 'John Rose's dark skin glistened in the heat. Tom noted he looked considerably younger than Plank, though Tom understood the three of them were about the same age. For certain, John had watched his diet and exercise more than his friend and Virginia's cousin.

Tom noticed the man's unwavering stare over at Virginia as she stood by the truck. "Lordy, I remember seeing Miss Virginia at the big house back in the day.

Everybody called her the princess."

"Oh, yeah? Did you know her back then?" Tom asked

"Oh goodness, yeah. My folks worked for Ginny's family. My mama was a maid, and papa was the overseer on the farm."

"I never knew that, never heard her mention that. Gosh, it's mighty good to meet you. And I bet you have some tall tales you can tell about Ms. Ginny. We'll have to talk more about the Princess when she's not around." They both laughed.

"I really want to thank both you and Plank for all you're doing for Mother. She couldn't have done anything without your help."

John Jr. shook Tom's hands, a bit less gregariously than his partner. "That's mighty kind of you, Tommy, but we're happy as hens to restore that old house – we been hoping for years that some of y'all would come back and bring that house to life again. It was in some terrible shape…thought it might fall any day.

John Jr. stared wistfully at the old home. "I don't guess you saw it in its heyday.

Well…it was a most magnificent piece of property, that's for sure. I know we likely missed a few points, but it wasn't due to our not trying…we did the best we could to get it back where it was, for Miss Ginny."

The man walked over to where Virginia stood, quiet and content beside Tom's truck, taking in the area and offering small bits of responses to the conversation.

"Miss Ginny, if you ain't as pretty as you were when you left here all them many years ago!" He laughed under his breath at her surprise and how she blushed.

"Well, I declare if it ain't John-John…it's good to see you! I was trying to figure out how I could get here without worrying Tommy, but it turned out it just wasn't in the cards. I hope he didn't mind too much worrying with his old mama.

"I tell you one thing…I'm ready to get down here and move in, lock, stock and barrel as soon as you boys say the word." She grew quiet for a moment, then.

"I can't thank the two of you enough for doing all this for me…you just don't know how much it means…"

Tom was surprised but touched by the emotion in Virginia's voice. John Jr. patted her lightly on the shoulder just as she swiped a tear from her eye.

"Oh, Shush, Ginny. We're doing what we do around here. Besides, it's a lot more fun to be doing this for somebody we know, rather than for some old rich codger we don't know from Boo. We're just happy you decided to come home. We always hoped you would."

By the end of the week, the contractors had listened to Virginia's directions for the bathroom and kitchen, taken notes on the appliances and hardware, bought the tile, taken it back, and brought in a handful of painters, to begin with, the kitchen walls.

Virginia kept shaking her head. "I just can't believe it. How in the world were y'all able to restore the place so perfectly? Especially the small details like the baseboards and fluted book casing! Where did you find these double-paned windows?"

Virginia recalled sending Plank the early photos she found of the home, but they had gone well beyond what the photos offered. She had given them free rein to investigate every inch of the house – from the attic to the old play area below the porch.

They told her they located the original blueprints at the courthouse and even some notes from her father's files. They had taken on the project as something very near a labor of love—each, for their own separate reasons. Virginia was dear to them both. She represented their past, as much as she did the past of Shreveport.

To Tom's complete surprise, he fell into the spirit of helping the two men as they worked to revive the old plantation home he'd heard so much about. It didn't take him long to realize it wasn't just that Virginia loved this large southern mansion, but it was what the home and the land it sat on represented for her. It was part of who she was before Thomas came and swooped her away.

Tom was enjoying this time mostly because he was learning so much about his mother he'd never known, maybe never taken the time to know. He'd come as close to hating her for her contempt for his father as any son could. Maybe, now, he would get a chance to reassess everything he thought he knew about Virginia Mallory.

To be sure, he was enjoying the manual labor, using every muscle in his body as he unloaded and carried lumber to and from the house, helping hammer in nails and even doing a bit of painting. However, he noticed the two men coming behind him to check his work. He wasn't beyond even running to the hardwood store on errands.

He couldn't believe these two 75-80-year-old men, older than him by almost 20 years, could scramble up ladders, balance themselves on the roof and bend to walk below the house like age was indeed just a number.

In the middle of his second day there, Tom realized he was as close to content as he'd ever been with Virginia. They hadn't scraped each other's nerves raw. He'd never done much carpentry work in his life. No working up a sweat and getting his hands dirty. He even whistled and smiled as he cleaned up after his second painting session.

Tom had spent most of his life sitting on his duff in a sheriff's office, talking on the phone, telling people what to do. The rest of the time, he'd walked from his truck to his house, or his office and the downtown buildings where he sat on his duff hours at a time, in meetings.

Amazing. He'd never really thought about his life quite that way, quite so boring and ordinary. There were so few instances in which he had exerted any real energy. How could a man go through his entire life – 60 long years—and not climb on top of somebody's roof, hammer a few nails, lay a tile or two, or at least paint the rooms in his own house?

There shouldn't be jobs that never called for a man getting a stain on their shirts from underarm sweat. He was befuddled about this thing that he hadn't known he missed for all these years. And, suddenly, a thought came out of nowhere, fluttering lightly but ominously around his brain: If he had married... Marriage would have changed his life alright. He would have experienced all of this and more. There would be Maia...or someone, reminding him to cut the grass, fix the leak in the roof, or paint the kitchen yellow, then blue.

There likely would have been sons he'd have taught to play football or baseball...as if he'd ever really learned himself. Or girls that he and Maia would ride bikes with on the weekend; or walk with down the road to the park, where they'd push them on the swing. There would be a life outside the office and his truck.

Maia. Tom frowned. A family was what she'd wanted for almost as long as they'd been together. Only a few times had she said so, but it was always there. And, he had pretended for over 25 years that she liked things just the way they were because he did. Deep down, he had always known. If Maia and he... Tom closed that thought off and moved from it to more comfortable thoughts, like what he could help the builders next.

* * *

PART XII: The Haunting of Old Times and Places

CHAPTER 20

A Mother's Cry for Help

Tom had been asleep for a couple of hours when the ringing began. As he slowly realized what the sound was, he remembered that his cell phone was in the pocket of his now-filthy jeans. Not much for packing, Tom had only brought two pairs of pants, and once he'd chosen the jeans, he decided they were just at the comfortable level he liked. Virginia had been tickled to see him walking around in not-so-clean jeans and a t-shirt.

"Lord, we got us a whole new Tommy down here in Shreveport." She tousled his hair and laughed. "I like him...this new Tommy." He grinned and shook his head. "Do you?" Tom looked up at Virginia and quickly away, embarrassed, but hell bent on not showing it.

"Do I what, Mother?"

"Do you like the Tommy you are down here in Shreveport?"

Tom shrugged and took a sip from his coffee, then leaned back in his chair to peer into the seamless beauty of the Louisiana sky. He understood why his mother loved the place. He could see himself loving it if he let himself. But he wouldn't have time to do that.

"I will say this, Mother. It's been a good two days. I didn't know it would be."

The phone stopped suddenly, and Tom settled himself in anticipation of a return to dreamland. But soon, the ringing resumed, causing Tom's eyes to flutter open and a frown to further crease his face. Was Daphne business following him to Shreveport? He imagined it was Maia or Mayor Simmonds Calling to tell him something was happening back home.

"H'lo... Sheriff Malloy speaking."

"Tom? Tom, this is Delia."

Tom slowly sat up, letting out a long breath before greeting Delia.

"Hello, Delia. How in the world did you get my cell phone?"

The older woman lightly soothed his ruffled feathers with the throaty laugh he recalled from the olden days. "You know me, Tom...always been pretty resourceful when I had to be."

"Delia...I thought we agreed I'd call you once I got back to Daphne. I won't be back for a couple of days."

"Of course, Tom. I know you're busy, and I'm sorry to bother you. The lady in your office told me you were traveling to Shreveport. And, since you're already down this way, I thought you could just come out this way to see me before you leave."

Tom was quiet for a moment, trying to pull his still half-asleep thoughts together. Maia. She'd get a good talking-to when he got back. He took a deep breath to keep from getting upset.

"Please, Tom. This means more to me than you'll ever know."

Tom looked over at the luminescent face of the clock that told him it was 1 a.m., already tomorrow. And now he was working out in his head what tomorrow would be like. First, he would finish this conversation with Delia. He'd tell her he would try to get over to see her late tomorrow; then he would return to bed and go back to sleep-- maybe for another five hours. Then, he'd spend tomorrow morning helping John Jr. and Plank on the house if they'd let him. Tomorrow evening he would tell Virginia he needed to drive into town to see an old friend who'd lost her daughter.

"I'll see you tomorrow evening Delia. Are you still at the big house?"

"No, Tom. I'm a respectable married woman now. I been married for about ten years now, and my husband and me built us a house on the other side of town. The big house is now Calli's, and my Lord, if she hadn't worked magic on that old place, spent all her spare time fixing it up one way or another." She was sobbing again, now.

"We're so tore up, Tom. You don't know the Calli we know. She really made something out of herself, after… She's a very special person here in this part of the world, a wonderful woman…a minister, no less."

"Oh Tom, we just have to find her. Nobody has any idea where she might be…it's just not like Calli. That part about her never changed. You could always set a clock by that girl.

"She was supposed to be here with me, was coming out to spend a few days with us, to rest up after her two weeks in Africa. We waited for hours before we finally called and didn't get her. Talked to her driver, Saul, and he said he had waited for her call, but it never came. He figured she had changed her mind and decided to rest at home.

" Lance and me drove out there, and her house was all locked up, had to get the police to let me in. Couldn't find a thing out of place, not a thing, Tom."

Tom could hear the sobs becoming uncontrollable. He remained silent until Delia was able to talk again.

"When was that, Delia, and where was she coming from?" "She

was driving in from the house, just a 20-minute drive."

Tom couldn't even imagine the Calli he remembered being a minister. Never recalled her setting a foot in church all the years he knew her.

"Yeah, God works in mysterious ways, huh, Tom?" Delia's weak chuckle failed to hide the sobs still in her throat. "My girl's turned out to be one of the biggest preachers in this area and has one of the largest congregations in the southeast part of the country.

Oh, Tom...she's really become something special."

"There is just too much we didn't say to each other...that I didn't get to explain to her about...me, about why I wasn't what she needed all those years. Monday, Tom, and I really need you to be there with me...we can talk about it tomorrow, but it would just make all the difference in the world to me...and, to Calli, I know."

By the end of the next day, Tom had worked off most of his frustrations and fears about seeing Delia on Saturday evening. He wasn't looking forward to reliving the past he'd shared with her and her daughter. He hated himself for thinking it... but this wasn't something he wanted to do. There were all kinds of reasons why.

Delia wouldn't have believed the things Calli had shared with him about the life her mother had lived most of her young adult life. He'd tried not to judge even at his young age. She had learned how to make ends meet as a young mother, then realized she was good enough at it that she could get more out of it than just what she needed.

"Who is this friend you're going to see down here in Shreveport tomorrow night, Tommy? I never knew you knew anybody down here."

"Delia Deveraux. Well, she married some time ago, but I don't

know the new last
name."

Virginia sat still, her face in a query. "I know that name…I've…Oh, Tommy!

Delia Deveraux, it was Tucker before. Her father was Billy Tucker, the town drunk. Everybody knew him. He beat his wife…everybody knew about the Tuckers. They had one daughter, she was a few years younger than me, but I remember her. She was really pretty, but…well, the students laughed at her and made fun of her father. Called them poor white trash. How in the world did you become friends with a family like that?"

Tom wouldn't discuss Delia, and certainly not Calli with his mother. He had promised Delia he would see her tomorrow, and he meant to. He didn't need Virginia making this harder than it was already. He was leaving for his room when he reminded Virginia to pack up tonight, so they'd be ready to leave after breakfast tomorrow.

"I wish you wouldn't drive back down here to meet with that woman, Tommy. I got a bad feeling about you getting mixed up with that family."

"Mother, go to bed and try to get a good night's sleep."

Virginia let out a long sigh. "You know, Tommy, I almost hate to leave here…I really do."

*　*　*

CHAPTER 21

Delia's Place

Tom Mallory's eyes opened on their own, against his will. After the three days of manual labor, he was just now feeling the recriminations from his body. Something so foreign to him that he imagined his bones were asking, 'How dare you?' After 60 years of non-use, how dare he put them through the antics he had these last few days.

Tom hated being reminded that he was getting older. Surely if he was 30 or even 40, he could get through these days with a lot less pain.

It was a mild Autumn morning, but Tom expected it would be warmer through the day. He hadn't brought a jacket or sweater on this trip but hoped he wouldn't be spending too much time outside now. The weather, though, wasn't his main concern. It was the ominous feeling he got when all signs pointed to something life-changing happening.

Tom willed himself to lie just a bit longer in the too narrow bed. He felt he would need every ounce of rest he could get this morning. But he wouldn't be able to sleep. He needed to call and check on Virginia to make sure she was fine and ready to travel.

He had been nervous about letting her leave with her cousin this morning, but they had told him it just plain made sense. He just wanted to make sure they arrived home safe and sound. He chuckled to himself, remembering how excited two old men were to spend more time with Virginia.

Her cousin Plank treated her like a dainty China doll. He'd overhead Tom and Virginia talking about the trip, and him driving back to Shreveport and immediately offered to escort Virginia back to New Orleans.

The big man had thrown his log-sized arm around Tom's shoulder and smiled like a Cheshire cat up into his face. "Tom, there is no need for you to be hurrying to take your mama home, then driving back here for your meeting. There's no need in all that back and forth. For that matter, John Jr. and I don't have a thing to do this evening or tomorrow. We're more'n happy to get Virginia back to New Orleans. Besides, we can spend that time planning out this project. You go ahead and take care of your business!"

Virginia, though, made him feel as if she was being abandoned. She didn't even try to understand why he felt an obligation to talk with Delia Tucker about her daughter's death. "Don't they have police here in Shreveport, or over there in Blue Bayou, for God's sake? Why would the woman need to call all the way over to Daphne for you to come see about her missing daughter?"

Virginia's chagrin at the brazen woman was unwarranted, Tom thought, indicative of a spoiled child, angry at sharing her friend with someone new. She had pouted when he'd told her he would get up early the next morning to come back and talk with Delia about her missing daughter. That was all he'd told her. He wouldn't dare share anything more. It wouldn't be Virginia, though, if she didn't demand a further explanation.

Most times, the fact that Tom was spending the night at her home was the reason for a smile from Virginia Mallory. This time, it was cause for suspicion and belligerence. He mentally kicked himself. Why didn't he just tell her he was heading straight for Daphne from her house? But Tom had never learned to lie to his mother. Plus, he suspected she could read his mind even if he tried.

"Mother, let's leave remembering that this has been one of the best times we've spent with each other since I was a child...no, ever. I'd like to think this is a turn in our relationship. But you'll have to meet me halfway.

"I tell you what...if you'll start practicing up on your best crème Brulé, I'll start making plans to spend Easter with you in New Orleans. I'll save my appetite for the whole week before I drive down that week. And, if the timing works out, maybe we can spend that weekend after Easter moving your things down to the house in Shreveport...that is if your cousin and his partner keep on schedule."

Tom knew he had bitten off a lot more than he really wanted to do, but those were the compromises one had to make to keep peace with Virginia Mallory. Besides, the combination of tending Delia's despair about Calli and his mother's sensitive needs was nearing his exasperation point.

"Look. Tom...me and John are happy to run Ginny back to New Orleans, get her settled, and be back here sometime tomorrow," Plank had chimed in.

"Plank...I sure do thank you both. I feel terrible letting you all do this, but it sure will help me out. I just hope it's not taking you all away from things here to do.

"Not a problem Tom. Plank and I will switch up driving down

there and back.

"Two drivers always better'n one!" John actually had a glint of excitement in his eyes as he spoke up. "Besides...I'm always looking for excuses to get over to New Orleans. This is perfect timing!"

John Jr. was making the drive sound like an opportunity of a lifetime. And, truth be told, Tom was grateful, though he tried hard not to show just how relieved he was. "Mother...what do you think? You know I'm happy driving you back. I still can."

Tom sensed Virginia's emotional conflicts. She knew and liked Plank and John, but...still. She just didn't like changes in plans.

"Tommy, I just don't know...I sure don't want us to be a burden on Cousin Plank and John after they've gone so far out of their way to help with the house."

Plank placed his arm lightly around Virginia's shoulder and led her a little to the side, whispering loud enough for Tom to hear most of what he was saying... how they could spend most of the drive talking about the final plans for the house, and some about all the changes in the town since she'd left, and the people she needed to know.

"Virginia, there is lots of things we need to talk about that we didn't get around to during these last few days. This drive is a good chance for us to do just that." Plank turned and winked over at Tom and John.

Virginia looked at Tom, then back at Plank. "I guess you're right. There probably are lots of things we need to discuss before I move back here, Plank." She sighed and looked beseechingly, questioningly, at Tom.

"I... I know it will be fine. I just don't want to be a burden,

Plank...John-John. I know there's plenty of things you boys could be doing here while driving an old woman from one side of Louisiana to the other."

"Ginny...I'm speaking for myself here. There ain't one thing I can think of that I'd rather be doing than driving you across Louisiana...not one," John said, with a straight face but a strange glint in his eye.

Virginia laughed despite herself, and the two escorts laughed with her as they began preparing for their trip across Louisiana.

* * *

After breakfast in the hotel, Tom went back to his room and grabbed his bags. He took Virginia's two bags out as John pulled the truck around. Plank took the bags and threw them in the trunk before walking to the driver's seat. Tom pulled the passenger door open, kissed Virginia goodbye, assured her he would call as soon as he was back in Daphne, and helped her up and comfortably into the truck. He walked around to the other door, shook Plank's hand, and then reached back behind Plank and shook John's. "No more thanking us, Tom," John laughed. "We feel lucky to be spending more time with Ginny."

Minutes after they drove off, Tom walked back inside the hotel and paid the bill for his and Virginia's two nights' stay. As much as he dreaded spending the night with Delia and her husband, he couldn't imagine he'd feel up to driving the four hours back to Shreveport after their meeting.

He took his bags to the truck and sat for a while before leaving. Tom was mentally preparing himself for seeing a woman he hadn't seen in 45 years, who had loved him like a son for a while, then hated him as if he was an enemy when he and Calli fell in love. Delia was kind to offer him a bedroom at her house. He had said yes but was now wondering if he shouldn't find a motel somewhere in town.

Truth was, Tom didn't know which part of staying there caused him the most consternation, having to deal with the woman's emotions or having to deal with his own memories.

Tom wondered if the Daylight Inn was still there. Back then, it was the only motel between Shreveport and Blue Bayou. The motel and Tom had had a brief history, one that made him blush, almost 45 years later. His cell phone went off, bringing him back to the matter at hand. He expected it was Virginia with some last-minute commands. He hoped she hadn't gotten down the road and changed her mind again.

"Hey Tom, it's Delia. I forgot to tell you about a community gathering at the church. Nobody knows what to call it since I'm not declaring my daughter dead, but she's been missing long enough that we want to observe it in some way.

I'll likely be there a few hours, but I'll meet you around 4 pm at the Tavern. I told Charlie to reserve us a spot for an early dinner, drinks...and quiet talk." Delia's voice was tired, much older. He imagined this was wearing her down.

* * *

Tom arrived in Blue Bayou just before dark. How well he remembered Delia's Tavern on Westwood Road. As he made his way down the dark, narrow road, Tom thought of just how bizarre this whole thing was. It wasn't a conscious choice to be in Blue Bayou,

Louisiana. Circumstances had made that decision for him. He couldn't think of another reason under the sky he would have set foot back in the town.

Delia…more so, Calli, was the only reason he'd returned.

* * *

CHAPTER 22

Coming Home to Good friends, Hard Memories

Delia's Bar & Tavern was a typical Louisiana honky-tonk that miraculously weathered the economic storms over the last 45 years. As Tom parked, it felt eerily as if time had stood still ...as if he was walking back in time some 40 years, when a barely- legal aged Tom had been introduced to the Tavern.

The place was, in fact, an old barn that was long ago refurbished, painted a deeper red on the outside, whitewashed inside, and filled with tables, chairs, and an oversized bar. The only addition Tom noticed was a raised stage, shiny hardwood flooring.

The place still catered to much of the same crowd but had also expanded its clientele. The Louisiana red necks and gut-bucket blues-ers were interspersed among the lawyers, students, and investment bankers. My, how times have changed, Tom thought to himself. This mish-mash crowd took up just about all the free space in the large establishment.

After all these years, Tom smiled. It was still one of the most popular eating and dancing places between Baton Rouge and New Orleans. Tom knew that part of the magic of the place was Delia's oversized personality and her irresistible magnetism. The other part, he thought, had to be that the regulars found something here they didn't find anywhere else...something they were all looking for: a way to forget the things they didn't like about their lives. Some of them might even be able to find something to replace it with inside these old wooden walls.

Charlie, the bartender, yelled across the room to Tom, then waved him over as Tom looked his way. Charlie had been the lone busboy at this place 35 years ago. Just a few years younger than Tom, town gossip was that he had left home as early as 12-years-old and arrived in Blue Bayou to live with his aunt and uncle.

His family had been sharecroppers for a plantation owner back in Tupelo, Mississippi, who had followed their son to Blue Bayou after his father was threatened by the landowner. . When asked how he ended up in Blue Bayou at such a young age, Charlie said he'd come to the town to find a place for his parents to move to after they learned the white landowner had been cheating his father year in and year out.

Before his parents arrived, Charlie's aunt and uncle enrolled him in the public school in Blue Bayou. It took him a little while to catch up with his class, but his teachers found him bright and a fast learner. With his inviting personality and his parents' work ethic, Charlie always kept small jobs to keep change in his pocket and help his parents out. His mother Rosie went to work for Delia in the restaurant, and Charlie came with her, bussing tables and even cooking a little when Rosie, her full-time cook, fell sick.

'Man, it's good to see you, Tommy ...I couldn't believe it when Dee told me you would be coming. I hear you a full-blown sheriff now. Life show is something, ain't it, man?" Charlie grinned with his whole face, baring the almost perfect space between his top row of teeth that had caught Tom's attention some 45 years ago.

"Charlie, I can't believe you right here where I left you, either…except, I see you've moved up in life." Charlie chuckled as he drew a beer and set it in front of Tom.

"On the house, man…you Dee's guest, tonight."

"It's sure good to see you, Charlie. Looks like you running the joint these days." "Just when Dee ain't here. She been real good to me, Tom. But, you know that.

I started tending bar about ten years ago. She let me take care of the place when she's off sick or on vacation."

"Dee knows when she got a good thing, Charlie…you always been a loyal employee. Somebody she can count on and trust…that's important in this kind of business."

Charlie smiled and shrugged.

"What's it like being a sheriff up there in Daphne, Tom?"

"Well, Charlie…it ain't a big town; a pretty small town, a few miles outside Mobile. Not too much crime, though…except every once in a while. Seems about every few years, something bad happens and wakes the town up, let us know we can never get too comfortable.

"…like a murder that took place about five years ago; a young girl raped and murdered…" Tom's voice trailed off as he remembered the case that still left a terrible feeling in the pit of his stomach. He didn't want to go into the details with Charlie.

"I have to say, most of the time, it's a quiet place, trying to keep up with the rest of the world. I guess, like a lot of small towns, we're going through a few growing pains.

Nothing serious, though."

Charlie stood listening to Tom, except when he was serving new customers who walked up to the bar.

"So, you been at this for 45 years, man? You got a family, children?"

Tom ducked his head, then shook it.

"Nope. Who gone put up with an old, broke down lawman like me, Charlie?" Charlie cocked his head and chuckled half-heartedly.

"You know, Tom…I remember you and Calli. When you left, man. She still loved

you, man. I think it took her a long time to get over you…"

Charlie knew right away that he had said too much, could see his old friend's discomfort, and that made him sorry he had brought the girl's name up. Tom drained the last of his Pabst and sat the glass down.

Charlie was remembering the last time Tom had walked into this place and crawled up on a barstool. Calli Tucker had been right there, like his shadow. The two of them. It was almost as if she was breathing in each time he breathed out.

"Still a Pabst man, huh, Tommy? Dee called just before you walked in, told me to let you know the candlelight vigil got started a lot later than planned 'cause they couldn't find Reverend Laing. They ended up having to find another preacher. She said she'd be here as soon as she can, but if she don't make it inside a couple of hours, go on and eat. She asked if I would take you out to her house if she's too late, give you a chance to rest."

While Tom was a little disappointed, he was also relieved that he was being given a reprieve. He might not have to come face to face with what had happened with Calli until tomorrow.

Old acquaintances he would have sworn he'd never see again stopped by to say hello. Some of them, he would have bet his last dollar, were either long gone from this part of the world, or just plain gone. Everyone had heard he was back in town, there for Calli's memorial service. After 30 minutes of catching up with folks he'd known back then, he began to get restless, checking the door to see if Delia had made it in. She hadn't.

Tom sat a little longer at the bar, reliving part of his past with Charlie as the rest of the old-timers listened in. He was drinking more than he had in years. It was getting later, and night was becoming a blur. Neither his speaking nor his listening was as clear as it had been when he'd walked into the place. Yet, he couldn't make himself admit he was ready to leave. He'd wait around another hour, at least, to see if Delia would make it. Tom stuck around, listening to the old stories and joining in the camaraderie as the men threw back beers and swapped tall lies.

There were, in fact, only a few men in this crowd that Tom would have called friends during his years in Blue Bayou. Other names were vaguely familiar, but there were no memories of them. Tonight, he was mildly humored by the old, grizzled men who had been young and full of vim when he was young. They were, he imagined, mirrors of who and what he had become.

Most of the conversations eventually evolved into debates, and most of those were shouted and slurred. As the night grew closer to an end, the conversation had grown quieter, and it was all coming down to the reason he was there...the recently departed Calli Tucker. Without forethought, many of the men thumped Tom on the back, sympathetically, when Calli was mentioned. It was as if, in their minds, nothing had changed; 40 years had not happened, and Tommy and Calli were still Tommy and Calli.

* * *

Tom awoke at Delia's house in a fog, remembering last night; how he'd been caught up in the community's grief and how he'd dealt with it the only way men of Blue Bayou knew to deal with grief. He'd drunk too many beers to see clearly or walk straight by the time Charlie escorted him out and into his car. He didn't remember the route they took home, or even having a conversation with Charlie on the way there. Who undressed him and got him into bed?

Now, he was smelling the stale odor of beer that saturated his skin. He wondered if his snoring kept Delia and her husband awake. He imagined they were as knocked out as he was…theirs from exhaustion and grief.

Tom had always been an early riser, no matter how late he laid his head on a pillow for the night. He realized he didn't remember the last time he'd taken his blood pressure medicine. He decided he hadn't taken it since arriving in Shreveport. Three whole days without taking his medicine. Wouldn't that be a story! Sheriff suffers fatal stroke in the place he'd fallen in love and lost the most important love of his lifetime.

The thought rattled him, so he got up to find his old, worn-out medicine kit. He still couldn't believe the doctor had diagnosed him with high blood pressure ten years ago. He'd not been sick more than a handful of times in his life.

He groaned as he dug in the shaving kit for his blood pressure medicine. As he rifled through the case, Tom remembered the surprise in everyone's faces last night. Seems they all must have heard about his vow never to set foot back in the place.

He imagined the whispers had already started up this morning. While everyone was plenty friendly enough last night, sober, they would remember the way Tom Mallory had left Blue Bayou and that the woman they held the vigil for was once that sweet young girl whose heart he'd broken.

Would they question the sincerity of a man who never set foot back in the town that was so good to him and a family he had pretended to care so much about, without a look back, all these years?

Whatever grudge Tom felt for this place, he was now too old, and the town was too inconsequential for him to hold on to that grudge. After such a long separation, he and Blue Bayou might just as well make peace with each other, Tom decided. He hoped the people of Blue Bayou saw it that way, too.

Tom found an empty glass on the night table and headed for the bathroom sink, loudly gulping down the pill, then the water. He admonished himself for playing with his health this way...the pills, as troublesome as they were, certainly were the lifelines to his health while he was here.

Tom splashed cold water on his face before settling atop the bathroom commode.

The long night and the two days of "real" work were taking a toll on his not-so-young body. Finally, he stood and dared stare into the mirror.

"My God," he blurted out loud as he stared into the face of the tired, aging man looking back at him. As he moved back into the bedroom, Tom realized something that had escaped him last night. Despite what the mirror told him this morning, he had once been a young, still innocent boy, and he had spent his last night not just in this town, but, in that one motel in Blue Bayou, with a girl, he had loved beyond words.

He had been so thorough in erasing the evidence of his and Calli's love from his conscious that he had buried the memories of their last night together. Now, he was finding it painful to pry the memory from its resting place.

Tom remembered the girl's tear-stained face and her wrenching accusations that he was leaving her there to "rot in my misery." He didn't allow himself to think that night, about how much young Calli Tucker needed him, depended on him for her protection from herself and others, even for her happiness. Though they were young, their love had been complicated, and he'd finally realized it had been more than he had bargained for or could handle.

"Now, what, Tom Mallory...what becomes of poor little Calli? What do I do with my life? You're the only one who really mattered...who really gave a shit." The tears had finally stopped, but in their place was a pitiful look of defeat, hopelessness. More than the fear of what leaving would do to him was what it might do to Calli Tucker.

"Come on, Calli. You're just 16. You have the rest of your life. Give yourself a year, and you won't even remember us. There'll be all kinds of boys running after you...hell, there already are."

He'd tried snickering, but it was no more real than the words he was reciting. He reached for her hand, but she snatched her body away, not looking at him. Not a hint of a smile touched her face as she walked to the window and stared out.

Tom had run out of words. Never a talker, he had said more than he'd meant to. He wouldn't change his mind, but he hated himself for it. What did she mean that he was the only person who cared? What about Delia, her mother? He didn't ask. Tom knew that Calli didn't count Delia's kind of love as either "motherly,' or nurturing.

He stared into the mirror, now, looking past the face that was etched with pain and self-recriminations. He remembered how easily the sixteen-year-old girl shared hers and her mother's darkest secrets with him, stories he hadn't asked and should have never learned.

Calli was a study in contrasts – both soft and hard; innocent and world-wise. At sixteen, she had experienced too much in life, seen too much...secrets that made her distrust. Tom's heart ached with guilt that he'd added to her distrust. It might have been different, he thought, had his own childhood been different. Had he not been programmed to escape the embers before the raging flames consumed him. He had walked away from Calli, Delia, and Blue Bayou because he was unwilling to get sucked into another complicated love.

He recalled every second of that evening, now. She wouldn't know how his heart had broken into tiny pieces as he said goodbye. He recalled that he'd slipped the simple turquoise friendship ring she'd given him months ago, from his finger, into her jean pocket. She had laid still, next to him that night.

"Tom...just keep it. You told me you'd never take it off."

"Calli, will you keep it for me? If... I ever come back, I'll want it back, I promise." She had not answered but stuck the ring back into her pants pocket.

Without the ring, Tom truly felt as if he'd lost everything.

"Tom, don't think I don't know why you're leaving. You started listening to what the others say about Mama...and me. I know that's it, and I guess I can't blame you for running scared." There was childish petulance, a tremor in her voice that came before the tears.

Tom fell back onto the bed, his folded arms hiding his face. He didn't know what he was feeling. He understood the sadness, but why was there anger, and who was the anger directed toward?

"Calli, it's a whole lot of things, what you've told me, the things other people remember about Delia. As much as I love you, I'm beginning to feel overwhelmed.".

Calli flopped onto her back, looking over at him. "If I'd known you were going to hightail it out of town like this, I never would have told you anything. Both mama and me thought you were somebody we could trust. that you loved us..."

" Calli...I'm on my way to becoming a policeman. I need a clean slate. I do love you...and Delia, but right now, I've got to get on my path to being a lawman."

"Alright, alright..." She turned from staring up at the light bulb fixture in the

ceiling and stared hungrily at his profile.

"I understand what you're saying, Tom, but why does that mean you have to leave me? You love me. I know you do. And you were the one person I thought I could always count on in this world. Now, what am I supposed to do? What in the world do I have to look forward to?"

For the first time since he'd met her, Tom didn't have the right answer for Calli Tucker. He turned back onto his side, facing her. He wrapped her in his arms and let her cry big, wet tears on his shoulder.

One or both of them finally remembered this was their last night together, and they had one last thing to do. It would be the last thing they'd do, the one thing that had always come so easy for them when words didn't work. Tom knew for certain it would never be the same with anyone else.

Tom had awakened before daybreak the next morning. He quietly dressed and left Blue Bayou and Calli before she woke from her sad slumber. As he slowly walked the half-mile to the bus station, carrying his single suitcase, Tom let the long-repressed tears bathe his face. It wasn't until he was near the bus station that he dried his eyes and wiped his face.

It was that day that Tom allowed, for the first time, a rare look inside himself.

This thorough self-examination, he knew, was long overdue. He'd gone almost 20 years with not one reflective spell. But, if not now, when? He was walking away from the second most important chapter in his life and on the brink of starting the next. There would be no better time to try and figure out who he was.

As he climbed up on the Greyhound bus, Tom Mallory felt ten years older than his young age. He imagined that old men who had lived much fuller lives than his must feel this way after some huge disappointment in life. Was love supposed to hurt this way, he wondered as he walked listlessly down the aisle,

Maybe it wasn't love as much as it was his decision to walk away from it. Or, maybe it was the fear of not being able to live up to it that hurt most. Maybe it was just plain old exhaustion from life, the running away from a life that hurt.

Tom settled into a seat in the middle of the bus, threw his suitcase in the overhead compartment, and his jacket on the seat next to him to discourage a seating mate he might have to talk to. The last thing he wanted was a talkative seatmate on this trip.

He pulled the fare from his pocket, so he wouldn't have to search for it when the driver walked back. Taking a deep breath, Tom sneaked a look out the window, hoping he wouldn't see a familiar face. He was too tired to be happy or sad by seeing someone he cared about.

The bus took off slowly, and Tom leaned his head back, closed his eyes, took a deep breath, and prepared to take a good, long look inside himself. He already missed Calli. He had failed her but leaving was the only way to become something better.

Tom knew he had stayed too long. He shouldn't have fallen in love and let the girl fall in love with him. He should have left the moment he realized their relationship had been rigged up for Delia's benefit. It wasn't a simple friendship, but an assignment, all by design.

Delia never admitted her plan in so many words, but she often hinted of Tom's role as the girl's protector, a distraction for the child as Delia resumed her life. "A ready-made big brother," was how she described the new addition to their family. Too late, Tom found himself too enthralled by the Tucker family to see that different isn't always better.

"There's something different but good in you, Tom Mallory," Delia often told him as they sat playing a Saturday evening game of Gin Rummy. She said later she could never determine whether the boy's oddity had more to do with the strange New Orleans culture or something else. Whatever it was, Delia decided he would be good

ONCE UPON A TIME THERE WAS A GIRL...

for Calli.

* * *

CHAPTER 23

Growing up Delia

Delia's wisdom was based mostly on the will to survive and on having no one in her life to fend for her. Growing up in a hopeless home life and the hardscrabble part of town meant Delia did less daydreaming and more scheming for survival. Her environment had sharpened her insight into people and toughened her resolve to use what insight she had to get out of the environment in which she found herself.

What she failed to learn about love from her parents, she would learn from the fine upstanding men who gave her envelopes for 15 or 30 minutes of her time in their beautiful plantation homes, or her back porch...as her mother slept off her night's drunk in the room next door or made her daily rounds to the corner bar.

Delia didn't fool herself or try to fool others about what she was. It wasn't her fault that her parents were what the good people of Louisiana called white trash, and that turned their heads rather than offer a "good morning" to the town drunk and his wife.

The girl had been just five years old when her parents moved up from the swamplands of Louisiana with their only child and rented a home on the edge of Blue Bayou – the edge where they could afford to live, usually next door to poor black families.

Billy Tucker was a tall, good-looking young man with a strong build meant for hard work. No one ever told him. He was known for his strutting, devil-may-care attitude. His wife, Sallie, was pretty enough to catch Billy's eye and docile enough to be led without questioning.

By the time they settled in Blue Bayou, Sally had tried hard to make a home for her husband in three different towns over five years. Billy's drinking buddy back in Alameda had promised Billy a job at his daddy's sorghum mill in Shreveport, and Billy had quickly uprooted his family to follow the new job. Billy worked only when he had no choice. He stayed a good year at the sorghum mill.

Billy told his friends, hardly seeing the need to say it to Sally, that he was born with a restless spirit and easily bored of jobs, places...and, to some extent, people over time. When his restless spirit got the best of him after spending two long years in Blue Bayou, Billy decided he wouldn't uproot his family again. His daughter was growing fast, and he figured she needed some stability in her life.

He promised Sally he would find his way back home before she missed him too much. Billy wasn't much on telling things exactly as they were. He was mostly gone for weeks at a time, returning to Sallie and Delia with presents from the places he'd been but no explanations.

Sally knew she wasn't to ask where he might have settled for all the time he was gone. After a year of coming and going and seeing the unasked questions on his wife's face, Billy's leavings lasted longer and longer. It was a beautiful spring morning when Billy's letter arrived, telling Sally he'd landed a job with the oil riggers in Bastrop, where his parents lived and were staying there for the time being. He promised to send money when he could, and that was the one part of his promise that he kept.

Delia was almost eight when her mother called her into hers and Billy's bedroom, too distraught to talk clearly...but enough so that Delia understood that her father wouldn't be coming back. He'd been killed down at Bastrop, near his parents' home.

Delia and her mother traveled the five hours by bus from Blue Bayou to Bastrop, Mississippi, for her father's funeral.

After a year of lying in bed and crying herself to sleep each night, Sally Tucker got up one day while her daughter was in school and made her way to the nearest liquor store, where she used most of the money she had to purchase a bottle of liquor. Delia was nine by then. It wouldn't be long before she realized her mother's propensity to drink while she was away at school. That year was the last time Delia would ever see Sally Tucker fully sober.

Miraculously, Delia remained in school through the ninth grade. However, by then, her mother was in no shape to take care of herself. She had watched poor Sally crumble under her sadness. As she took over the household, Delia realized she was more her daddy's girl, then Sally's. Like Billy, Delia had a love for life. What's more, she had Billy's guts to take chances, to find a way to get a little bit of what life offered. She was determined to make her life better than the one she had with Sallie and Billy Tucker...and to make good and damn sure she didn't die with that same nothing she was born to.

Delia was the spitting image of the handsome Billy Tucker, a shaggy-haired blond with an athlete's body, though he never played organized sports a day in his life. Boys her own age, and men old enough to be Billy's father, were struck by Delia Tucker's beauty and were quick to tell her so. Even as a youngster, Delia had no delusions about what they were after.

Delia Tucker never feigned innocence, even as a young girl. She wouldn't blow smoke up anybody's backside about just how far she would go to get what she wanted. Even in the early – for some, the innocent, teen years-- Delia hadn't a thing in common with the Donna Reeds of the world. And, the Donna Reeds of the world wouldn't have been caught dead palling around with the likes of Delia Tucker. Even so, Delia was the kind of girl who might have seen fit to bed the slightly attractive Warren—Donna's husband – if the urge hit her.

No one in Blue Bayou was really surprised when Delia turned pregnant or when her daughter Calli was born with no husband or father in sight. The whispered question was, of course, `whose child is it?' There were many a wife who was extremely anxious to get a sneak peek at the child.

Delia Tucker's penchant for older, well-situated, married men was pretty much common knowledge by the time Calli was born. Delia was simply playing out what the better class of people in Blue Bayou had already predicted about this Tucker family—with no class or culture to speak of.

But whose child was young Calli? That was the question on everyone's mind. When the child was old enough for Delia to take out with her, the townspeople stopped and stared in awe, looking from the mother to the daughter. The girl was exquisitely beautiful.

Though Calli wasn't the biggest mistake Delia had made during her young life…the child would be the most permanent and the one thing that made her reflect on her life, even slowing her down for a time. However, no one would ever get the truth behind the girl's parentage. The proper women wondered how in the world Delia had the nerve to parade the child around town like she was not a bastard.

To her own surprise, Delia was a remarkably responsible young mother. Lord knows she hadn't picked that up from her own mother. Though the child had not been planned or wanted, she would sleep in the bed she'd made. And, besides, the little thing didn't ask to be here. She'd stare into the girl's beautiful gray eyes and thought they were both misfits, thrown together by age-old mistakes between men and women.

The only time she thought seriously about whether she should keep the child had been one of her afternoons with a respected local doctor. She was six months pregnant at the time. As he dressed to return to his office, he put extra bills into her envelope and told her how easy it would be to either give the child away or not bring her here.

Delia knew there was no one to help raise her child. The father was something more than a one-night stand but certainly not a keeper. Her own mother had only known how to care for the man she married, and he neither wanted nor needed her kind of love. She had tried to blame Billy Tucker for her mother's descent into the dark hole she eventually fell into. Sally Tucker's drinking had caught up with her. She was either in bed coughing her lungs out or hanging out at one of Blue Bayou's half-empty bars. The few times she woke up sober, she would drag herself to the home of the old woman who hired her out for housecleaning.

"Getting knocked up… I just don't understand it. I thought you were smarter than that. How you gone take care of a child, Delia? All we got between us is the little social security checks left from your daddy and that part-time job you have at the Creamery." Delia sighed, looking away from her mother. There she went, still pretending she didn't know what her daughter's part-time job really was or the source of the money that kept their lights on and food on the table.

No, Delia had no option but to try to be a mother to her child. She had had so little example in how to mother, at least since her father died, and her mother took up with the bottle. It had become abundantly clear shortly after the child was born that Sally Tucker had not only forgotten how to be a mother but had lost the softness she once had during Delia's youngest years. Calli wouldn't grow up with the doting love of a grandmother.

The teenage mother was forced to make things work for the child's sake, and she promised herself she would be the best mother she could be for as long as she could, even if motherhood bored the hell out of her most times. She fell in love with the beautiful child, and, despite all the other things she was, she was a young woman who kept her word.

* * *

When Calli was 10, Delia met a customer at her part-time job who took a liking to her right off. The relationship was one of the easiest and most lucrative she'd ever held. In time, it would become something more. The handsome bachelor from New Orleans asked her to marry him, and without much introspection, she said yes.

John Deveraux was a wealthy businessman from New Orleans, a wonderful man who admitted he had always been more interested in friendship than sex. Their wedding was a quiet event with Calli, John

Deveraux's two sisters, and the justice of the peace.

It was a strange but mutually satisfying relationship for both parties. John adored Calli because she was Delia's daughter. He made Delia promise him that the girl would never want for anything. The marriage was three years old when John fell ill with a heart condition he'd never told Delia about.

While they no longer had a physical relationship, their friendship blossomed, and Delia admitted one night, she had allowed herself to fall in love with her husband. He was everything she could have ever dreamed of in a man.

When John died suddenly in bed, Delia felt a loss she hadn't felt since her father walked out of their lives. For the first time, a man had loved her unconditionally. She was grateful that John's family had accepted her from the beginning despite their untraditional relationship.

After the funeral services, the family met in the mortuary's office. While family friends enjoyed the meal and caught up with old friends, the immediate family met with Delia with John's lawyer. He shared John's last wishes, including funds disbursed to his sisters and their children. However, the bulk of his vast account went to his wife and her daughter. Delia learned that day she was suddenly a rich woman. Not one family member contested their brother's will. No one was more surprised than Delia.

For the first time in years, Delia cried uncontrollably when she returned home. That night, she fell to her knees and thanked God for finally fulfilling the dream that began when she was no more than Calli's age.

John's trust paid for the house Calli grew up in and the business

--Weston Road Restaurant—she bought from her boss, who was retiring. One Saturday morning, she walked into his office with an envelope filled with cash. He counted out the $50,000 gave her $25,000 back along with the keys and the deed to the business he'd owned most of his adult life. That night, again, Delia fell on her knees, thanking God for his goodness and crying herself to sleep filled with gratitude. It was that night that she promised God she'd become the best mother and human being she knew how to be. She kept her promise.

Now that she'd bought the restaurant, Delia would no longer be the nurturing, full-time mother she'd forced herself to be up to now. She needed to throw herself into turning the restaurant into the kind of business she knew it could be. She knew what it would take, her getting in before daybreak and leaving well after midnight. She was full of guilt but admitted she was burnt out on mothering, something she'd done since she was a child herself—first her mother, then her daughter.

Just months after she became proprietor of the restaurant, a young police cadet named Tom Mallory breezed into Blue Bayou for a Saturday evening dinner. Delia Tucker Deveraux worked day and night at the restaurant out on Wesley Road. She waited on the young man herself and was impressed at how polite and well-mannered he was.

When he came in a few weeks later, she introduced him to her 14-year old girl, Calli, who was at the restaurant helping out. Calli was always there when Tom showed up, and Tom began showing up in the middle of the week, not just on weekends.

Delia quickly sized Tom up saw he was a young man she could

trust with her daughter, someone who could not only be a friend but a protector when she wasn't around. Delia's fine-tuned sense of people allowed her to realize the boy was innocent, naïve enough to not understand the power he had in his hands when a young girl was in love with him. He was a young man who needed something, which worked in Delia's favor.

* * *

CHAPTER 24

Missing You. Missing Me

Tom had missed the candlelight vigil, but wouldn't be able to skip the church memorial, today. He had eaten breakfast alone after reading the note Delia had left saying she and her husband had to run to the church before the memorial. Tom was embarrassed at how relieved he was. Delia had left directions to the church, telling him she would meet him there.

Tom pulled onto the narrow street that was already overcrowded with automobiles belonging to relatives, neighbors, friends, strangers, and the media who were all obsessed by the story of the woman minister's disappearance and possible death. At least half of the people present had never met Callindra Tucker. They knew her story that she was a revered and much-beloved evangelist.

Tom squeezed his small Honda Element into a tight space left by the haphazardly parked cars on the side of the road. Every style and model of automobile imaginable—fancy sports cars, old clunkers, stylish SUVs, and hard-riding long haulers—and every one of them deserved a 50 dollar ticket, Tom surmised.

Tom sat for a moment, willing the strange exhaustion in his bones to stay put for the next few hours. Amazing, in all those Sundays, he'd sat inside Delia Deveraux's home and watched the church-goers piling into the church. He had never thought twice about the irony of Delia Deveraux's home sitting right across from the town's main Baptist Church and her never visiting there.

Tom could have stood at Calli's bedroom window and fobbed a rock –if he'd done it with enough force – right into the minister's office window. Even being that close, he couldn't remember Delia ever donning her Sunday best and going off to church or even talking about it.

As he stared over at the old Deveraux house, he wondered that Delia would so quickly give it up, even to her daughter, after she'd married. The home must hold so many memories for her. It was their first home after her husband passed. Maybe the memories were his, as much as they were for Delia.

The house looked the same but a prettier, fresher version of itself. Calli had somehow brought the tall gray colonial back to life. There was no fading gray paint and no cracked, stained windows anymore. The attractive, floor-to-ceiling picture windows framed the home perfectly. There was a front porch now, the old southern-style wrap-around porch. The swing was still there, but now it seemed perfect for the home. It was an alluring home that fit for a prominent evangelist.

Tom had never imagined Calli as an aficionado of home décor or caring one toot about what a house looked like from the inside or out. Now, the landscaping job was a head-turner. Lush, pink, and white rose bushes accented the stone and wood. When had Calli had time to do all of this if she worked as much as he'd read about?

He wondered...the stone-paved walkway and a lipstick red entrance door, to boot. Then, he remembered...she had had thirty whole years to work at perfecting the house that she only lived in for weekends at a time. She must have paid out a load of cash to transform the old, stately house into this beautiful, elegant one. He wondered whether she had done it to capture the good old memories or erase the bad ones—especially their shared memories.

Now, as he forced his eyes from the home and the memory that he'd been almost a full-time guest at the home, Tom found himself focusing on the sad faces, listening to the whispers about Calli. He realized he was there to learn as much as he could about the Calli whose life he was not a part of, not the girl he had loved so much that it hurt to remember.

Tom's spirits began to take a dive when he realized this service might be a final goodbye, not just a memorial. This trip to Blue Bayou might truly be his last. He would return to Daphne tomorrow. Would he be able to forget what he thought he had?. The happiness and love shared inside those walls, the nights he and Calli laughed so hard, their hearts felt as if they would jump out of their chests, the endless conversations about their future? He'd slept in that very home many nights, sat at the breakfast table the next morning with the woman and the girl.

Tom wondered, a fleeting thought, which Calli Tucker had turned out to be. Had she found love? Surely, she would have. She would have been such a beautiful woman...had been just a few years away from becoming that woman, the last time he'd laid eyes on her.

He spotted Delia Deveraux-Belson and smiled despite the occasion. Only Delia could look so alluring in a simple dark dress and a strand of yellow pearls lying loosely around her thin neck. She was escorted into the church by a tall, thin man with salt and pepper hair and a thinner, taller man held tight to his bible.

Tom had learned last night that Lance Belson had grown up in Louisiana but had gone away for college and stayed throughout a career in Chicago, where he worked as an engineer for one of the large tech industries.

He'd returned to Louisiana to retire, fish and hunt. He'd learned that Blue Bayou had one of the best fishing holes in the actual bayou and pretty much any small animal one would want to run into during a hunting spree. He had lived in the town a few years before a group of new friends recruited him to run for Mayor. After months of saying "absolutely not!" Lance gave in, said he'd throw in his hat, but he was sure no one would elect a stranger as their town mayor.

He'd had several fundraisers at Delia's Bar and Tavern. Not only because it was a perfect gathering place for his events, but he liked coming out to spend time with Delia after the fundraisers were over. He never let her forget that he'd been eating at the place for weeks before he learned that she wasn't a worker there but the owner. Delia never stopped taking orders and delivering food to the patrons.

The small talk from last night also included the fact that Lance and Delia's courtship had caused some heads to turn. The fact that the fine, upstanding Lance was getting into a relationship with a woman with a past, like Delia Deveraux.

The couple eloped just a year after they began dating. Lance had heard all the rumors and never mentioned them to his wife. He loved her for the woman she was, not the mistakes she'd made in her life. To him, Delia was a fine and valuable member of Blue Bayou's community.

Delia, Lance, and the other man were walking his way. Tom now realized it was old Pastor Laing with them. They stopped. Delia was talking directly to the minister. Tom could have sworn that the minister was delivering a sermon the way he stood wide-legged and pompous in Calli's yard. Delia and Lance simply looked on.

Delia's still-thick mane of hair was now silver. It lay, gathered seductively across one shoulder. She leaned onto her husband as he softly caressed her shoulder. Men had always liked being near Delia. But, as far as he'd heard since hitting the town, Delia Deveraux Belson was an upstanding married woman now, leaving the old lovers to their bygone memories.

It had been thirty years, and Delia was the spitting image of the old Delia Deveraux that Tom had known and loved. Except for the silver hair, and a few pounds that miraculously appeared in places where most people wouldn't notice them, she hadn't changed a whit. Neither the silver nor the pounds, Tom noted, erased her beauty.

The woman must be nearing 75 now. She'd miraculously held onto youth the way few women were able to...something more likely to do with plain old bull-headedness, rather than DNA, Tom thought. Delia's eyes widened as she spied Tom. She whispered in her husband's ear and lightly patted the preacher's arm as if to say, "I'll be back." She moved with purpose toward Tom.

Lance Belson glanced briefly over at Tom but continued talking with the minister as Delia walked down the steps toward the line of cars and Tom. Tom remembered in that instant what a maestro Delia Tucker had always been at walking away smoothly, leaving men wishing she'd stayed.

"Tommy...Tom Mallory. I'm so glad you came!" her beautiful, sad eyes drank in this older, taller friend. She stood before him with her arms outstretched and her head sadly shaking. It was as if she could hardly believe he was the same Tom Mallory who had left Blue Bayou 45 years ago, a disillusioned, broken young man.

Tom swept Delia into his arms, his grief and sadness now real, overshadowed only by awe at this septuagenarian's grace under such circumstances. Delia was more than a beautiful older woman; she was the mother of his first true love. Delia had been the reason for that love and something of a second mother to him.

"You look damn good, Tom...been taking care of yourself. Or...somebody has. I knew you would come. I don't know why...I guess I shouldn't have expected you after all these years. But Calli was special to both of us, even if you tried to forget her. You always made things right for her when nobody else could."

"Of course, I was coming, Delia. You know what you and Calli meant to me..." he couldn't hide his emotions now. It was like a cascade of memories that flowed over him all at once. Funny time, thought Tom, to be remembering his last summer here, how he and Calli had skinny-dipped in the town's historic bayou. Damn this suddenly overactive memory bank, Tom thought. He straightened himself, took a deep breath, and let go of Calli's mother.

He looked over at Lance and the minister still standing in the same spot. He cleared his throat and let some memories disappear. Poor Lance was still listening and nodding as the minister talked. He saw him peer over their way every few minutes.

"I heard last night that Lance is a blessing to the town. The city boy come to save this hick town. Delia smiled sadly and looked over at Lance. There was real love written on her face. It surprised Tom to witness Delia in love...with her own husband.

"Yeah, we had some hard times early on, but he's that person that can always make things right. I'm a very lucky woman, Tom. I've had two men in my life who have loved me unconditionally…that's more than some women can ever say."

"Small towns will be small towns. Some people tried to start up some foolishness, but it came and went pretty quick when they saw neither one of us was paying them any attention." They both smiled.

"And… old Preacher Laing, I can't believe he's still around after all these years. He must be 90 if he's a day." Tom was unaware that he still held one arm around Delia's shoulder.

Delia sniffled and giggled some as she dabbed at a few sparse tears that had surprised her. "Oh yeah, Laing is still around, alright. I guess he must be around 85, for sure, but he still preaches most funerals in Blue Bayou since we haven't found anyone to preach better or shorter funeral sermons than him. His problem these days seemed to be the bottle…makes him forget some commitments, like the candlelight vigil last night."

Tom remembered a younger Preacher Laing who had a few other problems, then, too. It wasn't the bottle, as far as he knew, but women…mainly underage ones. The man must have substituted one habit for another.

"Tom, do you know she never stopped loving you…not in all those years?"

Delia gave a throaty chuckle. "A mother knows. It wasn't until this year she met someone I believe might have been the one for her. You could feel something in the air when they were together. But, then…just like that she disappeared…."

Before Tom could ask her questions about this new person in Calli's life, Tom saw Lance making his way over to them. He removed his arm from Delia's shoulder and reached out his hand. "Tom Mallory. It's good to see you. Delia told me a lot about you, about what you meant to Calli...and, to her."

Tom shook the taller man's hand. "Pleasure's mine, Lance. I'm really sorry we have to meet on such an occasion."

The mayor nodded. "Well, we'll make sure we get to know each other better when this is all over." He reached for his wife's hand.

"They're forming the line now, honey. I think we better get on over there."

Delia and Lance were ushered to the front of the line of family members and directed on how the procession should move inside the church. Delia looked around to find Tom and whispered loudly, "Me and Lance want you to sit with us, Tom."

He shook his head, "No," and waited for the line of family members – some, obviously Lance's family-- to walk to the front of the church before he and a few straggler relatives took up the rear.

Tom took one of the candles being passed out by the ushers, joined the line taking the candles to the front of the church, and was surprised that his eyes were watering up when the girl lit it. He wanted to remember Calli as...he now remembered her. He deposited the candle and followed the receding line to the bench two rows behind Delia and Clyde. He felt Delia's eyes on him and decided he should sit with the family, just not next to Delia.

The emotions were hot and cold inside Tom as he sat staring at the beautiful array of candles of every color and size. For the first time in more years than he could remember...no, since he left Blue Bayou 45 years ago, Tom's eyes filled with tears as he remembered Calli.

As the memorial service began, Tom remembered the girl who he had foolishly chosen not to remember, not to wonder about, in all these years—who she had become, how her life had turned out. Now, sitting here, battered by tears that threatened to drown him, and hot and cold emotions that made him feel feverish...he knew without surprise that he couldn't leave Blue Bayou until he knew who Calli Tucker turned out to be... and why someone had abducted...and possibly, killed her.

* * *

The emotional memorial service was over in one hour, shorter than most Tom had attended over the years. Tom would have bet a hundred dollars that was Delia's doing. For as long as he could remember, Delia Tucker had damned pomp and circumstance, describing those who thought differently, "high falutin' show-offs."

After following the long line down the front doorsteps, Tom didn't get much further than the walkway he'd landed on. Some in the crowd knew who he was; a few remembered him from all those years ago, more remembered him than he could remember.

Still, their comforting and sympathetic eyes, even the quiet, kind words, discomfited Tom. He didn't deserve the sympathy of the people of Blue Bayou. Surely there was someone else in all these years that deserved it more than he.

As if she could read his mind, a pretty, older woman stopped just inches from Tom. She stood looking up at him with a strange smile on her face as she slowly shook her head.

"Tom Mallory, it's you. Oh, Calli would have been so happy to see you. You know, the Lord blessed her so, you would have been so proud of who she became."

The woman patted Tom's arm gently, then turned and walked away before he could say a word. It wasn't until she had turned the corner and disappeared that Tom remembered those beautiful brown eyes and that sweet smile. Miss Mary Winston. He wondered if she still lived just a few blocks from Delia's home; and if she and Delia were still best friends. He remembered, now, the endless Saturday evenings he'd sat at the dinner table with Mary Winston, Calli, and Delia, as they played Tunk, or Dirty Hearts, for pennies or sometimes nickels.

Tom remembered those evenings with fondness and nostalgia when Delia and Lance walked out the church door. He heard the loud, heavy sigh as it forced its way out of Delia's heart. She looked as if she had had more than enough grief for a lifetime, but Tom knew the day wasn't over.

As her grey eyes spotted Tom, he realized she wasn't looking at him at all. Her grief for her dead daughter had blinded her. And, as much as he wanted to console her, Tom reminded himself that Lance was her husband, now, and the best person for that job.

Tom Mallory had never felt at home inside churches because he hadn't grown up attending church. The possibility that Calli Tucker might be dead unsettled him. He understood the need for the community to have an outlet for their fear and grief, but he would just have to find out more about who she was, now, to get any real hold on what this could have been about.

Restless now, Tom needed to move away from the over-populated churchyard. He was amazed at the emotional transformation of men and women who had been saddled with grief just an hour ago. They now walked as if a weight had been removed, energized no doubt by the beautiful, crisp winter afternoon.

Most mourners were now flush with warm smiles and even quiet laughter. Surely, Tom thought, this was a good thing, having nothing to do with whether they truly loved Calli or would miss her, but moreso about the memorial service expunging their grief.

PART XIII: A Storm in the Forecast

CHAPTER 25

Looking Backward through a Broken Mirror

Tom sat, exhausted and filled with emotional turmoil. He had had no idea this event would be so heart-wrenching. He shook his head slightly, torn between going and staying, cursing himself for the things he should have done earlier today. He should have packed before leaving Delia's home this morning, so he wouldn't have an option about leaving. He should have checked in with Virginia by now, making sure she'd arrived back in New Orleans safe and sound with her Plank and Buddy.

And then there was Maia. Tom took a long sip of the tea Delia had offered him, and his cheeks burned red with guilt. Maia. He hadn't called her once during the time he'd been away. She would never mention she was hurt by his ignoring her, but he knew she would be. She would know, though, that it had been the fault of his oversight, not purposeful. He'd call tonight…and say what? That he seemed unable to leave this place –the site of his first, and maybe deepest love?

Maia had no inkling of who Calli Tucker was. He'd never mentioned her name, never told her how that love could have easily been the ruin of him if they'd let the fire continue to burn out of control. Poor Maia knew only part of who Tom Mallory was – only the part he chose to share with her, and she loved him despite it.

He had told himself hundreds of times that he didn't deserve a woman like Maia...who would put up with his inability to commit wholly to her. Like this trip, she had no idea where he was or what he was up to. Tom knew he wasn't being fair, but he seemed unable to change old habits, especially this reluctance to share himself with the woman who had shared his life and his bed for more than 20 years.

"I'll call her first thing in the morning," Tom mumbled to close off the thoughts that pointed accusatory fingers back at him. Delia had told him to go on out to the Tavern and have dinner. She and Lance would meet him there in a couple of hours once the visitors had all gone.

Tom scooted closer onto the time-worn bar that he imagined had held up more men with guilty hearts and broken lives than anyone would want to count. Nothing seemed to have changed much in Delia's place, while so much had changed in the rest of the world.

Tom's mind waded back to the Memorial Service, the sad eulogies, the surprisingly brief sermon. Surely, every soul in the town and the surrounding towns had found their way to the service. Most of them had stood up to "remember" Calli Tucker. The articulate, and not so articulate. The funny, the sad... even the morbid. Only in small-town America was freedom to speak practiced so democratically.

Tom had never been one to shine a light on himself in a crowd. Certainly, not someone he hadn't interacted with in 45 years, and most definitely, not Calli Tucker's. Besides, what could he have said to the hundreds of people there to memorialize Calli? He could never have told them what kind of girl Calli was, so kind and open and full of life. A girl wiser than her years and knowing more than was good for her. Should he have told them how looking into her eyes, he sometimes believed she had bewitched him and how her laughter could erase any hurts.

Calli. Tom had loved her from the moment he laid eyes on her, and that love had only grown stronger, deeper each day. So strong that for the last year of their love, he believed they would spend the rest of their lives together...couldn't imagine anything changing that.

Yet, for all that love, he hadn't known Calli Tucker, the woman, the outstanding evangelist the church had eulogized today. Tom had never expected to set foot back in Blue Bayou in a million years. God knows he wouldn't be here today if Delia hadn't picked up that phone in desperation. Calli would have been gone, and he would never have known.

But he wasn't wrong to run away...he still believed he did what he had to do. Their love had been dangerous, and that had scared him so badly that he erased its memory, its existence. He'd almost fooled himself. For these last 45 years, it hadn't been real. But sitting here tonight, Tom knew just how real it had been. There was no denying a love as strong as his and Calli Tucker's.

And, now Tom was feeling as if he was cemented to the stool. The longer he sat, the more he began to get the feeling deep down inside that he should leave, that 45 years wouldn't have allowed Calli Tucker to remain the girl she had been. That, he wouldn't find his Calli in the end. It was a feeling of dread...maybe that he might end up asking the wrong questions and get answers he would rather not have learned.

How was it possible that his Calli Tucker had become an evangelist, known around the country for her good work? As much as he'd loved her, Tom never saw her as anyone's saint. It didn't surprise him in the least to know she turned out to be a beautiful, bright, charming woman...but an evangelist? His imagination just couldn't stretch that far. But then, 45 years was a long time. A lot of changes could happen in that many years.

Tom's thoughts suddenly settled on Delia. He was sorry to see her so filled with grief. Was she now accepting that Calli was, in fact, dead, or were these last couple of days just a way to close some doors, to stop the questions he was sure she was getting nonstop?

He was both looking forward to and dreading their talk later this evening when he met her and Lance for dinner?. Would Delia tell him she wanted to call the investigation off or feel that somehow closing down the investigation would disrespect her daughter's memories? Would a mother's need for the truth about her daughter's disappearance compete with her desire to allow her child to rest in peace? Tom would certainly understand if Delia told him she didn't want to pursue an investigation.

Yet...Tom wondered, who would kidnap and kill a pillar of the community, a woman who had given so much and asked for so little in return, according to the endless eulogies? What kind of man or woman could hate or love Calli Tucker so much that they'd bring this kind of pain on her mother and possibly want to see her dead?

Tom had resisted Delia's urging to attend the after-church gathering at their home. He wouldn't participate, knowing that their raw emotions would be smarting for days to come. He didn't want to be a part of keeping the wounds open longer than they needed to be. Besides, he was in no mood for socializing. He was sure Delia remembered how he didn't grieve the way other people did...had his own way of dealing with loss. Or was it that very stoicism she was counting on when she called him last week?

Tom felt weary. His emotions were raw. And even though he knew it was all sparked by what he'd heard and seen today, he couldn't ignore it. Couldn't stop the memories flooding his mind and heart. Tom looked at his watch. His dinner meeting with Delia was about an hour away.

The Delia he remembered was a strong, resilient woman and, he knew the Delia he saw today would be fine in the short run. In time, however, it would all take its toll. How could it not? Delia had lost her only child at a time in her life when there was no guarantee there was time for the hurt to heal. Age had surely softened her and lessened the resilience and stamina necessary for healing the heart.

Calli had been a mirror of Delia Tucker in many ways, a reminder of who and why she was. Now, that mirror had shattered was no longer usable. The poor woman had lost the one person who knew her better than anyone, the child she had grown up with, who had been more like a younger sister than a daughter. And, from what Tom saw and heard today, the unique mother-daughter relationship had blossomed into something he was certain neither could have imagined 45 years ago.

Tom studied the bottom of his beer mug, seeing and not seeing. He was surprised by the strong desire he finally admitted, to learning who Calli had become and what her disappearance said about the person she'd become. Was it murder, as Delia had intimated just one week ago? Could Calli's disappearance be the result of some sadistic envy, hatred, or some other crazy relationship gone bad?

After today's shared memories, how could any of these be the impetus for Calli's disappearance? It seemed she had not one single enemy in the county…hell, in the whole state. Chief Tom Mallory could count on one hand the number of murders he'd investigated in his small town. He snorted, `how many lawmen, these days, could say that?'

Even with crime going up slightly in his town over the last few years, the crime rate in Daphne was still light years behind the larger southern cities like New Orleans, Houston, or even Mobile. No, Daphne, Alabama was still a small town, with small crimes that seldom resulted in death, and certainly not murder. And Tom Mallory was fine with being just a small-town police chief.

Tom jumped as he felt a soft but firm clasp on his shoulder. He turned to see Lance Belson's smiling face staring right back at him. "Lance…I didn't expect to see you out here this evening. I figured you and Delia would want some time to yourselves this evening before our meeting and dinner. I know today was a lot for you guys to go through."

"Nothing I'd wish on anybody else, that's for sure…but, it's life, right? What does the bible say, `what the Lord giveth…the Lord taketh away?' Calli was a joy to us and everybody she knew, but in the end…we all gotta be ready when the maker calls us."

After such a gut-wrenching day, Tom tried not to show his surprise that Lance was up to spouting philosophical rhetoric. But everybody had their way of dealing with grief. He reminded himself. "Well…I know you're right, but that never makes it any easier. At least for most of us. I just want you to know how sorry I am for your and Delia's loss."

Lance nodded, then turned and subtly motioned to Charlie. Tom realized that Lance's favorite drink would be well-known here. He scooted his stool closer to Tom's and fiddled with the napkin that sat in front of him.

"I tell you, Tom, we're really grateful that you came. If there was one bright spot in this day for Delia, it was having you here...you made it easier for her."

"Thank you, man. But I have to be honest. I tried every way possible to talk myself out of coming. Delia and Calli are...were very special to me. I had to come to pay my respects and do whatever Delia wanted me to do to find out what may have happened. It's the least I can do, even if it is 45 years too late."

"Yeah...45 years is a long time, but I don't think those years dampened Delia's feelings one bit, man...and, I don't think she'd mind one bit that you had your own motives for coming. The important thing is, you're here."

Tom sipped from his beer as Lance chatted lightly with Charlie, clearly torn up by today's affair. He had spied Charlie towards the back of the church before the memorial service started, but he noted his old friend had left by the time the service was over. Tom was sure he was hurrying back to open up the tavern.

"I've found that everybody grieves in different ways. I put Delia to bed as soon as the last guest left the house. She'll feel some better after a couple of hours of sleep. Mostly, she needed to get past today, needed to accept that her daughter may not be coming back.

"Now, I grieve different from Delia. When I'm at my lowest,

that's when I got to find something to keep me busy. I need to feel like I'm out in front of what's bothering me. The last thing I want to do is sit in one place and think about my sorrows. Coming here tonight...I know it looks strange to some people... but it helps me to lose myself in other people's lives."

Tom nodded, understanding. "For some reason, Lance, it seems so natural that you and Delia found each other. I didn't know you when I lived here, but I knew Delia...and I only have to remember her then to see how the two of you would have liked each other once you met."

Lance laughed softly. "Yeah, except we both skipped the liking part and went straight for the hard stuff. Man, I fell hard for that woman so quick. I was sure she had worked some Louisiana voodoo on me.

"Same thing with her...at least that's what she tells me. We decided right away we were meant for each other." He laughed, showing deep dimples that Tom knew women liked.

"The fact that you and Delia have been married and still living here in Blue Bayou for the last 15 years tells me just how long it's been since I lived here and just how much things must've changed in Louisiana since I was here." Their embarrassed laughter lightened the day's load.

"Well...that's what everybody except Delia seems to think. She says folks here are still no different inside...they just do what they have to do and grin and bear it. And, I know in some ways, she's right. But I don't really ask any more from folk…you can't force folk to like you. Just ask them to treat you decent."

Tom looked over at Lance, nodding. "Delia and Calli's

relationship must have changed into something pretty special, huh? I mean...they were always connected at the hip, but it wasn't always a good connection. I guess I wasn't smart enough back then to realize that most teenage girls hate their mothers. I don't think Calli understood it was a natural animosity either. Boy, they sure locked horns back in the day. Even then, they loved each other and really needed each other."

Lance smiled and shrugged. "I always told Delia her daughter was more like her than she wanted to admit. Calli could be just as bullheaded as her mama when she wanted to be."

Tom nodded and looked off onto the dance floor. As desperately as he wanted to learn who Calli Tucker had become, he wasn't about to delve deeper than what was being offered by her stepfather.

Tom stared over his beer at the expansive array of liquors and wines decorating the bartender's cabinet. Tom's stare lingered for a while on a reflection in the mirror of a young woman on the dance floor. Besides not eating today, Tom was exhausted and in bad need of a good night's sleep. He blinked his eyes, then turned to take a better look at the young woman.

The woman could have been Callindra's sister! Tom wouldn't have known what Calli would look like by the time she was this woman's age, around 40, but there was the same full head of dark curls, the same tiny but curvy body. When she threw back her head to laugh, the laughter was Callindra's. As Lance touched him gently on the shoulder, he realized that he was staring and muttering to himself.

"Looks a lot like Callindra, don't she?" Tom's daydream slowly evaporated as he looked over at Lance, chuckling. I know, everyone says the same thing when they see her. Charlie says the girl's name is Lucy, and she's a New Orleans girl. So is her pretty little friend over there. They're both nurses but like to come down here to let off steam. She does look a lot like Calli, but Calli would have had every head in the place turning about now," he smiled, "still…at 40 years old."

Tom swallowed. There was a tinge of discomfort, listening to Clyde describe the woman he never had a chance to know. Callindra had been sixteen when he'd left, and up to now, that was how he remembered her…as if time had stood still.

"I never saw her at 20, let alone 40…had she changed very much?" Tom hated himself for having to ask, needing to know.

"I didn't know her at 16, but I know she grew more beautiful. When I started traveling down this way from New Orleans on oil rigging business, I met Calli before I met Delia—I'd run into her right here…usually having a pretty good time, laughing and joking with Charlie, and every once in a while, dancing with one of the customers."

"Once I started dating Delia, Calli was in and out of the house visiting with her mom, but not a lot. That was before the Lord called her. She was kinda reserved, stand-offish, but she'd come out here and have a good time. She and Charlie were always big buddies."

"Calli was never a party girl. It's really hard for me to imagine her becoming one in just a few years. He looked over at the good-looking woman on the dance floor dancing with her friend, having a good time. None of that reminded him of the Calli he'd left behind.

"Well…I don't know how she was at 16, Tom…but people who do know say your leaving might have had something to do with the changes they saw in her." He hesitated, silently gathering his words before going on. "Don't get me wrong, the Calli I met 20 years ago was a real sweet girl, but according to Delia, she wasn't the same Calli you walked out on."

Lance was caught off guard by the sudden hurt in Tom's eyes as he took a drink from his beer mug. "Tom, please don't get me wrong. I didn't mean nothing by that. Delia just described her as an older, wiser Calli who looked at life different, with a new determination; as if she was out to prove something."

Tom was silent, inside his own thoughts and memories, but listening to Clyde with all of his will. This was something he hadn't allowed himself to think about in all of these years. But, when he remembered the look in her eyes, the older smile she had given him as he walked out of that hotel room, he understood who she might have become.

He looked over at Lance as the man cleared his throat. "I tell you, we all witnessed the greatest change in Calli once she found her calling. It was as if her life had completely turned around. She used to tell her congregation God had finally found after running after her all those years."

Somehow, that made things easier for Tom, to know she'd found something to believe in and devote her life to. Now, he just had to be able to compartmentalize the two—the girl he'd loved and the evangelist who loved God.

However, he found it hard to imagine Calli as a woman of God. "It's been a long time...but there are some things I remember as if it was just yesterday. That woman just brought it all back to me, but I don't have to look long to see she and Calli don't have a lot in common except their looks."

Tom grew quiet, watchful, his thoughts more scattered as he tried to hold on to his memories and at the same time to figure out which Calli it was he was here to vindicate the sixteen-year-old girl he'd loved or the woman who had relied on God for all her needs. If she was murdered, that death deserved vindication just as much as the other Calli's would. Lance understood his pensive mood and let him drink in silence.

As many bars as he'd visited over the years, Tom had never noticed how alluring the colors of liquor were or how sensual the shapes of the bottles were. How many young men take their first drink because they subliminally equate it with sex, women, or both?

CHAPTER 26

A Healthy Serving of Memories

Tom followed Lance's black Volvo from the restaurant and bar to the home he and Delia had created after their marriage. He jokingly shared with Tom that he and Delia almost called their wedding off after weeks of arguing over where they'd live. Delia had demanded they live in her old home, or at least build a new one in Blue Bayou—even if it meant Lance would be driving between there and New Orleans on frequent business trips.

"I ain't leaving Blue Bayou, Lance. I'm okay with a second smaller home in New Orleans, but you know I'm not a New Orleans kinda' gal. Blue Bayou is home and always will be." Lance could see the case was closed. They built the 30,000 square foot contemporary mansion and loved it.

A few years later, the town needed a mayor after the previous mayor died after serving just one term. Lance's name was thrown into the basked with just a handful of names in it. Business leaders thought he was the best choice, given his business background and no-nonsense apolitical sense. He'd won by a landslide against a younger opponent who returned to the town after living in the north for years.

As Tom drove into the half-mile circular drive, he smiled to himself. "High cotton, here," he mumbled. Delia had won that fight, big time. As he followed Lance to the door, it opened right on cue.

His old friend looked refreshed and rested. Lance was right; all Delia needed was some time alone away from everyone whose own grief was adding to the poor woman's distress.

"Oh, my goodness, Tom, I'm so glad you're here." She hurried through the door to give the tall younger man a warm southern Louisiana hug. Tom was surprised to find he really had missed the old Delia despite their tattered relationship. She was still one of the best hugger he knew. He had a theory about southern huggers. It was as though they were so generous that they gave part of themselves as a gift during the exchange.

"You're still looking mighty good, Delia. And, for sure, I can see you're more rested. I just wish my reason for being here was a different one."

"Well, it's all a part of life, Tom. And, as my daughter often said – everything in our lives, the good and the bad, are part of God's divine order.

"Tom, you know I don't want to talk about Calli's disappearance any more than you do. God, I wish I could just have a good time with you tonight, catching up on our lives; go to bed tonight and have a good, long sleep, then wake up in the morning, turn over and look at my handsome husband and he'd say, `Honey, you just had a really bad dream.'"

"But you know, and I know that won't happen, Tom. Calli's gone. Disappeared.

And not one word from anyone of what might have happened."

"I just hope I can be of some help, Delia…given that it's been over four weeks, now, since Calli's disappearance." He was sorry to bring that up, but it had to be addressed sooner or later.

"Oh, I watch CSI, Tom. I know the chances of us finding Calli alive lessens each day. She was a woman who lived by her faith, and I'm gonna live by that same faith for now. I'm just not gonna close her case until I'm convinced it's time. I have to find out what happened, Tom, and I know you feel the same way."

Tom offered her a faint nod. "Course I do, Delia." There was no need of him pretending otherwise. He wouldn't rest until he found out the truth behind what had happened to his childhood love.

"I hope y'all didn't eat a bunch of Charlie's delicious small bites over at the tavern, Lance. Dinner's ready, but I thought we'd settle ourselves and have a drink before we set down to eat. I want you to say hi to Alana, Tom. You remember her, don't you?

She's Charlie's first cousin and Calli's best friend.

She was a few years behind Calli but caught up real quick after they both became teenagers. You may not remember it, but Alana and Charlie McGriffin grew up with us at the tavern. I know you remember her aunt, Rose McGriffin. She raised

Alana from a child. You remember Rose was our head cook at the tavern all those years. Then, we hired Charlie when he was still in school.

"I always felt guilty that Charlie didn't do more with his smarts. He was a good student and could 'a gone on to college and made something more out of himself. He never liked sitting inside a classroom, though. He told me he was doing exactly what he was put on this earth to do: Restaurant work.

"He was such a fast learner and could do just about any job in that restaurant. But, you know, Tom…I'd watch Charlie sometimes and noticed he had this charm about him that almost put people in a trance. After a while, I decided that the best place for Charlie was behind that bar. I made him head bartender about 10 years ago. He took to it like a fish to water. You'd thought he'd died and gone to heaven.

"People just love him…I think some of'em come in there just to hang out with Charlie. I'm really lucky no one has stole him from me."

Tom laughed. "You know, I do remember that in the summer times, Calli hung out at the restaurant most times. And I vaguely remember little Alana. I guess that made sense. Why spend extra money for babysitters when they were just as safe and could have fun right there?"

"I think it worked out just fine for both the girls. Calli was older, but it worked out fine. It was funny how after Alana had run after Calli all those years, they finally became best friends. She was the first person Calli hired after she opened the church.

Before that, Alana worked as a nurse at the Shreveport hospital. But, Lordy, did that girl follow in her aunt's footsteps when it comes to cooking! I told her I can't pay you as my daughter does, but when I'm in a pinch and needing someone to cook for a dinner or gathering, she's never too busy to help us out."

"Alana!" Delia hollered into the kitchen, "Come say hi to an old friend!"

Tom looked up, squinting in disbelief when he saw the tall, attractive woman standing just inside the door to the kitchen. "Come on in. I know you remember Tom Mallory, that handsome young man who used to come to the Tavern a lot with Calli. You were still in pigtails and plaits, but I thought you might remember him."

The stunning woman with long, flowing auburn and gold braids looked at Tom with a big smile on her face. Tom noticed the resemblance to Charlie, the same caramel complexion and hazel eyes, except hers were softer. Little Alana, all grown up, Tom thought. The bright coral shimmered on Alana's lips as she smiled from the kitchen door.

"My Lord, this can't be the same little girl I remember." Tom stood and walked to the door. They were both staring and grinning, obviously pleased to see each other again.

"Tom Mallory. My lord. Did I have a crush on you?" Tom blushed as Alana went on, "Do you really remember me? I was just a snotty nose following behind Calli, back, then. But I sure remember you…seems like one minute Calli was taking up time with me during the summer, then all of a sudden it was Tom and Calli. I had a ball spying on y'all when you thought nobody was looking. "

Tom's face reddened, and they all laughed. Tom gave the woman a big hug. "I remember you alright, Alana…but why is it that I look like an old man, and you look like you barely skimming drinking age?"

Alana laughed. "I can't answer that, Tom. Good living, maybe? Both you and Calli were a bit older than me, but not by much. From what I hear, Tom, you've had a life of real adventure, hunting down criminals and putting your life at risk. I try not to do much of that."

Tom looked down, and a palpable silence followed. Alana offered an apologetic smile. "Sorry…sometimes I speak without thinking. I'll go and get drinks for everyone" The conversation was resuming when Alana returned with a tray of drinks. Tom chose water with lemon, while Lance and Delia chose the prettier cocktails.

"Charlie told me you were by the Tavern last night, Tom," she said, an octave lower. "You should'a seen that big ole smile on his face when he said it. He sure was happy to see you."

"Well, it was great to see Charlie. You never know how much you miss someone till you don't see them for 45 years. Hard to believe it's been that long. I remember we had some good times, a lot of late-night talks…about life.

"But you tell that rascal he's the cause of me drinking like a fish over the last couple of days…now, I got to go back home and dry out."

Alana laughed, "Don't go blaming poor Charlie, Tom. He's just doing his job, and Delia wouldn't have it no other way." Tom felt drawn to Charlie's beautiful, younger cousin, her easy laughter, and how her face lit up when she smiled.

Delia stood and motioned Tom to join her in the sitting room while Alana prepared the table. "Since you've not visited us before, Tom, we'd be happy to give you a tour of this place. Sometimes I wonder what in the world were we thinking, building a house this size. Neither of us is spring chickens, you know.

"Truth be told, I haven't walked through all these rooms since the first year we moved here. Lance still loves all this space, though. Give him time, and he'll hand me a violin to play while he tells you how he grew up with five children and two parents crammed into a two-bedroom house. I don't think he'll ever have to live like that again."

Lance laughed, smoothing Delia's hair. "Let's do the walk-through after dinner, honey…if that's okay with you, Tom?

"But, before we go into dinner, take a look up there at that painting, Tom...does that look familiar to you?

"It's old Blue Bayou on a moon-drenched night. There's nothing quite as beautiful or as haunting at the same time, as nighttime on Blue Bayou. You know we get to look out at it from our bedroom window? It's just about 100 feet behind the house.

That was one of the reasons Delia wanted to build right here."

Tom stood and walked closer to the painting. He stared longer than he realized. He was remembering Calli and him taking a boat out on a night that looked so much like that. The moon, he recalled, looked as if it took up half the sky. It was as if it was just yesterday. He wondered if the memories were so real because he was so near where it all happened.

"You know what's funny, Tom? Calli's house is backed up to the very same bayou, just about 20 miles from here."

Silence. No one could find the right response.

"Tell you what, Tom...let's go in and eat dinner. If you up to taking a tour of this big ole house after dinner, we'll do it then."

"Sounds like a plan, Delia."

***

Tom's stomach growled. He'd been smelling dinner all during their time in the sitting room. He remembered Miss Rose's cooking at Delia's Restaurant and Tavern and imagined that Alana's dinner would be just as delicious by the looks of it. Alana must have watched and learned all her secrets.

"Alana started cooking in high school, you know, Tom. She worked weekends at the Tavern when we were short-staffed, or Rose needed to be off. Alana stepped right in there and didn't miss a beat."

Lance chimed in, "And, she likes to test her new recipes on unwitting visitors!

Lordy, Alana, whatever it is, it smells wonderful!"

Lance helped Delia into her seat before sitting at the head of the table. Tom sat directly across from Delia. As he looked across at her, he remembered the many nights he had sat with her and Calli for dinner. How comfortable he always felt in that home, so much more than he'd felt in the place he'd called home.

His thoughts darted between the past and the present. Their small talk, he knew, helped keep them from piercing the dark cloud that surrounded them all. Delia talked and laughed almost like old times, even throwing in a few curse words here and there to make things seem normal. Lance was wonderful in his attentiveness to his wife. It was as if he sensed her need before she realized it. Tom saw, too, that he was worried about Delia, whether she would get through this hard time, okay.

"Alana, you prepared this sumptuous meal and made us eat it all by ourselves.

You could have joined us and helped us eat it." Tom joked.

"We always invite her to do just that, Tom, but she's always running, so... never takes us up on the invitation."

Alana smiled and shook her head. She saw that everyone was finished with their meal. She walked in and set the tray of peach cobbler at the corner of the table. "Y'all heard the old saying that a cook rarely eats her own cooking? Well, I have to admit I do sample a bit while I'm cooking and am always too full to sit and eat afterward. So, y'all go on and enjoy yourselves, and let me know if you need anything else."

Tom took a bite of the peach cobbler, closed his eyes, and savored the taste. "The cook absolutely deserves a tip. Alana, you absolutely put your foot in this dinner."

"Thank you, Tom, but no tips accepted here. I'm just happy you enjoyed it…and I'm so happy to see you again." She retrieved the almost empty plates from the table.

"I'm going to tidy up the kitchen, Delia. Then, I'll be on my way. I told Charlie I'd come by the Tavern for a little bit before they close. I can let myself out.

"Tom, you are sho' nuff a sight for sore eyes. It was so good to see you…and remember the good old days." Tom walked over and gave Alana a quick hug before she left. "The pleasure was all mine. Alana."

"Goodnight, Delia. I'll call you tomorrow morning." Delia dropped her napkin and hurried after Alana.

Tom looked over at Lance and smiled. "I know you couldn't be eating like this every night. You wouldn't have that boyish physique if you did."

Lance laughed, "Nope, at 75, almost 76, I have a few health issues that definitely require me to watch what I eat. This was in your honor, but truth be told, we enjoyed the dinner at least as much as you did, Tom."

Delia returned. "Okay, if everybody is as full as a tick, let's all go into the living room, unbutton our pants, and have another drink while we talk about the thing none of us want to talk about."

The lightness in the air all but dissipated. Delia took the amber-colored drink from Lance, who had comfortably taken over as server now that Alana was gone. Delia sat back in the soft blue leather chair and sat her drink beside her. Tom decided to try his luck with a gin and tonic. He was afraid he'd need it to get through this conversation. He settled on the end of the sofa nearest Delia.

Lance stood for a moment behind Delia's chair, massaging her shoulders. "Are you up to this, baby?"

'Oh, yeah, I have to be. If not, I won't be able to get to sleep tonight."

"You want me to stay? I'm not sure I have much to offer, but if you need me, you know I'm here."

Delia looked at Tom, then shook her head. "Honey, right now I think Tom and I will be okay. But if I need you, I know where to find you." Lance stole a kiss and excused himself.

"I'm so glad I got to meet you, Tom, after hearing about you from Delia. I just wish we could have met in different circumstances. Thank you for agreeing to help my lady and me. We both want to get to our Calli back, and I pray that you can help us do that."

"I'll certainly do what I can, Lance. I'll be able to tell you both just how much I can help after I get back to Daphne tomorrow."

"Oh, we were hoping you'd stay long enough for breakfast tomorrow."

"I'd love to, but my plans are to get up before daylight and get out of here, get back in time to get to my office before bright and early. I need to catch up on a bunch of business, but I promise to call Delia before the end of the day tomorrow."

* * *

PART XIV: Remembering Calli Tucker

CHAPTER 27

A Mother's Loss

Delia sat trance-like for about a minute before the sound of Tom's glass returning to the table brought her back. "Oh, Tom, I'm sorry. I'm just remembering these last 25 years and how life was so wonderful for Calli. I never in a million years would have believed we'd end up here."

Tom grappled with keeping his thoughts in some kind of order. Sitting here with Delia discussing Calli brought on so many memories. "I think it would be best, Delia, if we talk about those last 25 years. I'll also want to hear about the last time you saw Calli. How was she doing? Was there any inkling of something bothering her or any changes in her?

"Do you have any idea who the last persons was who saw her? I'll need a list of her friends, employees, and closest colleagues.

"We both loved her, and we both know what it was about her we loved.

But…we're talking about a grown woman, a successful evangelist. I really need to know who Pastor Calli Tucker was…is. I really need you to fill in the missing pieces since the time I knew her, Delia."

* * *

Delia covered her face with her hands and took a deep breath.

"Tom, if you hadn't already fallen in love with her when she was a girl, you'd love the Calli she became. My girl turned into something really special…and I'd be the first to say I had nothing to do with it. I didn't see it coming.

"You know, Tom, that my child suffered during her childhood, and I can hardly stand to look at myself in the mirror some days, knowing that I was the cause of most of her unhappiness. I was a terrible mother who should never have been blessed with a wonderful child, like Calli.

"Then, you came along, Tom. Innocent, naïve, ready to love someone. And I picked up on that right away. You became the one bright spot in that child's life, Tom Mallory."

She looked over at the tall, aging man who had once been a quiet, gentle boy when she knew him. "You were so good for her. I don't think you will ever know what you did for her. After you left… Calli went inside herself and didn't come back out for a long time. She even left home for a while…searching for you. She was gone for four months and three days. When God brought her back to me, I vowed on that day I'd try my best to be the mother the girl needed.

Tom blanched at this news. It scared him, even now, to know the young innocent Calli had been traveling alone to places she didn't know to find him. He looked at Delia. "I think we both let her down something terrible, Delia."

"I must have aged 20 years during those four months. It was the scariest time in my life. All those weeks not hearing from her, no letters or calls, not knowing whether she was dead or alive. That almost killed me, Tom. She never said it right out, but I know without a doubt that part of her leaving was to punish me. I think she blamed me for your leaving as much as she blamed you.

"After she came home, I became the attentive mother I'd never been before. I was afraid it was too little too late, but I had to try. I pushed her into things, mostly to get her past mourning over your leaving. Calli was always a pretty girl, so I got it in my head that competing in beauty pageants would be good for her. It would take her mind off you, and it would help her self-confidence.

"Can you imagine shy, introverted Calli competing in a beauty pageant? She didn't want to at first, but I pushed and pushed, and, finally, she agreed. And, like I always told her she would be, she was always one of the prettiest girls in the competition. Once she got into it, Calli started winning and kept on winning. She got college scholarships, cars, spending money, speaking opportunities.

"When she went off to Louisiana State, her heart wasn't really in it, but I was so happy. I never even graduated from high school, but here was my girl becoming this confident, beautiful college girl, finally pushing the memory of you into the back of her mind.

"I didn't even argue when she decided to pull out of the biggest competition of her career, the Miss Louisiana competition. I was disappointed, but I didn't push her anymore. You know who was in that competition, though? Alana McGriffin. She and Calli had competed together several times. And, for a couple of years, one or the other one was winning more beauty pageants than any girl in southern Louisiana. But for the big one, Calli pulled out, and Alana came in 1st runner up. You think she's something now, Tom; Alana was some beauty back then. Charlie told me Alana would never admit it, but the loss was a big blow to her, even though it paid for her college education.

"After graduating, Calli was courted by some of the Louisiana tv stations. They knew of her beauty pageant history and wanted her to be an anchor on their news shows. She wasn't excited about that either but finally agreed to try it. She was really good, and the viewers loved her. She was at KTAL for five years before she just quit one year, said she wanted to do something different. Just like that.

"That something was opening her own beauty school. She talked Alana into working with her, even though she'd just graduated from college. Alana has a natural knack for organizing and management, so she ended up as office manager at the beauty school. The school offered beauty services and classes on beauty and etiquette.

Calli said she wanted at least half the spots to go to girls from underprivileged backgrounds. They created a scholarship for girls who couldn't afford the tuition. Calli brought a girl out of Shreveport to teach dance to help girls with their posture and deportment.

"That place grew so fast. Mothers from all over this region were bringing their girls in for the classes while the mothers took advantage of the hair shop. She hadn't had the shop for five years when Calli decided she just wasn't happy doing it anymore. A company out of Shreveport wanted to expand and jumped at the chance to buy the company.

"Calli sold the shop, just like that. To everybody's surprise, Calli left town, went to New Orleans to a theology school, and was there for two years. That was a surprise to everybody, even Alana. She told me she had no idea that was what Calli had in mind or that she was seriously thinking of selling the beauty shop.

Alana loved the beauty school, and she and Calli worked so well together. It took Alana a while to get over Calli's decision, though she was quickly hired on at the Shreveport hospital as an RN. In time, Calli and Alana made up. I think we all understood that Calli was still searching for happiness.

"Then, after theology school, she came home for a while. I knew she was working on something but wasn't quite sure what. You know, Calli, she never was much on sharing her secrets. Well, she was working on starting that church. She and God, I guess. She finally told me He had directed her back to Blue Bayou and promised her that she would make a difference in people's lives, to give them hope and teach them of His faith.

"It took some work, but you know, people were coming out of the woodwork to help her get her church built. It was a small little building right off, and for months she hardly had enough members to have a service. Of course, she did – whether there were two or 20, there. I could see it in my baby's eyes, Tom. She was finally happy, finally doing what she felt like God put her on this earth to do.

It was like watching a miracle take place right in front of your eyes. It was like watching that…metamorphosis people talk about with butterflies. God came into her life, and before I knew it, she was this new Calli…still herself, but something so much more. So much confidence, but still love for everyone. She blossomed like a flower…it was truly a miracle to watch.

"She is a happy woman, a beautiful and happy woman with a heart of gold. Her whole life since that time has been centered around giving and helping others. You know she told me not too long ago that the Miracle Way of today, that big church taking up 50 acres of land and lake, was never anything she asked God for, not really something she cared about.

She was just praying, listening, then acting on God's directions. It was Him, she said, who wanted it for her. And He just kept on blessing her year after year! I can tell you one thing she wanted in Miracle Way was for it to be open to everyone, and I mean everyone, no matter how much money you got, no matter what color you are. She wouldn't rest until her church was truly filled with people from all parts of the community.

Now she has rich folks, middle-class folks, and just as many poor folks. She has black, white, Mexicans, and even some Asians. And, you know what? You never hear one word about problems within that church. Not one word.

"Alana was right there by her side, representing her anytime Calli needed to be two places at once. I think Calli told me Alana suggested the title of personal assistant. That suits them both because Alana is like her shadow all day, every day.

"Then, God sent Weldon. He was at the service, but I don't think you met him. He has been such a blessing for her, too. He's everything she isn't. A real businessman, a wonderful lawyer, and protective of her time and her money. When has Calli ever cared about money? Well, she needed someone who did, as the church began to grow like wildfire.

"Weldon is one of those people who know what you need before you know it. You ever had someone like that work for you? So, naturally, Calli began to depend on him more and more. Over time, they became closer, nothing romantic like some people whispered. There's was a business relationship. I know because I asked, and Calli told me without even thinking twice.

"You know, she used to laugh and say she had no idea she needed a Weldon in her life until he showed up and just started doing what was natural for him to do…take charge. That took so much off her."

Tom had been writing as Delia talked. Looking up, listening. He held his hand up. "Wait, let me ask a few questions, Delia. I get it that there was no relationship with Weldon, but…I don't know how to ask this, Delia, but what about Calli's…love life?

Was there, is there anyone else in her life?"

Delia shook her head. "Well, I don't know how to answer that question, Tom. What I can tell you is that Calli met someone just about two months before her disappearance. His name is Clyde Vann a very popular football player and now a rich businessman. He's a friend of Weldon's who was invited to come to the church. I think he must've enjoyed it because he continued coming for a few months before he got a chance to actually meet Calli during one of her pastor's receptions. Weldon set those up to make sure people like Clyde got a chance to know Calli close up. I was at that reception and actually met Clyde before he met Calli…and, I have to tell you, Tom, if I hadn't been married, I would have run after that man myself. Good-looking, charming, and just a really nice person.

"Well, I think Calli felt the same thing when she met him. In fact, I think all of us standing around when they met could feel something happening between them. I've never known Calli to take an interest in a man since you left Tom. Well, at almost 60 years old, I could see her falling for this man."

Tom didn't know how he should feel, but he knew Clyde Vann was someone he should talk to. "Where can I find Mr. Vann, Delia?"

"He works between New Orleans and Chicago. He travels all over the world, and half the time, he's not in the states. But, I have his phone number and email. I'll get that for you before you leave.

"Tom, You would think a woman like Calli, successful, beautiful, and giving, could have the pick of any eligible man in Louisiana. But, her focus for these last 25 years has been on that church and her charities. When I joke with her about it, she just smiles and says God is jealous, and she is too busy to think about having a man in her life.

"Of course, that was before she met Clyde Vann. I don't think she would say that now. So, I would say the two men closest to her would be Weldon, who's been there for about 15 years now, and now Clyde, who, according to Alana, was with her almost every weekend for the last couple of months and may have even spent a couple of nights at the house. She would never tell me that!

"I'll be honest, Tom, I'm happy for her. Real happy. I have a good sense of people, and Clyde Vann is good for Calli. She and Weldon could never be a good fit. He's too unbending, stuck in his ways. Anyway, rumor is Weldon has a woman friend somewhere in the county, but nobody knows who she is. He's never brought her around or introduced her to any of his church family."

Tom continued his questions for another hour. When he saw Delia fading and felt himself growing tired, he decided he'd better let Delia sleep. He'd take himself to bed too, and prepare to get up early and leave. He had learned plenty enough to keep him busy once he came back.

Tom tried not to think about it, but he couldn't help but wonder about Calli's decision to marry herself off to the church rather than a living, breathing man. Had she given up on love after that one try at 15? At least up until this past year when Clyde Vann walked into her life."

* * *

CHAPTER 28

De Ja 'Vu all over again in Blue Bayou

Tom woke from his deep sleep with sketchy visions of last night's dinner and conversation swirling in his brain. It was 5 a.m., time for him to rise and shine and prepare for his trip back to Daphne. He was ready to get back home, but for some reason, he knew Blue Bayou would haunt him until he was back here to help Delia figure out the mystery of Calli's disappearance. Tom couldn't force himself to think that Calli might be dead, though the logical part of his brain told him it was the most likely outcome.

His visit to Blue Bayou had brought back so many good memories, but some he'd just as well have left buried. What was surprising was how easy it was to rely on alcohol to dull the painful memories and...yes, illuminate the good ones. One thing hadn't changed. Tom snorted; Delia could still hold her liquor. He remembered the times when the little woman could drink most men under the table.

He remembered how he'd spent the first part of last evening at Delia's Tavern and Restaurant with Lance Belson and the scary feeling of DeJa'Vu when he saw the woman who was a spitting image of a young Calli. Lucy was her name, he remembered, and he'd self-consciously stared at her most of the night. He had to admit he'd enjoyed that the dancing and drinking had allowed him to forget the sad reason he was here.

The best part of the evening, Tom smiled, was reconnecting with Charlie and catching up on how life had been treating him. According to his friend, life was treating him very good. Twenty-five years ago, he'd married his high school sweetheart, and they now had three grown daughters, one married, one in college, and one "finding herself." Charlie and his wife Sandi lived on a small farm outside town. He still loved his work at the tavern where he worked as a bartender and restaurant host. "Delia's been more than good to me," he told Tom. "She's been a mother, a friend, and the best boss anyone could have. She's given me a raise just about every year I've been with her…and, you know that's been a long time, Tom."

The Country Slide…was that what they called it? He laughed out loud, remembering how he'd reluctantly allowed himself to be dragged onto the dance floor. He could only imagine what he looked like from the other patrons there, even the half-drunk ones. Tom was surprised that he didn't care. He couldn't remember the last time he'd danced.

Now, he did. the image of him and Calli Tucker slow dancing across the tavern floor as Karen Carpenter sang, "Close to You." Tom had told Calli he couldn't dance a lick, never took the time to learn, and she had been hell-bent on teaching him…right then and there.

Tom's heart fluttered as he remembered that night, what it felt like to hold her in his arms, to have her big, soft eyes glued to his. He remembered the sweet, peevish smile as she led him across the floor.

He hadn't been the only one to make a fool of himself on the dance floor last night. Lance had joined him there, just as tipsy and not much better at dancing. Tom was grateful Delia had sent Lance to keep him company.

The Calli-look alike had told Tom, "We been sitting there waiting for you gentlemen to come over and ask us to dance...but, since neither one of you had the courage to do it...well, hell; welcome to the new Millennium."

Lance looked over at Tom and hunched his shoulders in surrender. He was just tipsy enough to let Lucy grab his hand and drag him out onto the floor. He was happy to see that his new drinking buddy was making just as big a fool of himself as he was.

As the crowd grew louder and rowdier, Tom became soberer and began to feel his age. He apologized to Lucy, telling her he needed to sit and stop his head from spinning. He missed the simple two-step that Calli had taught him.

As he lay in bed, pushing back the need to get up and get ready for his drive back to Daphne, Tom's roving brain took him to the second part of the evening at Delia and Lance's home. He remembered his surprise that Delia and Lance lived in a house just one step from a southern mansion, even though the tour never happened.

He smiled as he remembered his surprise at seeing Alana – a definite sight for sore eyes. The last time he'd seen her at the tavern, she must have been nine or 10. He now recalled she was definitely Calli's shadow. Now, she was a beautiful woman. He wondered if there was a husband or children.

* * *

Tom sat up on the side of the bed, preparing himself mentally for the three-hour trip back to Daphne. From the corner of his eye, Tom saw the folded clipping Delia had given him from yesterday's newspaper. He picked up the crinkled clipping and slowly unfolded it. There it was, the photo he'd not allowed himself to look at last night. It was a headshot of Evangelist Calli Tucker. There were the same soft gray eyes and the winsome smile he remembered from 45 years ago.

He was afraid to take a chance at staring at that face last night with Delia sitting there. He'd skimmed the headline, then hurriedly folded the clipping and pushed it down into his shirt pocket. This morning he held the paper in front of him and noticed a slight tremor in his hands as he forced himself to stare back at the photo before reading the full article.

Popular Blue Bayou Evangelist Still Missing, Feared Dead

Evangelist Callindra Mae Tucker, 60, of Blue Bayou, Louisiana, is still missing after her disappearance four weeks ago. The police department said they are still following up on leads, but none have led to her discovery as of yet.

On June 25, 1942, Miss Tucker was born in Blue Bayou, Louisiana.

Her mother, Delia Tucker Vann, and stepfather, Clyde Vann, held a memorial at Great Albion Tabernacle Church on Sunday. The memorial was attended by local members of the church, and members of Evangelist Tucker's church, Miracle Way All Denominations.

Tucker founded the Miracle Way All Denominations Church, in 1985, in a mobile home outside Blue Bayou. In 20 years, the church grew from a membership of 10 to a congregation totaling more than 3000 members. Today, the church complex sits on 50 acres of land that includes a children's center, an eldercare center, and an education center, which includes a preschool and elementary school.

Ms. Tucker's ministry has taken her all over the world. A much-beloved community servant and philanthropist, she headed up the Annual Adoption Services' Christmas Charity Drive and founded the Blue Bayou Homeless Shelter Committee.

After attending Louisiana State University, she settled in Shreveport, where she worked for five years as a news producer and anchor at KTAL. She later purchased the Southern Belles Beauty Shop from a friend, operating it for five years before selling it to an out-of-town beauty chain. Tucker represented the state of Louisiana in many beauty pageants over the years.

According to officials at Miracle Way All Denominations Church, no plans are underway for a funeral service. "Like the rest of the county, we are awaiting the final outcome of the investigation into her disappearance," an unnamed official said.

PART XV: I am Calli

Calli lay quiet. Her breathing hardly there, slowing. It was dark again, damp, cold.

Slowly, slowly, her brain cells began to connect.

"My name is Calli. I am…Calli Tucker."

Her head turned slightly as if pulled by some unseen source.

She spied the small window of light, felt the breeze, and heard the sound of water More dreams?

There was not enough in her to raise herself or make a sound. Her will was depleted, closed away. When for how long?

She tried recalling the voice. The voices. Little more than whispers from some faraway place.

Voices she should know. Except her memory wouldn't hold onto memories. Gone, gone. Along with her voice.

I am Calli. I am Calli. I am Calli Tucker. "Callindra Tucker," was just a whisper in her ear.

The breeze again, and the sound of the water before her eyes fluttered closed, and her breathing became shallower, hardly a bird's breath.

CHAPTER 29

A Different Kind of Homecoming

Tom arrived back in Blue Bayou one week after he'd left Delia's home. He'd reluctantly turned over all his active cases to young Esau. "I'll be back when I get back, Deputy. Until I walk through that door, you're in charge. I need you to know I'm depending on you to take care of the city while I'm gone."

The young deputy tried to swallow past the lump in his throat. "I understand, Chief. I understand the responsibility you're leaving me with, and I promise to do you proud." Tom gave him a hard look, followed by a short nod.

"I'll check in with you. I'll try to do it at least weekly. If you get in a pitch, call me. Unless it's an emergency, Maia is the best resource in this office. Ask her anything you run into and don't know the answer to. I do." He smiled at the young man's raised eyebrows.

Tom was clear about one thing – Calli's case had him not thinking as clearly as he should. He hoped he'd get to the bottom of her disappearance sooner than later. He'd be in this hazy fog until things resolved themselves.

Maia noticed it, too. She had looked at him strangely as he packed to leave, asking him what kind of case was this to have him not sleeping at night. She was worried he was acting recklessly. Even though she'd pushed him to hire Esau, it wasn't like Tom to turn over his office completely to a newbie.

The Mayor was a little worried, too. During their breakfast on Wednesday, she'd asked him point-blank whether this was a personal thing. "Cause, if it is Tom, you and I both know that could be a problem. Your running out half-cocked to redeem personal guilt or loss is a dangerous undertaking. And it usually ends badly."

Tom knew she was right but looked straight into her blue eyes and told her, "I don't want to talk about it, Mavis." And that was that. For goodness sake, what was everyone getting into a tizzy about? Hadn't he always vowed to do his very best with everything he did? He wouldn't be very good at his job if he didn't. He had to be honest with himself, though. This was different. This was Calli. How could he not do all he could to find her—for him, Calli, and Delia?

The chance he was taking was that everything he'd gathered into his life for the last 45 years would still be waiting for him when he returned from Blue Bayou, no matter what the outcome was. He knew he was asking many people who cared for him to cover his tail every day without one complaint. Running off to Blue Bayou to chase the ghost of a girl he'd left 45 years ago. *You can't make it up to her, Tom. Too much water under the bridge*, he cautioned himself.

Every logical cell in his brain told him Calli was dead. It had been a month now.

Four weeks. 28 days. Whether it was a crime of passion, an accidental death, or a senseless crime involved with a robbery…whoever it was, they couldn't afford to keep their victim alive to tell the story.

The guilt he should be most concerned about, Tom told himself, should be about Maia. Sweet, wonderful, no questions asked, Maia.

Most things she knew about Tom, she wasn't 100% sure of because he'd never felt the need to confirm or deny what she'd heard. And while she had no clue about Tom and Calli's history, she did know this Blue Bayou case was trouble for him.

Something or someone was haunting him, something terrible. His sleeping had gone from bad to almost nonexistent. His blood pressure had shot up higher than it had in years. That long-ago habit of averting his eyes as a sign he didn't want to talk was back. It wasn't in Maia to come out and ask, but it was ringing in her head, on the tip of her tongue, "What kind of hold does this case have on you?"

Tom's only response to this tension between them was to hold her closer, more tenderly than he had in their long relationship. The night before was something she would remember for as long as she lived. He'd uttered the words. Actually, looked into her eyes and said, "I love you." She should have been over the moon, grinning from ear to ear.

Instead, it was one of those gifts that you're afraid to unwrap.

After Maia finished fixing her bed, she'd touched it lightly, smoothing over the side where Tom had laid. Maia would give all the world to be happy at this moment. But Tom was leaving for Blue Bayou. He'd packed enough clothes for a week or a month, or forever. She wouldn't feel settled until he returned.

As they stood at the door, Maia's face was dripping with tears. She swore she couldn't explain why. Tom found himself more annoyed than he wanted to be. Maia seemed petrified as the tears streamed. She felt in her bones Tom Mallory might not be back, or maybe he would, but he'd drag something heavy back with him. Something invisible, but she'd know it was there. She had a feeling that everything that mattered to him now would no longer matter after this trip. If she'd asked this time, maybe Tom would have told her. Spilled the whole story so she wouldn't have to ask again.

* * *

Tom was nervous, experiencing that outer body thing as he tried to make himself comfortable in the hotel room he'd be spending the next week or two…or maybe more. He went through the notes from his dinner with Delia and Lance. He was reaching out to local law enforcement offices for the next hour, introducing himself, telling them why he was in their jurisdiction, and asking for their help.

He called back to the office before closing time. Maia picked up the phone before Esau had a chance. It was a short conversation. There was nothing new to share with her. She told him she already missed him. He grunted and said, "Thanks."

"Is Esau around? Just wanna check in with him, make sure he's feeling comfortable there." She told him he was out running down a suspect who drove off without paying for gas at the Stop & Go.

Maia had brought him up to date on everything going on in his office and the city. He told her he'd call Esau back tomorrow. Maia had given him a good report. "That boy is really working hard to earn your favor, Tom," she'd giggled. It was after that she'd whispered how much she missed him and how much she'd like seeing him just for the weekend. "I can drive over right after work tomorrow, Tom, and get back here first thing Sunday morning."

Tom's "No," was final, no room for argument. He couldn't explain it to Maia.

Him, with another woman in Blue Bayou would be like

sacrament. As crazy as it sounded, this had been a magical place for him and Calli, and even now, it would feel like he was doing something wrong.

Tom told her he'd call back in a day or so before he flipped the phone shut. He shook his head. Women. They never seemed to be satisfied with the part of you, you willingly gave. They always seemed to want a little bit more. He couldn't. There wasn't enough of him to give away. Too much of it had been left in New Orleans, then in Blue Bayou...a lifetime ago.

He sat for a moment flipping between the channels of the hotel TV. More television church programs than he knew existed, but no Miracle Way All Denominations program. The knock at the door was the cleaning woman he'd sent away two times already today. "Come on in...I'm half-naked, but I'm sure it's nothing you never saw!" He chuckled, sure that would turn the woman away again.

He was surprised to hear the keys rattling in the door, and then the door to open enough for the hotel worker to push her smiling head inside the room. "Want me to come back?" He shook his head, laughing. "You better be glad I was lying. I think we would have both been terribly disappointed."

"I'm going to dinner. Thanks for letting me hang out here unbothered today." She smiled and nodded. He wondered how long she had cleaned up after people like him, how many men and women had set in this very room, sprawled in the easy chair, slept – or not – in the bed he had slept in for almost a week, now.

Thomas Mallory was feeling every second of his years. It was the mental part of growing old catching up with him. Him having to constantly duck the hopelessness of a job like this. The 'what difference will it make?' The urge to give up on what looked like an endless tail spend. He had to keep reminding himself that Calli could still be alive while his mind's eye looked him straight in the face and asked, "How?" No matter what he learned, he couldn't leave here without learning what happened to Calli Tucker.

He was trying hard not to give up hope as he began following up on the names Delia had supplied him with. He'd reached out to just about everyone she'd connected him with, including the elderly church members who had long ago lost the energy or health to get up on Sunday mornings and drive to Miracle Way. Each one, though, were still connected to Calli from her visits and cards.

They all shared the same refrain, "Lord, how could something like this happen to someone like Pastor Tucker? Who would want to hurt this good woman of God?" Tom was always respectful and quiet, listening for any tidbit of information that could help his search. Pastor Tucker walked on water, had no enemies, was loved by every resident of south Louisiana. She was a living angel on earth.

With nothing inside this room or his head to buoy him, Tom decided to break his promise to himself and drop by Delia's Place for a drink and maybe dinner. Why not? He needed to eat, and the Tavern was beginning to feel like a home away from home.

Besides, Charlie was always medicine for his soul. He needed a little medicine tonight. As Tom walked in, Charlie laughed with a couple of cowboys who looked like they'd just ridden in on horses from Southfork. Authentic Texas Cowboy hats, well-used but shiny boots and all. They were throwing back the hard stuff, taking up more space than they should, one leg each propped up on adjoining bar stools, and voices rising in decibels each time they took a drink.

Tom was glad he wasn't officially on duty here. His instincts told him these two might be packing, and things might get out of hand before they walked out the door. Charlie slapped the bar in front of his two wranglers and winked before leaving them to wait on Tom.

"Hey, man, you're a sight for sore eyes! I was wondering when you'd be back in to get that other half of the drink you left here a couple of nights back. You eatin' or just drinking tonight? Delia won't be too pleased when I tell her you haven't been patronizing the best tavern this side of the Mississippi."

Tom offered his friend a weary smile. "I've been working, Charlie. That's still how most folks get paid, remember? I don't get to stand behind a bar and have fun with customers all day and night, have pretty girls stretching over the bar to show you their cleavage, and all. We actually have to work."

Charlie laughed that Charlie belly laugh that always made Tom smile. "Well, I do work sometimes, buddy, though I have to admit it has its perks. But, seriously, I hope things are going well, that you're making some headway. I can't tell you how many people come in here in a good mood, then get to talking about Calli and leave here in tears, or more depressed than they meant to be inside a bar."

"I've heard that sadness since I've been here, Charlie. So hard to connect the woman they talk to me about to the Calli we all knew…and loved. Kinda hard to put my head around it."

"Well, let me tell you this, my friend. There ain't one person in this world Calli would rather have looking after her than you. You know that, and I know that. That thing y'all had back then? It was the real deal, Tom. Whatever happened to cause the split happened. But it was the lasting thing that you can't shed yourself of, even if you try a hundred years."

"Maybe, Charlie. But, right now, I feel like a dog trying to catch his tail. Nothing I have is leading to much. There's got to be something I'm missing."

"Sounds like you need a double of whatever it is you're having, my friend. Will it be your gin and tonic?"

"I'm so glad you asked, Charlie. A gin and tonic is exactly what I need." Charlie laughed. When he brought Tom's drink, he stood back and watched him for a while, realizing that Tom was in a mood to be alone and wrestle with his troubles. Man, what troubles.

Charlie eyed the new customer at the other end of the bar, slapped the bar, and grabbed his friend's arm. "I'll be back to check on you, Tom. And look…I hear you still the baddest Cajun lawman in the south. You'll figure it out. I know you will. Remember what they say on Columbo? 'It's always the ones you least expect.'" And then he was off to be Charlie, the lovable bartender to his new customer.

Charlie had stopped back by, done a bit of small talk, and set Tom's second gin and tonic in front of him. Just as Tom raised his glass, he felt a soft grasp around his shoulder.

"If it ain't the most handsome Cajun lawman in Louisiana." He knew the voice but couldn't put it to a face. As he turned, he quickly connected the dots. Alana McGriffin. She bent and gave Tom a cross between a sisterly and not-so sisterly hug before sitting at the stool next to him.

Charlie was back, asking Alana what she was drinking or if she was here for dinner. "Both, cousin. Right now, I want to have a drink with our old friend Tom Mallory."

Tom smiled. Pleased. Yes, he'd wanted to be alone with his drink and his thoughts, but…the thoughts could certainly wait until he returned to the hotel room. Alana was a sight for sore eyes.

"Let me do the honors, Ms. McGriffin. What will it be?"

"I'm having what Chief Tom Mallory is having. Gin and tonic, right Tom?" He nodded, finding himself a little tied-tongued. From the drink? He kept surprising himself.

"Well, tell me how things are, Tom. Delia told me you have been a very busy man. We've both been trying hard to hold each other up through this terrible time. I know she put on a good show the other day when you saw her, but Tom, we're all worried about her, keeping an eye on her. Lance is good, but he's the mayor. He can't sit home and babysit his wife. Weldon and I go over a few evenings a week to make sure she's eating and taking care of her health.

Though he was a little surprised to hear it, Tom was happy to know Alana was there. "I'm really happy to know you're here for her, Alana. I've never been good with the 'taking care of people' part. I'm just happy she has someone she can depend on to check in on her. And, about Weldon…"

"You know, Tom, Delia has been my "other mama" for most of my life. I think I'm a lot more like her than I am like Aunt Rose, who raised me from a baby. And Calli? That was my girl, my sister from another mother, that I never had. Maybe something better because we had all the good and none of the bad most sisters go through."

Tom looked down when he saw the tear glistening in the corner of her eye. This was the other thing he never was good with. women who cried. "That's pretty amazing, Alana, the fact that you all never had a falling out, given all the time you knew each other."

Alana rested her face in her hands, rolling her beautiful hazel eyes. "Oh, Ok, Mr. Sheriff, you know I don't mean we never had a disagreement in all those years. Just that, when we did have words, it was always something small and insignificant and never lasted. Calli didn't hold grudges, you know. You, of all people, would know that about her, Tom."

"You know folks think she still loved you, Chief Mallory. Can you imagine that, after all this time?" Tom tried hard to ignore the guilt he'd been walking around with all these years, trying hard to ignore for 45 years. He looked over and waved at Charlie.

"I'm gone get out of here, Alana, before I end up as tore up as I was the last time I came in here. My friend Charlie was absolutely no help, either." The two cousins laughed before turning to see the new customer sit next to Alana.

Tom recognized the good-looking woman who had reminded him so much of Calli. Lucy from New Orleans. The nurse smiled over at Tom.

"Hey, y'all. What you drinking, Alana? Whatever it is, I think I'll have a double." She laughed and waved at Charlie.

"Hello, Sheriff Mallory. I heard you were back in town. I hope you're enjoying yourself in this little Louisiana town. Like I told you, if you want to have some real fun, you gotta come on over to New Orleans." That smile. So familiar.

"I'm afraid my body fits better in small towns like Blue Bayou than in big cities like New Orleans. I actually am enjoying all the things I loved about it back then, the beautiful landside and the friendly people. It's always good when some things remain the same."

Lucy looked over, hesitant. "Alana told me you lived here for a time, and…that you and the woman, Pastor Tucker, were madly in love." Tom wondered if his face was as flushed as the younger woman's face.

"Calli Tucker—that's who I knew her as—we were very close back then. That was a long time before she became Evangelist Tucker."

Tom wished he'd escaped before this conversation began. He never felt comfortable sharing personal information with strangers, no matter how beautiful. He stared into the younger woman's eyes and realized they were filled with sadness.

"Did you know Pastor Tucker, Lucy?"

She shook her head back and forth as if she'd been caught off guard. " Oh no, no…I never met her." Lucy offered him the smallest of smiles, then got up and walked further down the bar.

Tom's eyes followed the young woman who seemed to have completely changed from the fun-loving party girl of the other night into one who seemed to be dealing with something.

* * *

Alana promptly filled in the empty space left by Lucy. She noticed Tom's eyes follow Lucy and lightly shook her head. "She'll be fine, Tom. Lucy has…some personal things going on. She'll be fine."

"It seems that a lot of people are effected by Calli's disappearance, whether they know her or not."

"I was just wondering, Tom, how things were going with the investigation.. Have you landed any good leads yet?"

"None. Not yet. I figure I'll be here a little longer than I'd planned." He saw Lucy turn slightly toward them as they spoke.

"Well. Good luck, friend. I'm sure we'll be seeing each other quite a bit before you leave, although I don't seem to have half the free time I did before.

"My role at the church has expanded quite a bit, but you can always call me if you need me, Tom. You can always find me there. Weldon and I are doing our best to hold things together until we get some finality about the future."

"Well, maybe you can help me with at least one thing, Alana. I've been trying to get ahold of Weldon, but I hadn't been able to so far. I hear he's doing quite a bit of traveling, but I'd really appreciate it if you would encourage him to give me a call. Let him know I'd love to chat with him when he gets a spare moment?"

"Of course. I'll let him know, Tom. He should be here most of next week. I'll make sure he gives you a call." She hopped off the barstool and gave him another hug before walking down to sit next to Lucy.

CHAPTER 30

Telling the Tucker Women's Stories

Tom felt the days whizzing past him, and he had no more information than he did the first day he returned. He had met Lance Belson at Delia's Tavern for dinner and drinks. Lance complained of a long day, as Tom complained that he was no closer to finding leads in Calli's disappearance than the day he arrived back in town.

Lance smiled apologetically as he took a sip from his drink. The two older men had settled into a mutual admiration club. Delia, of course, was the centrifugal force. "You know Lance before I forget to say it, Delia done good by choosing you—or letting you choose her. You all seem mighty happy and mighty good for each other." Tom was thinking of the old Delia. The change was miraculous. Maybe there was something to that immaculate conversion.

Even with her evolution, the couple was still completely opposites. That was the attraction, Tom guessed. Delia obviously needed a reserved, levelheaded man who would give her a sense of security, while Lance might have simply been attracted to the good-looking woman with the ageless sex appeal.

"You know Tom, Pastor Callindra is pretty amazing, too. Not just because she's Delia's daughter, but because she's the most genuinely good woman I've ever met. Never an agenda to her good deeds. I really think it was her watching the way Callindra lived her life that made Delia start rethinking how she lived her own. People who knew her back then says she actually grew into motherhood well after Calli was a young woman.

"Calli has helped change us…south Louisiana. You know our history, Tom. We hadn't always had the best reputation for tolerance of others, accepting people's differences. Well, Miracle Way is truly…well, miraculous in how they make sure they do the right thing by just about anybody, no matter what their stripe. And do it without ruffling the power folks' feathers in this town. They're teaching us something our own history should have taught us.

"If you have a chance, Tom, have Alana take you round to visit their programs for young people, the homeless shelter, the food pantry. All these services that the church runs really helps the city in all kinds of ways. One thing is, we have more leeway in how we spend our social services funds. Calli's mission, no 'her mission from God,' is to bring people together. All people.

"The city gave the church 20 acres of land out there near the Bayou. Land was all grown up, and the owners long gone. We told Calli and Weldon they could do what they wanted to do with it. I'll be damn if they haven't created one of the most beautiful, productive crop gardens in the county – what we grew up callin' truck patches.

"Calli has this gift of bringing out the best in people, Tom. Old folks, young folks, black folk, white folk, our Mexicans… The young folk are learning about growing their own food, making their own clothes; boys learning about welding and building…then, to turn around and let them sell it and get half the profit. If we lose Calli Tucker, we've lost a valuable resource in Blue Bayou. She's the epitome of God giving us the fishing pole, then teaching the rest of us how to fish."

Tom's mind was on the past, the young Calli as he stared back at the Mayor. His walks down memory lane had been regular and often since his return to the town. Sadly, they hadn't been helpful to the investigation. Between bites, he looked around the beautiful tavern that was now a full-blown restaurant that could hold its own in any large town in Louisiana. Delia had built the Blue Bayou Tavern from a small 'stop, eat n' drink,' nook to a destination establishment consistently voted by Louisianians as one of the "Best little food and drink restaurants" in the county.

After a delicious dinner, the mayor's steak and potatoes, and Tom's seafood and country greens, the mayor insisted on picking up the tab as they finished their discussion on politics and sports. "Does the name Clyde Vann ring a bell for you, Tom? Just wondering if anyone mentioned Clyde to you?

Tom nodded. "Yes, Delia told me Clyde Vann and Callindra had grown close the month or so before her disappearance. Of course, my ears pricked up when I heard that. But, in talking to folk who know them both, his reputation is about like Callindra's, sterling.

Sounds as if he'd be the last person to do anything to harm Callindra.

"Even so, I'll still need to talk with him when he returns to his office. I'm guessing that'll mean I'll need to drive over to New Orleans to either his office or his home."

"Clyde is Louisiana's "local boy done good." We love to share his story with the rest of the south. He came from a good, but really poor family down in west Louisiana. I hear he was a good student and an even better athlete who got a football scholarship to Tuskegee down in Ruston. He was good enough there to have scouts from all around the country courting him.

"I understand he and Weldon were friends, and Weldon introduced him to Callindra."

"That's right. He had started visiting the church some months earlier before Weldon invited him to one of the pastor's receptions after church service. Delia met Clyde that same time, and she couldn't stop talking about him when she got home. I think she was almost as taken with the man as Calli was!" Tom laughed to see Lance try to restrain his jealousy.

"Anyway, from all I hear, that one meeting kind've changed things for Calli. I think they probably saw each other most every week after that. They were out to our house a couple of weekends. It was almost like they'd known each other for years."

Tom had done his own reconnaissance on Clyde Vann after Delia told him about the man. He found nothing much different from what both Delia and Lance said. A young man who had grown up in poverty and worked his way out of it.

He learned he'd dreamed of becoming a New Orleans Saints all his life, and when the scouts came calling, he never even considered any other team. He was an immediate star and won every award thinkable. When he retired about 20 years ago, he turned to business, and lo and behold, he was a brilliant businessman. His popularity had only soared over the last decades as he became a very wealthy man.

The two men finished drinks, stood, and were on their way to the parking lot. Tom walked with his head down as Clyde continued to share what an exceptional man Clyde Vann was.

"He certainly sounds like someone Louisiana ought to be touting, but believe it or not, I never keep up with football or any sports, to be truthful. I don't mention that too much anywhere in the south. Of course, I'd heard Clyde Vann's name, but I admit I didn't know who he was."

Lance grinned. I'll keep that secret close to my chest, Tom. Not something you want folks to know…your not being a sports fan." They laughed.

"From what I hear, Clyde was a real 'catch' for the church, and Weldon made sure Calli knew he'd recruited one of the most popular men in the region to join her church. He used these little tete a tetes to connect select visitors with Pastor Calli?"

"Something like that. I don't think there was anything nefarious to it, but Weldon was all about keeping the church and Calli in a good light. You remember Calli, she wasn't someone who loved a lot of hoopla, and I'm sure she was bored stiff at most of those things. Maybe Clyde was the one time she was pleased with Weldon's little gatherings."

Tom was glad that nightfall had covered him, and Lance couldn't see the color in his face. He wouldn't have known how to explain this unexplainable emotion. He needed to get back to the hotel. He needed to figure out what it was he was feeling right now. Of course, Clyde Vann was most certainly someone he needed to talk to, but that need had to be for the right reason.

"If you have any problems getting ahold of him, let me know. Between Delia and me, we can make sure you connect to him. But Tom…I really don't think anything points to Clyde as a suspect. He's a genuinely good guy, and I can tell you there were sparks between him and Calli. Delia said it was like they both had found the other part of themselves."

Crazy as it felt, and the mayor wouldn't know it, but that piece of information was like a hard jab in Tom's side. Tom was jealous of a man he didn't know and a woman who no longer sounded like his Calli.

"No, I agree, Lance. I just really need to have conversations with the two men who were closest to Calli before her disappearance and may have been two of the last persons to see her. Whatever you can do to help me with both or either, I would greatly appreciate it."

"I've been trying to meet with Weldon Solder since his name was one of the first mentioned to me as the closest connection to Calli, other than Alana. I just thought he might be able to tell me something nobody else has been able to tell me. My guess is that he is as interested in getting to the bottom of all this as I am."

"I'm as surprised as you are that you haven't met Weldon yet. We met him at the church years ago, and he's been out to the house with Calli. Weldon is one of those people, nice enough, but you are never sure that you really know them. You know how some people just keep themselves close in check. He doesn't share a lot with you, but from all Delia says, he's a lifesaver for Calli. She doesn't think her daughter's church could have grown half as big as she is without him."

"Wow…that's quite a recommendation for the man and his skills. Do you agree with that?"

"As I said, Tom, I really don't know him and can't speak to his skills as a counselor. I mean, he worked at the biggest law firm in Louisiana, that has to count for something."

Tom noted the mayor's slight hesitation in his recommendation of Weldon Solder. "Thank you for coming out and having dinner with me, Lance. I sure enjoyed it. And… I apologize for that pre-interview on Solder. I'll just have to bide my time and wait until he's not so busy and come up with my own assessment of the man."

The two men shook hands and walked in different directions to their cars.

* * *

Tom turned over and cursed when he saw it was already 9 a.m. He quickly searched his memory for what he'd planned for the day. He was meeting Delia for breakfast 30 minutes from now. After five minutes of staring into the sparse line-up of clothing he'd brought, he decided on a pair of dark corduroy pants and a jacket since it was Sunday, and in southern Louisiana, you dressed up on the Lord's day.

Delia's expansive and convivial mood filled up the room as Tom walked in. "Tom, I really considered calling and telling you to meet me at Miracle Way. Alana invited me to their monthly after church reception since she and Weldon decided to resume them. Delia frowned. "Just something strange about having the pastor's reception when she's not there to host it. I didn't tell Lana, but I just don't feel comfortable going. Most folks are still too raw for that, right now."

Tom gaped as he followed Delia into the dining room. "My goodness, who prepared this Louisiana spread, Delia…was Alana recruited again? My Lord, if I'm not getting a flashback to Miss Rosie's Sunday brunches at the Tavern."

Delia laughed and shook her head. Tom was pleased to hear that old Delia belly laugh again. He hadn't heard it enough since he's been here. Clyde looked at him as if to say, 'Thank you.'

"It wasn't Alana this time, Tom. This is all little old Delia's doing. I admit I had to get started last night. Of course, it's nothing like Rosie's...that woman could come in two hours late and still get a breakfast like this ready to serve up, in no time flat. Even Alana is not that good."

Tom took time from his eating to look over at his hostess and smile. "You know, I can remember you whipped up some pretty amazing meals at the house more than a few times, Delia. Don't sell yourself short when it comes to southern cooking."

Delia laughed. "You know, now that you mention it...I did, for sure. But, the truth is, I did try and get Alana to come over to help out this morning, but she told me she had too much to do to prepare for service this morning.

"I hear tell she's running that church pretty much single-handed these days. Well, her and Weldon. But, from Alana's mouth, Weldon is having to travel more than he did before." Delia's face clouded over some as she picked at her omelet and sipped her orange juice.

Tom listened as he ate, not slowing down but listening still. "What is it you told me about Weldon's background? I was trying to get that straight last night. Is he from up north? And, what about that powerful job he left...anybody know exactly why he left there? Was he looking for a job when Callie offered him the job at Miracle Way? I imagine the church was much smaller, then, than it is today."

Delia shrugged. "I think he grew up in Illinois. He told us once, but that's been years ago. Alana will know. But I have to tell you, Tom, the man, is smart as a whip and knows how to grow that church. You'll meet him. You'll see what I'm talking about. It was like he walked in there and in no time flat, he knew exactly what that church needed and went about making it happen. It's been growing ever since."

"What's more, he saw what Calli could become. He believed in her. I tell you, the way he'd look at her sometimes, you could just tell he truly believed God had chosen her and that church for great things in southern Louisiana. Who can argue with him, now? He just saw it before everyone else did…except Calli."

Lance nodded in agreement. "Within months of him coming there, Miracle Way's congregation probably doubled…probably grew faster than even Weldon imagined it would. People from all over began flocking to that church. Nobody expected all that, but they believed in Calli. And, after Weldon came, they believed in him.

"Right now, those poor people at Miracle Way are hurtin' almost as if she was their daughter, or mother or friend. And, I know that includes Weldon, too."

Tom never stopped eating and listening and wondering, "I imagine this is painful for him, but I really need to talk with him. He could be invaluable in this…search. It's likely he may know something he doesn't even know he knows…someone who might've come into Calli's life, into the church, that we hadn't talked to. What he knows could be invaluable.

"I'm hoping I'll catch him at the church today. Alana said she'd do her best. If he's not there, I think I'll just stop by his home this afternoon to see if I can catch him either coming in or before he leaves on another trip. He hadn't come to the mountain in all these weeks of my asking. I guess the mountain has to make a trip to him."

An hour later, Tom stood, rubbing his stomach with satisfaction.

"Delia, between you and Charlie, I'm gone be a fat drunk when I leave Blue Bayou. There's no way I can keep eating this kind of good south Louisiana food and stay halfway healthy. I have no idea how you and Lance do it."

Delia laughed. "Before long, your taste buds take over, and you just say, `to hell with that shirt or those jeans that I like so much.'"

He was grabbing his hat, and Delia was standing in front of him, laughing. "Believe me, I got a few of those dresses, Tom. The ones that used to be so easy to slip on. I find myself fighting with them for an hour now…that easy relationship we had ain't no more."

As they walked to the door, the three swapped stories of how the southern cuisine was not for the faint of heart and how New York snowbirds had to fly in their chefs if they wanted to hold on to their skin and bone physiques.

"Lord…some of'em lose the battle, I'm afraid. Those are the ones who never go back home. My guess is they're too ashamed of how they've let themselves go."

Tom hugged Delia long and hard, thanking her for the delicious breakfast and allowing him this moment to remember the old Delia with warmth and love. As he slid into his Element, he decided he'd wait until after he stopped by Miracle Way to decide about driving out to Weldon's home. He hadn't decided yet whether he'd go inside without a warrant. But he'd been sending him messages for weeks now. Maybe he could justify it.

* * *

CHAPTER 31

Inside Calli's World

Tom tried to ignore the stirrings as he got out of his car and headed for the entrance to the church. The church that Calli had built. Calli and Weldon, to be honest. Finally, he visited the place Calli had called her home for the last 30 years. Was it fair to believe that this was what had taken his place?

Certainly, it was a representation of who Calli Tucker had become. The best indication she was no longer the simple, sweet irreverent girl he'd known and loved. She had found something that demanded her reverence, and because she was a woman in a highly male-dominant role, she had put to good use that steeliness she'd inherited from Delia. Miracle Way represented the woman whose life he might have shared, but who, without him, had grown into someone so special, so loved and, obviously, fulfilled.

Tom frowned. He was being maudlin. To be fair, he had a full life in Daphne. He was loved and well-respected in his community. There were even a few people who told him they loved him, and the city couldn't get along without him. And then there was Maia. Maia, who had been in his life for almost as many years as Calli had had the church.

As planned, Tom arrived at the church just as the service was ending, and most of the visitors and members were heading for their cars. The somber look on most of their faces told him Delia had been right not to come this morning. He walked against the crowd and into the church lobby. He hoped Alana hadn't forgotten he would be there. She'd promised to show him around the complex before introducing him to Calli's staff.

"Tom! Tom...there you are." It was Alana hurrying out of the sanctuary and toward the other side of the church. She gave him a quick hug and gently nudged him to follow her. He could tell she was in a hurry, though she'd promised to introduce him to some of the members today, the staff and workers who came in contact with Calli on a day-to-day basis.

More important than anything was whether Alana had tracked down Weldon. He saw that a selected line of parishioners was lining up to join Alana in the room he finally figured out was the pastor's study, given that it was etched above the door. Tom worried about how long the reception would last. He hoped she'd been able to track down Weldon, and encourage him to meet him at the church, today.

Alana's eyes swept over the setup quickly. Satisfied, she directed staff to keep the guests entertained until she returned. "Come with me, Tom. Let's walk around the backway. I'll give you a dime tour of the complex and a stop by Calli's office. I've also set up a place for you to chat with a few people who worked with Calli."

Tom was grateful but still wondering about Weldon. As they walked around the complex, he was amazed at the variety of programs sponsored by the church. An education wing, a music and video studio that was comparable to most he'd seen in Alabama. The library up on the top floor was top of the line. There were young and not so young visitors already there reading or checking out books.

Tom was moved by the good work he knew went on here. Some of his questions, now, had nothing to do with the investigation. He realized that his breathing was suddenly labored. Delia's and Alana's meals were catching up with him.

"This is some church complex, Alana. I've never seen anything like it. But why don't we break our tour up into two nickel ones rather than one dime tour?" Alana laughed so hard she found herself gasping for breath.

"Calli and I came out here three or four times a week to walk or jog around the trail. That was the only way we've been able to get around this place without passing out."

"It's truly amazing. How long did it take to pull all this together?"

"Oh, a good five years. The sanctuary was operational after the first year to 18 months, but the construction workers were steadily working every day except Sunday. It wasn't until Weldon came on that things got into high gear. Thanks to his job with that big law firm in New Orleans, Weldon had a relationship with one of the most prominent construction and architect firms in the south. Between Weldon and Calli, they sold the company on the vision lock, stock, and barrel.

They finished the complex in half the time and for half the quoted cost. Believe it or not, Tom, everything you see was Calli's vision, not there's. She would come in one morning and sit down with Weldon and tell him in detail how she wanted parts of the building to look and feel. Whenever he asked where she'd learned all she knew about building, she would smile and say, I don't…but God does."

Tom shook his head in amazement. "So, is it true that the original vision God gave her was just a little church beside the Bayou?"

Alana laughed. "Tom, you really don't know the Calli we all know. Yes, that was her original vision. I'm not so sure it was God's. If it was, He simply changed His mind. We've all decided that God really, really loves Calli Tucker. And, once He let her know what he had in store for her, she couldn't say no, now could she?

Would you believe, Tom, that most of the furnishings in the church, all high end if you notice, came to us without a price tag. Most were love offerings, gifts, donations from around the state. A lot of the work was done by members or people from the community who just wanted to help Calli realize her dream."

Alana checked her watch. "Oops, let's get back over to the study. Most everybody should be there by now." As she began to walk, Tom couldn't help but ask. "Alana, you think Weldon will make it here, today? I mean, I understand these gatherings were his own creation.'

"Tom, I talked with him last night. He called from the road and promised me he'd be here. He wanted me to go ahead and get started but said he'd be here by the time most of the visitors arrived. She gently took Tom's hand and hurried into the study that was already filling up.

***

As Tom stepped into the large space, he imagined this was what a CEO of a Fortune 500's study would look like. Expensive and perfectly appointed furniture. Paintings that looked authentic, even if they weren't. A space fit for a Southern Living magazine issue on contemporary churches. Not one thing out of place. He spied the 16-foot table that stood in the middle of the floor, brimming over with enough reception goodies to feed an army. Two servers stood post on opposite ends of the table, ready to accommodate.

"Well, I'll be damned," he muttered to himself when he saw Charlie standing behind the bar serving light refreshments, tea, lemonade, and water. Charlie smiled over at Tom and shook his head as if he knew exactly how ridiculous he looked. "Alana made me do it," he mouthed over to Tom.

Tom excused himself as Alana began to welcome the guests into the room. He felt the quiet wariness in the air. The guests were happy enough to see Alana but as lovely as she was, Alana was not Calli. No one was. Tom made his way to the table and picked a few grapes from its bunch. He looked back at Alana, wondering what she was feeling, knowing she couldn't take the place of a woman like Calli.

Tom couldn't help himself. He sauntered over and put a dollar on the bar in front of Charlie. Charlie tried as hard as he could to ignore the gesture, but they both ended up laughing.

"Once a bartender, always a bartender, Man," Charlie sputtered as he set a tall glass of lemonade in front of Tom. Tom drank the glass halfway down.

"You make a mean lemonade, Charlie McGriffin." He dipped his head and walked away.

Tom had to admit that Weldon Solder was one of the most handsome men he knew. He watched the man walk through the room over to where Alana stood. There was no real reason Tom should know who the man was, but for some reason, he did. It was the man's subtle control overshadowed by his charm. He imagined women found that mixture pretty irresistible. From all he'd heard, though, Calli hadn't.

As Weldon smiled at the guests who walked up to greet him, his eyes were measuring, rating – checking out the food table, the bar, the stature of the crowd—and searching for Alana, who was standing in the corner surrounded by guests.

Tom set his second glass of lemonade down on Charlie's play-bar and walked toward Weldon. He was certain he might not have another opportunity if he didn't get to him now. And he needed to get his dibs in before the man got wrapped up in the church business or became the center of everyone's attention.

As Tom walked toward him, Weldon turned on cue and acknowledged him. He met Tom halfway. They both were standing in front of the buffet table.

"Tom Mallory. Weldon Solder." He proffered his soft, manicured hand. "I'm so sorry it took us so long to meet…but I'm sure you've heard how things have been so busy these last few months. None of us could have imagined it."

Tom nodded. "Mr. Solder, the pleasure is all mine. Yes, I certainly understand how busy things have been for you. Alana has told me you're burning candles at both ends. I really appreciate you making yourself available to me today. Is there a chance we can find a spot away from the reception?"

Weldon smiled and nodded. "Sure, we can. Just give me a minute to make sure Alana doesn't need my assistance here."

As Tom watched the man walk over to Alana, smiling and greeting visitors who came up to him, he was grateful Alana had finally convinced him to talk with him. He watched as Weldon softly touched Alana's arm and guided her away from the crowd, and as they stood talking, he noted the serious look on each of their faces.

As Weldon and Alana walked back towards the visitors, Tom

noted that both smiles magically reappeared. "Tom, let's walk down the hall. My office is right around the corner. Alana can handle the reception without me. It pays to be Calli Tucker's understudy most of your life."

Tom followed the fast-walking Weldon Solder down the wide halls that bore beautiful pictures of biblical characters and stories. Tom recognized most of the images from the Bible that sat in his parent's home throughout most of his childhood. He rarely saw either of his parents read the book, but he'd looked through it a few times and read stories with his Sunday School classes the few times his family attended church together. As his parents grew apart, so did traditions like church attendance.

"Recognize this one?" Weldon asked, stopping beside a large painting of a beautiful woman with dark hair, kneeling at a well. The question interrupted Tom's childhood memories of a faith-less childhood. "I'm gonna take a leap and say that's the woman at the well?"

Weldon smiled. "Touché! It's one of Callindra's favorites. She preaches from that story at least twice each year. Each time she passes the painting, she stops as if it's the first time she's seen it. I asked her once why the painting held such interest for her." Tom waited to hear Calli's response, but Weldon Solder kept walking. Suddenly, he stopped at one of the three doors at the end of the hall.

He nodded toward the door next to his. "That's Callindra's office. The door is usually open. Believe it or not, she never locked it. She doesn't like closed doors inside the church. Said it showed a lack of faith in human beings."

Tom felt a sudden urge to touch the door, turn the knob, and walk inside. He wasn't sure what he expected to find. Maybe there would be something to get him closer to the Calli she'd become. Would there be any small reminder of the girl she used to be? "Mr. Solder, I wonder if I could take a look inside …the Pastor's office before I leave?"

Weldon's look said "no," but he nodded. "Sure, why not? She wouldn't mind."

As Tom walked inside Weldon Solder's office, he was not surprised to find that it suited the man perfectly, the quintessential power office with the oversized picture window, plaques and trophies, a desk that took up half the corner it sat, and a plush sitting area.

Anyone who visited Weldon Solder would leave without any question about his power at the church. He was even more certain that Weldon Solder had directed the appointment of his office down to each book in the sprawling bookcase. This setting fit him perfectly.

Weldon pointed to the table in front of the window. "Please sit, Sheriff Mallory. Would you like something a little stronger than lemonade to drink?" He laughed softly. I know Charlie can make anything taste good, but I think I can do a little better than lemonade."

Tom smiled. "Thank you, Mr. Solder, but I think I better keep my wits about me. I've drank enough since I got here in Blue Bayou. Anybody with a little creativity could write a country song about me. You help yourself, though."

Weldon suddenly threw back his head and laughed. "Sheriff Mallory, you have a wicked sense of humor. I think I will get myself a drink. I'm scared that if I don't, I may just fall asleep. It's been that kind of week."

Tom sat across from the man, watching him as he fixed himself a drink. He tried to remember why he'd decided he disliked Weldon Solder before he actually met him. He decided there was no good reason to dislike the man. You couldn't hold a grudge against a man simply because they happened to be the closest person to the woman you once loved or that he happened to be the kind of handsome that could be mistaken for a movie star. All the things Tom wasn't.

When Weldon sat, he took a sip from his drink, set it between them, and waited. "I guess the best thing to do, Mr. Solder, is to start from the beginning. When you and Callindra Tucker met, how you met…then fill in as much as you can about your work together. Who was close to her? What took place the last few days, weeks, the month before she disappeared? Anybody new come into her life…anybody old? Old friends, old acquaintances she hadn't seen in years?"

Weldon Solder sighed, settled into his seat, drank slowly from his glass, closed his eyes briefly, then started from the beginning.

* * *

Tom Mallory looked down at his watch as he stood to leave Weldon's office. He couldn't believe he'd been there more than two hours. He looked down at his notes and realized Weldon had been very forthcoming, had been almost methodical in sharing his years with Calli. He was sure Weldon Solder was most definitely in the right profession. Smooth, persuasive, charming.

For two hours, Tom sat, entranced by the man's poignant story of meeting Pastor Calli Tucker, describing her with something akin to adoration, laughing as he shared how naïve she was about business, and frankly, people.

"It took Pastor Tucker a long time to learn that everyone simply aren't acting on their love and faith in God."

When Tom peeked at his watch, he realized he had spent much more time than he'd expected to spend here, and Weldon had been a willing interviewee. In fact, had offered much more information than Tom believed he would.

"You have been extremely helpful, Mr. Solder. I can't tell you how much this helps me understand who Callindra Tucker was...who she became, since the time I knew her as a teenager."

"Of course, I'm more than happy to help with your investigation, Sheriff Mallory. I guess I've been halfway telling myself that I'd walk back in here one day, and she'd be here. I haven't really allowed myself to think that she may not be coming back. Today, that possibility is finally settling in. I pray you'll find her and bring her back to us."

Tom nodded, convinced that the lawyer's emotions were real. He thanked him again. As he walked toward the door, he turned back and saw that Weldon was already opening his desk drawer and removing a set of keys.

"Let me open Callindra's door for you. I'll leave you there. Take all the time you need, Sheriff. If you would, just pull the door closed when you finish. I don't think we need to worry about anyone bothering anything there."

As Weldon unlocked the door, Tom thanked him again. "If it's okay, I'd like to give you a call if I find there's something I failed to ask you. Will you be available for the next few days?"

Weldon smiled. "I'm guessing you'd like for me to stick around for the next few days, right sheriff?" Tom looked down and back up at Weldon Solder.

"I'm really grateful that you found the time today, and I'm sure you need a bit of rest after your travels."

Weldon shook the taller man's hand. "Good evening, Sheriff Mallory."

Tom walked into the office and gently closed the door behind him. He stood glued to the one spot in the middle of the floor, looking around the room, imagining Calli Tucker walking through the room, sitting behind the big chair at the oversized desk, meeting with visitors at the sitting area.

He walked to the desk and peered at the photos there. Delia and Lance, children, and some other older people smiling or laughing. In several photos, Calli was with a group in what looked like a foreign county. There were men and women dressed in western wear, but some were dressed in foreign robes and dresses.

The pictures confirmed what everyone had been telling him. The church and her congregation were her life now. He looked at the books in the teakwood bookcase. Calli always liked reading, but he hadn't ever seen her pick up a bible in his life. There were bibles of every size and with a variety of covers. Even some written in foreign languages. There were more than a few books by some of the country's best-known evangelists. Some were inscribed with warm salutations to "Pastor Callindra Tucker."

Tom walked to the window and looked out over the bayou that everyone swore was, in fact, a mistitled river. The deep blue water shimmered under the setting sun. He was sure Weldon Solder selected this view. There was endless light streaming through the room, filling it with soft warmth.

As beautiful and inviting as this room was, the Calli he remembered wouldn't be at home here. This was all Pastor Callindra Tucker. He sat at the desk, wanting to find one thing that offered him a thread to the Calli he knew. Just one thing. He was surprised to find the desk drawers unlocked. As he looked through them, he understood Calli felt comfortable leaving her doors unlocked.

There was nothing helpful there—sermons, letters, church accounting files, personnel files. As he closed the bottom file, a piece of paper fell to the floor. Tom continued to peek into the files, deciding there was nothing remotely of interest there.

As he pushed the bottom drawer in, Tom picked up the fallen paper to put it back inside the drawer and realized it wasn't a piece of paper but a picture. Likely another doting parishioner, he thought. He glanced at the photo before dropping it into the drawer. It was a young girl. As he peered, the face looked familiar…he decided it must be Callie 40 years ago. But the girl's hair was black, dark. He stared.

Lucy! He said the name out loud, thankful that the door was closed. It was the nurse he'd danced with at Delia's place that first night back in Blue Bayou and the very one he'd spoken to briefly just yesterday.

The picture was of a much younger Lucy. But that wasn't what drew him. Tom's breathing slowed. The hairs on the back of his neck stood on edge. It was Lucy at the age of 15 or 16, just around the age he'd last seen Calli. It was Lucy, whom he'd thought, at first sight, had an uncanny resemblance to Calli—a much older Calli. The teenaged Lucy was the spitting image of the teenaged Calli Tucker.

Tom nervously tried to unscramble his thinking. Calli had no sister or brother, so this wouldn't be a niece. Could it be that Lucy was simply just a fluke – didn't everyone have a twin?

Then why had Tom's blood run cold? Why couldn't he move the picture out of his sight? He turned the picture over and saw the name on the back. L.K. Whittington. Tom stood and pushed the photo down inside his front shirt pocket. He felt its weight against his chest. Did Weldon know the girl? He already knew that Alana did. So did Charlie. He would ask them who this Lucy Whittington was.

* * *

Tom stood in the humongous church parking lot that had suddenly emptied while he was inside. He felt that out-of-body sensation he sometimes got when logic didn't exactly connect with reality. He couldn't explain exactly what he was feeling, but Lucy or L.K. Whittington was in the center of it all. His gut rarely fooled him, and his gut told him the photo was a key to something. Something. He just didn't know what.

Tom walked slowly toward the Element. The photo in his pocket now weighed a ton. He slammed the truck door shut and remained sitting behind the wheel without turning the ignition. Tom touched his shirt pocket, assuring himself that the photo was safe. He sighed, deciding he'd best get back to the hotel. Before turning the ignition, he spied Weldon standing beside a car across the parking lot, not more than 100 feet away.

He saw the tall woman walking toward Weldon and the car a minute later. Tom stared at the two figures. As she neared Weldon Solder, Tom realized it was Alana wearing the electric blue dress he had complimented her on that morning. The glimmer of the setting sun above Blue Bayou sent golden embers through her soft braids. He took in the two bodies as they moved closer and suddenly realized, with a jolt, something that never crossed his mind. Weldon and Alana. The two knew each other in the biblical sense. There was something palpable between them as they stood, so intently refusing to touch.

Tom watched as the two carried on an intense, private conversation. Was it a controlled quarrel of some kind, possibly, even a lover's quarrel? Was Tom's presence there today the subject of their conversation? Or, was it simply the de facto leaders of Miracle Way hashing out their strategy to maintain the church's success, given Calli's disappearance?

No. it was more. Weldon and Alana. It made perfect sense. They had worked closely together for years, drawn closer together given their roles for and with Calli Tucker. They were also amazingly attractive people. How could they not be drawn to each other? Alana was a beauty queen, and Weldon was obsessed with beauty and power. Tom got the feeling the two shared insatiable ambitions, as well.

Tom tried to still his thoughts, to put them in some kind of order. He touched the photo again as he questioned its role in Weldon and Alana's relationship? Did it? When was the photo placed inside the drawer? Why was it not a part of Calli's display on top of her desk?

Had Weldon met the girl, had he seen the picture? For certain, he knew that Alana knew her. How, if at all, did the girl's appearance in Blue Bayou connect with Calli's disappearance? Maybe, it didn't. Maybe, all of this was a coincidence. But Tom's gut, his old trusty gut, told him that wasn't the case.

If the girl was a relative, a part of Calli's life, why was her photo stuck down in the bottom of the bottom drawer? Why wasn't it proudly displayed like the other smiling faces on her desk? He realized that Lucy wasn't smiling. Hers was the face of a troubled young woman.

Tom watched as Alana placed her hand on the door that Weldon opened. He saw Weldon place his hand, ever so lightly, atop Alana's for just a moment. He waited for Weldon to leave the parking lot and Alana to return to her car and leave.

He needed to get to his room and think. This day that started without much hope for any new information had suddenly filled with questions, which in his line of work, was always possibilities for answers. And while his conversation with Weldon had been mesmerizing, it was one-sided and left room for more questions. These last few minutes were full of questions. Again, questions he hoped would lead to answers.

He silently thanked Weldon Solder for painting an intriguing picture of who Calli Tucker had become—or, at least, who she was in Weldon Solder's eyes. Tom decided that he could never really like the man, but he could appreciate his obvious admiration and care for Calli. He imagined the real emotion Weldon felt toward his boss might very well be something more complicated – something closer to love.

Even with his subtle arrogance, Weldon had done nothing to engender Tom's disdain other than stand him up over the last month. Tom admitted his feelings were unfair, built on male insecurities, maybe even guilt for walking away 45 years ago.

He was now remembering the look on Weldon's face as he

recalled meeting Calli. "You know, Sheriff, I never in a million years imagined I'd end up working for a woman like Calli Tucker. I left a six-figure job with all the perks you can imagine to help this woman build up a Baptist church in southern Louisiana. God must still be laughing,"

Weldon had shared with Tom how he and Calli had worked long hours, held endless planning meetings to create the kind of church that Callindra Tucker deserved. She hadn't always seen the need for the beautiful art, marble desks, most upscale furniture of any church in southern Louisiana, but Weldon ensured her they needed it, that it added to the story of God's favor. Tom wondered if his Calli would have ever fallen for that?

Tom arrived back at the hotel right around dinner time. He hadn't really eaten since breakfast. He went to his room to change from his Sunday-go-meeting-clothing and into his jeans and shirt. He threw some cold water on his face and pulled a comb through his hair.

The restaurant manager and waitresses had gotten used to his solo dinners. They shared friendly chatter with him until his dinner arrived, then left him to dine unbothered. Tom coveted his time alone. Dinners were his time to revisit his day and glean through the information shared that might hold a few hidden clues. Tonight, though, he willed himself to put that off until after dinner. He wanted to eat in peace and enjoy his food. For some reason, he imagined this would be the last unfettered meal he'd have in a while.

Tom finished eating, left a generous tip, and said good night to the restaurant host. "Have a good night, Sheriff Mallory," she'd responded, smiling. Now, Tom willed himself not to jump in his truck and drive the ten minutes to Delia's place.

Beginning tonight, he promised himself, he was weaning himself off Charlie's addictively delicious drinks. He really did need to have all his faculties about him now that his gut was telling him something was right there beneath his nose.

Tom returned to his room and allowed himself an hour of news before shutting down the television. He walked towards the desk, sat, and pulled the photo out of his pocket. Holding his breath, he sat it gingerly on the wood surface. He grabbed his tablet and pen, then sat staring at the photo, turning it from front to back – wishing someone had written something more than the girl's initials and last name there.

Tom decided the first thing he would do tomorrow was find out more about L.K. Whittington. Had she purposely not mentioned her name when he'd first met her? Charlie would surely know. He prayed she had used a credit card rather than cash to pay for her drinks. He wouldn't ask Alana. Not yet. He hoped against hope that Charlie would know something more about the girl than her name.

By the time Tom lay down for the night, the now-familiar sound of hurrying traffic on the freeway had died down. He looked out the window and saw just a few headlights on the streets. He imagined most sane people had long ago turned in for the night. He'd lost track of time, lost himself in the questions and possibilities filling the pages. Possibilities based on his own swirling mind and the information Weldon had shared during their visit.

Maia had called during dinner. Theirs had been a short conversation, but he'd promised to call back before he went to bed. Now, it was too late. He promised himself he would find time to call her tomorrow morning before his day got too busy.

* * *

But Tom's day started busy. Delia was his first stop on Monday morning.

He'd not meant to see her until later in the day, but she'd called and invited him to breakfast. Tom figured it was just as well to start with Delia and get a delicious breakfast to boot. "We got shrimp and grits this morning, Tom…but you better hurry. Lance can never eat enough of 'em."

More than an hour later, Tom arrived at the Belson home. Lance and Delia had finished breakfast. Lance was putting on his jacket to leave for the office as Tom came through the door. "I'm so sorry I'm late, Mayor. My deputy called me just as I was walking out the door."

Lance smiled and shook his head. "No explaining needed, Tom. We're both in the business of running herd on small towns. Hurry on in there and grab your breakfast out of that warmer. If it don't fill you up, look through the refrigerator! I hope I'll see you later this week."

Tom promised him he would, then made his way toward the oversized kitchen. He wondered how Delia could have prepared breakfast, eaten, and already cleaned up, leaving a pristine kitchen?

"Tom! There you are. We tried to wait for you, but as I told you, shrimp and grits don't have much of a chance around Lance Belson." Tom laughed as he dished up a heaping plate of shrimp and grits for himself.

"I don't blame him one bit. I'm always good with leftovers, Delia; you ought to remember that."

They both laughed as Tom found a seat in the dining room, and Delia brought him a glass of orange juice and water, sitting them both down in front of him before settling herself in a seat opposite him.

"How was church yesterday? Did they have a full house?"

"Yep, sure was. Filled to the brim. I have to admit I was taken by surprise when I learned that Alana delivered the message. I didn't know she was a minister." Delia smiled and nodded.

"Yes. That child been walking in Calli's shadows most of her life. She decided she wanted to get her minister's license about ten years ago. She talked to Calli about it, and Calli, of course, told her it was a wonderful thing to do. She mentioned it in passing…not asking my advice, really.

"I have to admit I was a little surprised, about like you were. Ministering just didn't seem to fit Alana's personality, somehow. But, well, she convinced me it was a direct message from God. So, what can you say to that? I told her, 'If God's in it, I'm all for it, Alana.' "

"According to the congregation, she did a good job, and most importantly, she was true to her word, she delivered Weldon Solder. I finally got a chance to meet and talk with the man." Delia felt a levity in Tom's words. She stared over at him for a minute.

"And how did that go?"

"Believe it or not, Delia, it went well. He was very forthcoming and gave me a very moving, very compelling picture of your daughter. Frankly, I was surprised…but very grateful that he devoted so much time to me given how busy he seems to be."

Delia smiled into her coffee before taking a sip. "I'm happy you finally got to talk to him, Tom. I'm not surprised he gave you such a thorough picture of Calli. Weldon was definitely smitten with Calli early on, but I think once he realized that would never fly with Calli, things settled into the way it was supposed to be. Weldon became Calli's gatekeeper and protector. She depends on him for just about everything, runs every big decision by him. If anybody ever wants to get to Calli, they always have to go through Weldon Solder."

"I kinda figured that was how things were. You all had told me about this megachurch, and I thought I knew what that meant…but, clearly, I didn't. I was completely blown away by the complex. It was quite something. I could feel how proud Weldon was of it, too."

"Well, he has a right to be proud, Tom. He deserves a lot of the credit for that church growing into what it became. But the truth is it's Calli's church. The congregation is all hers, the music, the programs…all of that is her. Weldon took care of what the building should be to glorify her vision. She trusted him with that.

"Tom, the Calli we both know, would never worry about the right flooring or colors in the study. She never cared whose handprints showed up on things like paintings or church furniture. When she walked into that church on Sunday mornings, it was for one reason, to deliver God's message to her congregation. I'd say Weldon and Alana worried about the material side of things at that church while Calli took care of the spiritual.

"Point well taken, Delia. But, let me ask you this…and I guess it sounds more like gossiping than anything, but I just need your honest assessment. Since I've been here, I've been hearing that Weldon has this mysterious woman friend somewhere in the area, but nobody seems to know anything about her, and to my knowledge, no one has met her. Then, I'm also hearing that same thing about Alana – some love she's keeping out of sight. Is it remotely possible, remotely possible that the mystery woman is Alana, and the mystery man is Weldon?"

Delia stared, batted her eyes, then frowned and shook her head. "Oh, Lord, Tom. You are really reaching for straws, now. No. I don't think that's remotely true. No. I never in all these years saw those two people interact with each other in any way except business. Granted, I'm not very close to Weldon, but I am very close to Alana…and, I just don't see that being a possibility."

Tom frowned. "Maybe you're right. It's just a crazy thought I had, I guess." Delia laughed. "Well, you've been known to have a few of those in your time, Tom, but a lot of them actually turned out to be right if I'm remembering correctly. Still. This one…let's just say if this one turned out to have any truth to it, you could feed me crow pie for a week!"

Tom laughed aloud as he stood and took his plate and glasses to the sink. He shook his head as he rinsed the dishes. "Delia, I hadn't heard that one in a while…only in Blue Bayou!"

PART XVI: What Tomorrow Brings

CHAPTER 32

Nurse Nancy

Nancy Chancer paced across the hotel room, anxiously awaiting a phone call. He had promised to call this evening to update her on their project. Where was he? Timing was everything.

She walked to the phone and punched his number in. Nancy had never had the patience to wait for others to keep their promises. As the phone rang, she closed her eyes, her labored breathing sliced into the silence. No one answered. She slammed down the phone. She began her terrible habit of biting her nails as she stood and walked over to the window. If he didn't want to answer the phone, damn it, he needed to get himself over here so they could plan the next steps.

Nancy hadn't planned to get down into the weeds with this project. Her usual modus operandi was to deliver the source and let her colleagues do the rest. She was dealing with amateurs whose lives were centered around church and religion. What did she expect? Though she'd worked at a Catholic Orphanage most of her life, she hadn't walked into a church since she was a child. For what? He'd let her know very early that nothing was waiting for her in heaven—or, on earth, for that matter—unless she grabbed it for herself.

She gave New Orleans its props. It taught you how to survive…or else. It had even taught her how to take advantage of those who didn't know how to survive.

Something akin to a chuckle rose from deep inside her throat. The years of hard liquor and cigarettes had long ago erased the voice God had intended for her.

There was a soft knock on the door. She took a breath, went to her purse, and pulled out the gun she kept with her as a safety measure. She pushed it into the back of her pants. "Who is it?" she called. There was no answer for a while. As she walked toward the door, there was a low answer. "It's the church attorney." She recognized his voice even though she thought it was weird how he liked to use this code word rather than his name.

When she opened the door, Weldon Solder quickly walked inside, taking in the small dark area and imagining the endless people who had spent time in the room. He refused to sit on any surface inside the room.

"Where the hell have you been? And, why haven't you answered your damn phone, Weldon Solder?"

He winced at her use of his name. "I have a lot more to do with my time than you do, Ms. Chancer. I wish you'd try to remember that. I have a 24-hour job and endless responsibilities."

"Yes, and I guess you'll have a lot more responsibilities now that Pastor Tucker is out of the picture. I haven't talked to that woman of yours since everything went down. The preacher woman is out of the picture, right? Completely out of the picture? We couldn't just kidnap her now, not after she recognized me in the restaurant. For all I know, she has a photographic memory too."

Weldon refused to look at the woman. "To my knowledge, everything has been taken care of."

"What the hell does that mean, Weldon Solder, 'to the best of my knowledge?" "It means that Alana volunteered to do the job. It seems it was something she

relished. She has her own reasons."

"And did she get it done? That's the only damn question I need answered. By the way, where is Miss Black America?"

Weldon bristled at the snarling woman's depiction. "Please. Alana will be here. Don't get so riled up, Ms. Chancer. Why don't you have another drink and settle yourself down?"

"I have a feeling I should have followed my first mind…you just can't send freshmen to do a senior's job." She walked over to the bar and snatched up the small hotel bottle pouring it into a glass.

* * *

Calli Tucker lay in the pool of blood and vomit. She tried, unsuccessfully, to ignore the searing pain in her head. Her parched lips whispered the one word that resonated somewhere inside her. Calli. Calli. But, the darkness always returned. No matter how hard she tried, she could not hold onto the shrivel of light that sometimes came through and made sense of the shreds of memory that floated inside her. The darkness always returned, like an invisible thief snatching away the light and the memories.

Darkness won as the world continued without her. When she awoke much later, her memories were less foggy. She could hear her ragged breath smell the rancid odor of her soiled clothing. She had no sense of how long she had lay wallowing in her own filth and wounds, grasping at life without knowing she wanted to live. The light never stayed long before the deep abyss of sleep returned.

Slowly, there were images that became clearer in her mind…of Alana's smile. Weldon's cautious laughter. A young Tom's pensive stare. Had it been weeks or months since she'd seen these faces?

After another lapse in time, there were suddenly memories of her and Alana and Weldon enjoying dinner. And, after dinner, the woman...a tall woman with an angular, unsmiling face and a scar on her forehead. The scar and her unsmiling eyes were so familiar. She had looked away, and just that fast, the woman had disappeared.

Her silent groan was an attempt to see clearer, to understand the meaning behind the images. She shivered from the cold wind and from a dread the memory of the tall woman's face had created. As she fell again into the darkness, there was the sound of footsteps. More than one set of footsteps came to a stop somewhere further down the bayou bank. The wind brought their voices to her. First low voices, then louder, angry.

* * *

CHAPTER 33

What Loyalty Gone Wrong Looks Like

Alana and Nancy hadn't seen eye to eye about this project from the beginning. Nancy thought she understood what Alana's problem was. She wanted to be Pastor Callie. In Alana's eyes, Nancy was a crooked nurse who cared about nothing except making money off young mother's mistakes. The women's hatred for each other was like white-hot steel, and Weldon Solder made every attempt to stay out of its way. He had his own demons to tame. He'd done three things he'd sworn all his career he'd never do: lie, cheat and steal. And against a woman he had loved and still greatly admired. Greed had gotten the best of him, and he'd gone too far to look back, now.

"Why didn't you make sure? What? Do you think this is a game? You take your own life at risk when you half-do a job."

"I didn't half-do it. I did the job, lady. I even put that drug, Propofol, that you stole from the hospital in Callindra's drink at the restaurant…against my better judgment."

" "Ha… Your better judgment?"

"My first mistake, Nancy, was giving you the benefit of the doubt the same as I do for most human beings I deal with."

"You…"

"Please. Please. Can you two just stop it? Let's get this over and done with! Alana, did you get rid of the vial the drug was in? Have you talked with Lucy today? I tried calling her last night. She didn't answer, and she didn't respond to my voice mail. Have you been keeping an eye on her?"

"I haven't talked with her, but she should be meeting us today. She knows we need to tie up loose ends. Last weekend she told me she was on call and expected to have to work most of this week. And, yes, I threw the vial out in the middle of the bayou."

"Boo hoo hoo... poor little rich girl. I don't feel a bit of pity for Miss Lucy Whittington, daughter of the rich and famous. Little Miss Lucy is really making me nervous. It's like she's been all over the place since I met her. First, she hates the preacher woman who abandoned her. Then she decides the woman had her own issues she was dealing with, so she wonders if she has it all wrong about her. Somebody better get it into her pretty little head that we're too far down the road for her to get a conscious now. I'm beginning to wonder if we can even trust her to keep her mouth shut."

"Come on, Nancy, Lucy knows as well as we do that she's in this up to her neck. You didn't reach out to her, remember? She reached out to you. Besides, it's natural for her to be emotional and a little confused about how she feels about her birth mother. I would think right now she's wondering how this good preacher that everyone seems to love, can be the monster she'd imagined she was.

"What's more, she's bitten off a lot more than she bargained for...I guess we all have. None of us knew it would end up the way it has. And, the truth Nancy, is it didn't have to happen like this. You took it on yourself to show up at that restaurant. For the life of me, I don't get why you did."

Nancy's glare was hard and directed at Alana. "It's a free country, ain't it? As I recall, somebody told me it was a good restaurant. Why shouldn't I eat there?" Nancy's throaty laugh

"That's not really the answer, though, is it, Nancy? Not after I'd told you we'd be there with Pastor Callindra? I'm still trying to wrap my head around why you had to show up? Was it a power thing to show your face to her before you destroyed her life?"

"Don't hurt yourself trying to figure me out, Cleopatra Jones. Tomorrow this will all be old history, and you won't have to see this face ever again."

Weldon rolled his eyes and shook his head. He was weary of their stupid arguing.

Finally, enough was enough. "Look...both of you, just stop it. I'm sick of listening to both of you. We need to get this done and get out of here. Your snapping at each other is not helping us get this done."

* * *

It was a man's voice, now. A voice she knew. A voice she'd heard so many times. She tried to hold onto the light, to hear the voices. The women's voices, and the man.

The voices were somehow part of her life. Yes. Yes! She was screaming inside the darkness, but no one could hear. "Oh, my God, it's Weldon. My Weldon!" No sound left her body. Fear was suddenly part of the cloud that enfolded her. Fear, and a realization that the voices of conversation were about her, Callie Tucker, and the girl in the picture, Lucy. Oh God, no...it can't be. But, suddenly, she knew it was.

L.K. Whittington was Lucia Benet. The photo left on her desk the night

they'd had dinner. Yes, she'd quickly seen the likeness, but she hadn't allowed herself to even consider the truth. Weldon had walked to her door and looked in, and she'd placed the picture away.

Weldon had driven that night, as he always did, and Alana had sat in the back, hovering close between the two of them. There was small talk all the way to the restaurant. And more small talk and laughter before they ordered dinner. Alana wanted to hear more about the Africa trip. Weldon was quiet, listening.

As they'd walked out of the restaurant, Calli was thinking how blessed she was to have these two people in her life, such loyal friends and employees for so many years. But then, she'd begun to feel darkness overtaking her, just as she saw the tall woman with the scar on her forehead. They had locked eyes. There was no mistaking Nurse Nancy from the orphanage. The memories and the fear… was overtaken by darkness.

PART XIV: Luke 8:17

CHAPTER 34

Charlie's Secrets

This was the first time in a long time that Tom had seen Charlie McGriffin standing anywhere other than behind what had long ago been dubbed "Charlie's Bar." Now, a young white man stood there, watching the news and polishing glasses as Tom walked in.

"Good morning! You need a pick me up?" The young man chuckled.

Tom shook his head. "Too early for that, but I wouldn't mind an orange juice with a couple of lemon pieces thrown in."

The young man nodded. He noticed Tom's eyes scanning the place and pointed to the outside dining area. "If you looking for Mr. Charlie, you'll find him out there on the bayou." He handed Tom his orange juice and waved off his dollar bills.

"Thanks." Tom nodded, stuffed the bills in the tip jar, and took his drink with

him.

Charlie McGriffin was the permanent fixture at Delia's Place. No one, including

Tom, could imagine anyone else ever taking his place. From all accounts, he was always the first to arrive at the Tavern each morning and the last to leave, most times in the wee mornings, carrying bucketloads of customers' secrets home with him to bury.

Tom wondered just how many secrets Charlie had heard in his 40 years working at Delia's Place. He was remembering how Charlie leaned so effortlessly into conversations with his customers, drinking in their conversations as if theirs was the most important in the world.

There was an art to the way Charlie could loosen up the most tight-lipped customers, allowing them to comfortably share parts of their lives they'd never share with anyone else. Part of it, he imagined, was the deceptively powerful libations Charlie served. The other part was Charlie's ability to look into the customers' souls, to listen and impart a sense of guarding their secrets. A perfect listener, nonjudgmental, empathetic, and always at the ready with a hug across the bar or a pat on the back.

As Tom stood at the sliding door watching Charlie, he wondered about the man's other life. Did he truly have a life outside Delia's Place? How much time and attention could he really devote to anything else when he was at the Tavern 85% of his hours in the day. He couldn't imagine his friend doing the normal things everyday people did— fishing, hanging out with friends at a barbecue, bicycling along the bayou.

Charlie had married his childhood sweetheart, and they had three children. There was no question he loved his family. He remembered how he'd proudly pulled out his wallet and shown him his beautiful family. Yet, he knew Charlie's devotion to the tavern took up a huge chunk of his time and his life.

Tom walked outside the sliding glass door and onto the outdoor dining room floor. He smiled as he saw Charlie standing on the banks, skipping rocks across the water. It was an old game boys often played to see how many times the rocks would skip before sinking.

Tom and Charlie had loved competing at rock-skipping when they were much younger. Charlie was always the winner, with as many as seven or eight skips at a time.

As Tom walked down and stood near his friend, he realized Charlie was lost in his own thoughts. There was no inviting smile, no clap on the back, or the playful bear hug Tom usually got from his friend. Only a faraway look Tom didn't recognize.

" Hey, man, what you doing out here so early? We won't be open for another

hour."

"I know. I'm here to talk with you, Charlie, before you get busy this morning." Charlie looked hard at Tom, then turned back to the bayou. Tom had never seen his friend without a smile on his face or so deep in thought. His warm smile was a staple in Delia's place.

"Charlie looks like somebody stole that big ole smile of yours. I swear if I didn't know you so well, I wouldn't recognize you."

Charlie shrugged his shoulders. "Just woke up this morning with a lot on my mind, my friend."

Tom sat on a small boulder near the place Charlie stood. "Well, I'll leave you to those thoughts in a bit. I went to bed with a lot on my mind and woke thinking you would be a good place to start trying to resolve these things rolling around in my head.".

"Is this about Calli, or about someone else, Tom?'

Well, about Calli, yes. But, also about someone else. Someone, it seems you may know at least a little about…the woman named Lucy who hangs out at Delia's Place sometimes on weekends."

Charlie looked into Tom's eyes, then back out toward the bayou. "You know what I been thinking about this morning, Tom? How was it that those old folks were so wise…everything they ever told us seemed to be the truth, no matter how crazy it sounded at the time.

"Remember how at one time or another, the preacher or Sunday school teacher talked about Luke 8:17. You remember that verse, Tom?"

Tom chuckled. "You got to remember, Charlie, I was never a big bible reader. My daddy was Jewish, and my mama was Catholic, and I never figured out what I was. But please enlighten me, friend."

"Yeah, well. I was thinking this morning how Mama Rose just about lived in church and had us in there anytime we weren't working or in school. I guess I was there so much that the head deacon decided I'd make a good junior deacon. That was during my senior year, and I swear I didn't know whether to be mad or proud."

Charlie stood silent for a while. "Luke 8:17 says, "For there is nothing hidden that will not be disclosed, and nothing concealed that will not be known or brought out into the open."

For a second time in two days, the hairs on the back of Tom's neck stood up. A chill caused goosebumps on his arms, though it was already nearing 70 degrees. Secrets. There was something about the look on Charlie's face that told Tom his friend was ready to share more than he'd known to ask.

"What does all this have to do with Calli or Lucy, Charlie?"

Charlie looked up at his friend with a seriousness Tom had never seen on the man's face. "Well, think about it, Tom. You're out here so early in the morning to learn something about the girl you loved 40 years ago and the young woman you met just months ago. I'm guessing there have to be one or two secrets wrapped up in what you're seeking."

"Maybe you're right, Charlie, and I'm hoping you'll tell me what you know."

Charlie looked down, picked up a handful of pebbles, then slowly threw each into the bayou, dusted off his hands, and turned toward Tom. "Calli loved you more than any young girl should ever love someone, Tom. Your leaving came real close to destroying that girl. She was in bad trouble there for a while."

Dumbfounded by his friend's words, Tom resettled himself on the boulder, his eyes on Charlie.

"The craziest thing happened after you left. For whatever reason, I became the person Calli shared her hurt and her dark secrets with." He chuckled deep in his throat. "Not all of them, but most. And, it got real dark for that girl for a while, Tom. Real dark.

"I know what you're thinking, Tom. I asked Calli the very same thing. Why did she come to me when Delia was right there in the house with her? Well, the truth is Tom…and, I love Delia like a mother, but she never knew the first thing about being a mother to poor Calli…not until she was good and grown and made a life for herself. The strained relationship they had when you left was never completely resolved. No, Calli would never have confided in Delia."

"You know Lana; she never holds anything back. She was that same way as a child. Boy, did she razz me about Calli coming to me with her problems? Started calling me "the white girl's doctor." I just figured it was jealousy, Calli getting the attention Alana thought she deserved.

"The truth is, Calli spent most of her time talking about you, Tom. She was trying to understand why you left, and she felt comfortable enough telling me how much she was hurting. Every conversation was about you. Truth be told, I learned a lot more about your and Calli's relationship than I ought to know. Anyway..."

Charlie took a few steps closer to the bayou, stooped, and looked deep into the water as if there was a message there. "She loved you so much, Tom. I was just a sounding board that she knew she could dump her hurt and deep secrets. That was all it was.

"Then, one night, she and Delia had a fight. Calli called me at work, in really bad shape. She said she needed to talk to me. I tried to talk her out of it and told her to go to bed and things would be better in the morning. She wouldn't listen. So, when she asked, I told her Delia had just left, and I was finishing up cleaning and locking the place up. She knew her mama's habits like the back of her hand, knew that Saturday nights drained Delia to the bone, and she always came home and fell straight into bed. Nothing short of a diesel truck could wake her.

"I'll be there as soon as Mama falls asleep, Charlie," is what she said.

"You know, Tom, something told me that night of all nights wasn't a good night to talk to Calli. She sounded lower than she usually did. And, Lana, who loved Calli to the moon and back, had been in my ear nonstop about me spending too much time babying Calli. "Why don't you tell her to find some of her own friends to cry to?" She also said Delia wouldn't like me talking with Calli so much.

"Anyway, I finished cleaning. Looked out the window and saw an ugly rain and thunderstorm had come up. Just as I was talking myself into leaving before Calli showed up, she showed up. She had been crying like crazy, and she was dripping wet, so I told her to go find some towels in Delia's office, then dry herself off in the bathroom, or she'd end up sick.

"She did, and came back out, still crying and complaining about Delia. After about 30 minutes of listening, I realized I was drained too. It was Saturday, which meant I had been there for a full 12-hours. Lord, I was ready to get home to my wife and my bed. But I sat, and I listened until I found myself fading. Every 10 minutes, I'd have to shake myself to stay awake.

"I finally told Calli, "The only way I'm gone be able to keep listening is if I can lay down over there in front of that fireplace. Tom, you remember, in the fall and winter, Delia kept that fireplace going, and I hadn't put the embers out yet. Lord knows I didn't mean to fall asleep, but I did…must've slept for quite a while.

"When I woke, I jumped, couldn't believe I was still there. The rain had stopped, and I could see morning coming through the windows. When I went to turn, I found that Calli was laying there sleeping, tear stains all over her face. I lay there feeling so sorry for the girl. I thought to myself, it's like someone cut her heart out and left her to survive the best way she could.

"I tried to move her back so I could get up, but the more I tried, the more she clung to me. I was at my wit's end, and I swear to God my only thought was to let her sleep and get out of there and home to Sandy.

"That's not what happened, Tom. I still don't know how it happened, but somehow I realized I was holding her in my arms and shushing her crying. And, then she kissed me, and I was trying to…but didn't have the will. God forgive me. I didn't have the will.

"Tom, it was like something had been pent up in both of us for longer than either of us understood. I don't think either of us could tell you what it was. It wasn't love, Tom. There was no one but you, for Calli and Lord knows Sandi is the only woman I ever loved. Still, one thing led to another. And I've thought about it a million times since, and I know Calli has too. But what is done is done, and the truth is finally in the light."

Tom stared across at his friend, who was now standing, facing him with tears in the corner of his eyes. Tom couldn't put the two together, Calli and Charlie. He tried but couldn't. He put the story in the back of his mind, something to explore in detail later.

Right now, it was more than he could admit was truth.

Yet, he believed Charlie. Why would he lie about something that could harm so many people? Of course, it was human nature—two young people, one in deep pain, believing…hoping, that sexual intimacy with a friend might erase that pain. He believed neither of them had planned for it to happen.

Still, it was a lot to digest. Charlie and Calli. It made sense, he thought. How close they'd grown, how desperately she depended on him to help her get past her pain.

"Tom, that's only part of it…."

Tom saw Charlie's eyes move to something behind him. At the same time, he felt a presence. He turned and was surprised to see the young woman he was there to ask Charlie about.

"I heard the whole story, Charlie, and in some crazy way, I'm glad it happened the way it did. You saved Callindra when Tom Mallory walked away from her. And now I know what I've always believed is the truth…I am the result of that relationship. I'm happy that I'm the result of two people truly caring about each other. Even if it wasn't love."

Tom stood staring at the woman that now left no question of who she was. How could he have missed it the first time? Lucy wasn't just the spitting image of Calli, but the doe eyes, the curly ringlets, the tiny gap in her teeth were all Charlie's.

"How long have you known, Charlie, about Lucy?"

"Charlie didn't know all these years, did you? You had no idea that the sweet young Calli would go away, have your child and never tell you that you had a daughter."

"Charlie. All this time, you didn't know?"

"No. Not until Lucy came to town. And, no, she didn't know me from Adam, but after she began coming to Delia's Place, she eventually began to share her secrets with me, not knowing she was sharing her secrets with…."

"With my father," Lucy whispered

Both Tom and Charlie looked down at the words.

"Lucy told me what she'd learned about her mother taking a bus to New Orleans, being taken in by the orphan home there, and having her daughter who she left with the Nuns.

"You know, I was pretty good in math, Tom. Once she told me that whole story and her birthdate, I knew. You had been gone for months when all of that happened. I knew without knowing. Calli became pregnant the one time we…were together."

Lucy looked from Tom to Charlie. "Charlie, I had no idea who my father was before I came here, but I knew who you were, Tom Mallory. I knew that despite everything, Calli would have given anything for me to be your child."

Tom's questioning look brought a sad smile to Lucy's face. "Oh yes. It's fully documented. The woman paid to take care of her in the orphanage sold me my mother's diary she stole from her one night as she was sleeping.

"Tom Mallory, you were her one and only love, and she'd hoped a miracle would happen, and she'd be carrying your child…but it wasn't to be."

Lucy was now wiping tears from her eyes, shaking her head. Charlie went to comfort her, but she gently pushed him away. "I'm fine, Charlie. I'm just remembering how all those years I'd felt my adopted mother's resentment. But it wasn't until I overhead her nasty tirade against the orphanage that I realized that not only was I adopted, but I was adopted under what she described as "trickery." I was half-Black, not proper Whitley stock. That knowledge resolved something in me. In my mind, my birth mother had set me up for this unhappy existence.

"Not long after that, I began searching for my real mother. I was desperate to find her, to confront her, to tell her how much I hated her for abandoning me, for ruining my life. But also… to tell her how much I'd needed her in my life. All my life. Dreaming of who she was, of hearing her say she loved me.

"When I contacted the orphanage, of course, they wouldn't tell me anything, said it was their policy. And then, one day, as I continued to search the internet, Nurse Nancy Chancere reached out to me. I'd left my email at the orphanage. My guess is that's how she learned about me. Someone at the orphanage must have told her because she said she hadn't worked there for 10 years.

"Nurse Nancy? Who is she?" Tom asked, confused.

"She's a horrible woman I stupidly got myself entangled with. A nurse, no less. Makes me ashamed to know we share that distinction.

When I first met her, I knew that I'd made a mistake, but I looked the other way because she was the link to my mother. When I asked her how she knew my mother's secrets, she showed me the diary and admitted quite brazenly that she'd been an attending nurse at the orphanage when my mother was there.

"She also admitted she had stolen my mother's diary and learned all about who she was, where she lived, and who the father of her child might be. She felt no shame in telling me she'd read the young girl's diary from front to back—and remembered every word. She was very proud that she'd been blessed with a photographic memory.

"She kept Callie Tucker's life story inside her brain with the hope that it would one day be of use. My mother, a young, scared girl, had poured all her life into that diary…about her mother, about you, Tom Mallory, and about the boy, she said: "Saved her life." Even in her diary, she didn't admit that Charlie was a black boy. She didn't even write his name in the diary. I have to believe it was to protect you, Charlie, knowing that her mother or someone else might find the diary. Then, the problem would not just be that she'd had a child, but she'd had a black child. This is southern Louisiana."

Lucy stepped down to the bayou bank and sat, offering a place for Charlie to sit beside her. She stared into his eyes as the tears continued to fall from her own. "How can I ever repay you, Charlie, for saving my mother's life, for saving me?" Charlie looked down, shaking his head. He folded the young woman, his daughter, into his arms.

* * *

After a long moment of silence, Lucy stood and looked over at

Tom, bracing herself before she spoke. "Sheriff Mallory, I know what happened to Calli Tucker, and I know where she is. I'm responsible, at least partially responsible. I made a terrible mistake, and I know I have to pay for that. But, I will tell you everything I know."

Tom looked from Charlie to Lucy. He could tell by Charlie's face that this was the first he'd heard of Lucy's involvement in Calli's disappearance. "I need to know how you're involved, and you need to tell me where she is."

"My desperation to find the woman who left me at the orphanage and caused me to experience a horrible childhood led to this. I…never meant for this to be the outcome. For as long as I can remember, even before I learned I was adopted, I wanted another family, another mother. And then, one night, I overheard my mother on the telephone, yelling at the nuns for giving her a daughter…who was not what she expected. That phone call answered two things that I'd wondered about all my life—if I was adopted, and…I was horrified I was a mixed child, that my father was a Black man."

"I paid Nancy Chancere $20,000 to find my mother, and when she did, that should have been the end of it. But it all somehow went really wrong when Nancy, Weldon Solder, and Alana met. One night they were all here for dinner, and I'd walked over for a drink. The conversation stopped immediately when I sat there. I didn't stay long, but my gut told me something bad was about to happen.

"What was so strange was that Alana and Weldon, who I thought were Calli's friends, had suddenly become close to this horrible Nancy. I taught for a while in a school for the deaf and learned to read lips very well. So, after moving to another table, I could still look over and understand most of their conversation. What I overheard made me believe they had decided to harm Calli. I was terrified. If they would harm a woman of God, there was no limit to who they wouldn't hurt. I didn't drive back to New Orleans that night.

"I'd begun looking for my mother out of desperation to learn who she was. The problem wasn't the search but hooking up with a woman like Nancy. Then, once I'd paid her off, I thought that was the end of it. Instead, I learned that Weldon and Alana were lovers and had been cooking up a way to steal money from the Pastor all along. I couldn't believe the horrible spider's web I found myself in."

Charlie frowned. "Alana? And Weldon? I can't believe it. I was raised with that girl since we were children. She's like a sister, has been my whole life. Are you saying she is involved in a plan to hurt Calli? And Weldon? The two people Calli trusted most in her life?"

Lucy shook her head. "I'm sorry, but it's the truth, Charlie. I wouldn't lie. It came directly from their own lips. Weldon told Nancy they had been working on a way to steal money from the church for a few months. The kidnapping was their last-ditch attempt.

Lucy hesitated but went on. "I heard them says they had already begun manipulating the financial books to make it easy to take control of the account. They said millions of dollars were in that account, and Calli never bothered about the money. Besides, Weldon said he was the one who helped her raise the money over the years. Weldon and Alana aren't the people you think they are, Charlie. She was the one who hinted at the fact that you and Calli were more than just friends. That was before I knew who you really were.

"Lucy, I pray you got it all wrong. Weldon and Alana worshipped the ground Calli walked on. They were there whenever Calli needed them. All she had to do was call either one of them. Everyone knew that. It was those two who helped her build up that church, took her vision, and made it into a reality."

Tom interrupted the father-daughter conversation. "Lucy, all this you're saying…I need you to write it all down. And I think you better start giving thought to the likelihood that you would be a primary witness if…no, when this all comes to trial."

Lucy blanched. Fear and sadness filled her eyes. "I will, Sheriff Mallory. I will. And, I better tell you the last thing I learned from them. Weldon said no one but him knew that Calli had recently been left an inheritance of over 20 million dollars, plus a spanking new jet that one of her wealthy parishioners left her.

"They said the old man had joined the church when Calli had first opened it when it wasn't much more than a shack by a bayou. In his will, Weldon said, the old man called Calli his Angel, said she was the reason for his getting up every morning and staying alive as long as he did. In his will, he'd stipulated that Callindra could use the money for the church if she wanted to, but legally it was hers to use in any way she saw fit. After the old man died, Weldon had gone with Calli to the attorney's office. He'd directed them to share the letter and a copy of the will with her after he was gone.

"Did you get the name of the attorneys, Lucy?"

"No, I'm sorry, Sheriff, I didn't."

Charlie was back to staring out into the deep bayou, shaking his head as if he was trying to clear it of memories. "Calli was like the big sister Lana never had. She really does love her…but, it must be all twisted up. And I'm guessing Weldon and Nancy helped her get to that other side. I guess I was about the only one in Blue Bayou who knew about Lana and Weldon. Nobody knows how close we are, especially since Mama Rose died. We told each other most everything. The thing with Weldon and her just happened, she said. Wasn't planned. She used to tell me she didn't like the man…still, something happened. They fell in love."

As Charlie sat back on the big rock on the bayou bank, Tom wondered if God would answer his prayer if he sent one up there. He hoped that Calli was still alive. Yes, it had been more than a month, but miracles still happened. He found himself praying this would be one.

"Lucy, tell me the last time you saw Calli. What kind of shape was she in?"

"She was not well at all, Sheriff, in bad shape. Alana was supposed to shoot her. I still don't understand why she didn't. Instead, she hit her over the head with a stone. I'm guessing more than once. There was a lot of blood, a really bad gash to the head. But I don't think she had the nerve to shoot her friend as much as she told Weldon she would.

"After I followed them to the swamp site, I hid and waited for them to leave. I swear I thought the woman was dead. Her breath was so shallow. For the last few weeks, I've gone back to check on her when I could, taking her water and forcing soup with medicine in it, down her. She never knew I was there. She'd lost so much blood, but I was too afraid to try to take her to a hospital. I did what I could to care for her and keep her alive. I was praying every day that someone would find her.

After you came back to investigate, Sheriff Mallory, I wanted so bad to leave a message for you, but then…I knew enough to know I would be incriminating myself.

Tom was now on the phone, moving a distance from Charlie and his daughter. "Yes, meet me…let me get a proximity of where we will be going…."

"Lucy, do you have any idea what the address of this place we're going to?"

"Yes, sir. It's in my telephone MapQuest. I used it every time I went to check on

her."

Tom shared the address with the Blue Bayou police chief, who promised him there would be a force there to meet him when he arrived.

"We need to get there, now. After seeing Weldon yesterday, I'm afraid he felt the need to make sure the deed was done and probably had plans of destroy all evidence the best way he could. We can't wait. Lucy, if you can take us to her, let's go."

* * *

CHAPTER 35

No Way Back

Calli lay quiet. She felt the vibration of footsteps growing nearer. In time, she sensed they had stopped, and eyes were boring down on her. Something wouldn't allow her to connect the boring eyes with her lifetime friend, her loyal counselor, or the woman with the mark on her forehead.

Alana's voice held a tremor as she half-whispered, "She's right here, just like I told you." She stared down at the woman that had been her best friend for most of their lives. Hesitantly, she stooped down beside the supine body and lightly touched her. Suddenly, she was scooting back on her heels and screaming. "She's not dead! She's still breathing! How can that be, after four weeks?"

Nancy Chancere went rigid; her face a dark red. " Looks like our Superwoman lost some of her powers when it came to actually knocking off her preacher friend.

"Well, you know what this means, honey. Somebody has to finish the job, and I won't be the one to do it. We keep to the plan, and that means one of you take care of her...now!"

Alana now stood well away from the body. "I just don't understand. How could she have survived this long? This makes no sense."

"That's the difference between you and the preacher woman,

Alana. She really is a woman of God and looks like He wasn't quite ready for her. Whatever the explanation is, you need to finish the job you started. You, who made us believe you hated her with more venom than both of us put together. Not that I ever believed it.

"Both of you holier than thou-pretend Christians pretending to hate this woman enough to kill her and then half-do the job. Cowards. More than that, you both love this woman more than you let on…certainly more than you hate her."

Alana was sobbing, crumbling under the pressure of attempting to murder her friend, then failing. She stared pitifully over at Weldon, who was staring from her to the tall, haggard Nancy Chancere.

"*A-lana.*"

"*A-lana.*"

All eyes returned to Callindra.

"*I love you, Alana.*" her voice was so small, not even much of a whisper.

Alana turned away at the sound of her friend's voice, then began walking away, then running away from her friend, from Weldon and Nancy Chancere.

"Alana…come back!" Weldon was in shock. He started to run after her, but Nancy stood in front of him. Her face was full of dangerous hatred.

"You will not leave me holding the bag! Let that bitch go…all that bluffing about how she'd dreamed of this her whole life. Nothing but a lie."

Weldon walked close to the woman. "You have no idea what you're talking about, and we don't have time for you to stand here hating Alana."

"*Weldon. Weldon.*" the half-whisper again.

Callindra was still wallowing in her own blood. Her hair was matted and filled with God knows what.

"I won't do this. I can't.."

"Cowards! I was not supposed to be the one to take care of this. You two promised you'd be the one to take care of this!"

"Alana tried but failed. I never promised I'd do it. I knew I never could."

The woman pulled her gun from her purse and pointed it directly at the woman. Weldon turned away, refusing to watch. As the gunshot rang out, Weldon began to turn.

Only then did he realize it was him she had shot. A second shot rang out before he could speak, and Weldon fell ten feet from Callindra.

With labored breathing, Calli turned to see Nancy pointing her gun directly at her. There was not enough inside her to be afraid or feel sorrow at her own death. She closed her eyes and waited. The gunshot was loud as she held her breath and prayed her final prayer.

She heard the anguished scream, but it didn't come from her. The tall woman's body fell heavily just inches from where Calli lay. The gun touched her leg. Now, the only sound was echoes of running footsteps.

It was all too overwhelming. The footsteps were now faster and nearer. But already, the darkness was covering her again.

* * *

Epilogue: Again, With Love

It was fall, a southern fall which meant the temperature was a pleasant 69 degrees though it was early morning. The sunrise had begun more than an hour ago, and it now shone brightly above the trees outside the hospital window. As the nurse walked in with a pitcher of cold water, she liked looking across at the beautiful Blue Bayou. Often, white egrets flew in to catch fish or commune with the thousands of others settled around the bayou.

This morning, the nurse stopped abruptly as she walked into the door. The patient who had lain still, unaware of anything around her since coming in last week, was now turned toward the window, her hands moving up and down the bedspread.

Even in the dim light, she saw that the patient's eyes were open, and she was staring through the window. The nurse turned and tiptoed back outside and down the hall to the doctor's station without setting the pitcher down.

"She's awake. She's wide awake!" Dr. Pelham looked up at the nurse, half-questioning the validity of the nurse's words. But for just a moment. She was the best nurse on the floor. He hurriedly put away his paperwork and followed the nurse back to the room. In their wake were at least four other doctors and three nurses. They were all anxious to witness the miracle that was Calli Tucker, resurrected from what most had believed would be her death bed.

Tom Mallory and Clyde McGriffin were walking out of the elevator as the doctor and nurses hurried toward the patient's room. They were just back from their third trip to the cafeteria this morning for their third cup of coffee. Tom couldn't seem to quell the butterflies in his stomach. The out-of-body experience when he'd first lain eyes on Calli lying lifeless in the swamp area was still lingering. His life had suddenly turned topsy turvy, and he wasn't able to right it.

The two friends watched with alarm as the medical team walked into Calli Tucker's door. Neither Tom nor Charlie dared enter the door. They both stood outside, looking in and listening. Delia and Lucy noticed the commotion and hurried from down the hallway where they'd camped out most every day and night since Calli had been helicoptered to the hospital. Mayor Belson had just left after leaving them with a breakfast box.

As they arrived at the door, Delia noticed Charlie's eyes were as big as saucers. "Calli's awake. She's been awake for a while, the nurse said." Charlie and Delia hugged briefly before the mother made her way into the room.

The doctor spied on them and offered them five minutes before the room had to be cleared. He knew what they had gone through, then relented. "Ten minutes, and you go," he said. He knew Delia Tucker well, and his wife attended Miracle Way church.

He could only imagine what this family had gone through for the last two months. He looked quickly over at the younger woman. Gossip had it that she was Pastor Tucker's daughter. He didn't know, but he was hopeful the pastor would survive.

Delia stood in silent disbelief at the foot of the bed, looking from her daughter to the doctor. Lucy had settled into the farthest corner from the bed. She stood with her hands clasped as a new wave of tears streamed down her face. This time, they were tears of hope.

Calli briefly locked eyes with the younger woman before Dr. Pelham, and the nurse blocked her view. "Has she spoken at all?" Doctor Pelham whispered to the nurse.

"No, Doctor. She was laying quiet when I arrived."

Dr. Pelham nodded as he took out his stethoscope to listen to Calli's heart and her breathing. He lightly grasped her wrist, feeling for her pulse. He peered into her eyes…and a half-smile appeared on his face as he silently thanked God for this miracle.

"Doctor?" She couldn't stop her hands from trembling. Her girl was alive and awake. Admittedly, she didn't look so good…about like you'd expect a woman to look after going through hell and back. But thank God, she was alive.

"Does she recognize us, Doctor? Is her thinking …alright? Can we talk to her?"

"Mrs. Belsen, I'm afraid I can't begin to answer all of your questions right now. We are all hopeful, but right now, I'm going to have to ask you and the family to leave Pastor Tucker in our hands, at least for the next couple of hours.

We can't take the risk of getting her overly confused or excited. I will be doing a full battery of tests this morning, hooking her up to a few machines, forcing some more much-needed nutrients into her body, making sure the blood transfusion was successful. By the way, I can't thank you enough for that. By early afternoon, maybe even by lunchtime, I'll be able to tell you more."

Delia frowned. She was being asked to leave her daughter just as she was fully returning to her. Eight whole weeks of fearing the worst, going through the memorial service…and now, for the last week, praying the hopelessness that kept rearing its ugly head would go away, even as she realized how much her child had suffered. God had to let her survive. He just had to.

* * *

"Why don't we go and take a walk around the court, Delia. We could all use some fresh air and stretch our legs." Charlie walked over and ushered the woman who had been his boss, his second mother, and his friend for most of his life towards the door, gently prying her hand from the end rail of the bed.

"Lucy, come on, let's give the doctor room to do what he needs to do."

The younger woman reluctantly followed Delia and Charlie out. She was still quiet; tears remained at the corner of her eyes. Tom stood at the outside edge of the door. He had listened to the conversation but refused to darken the doorway, not ready yet to see Calli lying inert in the bed. He desperately needed her to be alright, had found himself doing something he seldom did…praying, asking God to intercede where the doctors couldn't.

Tom knew he'd have to get a handle on his emotions before he presented himself to Calli Tucker. He needed to say a lot to her beyond the long-overdue apology for his part in her years of unhappiness. It was Charlie who had made him painfully aware of just how unhappy she'd been. And how her despair had led to…hers and Charlie's moment of weakness that resulted in their beautiful daughter, and with it the years of guilt and secrecy for Calli. What a terrible avalanche of despair his selfish decision had wrought.

Tom knew it would take an even longer time for him to forgive himself. For 45 years, he'd pushed the hurt he'd caused back in his memory, allowing it to disappear over the years. He'd never be able to, again. Not now, after he'd been given this opportunity to make amends. He'd be damned if he wouldn't make good use of it this time.

* * *

The two women and two men made their way to the elevator, staking out separate spaces, ruminating in their own separate thoughts, avoiding each other's eyes. Lucy broke down in tears.

"Oh my God, oh my God. If He lets my mother live…I swear I will devote my life to serving Him and doing all I can to make up for my part in all of this. Even if it takes the rest of my life."

Delia patted the girl's back, pulling her into a tight embrace. Now, they were both crying, laughing, shaking their heads in disbelief. "I know exactly how you're feeling, honey.

We all know how you're feeling. We have all been praying that we weren't going to lose her. Calli's been living inside miracles for a long time now. God is just doing what he does when it comes to her. Now, we just need to keep on praying that Calli comes back to us just the way she left us."

Charlie nodded and let out a loud, deep breath. Tom's eyes seemed interminably glued to the floor, and his mouth glued shut. Delia didn't dare interrupt his thoughts. When the elevator came to a hard stop, Tom stood back as the three walked out. They all headed for the lobby, then outside the building.

Was it only their imagination that the sun shone brighter, the sky was bluer, that the birds' songs as they flittered from one tree limb to the next, engendered hope and joy?

They followed the path of the courtyard that took them to two benches on the bank of Blue Bayou. As they sat, each of them nurtured their own thoughts of Calli Tucker – the irresistible link that connected them.

They had sat and made small talk for little more than an hour when Delia received the text message. The doctor would like to see her. Refusing to go up alone, she invited the other three up as well. Only Tom hesitated. "Let's go, Tom. We need to make sure that Calli Tucker is back."

* * *

The miracle was real. Calli was back. She was bruised, stained, and in need of weeks of close care by her doctors. There was not a minute's hesitation as she watched the three people walk into the room. She held out her arms, and Delia was the first to fall into them. Charlie kissed her forehead and told her how happy he was to see her smile. Lucy stood back, nervous, unsure.

As the other two moved away, Lucy timidly made her way to the bedside. She sat gingerly next to the woman who was her mother. She stared into Calli's eyes—the eyes of the woman whose life she'd saved and whose life she'd put in danger.

"Lucia. How many times have I seen you in my dreams, spoken your name to myself?" Calli shook her head in disbelief that God had saw fit to give her this miracle. "I'm not sure I'd ever have the courage to find you, myself. But God decided it had been long enough. I'm so ashamed, and I am so very sorry for what I did, creating a secret to haunt both of us for all these years." She touched the younger woman's face, her hair. "You're so beautiful, yet I can see the pain in your eyes."

As Calli reached out to her, Lucy could hold in the tears no longer. The two women's faces were wet with tears. Neither seemed able to speak for a time. Finally, Lucy sat back and wiped her face. "I'm just so sorry about everything for allowing this horrible thing to happen to you. I never meant to hurt you…I didn't know it would come to this."

Calli touched her daughter's hand. "Don't, Lucia. There is more than enough regret to go around. Together, we will work through all of this…and my God tells me we will all be the better for it, on the other side. We have to catch up on so much, beginning with getting to know each other. This is a time for celebration, my daughter, and a time to say, "Thank You, that He finally brought us together."

Lucy nodded as she continued to stare into her mother's face. The woman she'd dreamed about so many nights as a child. The woman she had prayed she would find, just never this way.

Dr. Pelham walked in, smiling this time. He sensed the relief, the joy, and most of all, hope inside the room, this time. "I'm afraid I have to break up this beautiful gathering, everyone. Pastor Tucker will have to spend the rest of the night quiet, hooked up to those ugly machines. She's had a rough couple of months, and we have to make sure we replenish all she's lost."

Charlie walked to the door, looked out, then walked back in. "Tom's gone," he whispered to Delia. She shook her head. "It's fine, Charlie. He'll be back. I can only imagine what he must be going through."

"Mama, Lucia, Charlie…before you leave, please come here and pray with me before the doctor turns me into a Frankenstein? Let's not let this moment pass without saying, "Thank you for this miracle tonight."

* * *

It was early, and the sun was just showing itself behind the trees. The morning sky outside Calli's window was a beautiful ribbon of blues, pinks, and grays. The nurse straightened the covers on her sleeping patient and made certain all her wirings were still in place. She looked down into the woman's face and saw a remarkable change. The weariness and strain had all but disappeared. She'd heard of Pastor Tucker but hadn't met her before she became her patient. She was a beautiful woman and blessed to have so many people stopping by and sending flowers.

She smiled as she turned away. There was a God in the heavens. She'd always believed so, but this miracle made her know. Her next check-in would be two hours from now. She hoped the woman would be awake then so that she could tell her how many phone calls and visits she'd had since last week.

When the nurse returned for her check-in with Calli, she found the door closed but the sound of voices inside the room. Who could be here so early, she wondered. Surely Dr. Pelham wasn't already here. He wasn't scheduled to stop in until 10 am.

As she gently pushed the door open and peeked into the room, she saw the tall, handsome man they all called Sheriff Mallory. Tom looked up and began to stand. The nurse motioned him to stay put. Pastor Tucker smiled over at her from the bed. She or someone had placed pillows behind her.

It was obvious the two had been in deep conversation before she interrupted them.

"How are you, Pastor Tucker?" She checked the wires connecting Calli to the bags of liquid nutrients.

"I'm feeling almost normal. I can't thank you and the team enough for saving my life."

The nurse smiled, then quickly made sure there was still water in the pitcher and turned the thermostat a few degrees lower. "The whole hospital has been praying and pulling for your recovery. You can't imagine how happy we all are you're still with us. The doctor should be here in about an hour to give you an update on your status. If you need anything before then, just buzz us."

Tom had lain awake all night. Going over his life, over the time in his life when Calli was so much a part of it. Remembering the night he'd left, and the pain in Calli's eyes when he'd said the words. He was wondering now if there was anything he could say that would make a difference to her now.

Was his apology too little too late? Should he have just packed up and left? The local police would take care of things from this point. They'd thanked him profusely and told him he should feel free to get back to his real-life as soon as he could. What was his real-life now? he wondered.

He was thankful beyond words that two of the criminals were no longer there to cause a threat to Calli. No one believed Alana meant to kill the woman who had been her best friend for so long. But, right now, that didn't matter much. She had tried and been an accomplice, at the least.

She wouldn't rot in jail, Tom imagined, but she'd spend some time behind bars for the role she played in the kidnap and attempted murder. The policemen had also held Lucy for most of a day, questioning her and gathering information about her and the others' complicity in the crime. In the end, they had let her go, convinced she was at the most misguided and used bad judgment. Tom imagined she'd still be at the jail if Calli weren't revived.

Tom had walked back and forth in the hotel room, unable to sleep or settle down. Maia had called several times, and he'd refused to answer the phone, not at all sure what to say to her right now. There was nothing, he knew, that would make her feel any more secure.

Mayor Simmonds had called as well. He couldn't bring himself to talk with her, either. The deputy had sent him a note telling him what was waiting for him when he returned. He hadn't responded. Yes, Calli had been found alive, but that was only part of it. This trip was all the things that had made him hesitate in the first place. He could never be able to resume his life until he settled things with Calli and with himself.

* * *

Esau, his deputy, sent him a long weekly update on the goings-on over the past week and items that needed Tom's attention when he returned. Tom saved the note to his office file for a later response. He didn't blame them for not understanding. In their minds, all was well—Calli was alive and recuperating at her mother's home. In their mind, Tom's investigation was a great success.

Even the city of Blue Bayou had revived interest in Tom Mallory, calling him a hero for leading an investigation and rescue of the abducted and injured evangelist. There had been newspaper, radio, and television stories. National networks were falling over themselves to run the story, disappointed that Tom Mallory refused to interview with them. Tom couldn't believe that one New Orleans newspaper dug up the long-ago story of his father and even interviewed Blue Bayou residents about his and Calli's long-ago relationship. He turned his phone off in hopes of avoiding a call from Virginia Mallory.

* * *

Tom woke this morning feeling like he'd run a marathon and come out the winner. He almost looked over on the nightstand for his blue ribbon. He yawned and stretched with a small smile on his face. There was just a little humor in the fact that he'd found himself now including God in the equations of his successes. Here was a man who hadn't really prayed in his adult life, now convinced there was a power greater than himself. It was that power, he believed, that kept Calli safe for two long months. Yes, he'd freely give this new God all the credit for that huge success.

Another ribbon, he decided, was for his getting over the final hurdle, the most difficult he'd overcome in his lifetime—confronting his past, hearing from Calli's mouth how much he'd hurt her, then asking for her forgiveness. Tom had sat in Calli's hospital room and shared his hurt and pain from his childhood in New Orleans to his last days with her in Blue Bayou. He was a hurt and scared boy running away to avoid more hurt.

She had listened as he spilled all that was locked up inside him for more than 50 years. She cried. They cried together. She gathered him in her arms, realizing finally that her hurt in losing him could not compare to the hurt he'd experienced from growing up in New Orleans in Virginia Mallory's home.

"Thank you, Tom. You didn't have to share all you did, but I'm so happy you did. Not so much for me, but for you. I learned a long time ago that it is only when we unburden ourselves to God or the people God places in our lives that we will be free to move on.

Tom…there's something else. I need you to know I'll never stop loving you. In all these years, I never have. But God showed me something. That love comes in all manner of shades. My love for you is not the love of a troubled sixteen-year-old girl. It is a much stronger love, one that you can take with you wherever you go…that will never hurt you, but prayerfully helps you understand your worth. Finally, I'm able to love you from a place of wholeness, not hurt."

* * *

This morning as he walked out of the hotel to his car, Tom remembered how much he'd loved the beauty of Blue Bayou, Louisiana. Especially the autumn season when the air was crisp and cooler, the skies an achingly clear blue, and the songs of the birds were more poignant than any other part of the year. Autumn in Blue Bayou was for lovers, for couples who had grown old together, and for old codgers like him who had so much to be grateful for.

It was Sunday morning, and Tom found himself enroute to Delia and Lance's breakfast table once again. However, this time, he would be just one in a larger group of family and guests, there for Delia's famous Louisiana breakfasts.

As Tom rang the doorbell, he heard Delia's voice from inside the house. "Come on in, no need for doorbells and knocks, Tom Mallory!"

Tom walked in and dropped his jacket and hat on the coffee table. He smiled over at the roomful of friends smiling back at him.

"Good morning. Did I miss breakfast again?"

They laughed, shook their heads, but kept right on eating. "You know the drill at this house, Tom Mallory…if you are late, you are likely to miss out on a good meal. But, this time, you're lucky. There's more than plenty here, even for a growing boy like you."

Tom walked over and handed Delia a large box with ribbon and a bow.

"Tom, you know there's no gifts needed here. I should be giving you the gift! You found my girl. You saved her life...my life."

She hugged Tom and wiped the tear before it fell. And, guess what Tom? I've eaten two helpings of Crow pie, this morning."

Tom laughed, winked and then walked over to where Calli sat and handed her the other gift.

"Oh no, Tom. I wish you hadn't. Mama spoke for both of us...we owe you. You don't owe us."

"It's not about anybody owing anybody, you two. It's about gratitude. Something I've never said enough about, done enough about. It's something I wanted to do. You don't have to open them now...but please allow me this small pleasure."

Tom walked over to his friend Charlie and grabbed him up in a big Louisiana hug. "Thank you, brother. You know why. I won't ever be able to thank you enough, but you know where I am now. Call me if there's anything I can do to make your life better. And enjoy that gift from God. The wonderful addition to your family."

Tom looked into Lucy's eyes, thinking how close to being his she had come.

"You take care of your mama, grandma, and even that old bartender over there. Do it for me, will you?

"You know I will, Tom. They couldn't get rid of me if they wanted to. I've already given my notice at the hospital in New Orleans. Mama wants me to move in as fast as I can.

I'm in training to be the pastor's assistant. Wish me luck." Tom chuckled and winked. "You'll be amazing, Lucy."

"Get yourself a plate and find you a seat, Tom...seriously, there's plenty of food left," Lance smiled and patted his new friend on the shoulder. Tom shook his head.

"No...I thank you, but I ate before I left the hotel. I need to get home. I stayed longer than anybody expected, but I wouldn't have left before we found that pretty woman over there.

"Everybody knows I'm not much on talking, and I won't be changing that. But I need you to know that I feel like I'm at home for the first time in my life, and I'm with family. And, I can actually say this now...I love you all.

"Now, I'm going back to my life in Daphne, but I'm going back a hundred pounds lighter than when I came. I'm going back with a clearer conscious and a purer heart. And, I have all of you to thank for that. And guess what, Pastor Calli... I'm going back with something else, prayer in my heart and faith I never had before.

Calli clapped her hands and laughed. "Praise God, Tom Mallory. Praise God."

"Yes, this old Cajun Sheriff still got a few more rounds in him. I hope you all will let me come back and visit, sometimes. I think I need to come back and remember how love and family can be." There were sniffles and tears around the table as Tom gathered his things to leave.

He had packed his bags early morning, paid his hotel bill, and thanked the staff for hosting him for the last month. On his way to Delia's, he'd filled his gas tank for the three-hour drive home.

During the thirty-minute drive from the hotel to Delia and Lance's home, Tom had replayed his and Calli's time together yesterday. He couldn't believe that 24 hours later, he had a smile on his face, and all was well in his world.

Calli had forgiven him and given him his blessings to move on with his life. She'd done something more. Told him she loved him and always would. That was enough to sustain him for a good long while. She'd called it a "love endowed by God. The kind that never changes." The kind he'd been looking for all his life.

As Tom walked out of Delia's door on his way to his car, he almost bumped into a man walking toward Delia's front door. A tall, handsome man with a smile and a suitcase, who reminded him of Charlie, and strangely, given the man was African American, even a little bit of himself.

"Good morning. Don't tell me you've eaten breakfast and leaving already?"

"Well, I actually had already eaten breakfast, but yes, I'm on my way home."

"You're Tom Mallory? What a pleasure it is to meet you. I've heard so much about you from so many different people. Oh, by the way…I'm Clyde Vann."

Tom stared for a long time. Somehow, he knew. He smiled and offered his hand to Clyde Vann. "I've heard quite a bit about you, Mr. Vann. It's my pleasure, as well."

The two men stood smiling at each other for 30 seconds before Tom spoke., "I don't think I have to say it, but please take care of her for us, Clyde. Somehow, I know you will."

The other man nodded. "You can bet on that, Tom Mallory."